PART I:
CAMPUS COMRADES

Anxious Attachments

M. Ressina

AOS Publishing, 2024

Copyright © 2024

M. Ressina

ISBN: 978-1-990496-36-3

Cover Design: Jessica James

Visit AOS Publishing's website:
www.aospublishing.com

Chapter 1
First Impressions

Alexandra

Sasha had been doodling in the margins of her notebook when the monotony of class was interrupted by a knock at the door. Mr. Blunt abruptly stopped and announced, "Alas!" to a low chuckle from the room. Sasha liked Mr. Blunt. He was just young enough to find the subject he taught interesting but not so young that he tried too hard. Overall, not the worst Shakespeare teacher. He held the door ajar as the students fell into a lull of whispers.

Two boys were invited into the class, all eyes on them as they introduced themselves. She remembered being in their shoes, her heart pounding against her chest so loudly that she could barely hear herself think. Oral presentations were always a nightmare, but being the new kid at school and trying to make a good impression was worse. She put her pencil down to listen.

Gabriel Wells and Hale Yu were both handsome. It had been a long time since there's been anyone worth gawking at Saint-Ignatius. Gabriel was half a head shorter than the other boy, at ease with his backpack slung over one shoulder, long dark hair in a loosely tied braid, and his uniform slightly disheveled. He looked like he worked out, and spent much time in the sun, with olive skin and hazel brown eyes. Hale, taller and lanky, had the face of a Japanese pop star, dark eyes, high cheekbones and straight black hair falling into his eyes. His uniform was immaculate, every button of his school shirt done up, all the way to the top of his throat. He gripped the straps of his backpack, the tension evident in his shoulders, his eyes darting around the room.

Sasha had a seat by the wall, giving her just enough distance so as not to be overheard in the murmur of the classroom. She leaned to her left towards Eva, whose long red hair obscured her face.
"Whatcha think?" Sasha whispered to her friend.
Eva was staring at Gabriel, looking pale. Well, paler than usual.
"Eva!" she hissed quietly. Eva jumped, still staring at Gabriel.
Sasha repeated her question.
"They're both cute." she finally turned to look at her. "That one's a total player, though."

1

"He's barely said his name!" Sasha shook her head optimistically. Eva was quick to write someone off as being out of her league, which she felt was completely unwarranted. The fact that Pamela's group at the back of the class was less than subtle about noticing Gabriel didn't help either, and he noticed them too. He winked at Jenn, and the girls burst into fits of laughter, which Sasha thought a bit excessive. What a lame move. When they were asked to sit, Gabriel headed straight to the back of the room and let his bag fall to the ground, directly in front of the group of the loudest group of girls. Maybe Eva was right. Mr. Blunt shushed them, but it didn't stop him from pursuing a medium level conversation with Pamela behind him.

"This isn't my first rodeo, I know a guy like that from miles away." Eva confirmed.
"I like the other one." Sasha said, but Eva was still staring at the so-called player. Sasha turned her attention to Hale: he'd chosen a seat on the other side of the room near the door, making it hard to see him behind her classmates. All she could see of him now was a mop of dark unruly hair, his posture exceptionally straight.

Sasha sighed and returned to her math homework, which was due next period. She erased the doodling she'd done in the margins and tried to focus as Mr. Blunt went back to his lecture. Being new at their school was hard, she remembered that. When she'd moved from Montreal, everyone had known each other all their lives, except for Eva, making them quick friends– two frightened kids standing in front of the class just like Gabriel and Hale. The school had seemed so big and expensive back then, as though she'd never fit in. It had been completely overwhelming at first, but she'd found her footing. It was probably why she'd since started trying to adopt all the new kids until they found their places elsewhere. It seemed Gabriel Wells wouldn't need that kind of help, but Hale Yu just might.

Evangeline

Those eyes; where had she seen them before? Eva tapped her pencil gently against her notebook in rhythm with her thoughts. "That's it!" her brain cried, "but what is he doing here? Shouldn't he be...?" When Sasha's voice had broken her out of her reverie, she'd hardly heard her.

Memories of a little boy from the playground flooded her mind - tangled long hair with all sorts of things stuck in it, black clothing with holes and spots all over it. She remembered his voice too, moody, and angry most of the time when it wasn't sulky and remorseful. There was no way it was the same person...they said there had been no survivors after the fire. A coincidence? Was the boy also named Gabriel? She couldn't remember. She needed to dig up that old class photo. It was in the basement at home, along with all the other boxes of things that her parents never bothered to unpack. There was rarely a reason to unpack everything in a military family: You could move again at any time, but they'd been here for a while, so chances were that her parents just didn't want to see what was in those boxes. The way he fiddled with the tip of his long hair seemed familiar too. The kid she remembered didn't have any of that confidence though. Sasha was right; he was cute.

When the bell rang, Eva watched Gabriel Wells turn in his seat directly to the preppy girls in the back. Of course, the popular girls would be his type, she thought. Sometimes, high school felt like such a cliche.

Sasha was packing up her bag beside her and rolled her eyes. "Guess you were right about that guy. Cute butt though." she remarked. Thankfully after that redirection, Eva's concentration on memories flew out the door. She watched Gabriel flirt with Pamela, flashing a stunning grin, and Eva turned away.

"It's fine."
"You say fine, I say, a complete loss. Come on. This is just depressing."
Jason's gang and Gwen had also joined the group, and Sasha shook her head. "Should we adopt the other one, then?"
"You and your adoptions!" Eva laughed. "He's not a puppy."
"Nope, but he's cute."
Eva just shook her head. "If you want to invite him to eat with us, you can. We're used to it by now."
"I'm being nice!"
Eva batted her friend's arm. Their little group was always getting new additions as Sasha took it upon herself to herd over anyone sitting alone. "Think I should ask Daphne, Mel and Mila?"
Eva chuckled. "I think Daphne will like this one. Mr. tall, dark and handsome, though a bit too nerdy." She knew it came from a good place, but Sasha's habit of picking up strays generally led to them being stuck with people in their friend circle who had nothing in common with them and would probably have been happier elsewhere.
"Want to grab a coffee before our next class?"
"Sure, I definitely need a pick-me-up." Thinking back to her childhood had made her feel a bit shaky. She was glad for the distraction but still couldn't get the image of Gabriel Wells, back from the dead, out of her mind. She glanced at him one more time before they left the room and

3

he caught her gaze, recognition in his eyes. He pointed her out to Gwen, who was looking at his school schedule and she could see the other girl mouthing her name.

Why was he asking about her?

"Come on, Eva! There's going to be a huge lineup." Sasha was pulling her out into the corridor.

Alexandra

They waved at Mila and Shauna as they entered the crowded cafeteria. Both were way ahead of them in line.

"Guess we took too long ogling." Sasha sighed. "There's no way we're getting there before class."

"S'cuse me! Comin' through!"

Jason and his buddies walked past them as though they were invisible, while someone ahead waved to them.

"Um, 'Scuse me!" Sasha called.

Jason's friend, Eric, turned around, "What?"

"There's a line, in case you hadn't noticed."

"Enjoy it. My brother's saving us a spot."

"That's not a thing."

"What are you gonna do about it?"

Sasha crossed her arms. "That's not the point. We have friends up front too."

"Piss off." He turned and followed TJ and Jason.

"Oh, Sash, don't go looking for trouble," Eva said.

She huffed, feeling her cheeks burning.

"Did you honestly think they were just going to line up?" Daphne asked, lining up behind them. She and Mel had been in phys ed that morning and were wearing school shorts and t-shirts. Daphne's thick curly hair was pulled back in a ponytail, and her face was flushed. Sasha let out a breath. "I don't know. I guess I thought they might decide to be nicer for our final year."

"They're not so bad."

She knew Daphne's cousin played basketball with Jason's crew so that she might have known him in a different context, but as far as Sasha was concerned, they were obnoxious jocks.

"I guess it depends on who you're comparing them to."

"We heard there are new guys today," Mel said, changing the subject.

"Yeah, they're in our class English class. Gabriel Wells and Hale...something." Eva confirmed, trying to peer over the lineup to see if they'd moved. Sasha got up on her tippy toes, but even at her height, most of the guys at school towered over her.

"Do either of them look sporty? We're down a player since last year."

4

"Why don't you ask them?" Sasha teased, nodding towards Gabriel who was walking into the cafeteria with Gwen, Jason's sister.

"Wasn't he with Pamela five seconds ago?" Eva remarked.

Mila and Shauna passed their little group with their drinks, waving goodbye as they headed to their respective classes.

"I don't think we're gonna make it," Mel stated. Eva kept staring at the back of the cafeteria .

"He looks like he likes sports," Daphne said, following Eva's gaze.

They hushed as Gwen, Pamela, Gabriel, Genevieve, and Jennifer lined up behind them.

Gwen was holding up a folder, pushing her hair behind her ear and pursing her lips.

"Advanced mathematics, advanced physics, advanced," she sighed, "in everything."

"How'd you end up in that?" Jenn said, leaning over Gwen's shoulder.

"Bribery." Gabriel mocked. "Why? Do I look stupid?"

"I wasn't saying that!" Jenn retorted. "The only other person in all those classes is Gwen!"

"So would the rest of you if you apply yourselves. Anyway, at least I can show you where your classes are." It was hard to believe that a girl as sweet as Gwen was related to Jason and his crew.

"So it'll be the two of us a lot, huh?" Gabriel said.

"And the rest of the brainiacs. My brother's in some of them too. He's not as much of an idiot as he pretends to be, promise." Gwen clarified, smiling.

"Hey, Gwen!" Jason called from up front.

"Oh, thank God." Gwen said as the group moved past Sasha and to the front of the line.

"Jesus H. Christ." Sasha let out, exasperated. "I give up."

"Yeah, me too." Eva agreed.

As they began to head to class, Sasha turned back to give the group a dirty look, and caught Gabe looking back towards them.

"New guy is looking at us." She said to Eva.

Eva stopped to look back, but the moment had passed.

Chapter 2
Making Contact

Evangeline

It was weeks before Gabriel approached her. It was alarming how quickly a guy could make a reputation. It seemed like "Gabriel Wells" popped up in every conversation around her. Rumor had it that he'd already hooked up with Pamela, Jessica and Jennifer—or had it been Genevieve? It didn't particularly matter.

She'd dug up the photograph at home, along with shreds of other forgotten parts of her life. Her parents had stashed it all in the basement, all of the memories of her time going to school at the little church, and the tragedy she and her family had narrowly escaped. Her parents had kept newspaper clippings with the names of those who'd died. She found Gabriel Wells among them. Could it just be a coincidence? A namesake who looked like the little boy she remembered? He'd been a strange child, but everything that made him weird then seemed to make him popular now, from his long hair to his constant jokes. Inappropriate jokes weren't as funny in the third grade she supposed. Either that, or the trauma was finally catching up to her, which made her want to push it down further.

It was as though her parents had put her childhood into a box and sealed it with packing tape. She wondered if she should bring it up with them, but every time she'd mentioned that time in their lives in the past, her dad would either leave the room or find some excuse to change the subject. Whether she asked why they'd moved, whether they'd ever visit there again or even saying she remembered something from that time, tension filled the conversation, so she'd dropped it long ago. She used to think it was because her dad didn't like talking about moving or his job in general, but now she was beginning to think there was more to it. Her brother wouldn't remember, he'd been too young.

She considered bringing it up with Sasha, Daphne, or even Shauna, but what if one of her friends accidentally spilled the beans at school how she thought she knew the new popular guy? The last thing she wanted was to be added to the rumour mill and for any of that to get back to Gabriel himself. What if it had been him, and he'd somehow survived? Who'd want that kind of information out at a new school? She did catch Gabriel looking at her, or maybe it was because she was always staring at him. It felt as though he knew her too, but then he'd turn back to whomever he was talking to, and she'd feel stupid for having made such a leap.

Usually, on warm days, she and her friends could be found outside eating near the gazebo, but today, she really needed to focus on her Spanish test, so she'd headed off into the vast grounds in search of somewhere quiet to study. The school landscaping was beautiful and lush, with trees lining the long path that led up to the main entrance or down to the iron gates that led to the street, flowers carefully maintained, blooming through the seasons.

She found a spot and settled in contently. With the sunlight warming her skin, she spread her notebook on her lap and her lunch open beside her. Eva relished these quiet moments alone, mainly because they never lasted.

As if on cue, he found her. "Hey, babe!" Gabriel approached from the direction she'd come, not carrying anything at all, his hair looking glorious and silky in the afternoon sun. She propped herself against the elm's trunk and nearly choked on her sandwich.

Wasn't calling someone you'd never spoken to "babe" a little much? She concluded that his supply of girls must be running thin, and he was now moving on to deeper waters.
"What's up?" she asked as he sat down beside her, uninvited, and proceeded to swipe the other half of her sandwich from its plastic baggy. She had underestimated his 'muchness.'
"Nothing. Needed to get away from Jenn." He had a sideways grin, which she'd noticed many times before, but this was the first time it was directed at her. She'd seen it used on so many girls already but somehow, the effect wasn't lessened. Sitting down, the tip of his long, braided hair reached the ground. She wondered how long it took to grow hair that long. It looked well-maintained, unlike his uniform. He sat casually, leaning against the tree, very close to her. "Mmm." he commented on the sandwich. "What is this anyway?" he finished it in three bites.

This moment felt like deja vu, a confirmation. The boy sitting beside her was definitely the same one that sat near her at school all those years ago. It figured that he wouldn't remember her, or her mother's food. Hell, this kid couldn't even remember to tuck in his shirt.
"Peanut butter and honey sandwich." she sighed as she picked up her apple.

"Genius. My compliments to the chef."
He tugged his tie looser than it already was and leaned back, trying to get comfortable with all the roots underneath them. "So, why are you here by yourself?"

"I'm just enjoying the sun," she said, stretching her arms towards the warm light. "And you? Shouldn't you be off with Pamela?" However, his disheveled appearance distracted her. "Hold on, before you answer that I have to do something," she leaned over and neatly tucked his shirt into his navy blue pants. His apparent allergy to belts made it easy. "There, I just saved you from a demerit."

His eyes had widened when her hands reached towards his pants. He blushed.
"Thanks, mom." he laughed. She felt her cheeks warm too. Luckily, he picked up the conversation where they'd left off, so she didn't need to keep reliving the moment.

"Pamela? I think she can survive without me for a few hours."
"Whatever floats your boat," Eva said, still embarrassed. Pamela mostly hung out with the twins, Gwen and Jason, and their friends, TJ and Eric. The Jenns (Jennifer and Genevieve) were Pamela's entourage. Everyone at school knew them, and Gabe by extension.
"She's just insecure." Gabe shrugged. He squinted at the clouds. Eva followed his gaze. "Looks like a dog with its ears up." She said, digging around for something to say that wasn't gossip or embarrassing.
"Oh, and that one's a hunter!" he pointed.

She couldn't fathom which cloud was supposed to be a hunter. "I think it's a rabbit." lying flat on her back so she could see the clouds better. He followed suit. They were lying parallel, just far enough that it wasn't completely bizarre, though it still felt surreal.
"It's nice here." He said.
"Yeah. Kind of familiar, isn't it?" She goaded. She was almost certain; she just needed him to confirm it. Their whole class used to lie flat on the grass like this and watch the clouds as kids. The Church wasn't big on secular education, and "watching the heavens" was an easy way not to teach them anything in particular while still pretending there was some sort of religious connotation. There weren't many games that the nuns approved of, so they had to be creative.
"Not for me." He said.
"You've never done this before?" He craned his neck to look at her face.
"Nah. Never really been the type."

"What type is that?"
"Quiet."

That part was true: She remembered him as a child, angry and explosive. She could see his chest rising and falling under the school shirt from the corner of her eye. His arms were thick and muscular. The sudden silence surprised her, though, as Gabriel had said, it didn't last long.
"You sayin' I talk too much?" He finally said.
"No, just enough."
"How would ya' know? You never give me the time of day."
"Same goes for you, Mr. Popular."

He shook his head and propped himself on one elbow to face her. She kept looking up at the sky, glancing at him occasionally. His face was a little too close for someone who thought they'd never met.

"I've been tryin' to meetcha for weeks now!"
"Oh really?" She shook her head. "You play too coy then."
"Are you hittin' on me?"
"I wouldn't dream of it."
"Kinda forward, ain't ya?"
"You called me babe."
"You put your hands down my pants."
"That was, " she paused. "an accident."
"A Freudian slip."

She giggled. She liked that he referenced Freud. She liked that he had sought her out. It made her insides feel warm. Still, it all felt so sudden, so unlikely. He didn't recognize her, and his reputation preceded him. She didn't want to be another conquest on his list. A beeping noise came from the bowels of her backpack, reminding her that the school bell would ring soon. This had been fun, but he would return to his everyday life and forget her. He had never been popular as a kid, so he must love it now.

"We should get going soon." she heaved a small sigh. "Sorry about earlier. It's what you get for having younger siblings."

He sat up fully, shaking his head. "Nah! Don't sweat it, babe. You can stick your hands down my pants anytime."
She needed to get out of her head. Now that she'd officially "met" him, maybe she'd stop obsessing over whether he was the kid from the church.

Eva realized she'd been quiet for too long when he asked, "Any chance you hate Spanish class as much as me and want to go for ice cream instead?"

It was tempting, but she wasn't about to throw away the past few years of hard work for a date. Besides, would he still be interested if she made him wait, or was this just how he was now - flitting from girl to girl, easy come, easy go? There was only one way to find out, she supposed. "I really need to get a good grade in Spanish, but after class, I'd be down for ice cream." she offered.
"Alright." He surrendered. "Well, I don't need the grades, so I'm gonna go get the car, and I'll pick you up in front of the school after class. I'll be in the convertible."

Convertible? His entire story was fishy; she thought before pushing it to the back of her mind as she gathered her things for class. There were plenty of students with nice cars at their school, but she hadn't noticed Gabriel with one. She wondered if maybe he'd been adopted into a military family after the orphanage. It would explain why he'd have moved here in the middle of the year, and how he suddenly had the money for a fancy car.

The first bell rang. "See you later then, Gabriel." She quickly got up.

"Later, babe."
"It's Eva, Gabriel."
"It's Gabe, babe."

She shook her head and pulled her bag up on her shoulder, clutching her books to her chest and ran in the direction of the school, flashing him a smile over her shoulder. She saw him give an exaggerated wave and look up at the hunter-bunny-cloud.

***

"Bye guys!" Eva chirped, butterflies gathering in her stomach.
Shauna stopped as the rest of their friends waved, beginning the long walk down the school's tree-lined drive. "Where are you going?"
"Oh, I'm just meeting someone."
"Someone?" Shauna laughed.
Eva rolls her eyes.
"Do you need me to call midway in case it's a terrible date?"

"I'll be fine." Eva shook her head. She couldn't imagine a date with Gabriel Wells being the experience you'd want to bail out from. "I'll text you when I get home."

"You'd better!" Shauna called playfully.

On first impression, she was most certainly right. He was sitting in a red Mustang convertible, the roof down, the paint shining blindingly brightly. He was tapping his hand on the steering wheel along with the radio, his school tie disheveled, his long hair blowing in the wind as though he was in a music video. They were playing something upbeat from the early 2000s, which made the car seem all the more exciting. Eva stopped at the edge of the lot and stared. He'd said convertible, but this was ostentatious. What kind of seventeen-year-old drove that kind of car? She concluded it must be daddy's money, like so many other kids.

As she watched, a few of the guys from the football team gathered around and struck up a conversation she couldn't hear over the music, talking to Gabriel as though they'd known him all his life,which they hadn't,because they hadn't gone to school in the annex of a little church a lifetime ago. Could she be mistaken?

She felt someone stopping directly behind her and turned to see the other new guy, Hale, staring at Gabriel's car too. He looked bothered, disgusted even. She opened her mouth to say something but he turned and walked off. "Curiouser and curiouser..." she mumbled to herself. Gathering her courage and trying to contain the trepidation, she walked around the parking lot to reach the Mustang.

"Hey, babe!" She heard and looked up to see Gabe waving her over, grinning ear to ear. The other guys from the team mirrored the surprise she imagined on her own face. "Ready?"

She let herself into the passenger seat, feeling tongue-tied. Was he like this with everyone?

"See you guys tomorrow." He called to the crowd of jocks as they backed away to let them drive through the school grounds.

"How was Spanish?" He asked loudly.

"I'm surprised you remembered."

"It was three hours ago."

"It was fine. Guess you skipped school?"

"I figure I've already missed a month. What's another afternoon?"

"Won't you get into shit?"

"Did you just say shit? Nah. Nobody's worryin' about my grades."

"Oh, deary me, forgot to be a southern belle." She laughed, leaning fully into her Southern accent. He must have thought she was some sort of prude, too dainty to swear. "Shouldn't you be worried about your grades, though? College applications are pretty soon."

Eva kept her eyes on him as he drove. He was a natural behind the wheel, as though he'd been driving for decades, a bit like her dad, actually. He never slowed down preemptively, and he shifted lanes close to the turns. The stops were hard and he never waited at a yellow light. He exuded confidence. Her driving instructor might have called it reckless, but she never felt like grabbing onto anything, the way she did when she got into the car with some of her friends who had just recently gotten their licenses.

"I'll be fine." He dodged the subject.
"Okay." She mostly felt lightheaded, like this was some sort of daydream.
"So babe, where are we goin'?" The cadence of his speech was familiar too.
She paused. She thought he was the one guiding her. She stuck out her lower lip. "Ice cream, right?"
"Tell me where to go."

She'd forgotten he wasn't from here, maybe because he already fit in better as though he'd been here forever. Eva directed him along Ashford and down to Peaches & Cream, her favourite ice cream parlor. The shop was full of elementary school students and their parents. As they parked the car, she noticed Gabe smiling as he watched kids pushing one another out of line, the afternoon sun catching the highlights in his otherwise dark hair and picking up gold colours in his eyes. Being away from school, Eva definitely felt more confident. She hadn't particularly enjoyed getting into the car with everyone gawking at them. She'd come to this ice cream shop hundreds of times with Shauna, Daphne, Mel and Sasha. She'd even been here on dates before.

"So, where did you transfer from?" She asked as they got in line behind a rowdy group of kids.
"Pretty far. And you, where are you from?"
"All over the place." She said earnestly. "We've lived everywhere."
"Same." He answered, grinning. "Man! Check out the number of flavors in this place!" He was practically bouncing, pointing at the sign. She giggled; he was like a puppy. "Yup! I've tried most of them, except mint, nasty."
"Top pick?"

"Depends on what you like. Ever had a Georgia peach before?"
"Nah but y'all sure like naming things after fruit so I'm guessin' it's a good choice."
"My mom makes the best peach things...cobblers, pies, jam."
"Sounds like a peach." It was cheesy but the nerves made her laugh.

They got their ice cream and sat down at the little tables in front of the shop, but the kids had taken all the spots.
"Eat in the car?"
"Won't your parents be pissed?"
Gabriel laughed. "Nobody's gonna know what happens in that car."

The flirty note wasn't lost on Eva and he didn't disagree with her about the parents comment. Child-Gabe definitely didn't have parents, unless the so-called orphans at the church were living there for other reasons, which she realized was likely the case. He opened the door to the backseat, and they put their feet up on the dashboard. He asked her about her family, school, music, and she was happy to oblige. He was a great conversationalist and never let them lapse into silence. The sun waned in the distance kids went home, and the music kept playing. She wasn't sure how they'd slumped down so low that she'd propped her feet on his lap.

While she was happy to oblige and share about herself, he was dodging her questions left, right and center. He always had an easy but vague answer no matter what she asked about his past.
He was definitely the boy from the church. Did he honestly not recognize her or was he playing the long con? She told herself that was okay for a first date.

When they finished their ice cream, they lined up for another scoop and returned to their spots to keep chatting. Suddenly, she saw all of the lights along the road flickering on. It had gotten dark.
"Oh, crap.What time is it?" She asked, leaning forward to check the dashboard.
"I don't wear watches." Gabe shrugged, taking a swig from a bottle of water.
Eva squeaked. "It's 9:30!"
"Yeah?"
"I've got to get home!"
"Oh, overprotective parents?"

She wrinkled her nose as she dug her phone out of her bag. There were several missed calls and texts from her mom. Her parents were probably worried sick. A wave of guilt hit Eva. Why hadn't she come up with an alibi? She hadn't thought they'd be out this late. She quickly flipped her phone to airplane mode. She'd have to claim that it had died.

"Do you need to go home?"

"I can't pull up in front of the house in a car like this!" She cried, digging the palms of her small hands into her eye sockets. She groaned in frustration. "Okay, let's go. My house is that way." She pointed to the right.

She directed him for about fifteen minutes as the sky turned from pink to purple to a velvety indigo. They left the radio on to defuse the tension. "Stop here." She said firmly, as they turned onto her block. He did, pressing his foot solidly on the break and pulling the car into park. She shut off the radio.
"Bye, Gabe Wells." She said, pulling the door open and letting herself out.

"Um. Good night?" The disappointment on his face was priceless, but she didn't have time right now. With all her things, she began walking down the sidewalk, waving at him. He shut off the engine and hopped out of the car to follow.
"Where are you going?" He asked, catching up.
"Home."
"Which is...?"
"At the end of the street."
"Why are we walking?"
"I'm walking, and you're going to get back in the car and wait for me to go inside before my dad sees you and shoots you dead."
"I'm not lettin' you walk home alone!"
"Yes, you are." She said, stopping and turning to look at him. She reached up and put a finger over his mouth to silence him.

"And if you do. Maybe we can do this again." She smiled.
He smiled back, seeming to understand, "Good night Princess."
She laughed. "Is that an upgrade from babe?"

He shrugged and let her go, watching her walk into the darkness. Her street had no lights, but she knew the car was still off. She turned to find him sitting on the hood until she was on the threshold of her house, a beam of light pouring into the street as she stepped inside.

Alexandra

When Eva told them about her impromptu date, Sasha didn't know what to make of it. On the one hand, Eva seemed so excited. On the other, every interaction she'd had with Gabriel Wells, which, to be honest, was limited, had suggested that he was just a vapid, arrogant, self-obsessed rich kid. It didn't surprise her that he liked Eva, but for Eva to just go with it? She supposed it was none of her business, but she felt protective. It didn't help that Eva was so tight-lipped about her new relationship. She was even hanging out with Gabriel's friends, people they'd always avoided. Their mutual friend Mila told her not to take it personally.

Their school was small, and any new addition made waves. Gabriel was like a typhoon. The other new kid, Hale, less so. His only reputation was that he was rude. She never saw him speaking to anyone, but he paid attention in classes and was always among the first ones at their desk. Despite making up her mind that she wanted to meet him on that first day, it was a few weeks before Sasha caught up with Hale. She'd tried to meet him earlier, but he had the uncanny ability to disappear the minute class was over, regularly forcing Sasha to ask around for him. Her friends teased that she was stalking him and that he knew it.

On the afternoon when her luck finally changed, she had stayed behind to finish a science lab with Margo, her lab partner. Margo insisted that she was "so much help." though both girls knew Sasha had no idea what Margo was doing. All Sasha did was cheer at the appropriate times when whatever they were mixing turned the right color to warrant her name on the lab report. Having finished the lab, Margo stayed upstairs to work on other assignments, while Sasha shuffled downstairs, eager to get outside. When she walked past the cafeteria, she spotted a tall figure at the very back of the room. It was him!

Sasha smiled, stepping between the empty tables and making a beeline for the back of the room.
"Hello!"
"Hi." She had heard Hale speak before, and he always seemed frustrated, even at teachers. It was surprising how much derisiveness could fit into one syllable.
She sat in front of him, the white cafeteria table between them.
"Whatcha doing here all by yourself?"
"Checking my email," he stated flatly.

"Ah," she nodded. "From your friends at your old school? Must be tough." She leaned forward on one elbow; the back of the laptop screen obscured her sight of him a little, so all she could see was his dark eyes and the mop of dark brown hair.

"It's not that bad," he stated, with the same tone.

"Where'd you move from?

He paused, as though he was thinking about it. It struck her as odd not to know the answer immediately.

"New York."

"Oh yeah?" She grinned. "I've been to NYC. Where from?"

"Brooklyn."

"I have a friend who lives there! I mean, it's a big city, and you probably don't know her, but...?"

He stared at her with his fingers positioned on the F and J keys, his thumb shifting over the spacebar of his computer. Sasha realized how silly her question sounded. She decided to switch gears.

"Do you miss it? Our town must seem so small in comparison."

"It's fine." It sounded like a shrug, but his shoulders hadn't moved.

"Well, you're taking it better than I probably would. I'd miss my friends like crazy. Speaking of which, do you wanna come have lunch with us? I'm sure they won't mind, and it's a nice day out."

She tried to read his facial expression, it hadn't changed a smidge throughout their short exchange.

"I think I'll just answer my emails. I have an essay to work on anyway." This explained why he wasn't part of any of the groups yet. She didnèt believe him for a second. She wasn't in all of the advanced classes with him, but she knew they didn't have enough homework to warrant this kind of commitment.

"Oh, come on, Hale. You've got all day to do that. Besides, it's a total waste of recess to stay inside." She kept her smile unwavering, hoping to draw him out. She knew she was being pushy, but sometimes people needed to be pushed, in her humble opinion.

"Look, I'd rather get my work finished." His speech became strained.

She rolled her eyes.

"You're sure? Final offer now. You're going to get lonely doing this all the time. I don't mean go about it like Gabriel Wells, but, you know, there are worthwhile people here too. I don't even mean me," she put her hand on her chest for emphasis. "I mean that there are people you'll like. Some aren't even obnoxiously chatty!" Obviously, beating around the bush wasn't the way to go with this guy, and she was a little annoyed that he hadn't bothered to ask her name.

He heaved a sigh. "I'm positive. Alexandra, am I right?"

At least he knew who she was. "Yeah, pleased to meet you." She held out her hand across the table, eyebrows up, challenging him to take that tone with her again. He reached his hand toward her outstretched one and shook it firmly with a nod. "You don't have to wait around; I'm sure your friends are waiting for you."

Was it just her imagination, or was his hand calloused? It took everything in her to refrain from asking.

"Well, I'll be beside the gazebo by the tree at the far end. Seriously, come see us when you're done with your emails. We're not exactly the "in" crowd, but my friends will welcome you with open arms." She straightened and walked back out, waving goodbye.

Chapter 3
Rhythms and Rumours

Eva

She couldn't believe it was her last homecoming. Her mom had agreed to drop her off so she didn't have to walk all the way here in heels. Shauna, her usual ride, was ditching homecoming to spend more time with her boyfriend.

"At least Mel, Daphne, and Sasha will be there," she thought, as her mom snapped a photo of her with her phone.

"Mom!" she exclaimed.

"You get a lift, I get a photo. It's a fair deal."

Eva couldn't argue with that. Her mom was a little overbearing, but she knew it came from a good place. Having moved around so much throughout her childhood, and with her dad being deployed at various times in those years, there were times where it had felt like it was just herself and her mom, even after her little brother had come along. She knew her parents didn't like the idea that she was growing up so fast, so she let her mom indulge in trying to capture these little moments. She gave her mom a quick hug and stepped out of the car. "One last homecoming." She thought, inhaling the warm night air, the breeze carrying petals from the lilacs that bloomed around the gazebo.

"No later than midnight, okay?" Her mom chided from the window.

"Don't worry, mom, this isn't my first rodeo." She assured her. The lineup outside the school had already begun. She spotted Pamela and Genevieve at the very back. She waved as her mother reluctantly reversed the car out of the parking lot. Once she was out of sight, Eva walked to the back of the line by herself, her heels making a clicking noise on the pavement. She tugged at the red dress she'd chosen, it had ridden up in the car. It was too warm for her sweater so she rolled it up and shoved it into her purse.

Eva expected Gabe to ask her to go with him, but despite spending time together recently, he never asked, as though he didn't know homecoming was right around the corner. He spent a lot of time with Jason and Pamela's group, but he always found moments to drop in on her, and the unpredictability was both thrilling and frustrating.

18

Sometimes he caught her in the morning and honked for her to hop into the car. At other times, he surprised her outside of her last class and insist they go to the park or the movies. He'd often invited her to sit with the popular kids, but it never lasted long. It just wasn't her scene. She had no idea how he fit in so quickly. None of the jokes they told or the references hit right for her. His friends also loved to tease one another, which wasn't a dynamic she'd ever felt comfortable in, especially with random acquaintances. In this case, she would've liked to know if she'd be dancing with him, but she didn't ask, nor did he. She wondered if he'd be here at all.

She pulled her phone and texted Sasha, "Are you here?"
She glanced up at the sound of her name.
"Eva!" Pam smiled, wearing a tight silver dress. They saw each other out of uniform so infrequently that it was always a big deal. "They're still not letting anyone in. We've all been waiting for the DJ to get his act together. You look amazing!"
"Thanks, so do you guys." she said awkwardly. Genevieve mumbled a thanks and kept scrolling through her phone. "Gwen says she and the guys are on their way."
Eva supposed they knew about her and Gabe, which was why they acted so chummy. They had never been outright mean to her, but this was definitely beyond their usual level of casual friendliness.
Sasha finally texted back, "On my way. The buses are so slow at night."
Eva could finally hear the music blasting from inside the cafeteria and coloured lights were flashing in the small windows. The cafeteria was on the main floor, but below ground level. More people were arriving, lining up behind her. She felt the usual pre-dance jitters in her extremities.
"So, where's Alex?" Pam asked.
"Sasha?"
"No, silly! Your boyfriend?"
It took a moment for Eva to realize to whom Pam was referring. "Oh, we broke up a while ago."
"I'm sorry! What happened? You two were so cute!"

"No biggy." She shrugged. "Plenty of fish in the sea." Alex had been a senior last year and went to college early in the summer. She hadn't thought of him much since school had started. They'd dated for nearly a year, but by the time he'd left, she had already emotionally let him go. What little excitement had been there from the start was long gone, and they'd fizzled out so she'd expected it by the time the conversation about breaking up had come up.

Soon afterwards, he began posting pictures with girls from college, forcing Eva to delete him from social media. When she thought about it, it was more the idea of having a boyfriend that was fun, but beyond being nice, she wasn't sure what to say about Alex. It felt like a long time ago, though it wasn't really. Pamela and Genevieve nodded approvingly. She wondered how they even knew about who she had dated. She didn't think anyone cared beyond her own friends. She'd been careful not to share anything about him on her own social media. She didn't need the questions from her parents.

"Oh, there they are!" Gen said and left the lineup for the parking lot where a Lamborghini blasting music so loudly that all she could hear was the base had pulled up. She knew it belonged to Jason's parents.

Jason, Gwen, Eric, TJ and Gabe stepped out, passing a small silver flask back and forth. Eva bit her lip seeing Gabe in a black suit.

"He cleans up good, doesn't he?" Pam said.

"He sure does."

"So, are you dating?"

Eva shrugged. "So they say."

"I thought he liked Gwen."

"Not that I know of."

"And Jenn likes him. You know that, right?"

"That's none of my business." Eva muttered.

"Hey!" Sasha called, waving on her way up the hill. She was wearing a black skirt, a red tank top, and black ballerina slip-ons.

"Where's Mila?" Eva asked as she approached, grateful for the interruption. Pam didn't greet Sasha.

"Bailed. How about Shauna?"

"She said she'd rather spend time with her boyfriend."

"Final hurrah is on us then." Sasha said.

The lineup was finally moving as students showed their student cards to a volunteer up front.

Jason's group, including Gabe, ended up standing in front of them as Pamela waved them over.

"Typical." Sasha grumbled, but didn't make a scene.

Gabe didn't seem to notice them, which stung. She and Sasha followed the lineup inside to the gym, where the student society and alums had already set up the food and drinks. Teachers peppered the room while disco lights danced off the room's dark corners. It felt so much smaller than in previous years. The music bounced off the walls, filling the small room.

A crowd of dancers was already in the middle of the space, and another group backed up against a corner, probably sharing a joint.

"I'm going to go get a drink." Sasha shouted over the music. Eva nodded and headed to the dance floor to catch up with some of her friends from the yearbook committee, feeling much more relaxed now that she was with a group of people, though still irritated. There was a little dancing, a little bit of yearbook talk, and a few quickly snapped photographs. In the midst of a conversation about senior photos and their contrived poses, she felt a tap on her shoulder. "Hey, babe!"

"Hey?"

"Wanna dance?" Gabe stood in a white untucked shirt and black pants, the top part of the tux had somehow disappeared.

"You finally noticed me." She thought, but kept it on the tip of her tongue.

"Sure," She said instead, and allowed him to lead her back to his group of friends, who were already dancing drunkenly. Gabe didn't seem drunk, just excited and happy.

"So, who'd you come with?" He asked her, swaying to the music in a way that wasn't exactly dancing, more of a non-committal acknowledgment that there was music.

"Just myself. No one asked me."

"Is that right?" He laughed, "School full of idiots then."

"Idiots indeed." She agreed, watching his expression. He seemed pretty comfortable. She wondered if he'd ever been to a school dance.

"Can I cut in?" It was Jenn, stepping between them in a dusk-blue dress. Just then, as though on cue, the DJ chose a slow ballad, pushing all of the couples on the dance floor to get closer to one another and banishing the others to the sidelines.Gabe didn't protest and Jenn put both hands on his shoulders. She sighed, feeling small again and left the dance floor along with everyone else who wasn't in a couple.

As Eva approached the food table, Sasha handed her a cup of punch that smelled of alcohol.

"Looks like you need this." She said.

"The yearbook committee set this out?" She exclaimed in shock. Since they were all underage, if caught, they'd be expelled.

"No, courtesy of Evan's flask. It's terrible rum." Sasha said, sipping at her concoction. Evan was one of Sasha's friends who sat with them sometimes. He'd been new last year but he was closer with the kids from the band.

"I'm okay." She lied, watching Jenn pulling Gabe to her and whispering something in his ear that made him laugh, their bodies melting into one another.

"No, you're not. Gabe's playing you like a flute."

"Um. thanks?" Eva scoffed. She was starting to get more than a little annoyed at everyone sharing their unsolicited opinions.

21

"Sorry, I don't mean it like that." Her friend said, "I just think he doesn't appreciate you."

"How would you know?" Eva snapped and downed her drink.

"I would if you'd tell me about it. Also, I can see with my own eyes." She waved at Jenn and Gabe.

"You know what Sash?"

"What?"

She wanted to snap back, to tell her it was none of her damn business, but she realized it wasn't Sasha she was annoyed with: Gabe was over there dancing with all these other girls and she was here waiting for him to come towards her. Maybe it was time she gave this rumour mill something to talk about on her own terms.

"Never mind. I don't want to talk about it right now."

Jenn and Gabe had finished the slow dance, and the music had shifted to a low base again, the crowd shifting to make room for breakdancers and groups of people jumping. She left Sasha and headed towards Gabe again. He spotted her and grinned. "Lookin' to dance?"

"Actually, I thought we could go have a smoke." She pointed to the door. Gabe's eyebrows lifted in surprise, "you don't smoke!"

"You coming?" She asked, taking his hand and heading outside. Like a puppy, he followed her. Gen and Pam's looks were satisfying as she passed them by the door, but the fact that Gabe just went along with her request was even better. She didn't turn back to look at anybody else.

She led him just behind the school, and stood before him, looking up into his confused face.

"Are you going to keep playing hard to get?" She said, letting go of his hand.

"Hard to get?" He put both of his hands in his pockets.

"Yeah, you keep flirting with me. We go on dates. Are you going to do anything about it?"

"Like what?" He chuckled, leaning in.

She put a finger upon his lips. "Are you going to ask me out first?"

"Ask you out?"

"Yeah, as in - will you be my girlfriend, Evangeline?"

"Do you want me to?" The question didn't hold a hint of sarcasm. He was genuinely asking.

"Are you kidding me?" She laughed.

"No, but I just figured you weren't that kinda girl, you know?"

"What kind is that?"

"I don't know. I'm...I'm me."

She shook her head, leaned up, closed her eyes and kissed him. It took him a moment to do anything; not like him at all. She pulled back and looked straight into his eyes. Was this not what he wanted? She stepped back, feeling stupid. "Sorry, I guess I misread..."

"No, wait..." he stuttered and hungrily pulled her back towards him. She allowed him to kiss her, standing on her tippy toes and responding in kind. She felt the smile on his lips and tasted alcohol on his tongue. Neither of them pulled away for a long time, the school wall keeping them upright and grounded. She kept one hand against the gray brick, the texture of it keeping her from losing her head. When they did pull away, both were breathless.

"Are you okay with this? Even if I'm not makin' any promises?" He asked.

"I didn't ask for promises. I just want you to ask me to the next dance,that is, I thought you would've wanted to invite me."

He nodded. "Message received." and leaned forward again. Kissing in the dark was way better than dancing. There was still so much left unsaid but she wanted to silence the hamster wheel in her brain. She wanted this right now. The rest, she'd figure out later.

Sasha

It was a rainy, muggy day. Their school skirts clung to their thighs and their white polo shirts did nothing to keep them cool. The heat was oppressive and triggered her anxiety. Eva, Sasha, Mel and Daphne were stuck to their chairs in the tiny school library working on an English project, surrounded by the buzz of all of the other students. The school year picked up speed, and exams were already looming. She and Eva hadn't talked about what had happened at the dance, but she knew better than to confront her in a group setting.

After Eva had disappeared with Gabe, Sasha quickly found herself wanting to go home, so she did. She didn't love large group gatherings to begin with, even less so without someone to talk to from her circle. She'd spent the weekend complaining about it to Mila while they marathoned an old cartoon. Unfortunately, Mila wasn't usually one to chime in on these things. She'd essentially told her she was taking this way too seriously, and that was that. She'd been rereading the same sentence over and over again in her Social Studies textbook, something about land acknowledgements, but the information refused to sink in. She highlighted the sentence for good measure, hoping that would help.

"So," Daphne leaned forward conspiratorially towards Eva, "You and Gabe..."

Sasha looked up from her notes expectantly. If she couldn't study, at least she could hear more about what was going on with Eva. She wasn't a big fan of this new relationship. She had two pet peeves: arrogance and dishonesty. Gabriel Wells had both in spades, at least, that's what everyone said. Didn't Eva know that? Didn't she care? Hadn't they always mocked guys like that? Eva was asking to get her heart broken. The rumours were that Eva had kissed Gabe at homecoming, which didn't seem like Eva at all, but she certainly seemed ready to choose him over her friends these days.

Mel continued twirling her pencil between her fingers, her head still towards her notes.

Eva let out a huge sigh, "I don't get why everyone is making such a big deal about it. We're just hanging out." She leaned back in her chair, folding her arms over her chest.

"Jenn's saying you stole him from her." Daphne remarked. Sasha had heard the same, but she could see Eva's cheeks reddening. Mel kept quiet.

"What about you?" Sasha interrupted, turning to Daphne. "Do you like anybody this year?" There was only one way to get Daphne to stop talking about someone else; to make her talk about herself. She didn't want Eva to storm off and more than that, she wanted to see that despite her frustrations, she was on her side. Their friendship was bigger than some guy!

Debby tucked a stray strand of hair behind her ear. "Still working on Hale. He held the door for me yesterday morning when I came in. We both get here at like seven, so it gives us time to talk."
"I don't think anyone's getting far on that one." Eva shook her head.
"He's really shy." Sasha said supportively.
"Or an ass. Didn't he make Lucy cry?" Mel said. She'd heard that story too. Apparently, Lucy had been partnered with him in gym class and he'd said something offensive, though no one knew what it had been. The theories varied, but the consensus was that whatever it was, it was bad enough that she'd refused to partner with him again. Sasha wasn't sure what she believed, but she did find Lucy annoying. Her locker was directly next to hers last year and there had never been a day when Lucy hadn't been whining about something inane, whether it was the weather or how her aesthetician had done a bad job with her nails.

"Yeah, that wasn't okay, but he's gotten nicer since the first week." Deb said.

"Maybe he's just a loner." Sasha suggested.

"You have no leg to stand on Sash- everyone knows you like him too." Deb replied.

Sasha blushed. "Guess not."

"I think we just need a different approach." Deb suggested, looking conspiratorial.

"What approach?" Eva asked, looking calmer.

"Well, if you and Gabe are "hanging out," Daphne made quotation marks with her fingers. "Could you help with the roommate? Everyone knows they live together."

"How are they paying for a place of their own is what I'd like to know." Mel thought out loud, still twirling her pencil.

"I don't think so..."

Daphne looked impatient. "Eva, we're your friends. You don't have to hide everything from us all the time."

"I'm not hiding anything. We just don't talk about stuff like that."

"Sounds like you don't talk much." Daphne teased, though she sounded irritated.

Eva had had enough. "I have no idea where they're getting the money from," she answered Mel, "and as for Jenn, she can think what she wants. I really don't care. I've also never spoken to Hale so you're out of luck girls." She slammed her book shut and started putting her things in her bag. "I'm gonna grab a coffee before class; who's coming?"

Mel looked at Daphne, but Daphne gave Eva a disapproving look and shook her head. "No, I'll keep at this."

Sasha slung her bag over her shoulder. "I'm in. My brain is mush anyway." She hated when things got heated like that. She and Eva had discussed time and time again how girls could be petty and judgmental. She'd spent so much time trying to find a group of friends where she didn't feel they were setting each other up, but every now and again, especially when guys were concerned, it turned into the same catty bullshit.

Eva

Eva's life had both changed dramatically and remained painfully the same. Gabriel continued to push to spend time with her, and she accepted most of the time, even times when she already had plans. On his end, he was always being pulled away by his own friends, and she didn't much like being around that group. She also didn't want her friends to feel like she had ditched them, though she was feeling spread thin. It was enough that she had bailed on study sessions twice last week because Gabe invited her to "catch a ride" to Mel's but then drove her to get iced cappuccinos instead. It was hard to keep up with everything on top of school and her extracurriculars. Her mom was also getting huffy about how often she wasn't home for family dinner. The trouble was, even when she wasn't with Gabe, she was thinking about Gabe, or remembering moments from her childhood that she hadn't thought about in years. She kept trying to find the words to bring it up with him directly, but kept chickening out at the last minute. It was driving her nuts!

She tried not to let her mind spiral as she and Sasha left the library. The corridors to the cafeteria were full of students sitting on the floor, trying to cool off from the heat on the dirty tiles.

"This is the only time of year I resent having a historical building." Sasha said.

"I'm just tired of being accused." Eva said, hoping for some sympathy.

Sasha shrugged, "They didn't actually accuse you of anything."

"Thanks for the support." Eva thought, but she held her tongue. She didn't need confrontation, but she wished Sasha would cut her some slack.

As the girls made their way through the corridor and into the stuffy senior cafeteria, a loud and cheery "Hey!" could be heard from the back of the room. A group of cheerleaders, including Jenn, sat around Gabe as he leaned his back against the wall. Jason, TJ, Eric, and others joined him.

He waved both arms over his head towards Eva as though there was any chance that she couldn't see him. His shoelaces were characteristically undone, as were the regulatory top buttons on his school shirt. He had piled his hair on top of his head in the heat and secured it with his tie.

He looked hilarious and very pleased with himself. Sasha rolled her eyes, bristly. "That guy has no shame, none."

Eva chuckled, "None at all." She waved at Gabe as she made her way toward the coffee machine. As she stood in line, Daphne's words began to replay in the back of her mind. She shook her head. It didn't matter what Daphne thought.

Gabe bounced over to the coffee line just as they reached the front and slid two one-dollar bills into the slot.

"Where you been hidin'?" Jason was close behind. No one behind them said anything about the line having been cut, the power of seniors, or maybe of Gabe and Jason. Eva accepted the drink.

"Maybe you weren't looking hard enough." she said, trying to act nonchalant. When she was with him, it was easy to forget about prying eyes, judgements and rumours.

"So, you, me, Eric's party?" Gabe asked, getting himself a hot chocolate.

"Hey you." Eva turned to see if Jason was speaking to her, but it was Sasha he was addressing, who looked up at him, baffled.

"Hi Jason." Her friend mumbled, meeting Eva's gaze. They'd spent all their years at Saint-Ignatius in Jason's class, and the most he'd ever said to either of them was probably, "Can I borrow this?" or "When's the English final?"

Eva put the coffee cup to her mouth and turned back to Gabe. She'd completely forgotten his question. They moved out of the lineup to let Sasha get her coffee.

"Sorry?"

"Eric's party, you said you'd think about it?"

"I said I was undecided."

"You said you wanted me to invite you to the next dance, right? I'm inviting you."

"I have to see if I'm free that night."

Meanwhile, she eavesdropped on the conversation beside her.

"Guess you're buying me a coffee?" Sasha said boldly to Jason, nodding at the machine. "I like cream, no sugar."

Jason smiled and put in a coin. "You got it," he said with a wink. If Jason hadn't been so charismatic, that gesture would have come off as pathetic and cheesy. She wondered if Sasha could fall for someone like Jason, it sure would make her life easier if she could just merge friend groups. She watched Sasha pick up her cup.

"Thanks." She said, not making eye contact. "You didn't need to do that."

They moved out of the line to stand with Gabe and Eva.

"No problem. So, there's this party at Eric's this weekend. You should come." Jason said, shifting from one foot to the other.

Sasha laughed, glancing at Eva in bewilderment. "Won't Eric mind?" Eric's house was mere blocks from Sasha's, but neither she nor Eva had ever been inside. It was on one of the fancier streets in the neighbourhood, and they'd sometimes gone for walks there to see the elaborate Christmas decorations.

"Why would he?"

"Because you just invited a stranger to his house?"

"You're not a stranger, Alexandra. We've known you for years!" The fact that he had called her by her full name was a strong suggestion that they were strangers, Eva thought. Sasha didn't correct him though, which was uncharacteristic of her.

"So, you're sure he won't mind you inviting me without asking him?"

"Nah! It's cool." Jason said with a smile, "Besides, If Eric has a problem with it, he'll have to deal with me."

Sasha bit her lower lip. "I'll have to check what's going on that night."

"Hope you come!" Jason said with a coy smile at Sasha and headed back to his table.

"Still undecided babe?" Gabe asked Eva.

"Like I said, I have to see." Had Gabe asked Jason to ask Sasha to go so that she'd come?

"Alright; I'll meet you in the parking lot after school." Gabe said and pecked Eva on the lips, then followed Jason. TJ and Gwen had started a competition on who could balance the most sugar packets one on top of the other. He knocked over TJ's and announced Gwen as the winner, to which she clapped appreciatively. Eva couldn't believe he'd just kissed her in front of everybody like that.

Was this normal behaviour? They'd naturally gravitated towards one another when they were alone, easily moved from hand-holding to pecks on the cheek to full-on make-out sessions. Still, she wasn't sure how he felt about it happening in public, especially with the rumour mill churning. He didn't seem to care, acting as though they *were* alone.

Eva turned to Sasha, "Did Jason O'Neil just invite you to Eric's party? Is this real life?"

Sasha covered her mouth with her coffee cup, failing to hide the grin that crept across her face. Eva felt excited for her friend, though surprised. What if Sasha and Jason really did become an item? She'd have someone to hang out with besides the popular girls when she was with Gabe's friends. Besides, Jason wasn't a bad choice; a football player, charming, curly brown hair and massive brown eyes. He was cliché, but in the best way possible.

"No, I think we're getting heat stroke. I was sure I'd just seen you kiss Gabriel Wells publicly." Sasha said, checking her phone for the time. They began the long trudge up the stairs toward their classes.

"So, you and Jason, huh?" Eva said, mimicking Daphne's voice from earlier.

"Oh, come on, that's the most interaction I've ever had with Jason."

"Same. He was being nice, though."

"You're going to that party, right? I'm having flashbacks of all those movies where people get invited to parties as a joke and then come out tarred and feathered."

"I know. I keep waiting for something awful to happen." Eva said, taking a long sip of her coffee. She decided that a little honesty might go a long way with Sasha, particularly if she wanted her to attend the party too. "Gabe's been asking me to go, and since my parents are taking my brother to a basketball tournament, I can sneak out for the night." She said with a cheeky grin, "What they don't know won't kill me."

"You said you were undecided."
"Gabe isn't the only one who gets to keep me guessing." She dumped her empty coffee cup in the trash, mimicking dropping a microphone.
"Cheeky."
"You got Jason to buy you coffee!"
"Yeah, let's not take that seriously."
"If you say so. I gotta get to class," she sighed dramatically. "Text me later!" She called over her shoulder as she hurried out into the hallway.

Sasha

Sasha had science next, which meant that her having missed her "daily stalking" of Hale, wouldn't be a big deal because she shared her next class with him. Margo was away for an out-of-state math competition, so she'd need a lab partner.

She hoped he didn't think that schoolwork was why she kept hounding him to hang out with her. It wasn't. She just couldn't figure out why he was so averse to being adopted into the group. Mila kept saying to leave the poor guy alone - that between her, Daphne and Lucy, he probably just wanted some peace and quiet. Mila also said none of them had any gaydar. Sasha said that didn't matter.

She was still flustered from Jason suddenly taking an interest in her, but seeing Hale sitting quietly in his seat felt like everything had returned to normal. Without hesitation, Sasha plopped her backpack on the desk next to Hale when her cell phone buzzed in her bag. She popped it open briefly before the teacher could see her.
"He's going to get a restraining order." Mila's message read. She laughed, quickly glancing back at her friend at the back of the room, who was sliding her phone back into her anime-themed pencil case. She wiggled her eyebrows at her, making the other girl burst out laughing.

29

So far, her plan had been going well: Most people sat with their friends, and Hale sat alone. If she came in late enough, the seat beside him was the last one available. Today, it was just a fortunate circumstance. She greeted Hale cheerfully, laying out her books and pencils. She found it funny that around Jason, the most coveted guy in the school, she felt that she had to lay on the sass and put on a brave face, whereas around Hale, she kept finding new wells of enthusiasm. He nodded in response, not seeming to think it was worth using up breath on greetings. "I'm very caffeinated right now." She said, wiggling her fingers to illustrate.

"I see." He responded quietly.

He rarely engaged with what she said, unless it pertained to assignments, and even then, he kept it brief. He was organized, present, and unaffected by the chaos of school life, a steady rock in a quickly coursing stream. She was feeling jittery and it made her chatty.

"So, you and Gabe are roommates, right?"

"Right." His tone took that edge it had when he didn't want to discuss something, which was often. Glancing towards the door to see if the teacher had arrived, Sasha carried on. "Are you guys close?"

"No."

"I guess you're really different."

Another nod. She waited for elaboration, but none came.

"Do you hang out outside of school?"

"No."

"You don't like him?"

"I don't care." Nobody sounded this angry about something they didn't care about.

"Sorry, didn't mean to touch a nerve."

"Why are you apologizing?"

"Touchy subject?"

"No."

"How did it happen?"

"What?"

"You and Gabe living together." she clarified.

"We needed an apartment, living alone is expensive." Hale's voice went down a notch as though he was reminding himself how little he cared.

"Did you go to the same school before?"

"Yes."

She made a "go on" gesture with her hand, eyebrows up.

"We stay out of each other's way." He said, with a note of finality.

"What about his gang? Eric? Jason? TJ?"

"Idiots," He muttered.

"Hello, everyone!" The teacher came in at that moment, and Sasha didn't get to ask if he would be at Eric's party, though the answer seemed clear. Sasha felt Hale looking over at her when she finally looked up at the teacher. She debated passing him a note but thought better of it. He wasn't interested. She was playing with a black hair elastic around her wrist, creating a dent in her skin. She glanced over at him, and he looked away quickly. She smiled; at least she wasn't the only one staring.

Eva

"So, this is the infamous dwelling of Gabe Wells." Eva said, setting her backpack down by the door and slipping off her running shoes.
"This is it! Time for the grand tour." He spun in a circle in the tiny space. "Couch was here when we moved in, TV was here when we moved in, a pile of laundry that will probably be here when I move out, hallway, bathroom and shower's over that way and my bedroom's right here." He tossed his bag into the room, where it landed on the unmade bed with a thud. Eva let herself into the apartment and pushed the curtains back from the balcony door, flooding the room with sunlight.

"Nice view!" She unlocked the door and let herself onto the balcony in her socks. Gabe followed close behind, grabbing a pack of cigarettes and a lighter from a drawer in the tiny kitchen. She leaned onto the creaky banister and peered out over the rooftops.
"Doesn't the town look small from up here?" Eva remarked, looking out into the distance. Her house wasn't visible, and the school would be behind them, but she had a clear view of the base where her father worked. She could also see her little brother's school.
"I've lived in smaller. It's weird how there are always so many regular people living near military bases."
"Is it? Military families bring business, and the community just builds up around them. I've lived in military towns all my life; it doesn't feel weird to me." she said, closing her eyes to inhale fresh air.
Gabe lit his cigarette and offered her one. She shook her head. "No thanks. I've got both dance and swimming tomorrow."
"Didn't you say you smoked the other night?"
"That was me trying to get you alone." She laughed.
He chuckled. "And it worked like a charm. Do you mind if I smoke, though?"
"No, it's fine. How long have you been a smoker?"
"On and off since I was 12. I used to just to keep 'em for people but eventually tried it too. It ain't a big thing for me." He puffed little circles into the air, but it was too windy for the trick to work.
"Bad habit, you know."
"Yeah, I've got a lot of those."
"I'd kill my brother if he smoked. He's almost twelve."

"So, it bothers you?"

"No, it's kind of hot when you do it, sort of a James Dean thing."

"That's a good thing, right?"

She laughed. "You're not sure being called James Dean is a compliment?"

"Am I supposed to?"

"East of Eden? Rebel without a Cause? Giant?"

"Sprechen Zi English?"

"Oh my god Gabe, we have got to work on your pop culture references."

"Are these new movies?"

"Not at all, but most people have at least heard of them."

"I haven't seen a lot of movies, to be honest."

"So, what do you do for fun?"

"Hang out with you."

"Well, before I came along."

"I've never had as much fun as I have this year. Never in my whole life."

"I'm sure you say that to all the girls."

"It's true, though!"

He finished his cigarette and threw it off the side of the balcony.

"That's a bad habit too, littering."

"Sorry."

"Are you?"

"Sorry that it bugs you, sure."

She shook her head. "Will it make you stop?"

"Littering or smoking?"

"Either."

"Sure, well, around you anyway."

She shook her head. "You're too much, Gabe."

They returned inside in due time, and Eva had already pulled her computer out of her bag and was typing away. "We'll stream a movie and start your film education. What's your wifi password?"

"Uh..." He sat beside her on the couch and leaned over to type it in. They were so close that she could smell his shampoo. Before she knew it, they were curled up on the couch watching superhero movies, waiting for an all-dressed pizza. She was leaning against his chest, and his arm was around her. Sometimes, it was worth the rumours.

Chapter 4
Parties and Promises

Eva

The music could be heard down the street on the otherwise quiet suburban block. Sasha and Eva had decided that fashionably late was the best way to go. It would mean they didn't need to spend seven hours with people they had already seen a lot of at school.

They had spent at least two hours getting ready. Eva had settled on a form-fitting black dress and black heels, a choice that she regretted now. The heels were digging into the sides of her feet, and she wondered if she should have picked the white dress instead. With a deep inhale, she pushed open the door. "Let's do this," she said to Sasha, hoping to find reassurance in her friend's face.

She took a deep breath of stale, alcohol-scented air as the door swung open. As they pushed into the house, there were so many uncomfortable sensations in one shot that Eva almost turned around and went back outside, the music was deafening, there were too many people and too little space. A couple of kids they'd never seen before were blocking the corridor, holding beers.

"Ready?"
"No."
"Jason O'Neil invited you."
"That doesn't mean I'm ready. You know how I feel about crowds." Sasha said as another unfamiliar group of teens passed them through the doorway.

Eva took her friend's hand as they weaved through the corridor. The air was thick with summer scents: the sickly sweet skunky smell of pot, the sour smell of beer, too many perfumes mixing, hair spray and sweat. Eric's house was big, the main floor laid out perfectly for a dance floor in the open-plan living room and dining room, while the sound of ice hitting glass could be heard from the alcove kitchen.

Sasha stopped halfway into the room, and Eva stopped to check on her. "You okay?"

33

"Yeah, just a little claustrophobic! Let's just get this over with!" Sasha yelled over the music. Sasha took the lead and pushed ahead of her, firmly through to the open back patio door, where they could both make out the back of Jason's head over the crowd - height definitely played in his favour. If Jason was there, Gabe would be close.

"Hey, ladies!" It was Gwen, holding red plastic cups in one hand and a beer in the other. "How's it goin'?"
"Good! It seems like we got here right on time."
"Yeah, the music's just pickin' up. Here." She handed them each a plastic cup. "There's lots of stuff in the fridge and at the bar." She pointed at a mini-bar by the pool area. The pool illuminated from under the water, and a few people sat around the edges.
"Oh!" Sasha pulled a bottle out of her bag. "I have a contribution. It's vodka. My parents will never miss it. We don't really drink."
"Aren't you Russian?" Gwen asked, holding out her cup.
"That's a stereotype." Sasha corrected.

"Thanks!" Gwen put an arm around Sasha, which made her friend wince. Eva wasn't used to Party Gwen. This Gwen made a lot more sense as Jason's sister. School Gwen was serious and studious. Sasha's friend Margo was probably the only person who could beat her in grades. "Where can we get cups?" Sasha asked, extricating herself from Gwen's hug.
"Mini bar."

They headed in the direction she'd pointed and got themselves two red plastic cups. People were serving themselves. Eva wondered how Eric's parents were okay with any of this. This was definitely not the sort of party you could hide before the following day.

Sasha was going easy on the alcohol and closed the bottle after only a quarter of the cup. She made herself busy filling the rest of their cups with orange juice. "Screwdriver?" She asked, pushing the full cup into her hand. Eva took it and took a sip. There was shouting and laughing by the pool.

"There's Jason." She said to Sasha. It would be nice for her friend to finally go after a guy who was interested in her rather than having her chase all of these lone wolves. Sasha looked sheepish but followed Eva toward Jason and the group around him.

"Hey guys," Eva said as the two walked into the circle. TJ was in the middle of some sort of joke, and Jason was laughing so hard that he'd spilled liquid down his front, a dark stain on his light blue t-shirt. "Oh, hey ladies.'"

Eva looked around for the familiar long hair and dark eyes, but Gabe wasn't here. She wished she could call or text him, but he'd never given her a phone number in all the time they'd spent together. How had that not come up? She supposed it was because he seemed to just show up out of the blue whenever she thought about him, which was often. "Glad you made it." Jason said.

"I live three blocks away. I could've sleepwalked here." Sasha confessed.

The conversation turned to classes, and TJ started to recap the beginning of his sports-related story as Eva kept looking around for Gabe. A few people were in the pool, but none were short and muscled. "I'll be right back, bathroom." Eva said and started heading back into the house. Sasha was laughing with Jason and seemed content to be near him, so she figured she would be fine. She slid the patio door open again and stepped inside, where the music had turned to screaming techno that didn't qualify as music under any definition. She ran into Pamela in the kitchen, sipping on something fizzy.

"Eva!" Pamela cried, wrapping her arms around her.

"Pamela...hi." Eva pulled away, trying to gain some personal space.

"I've never seen you at Eric's house parties."

"Gabe invited me, yeah."

"Gabriel Wells is like, really something, isn't he?"

Eva had to agree. Of course, everyone else had noticed it too. "Yeah, have you seen him?"

"Oh." Pamela looked up towards the stairs. "I did...we danced briefly, and then he went off with Eric and Jenn."

"Where?" She tried to make herself heard over the blasting music, which someone had cranked even higher, the walls and windows shook.

Pamela shrugged. "Honey, you'd best not get too attached to a guy like that."

"Why? What's going on with him?"

"I saw him go upstairs." She repeated, as though that meant something specific that Eva was already supposed to know.

"I have to go." She said and moved on towards the stairs. She went up a few steps and almost tripped on a couple making out, spilling half of her drink, some on her dress and some on the ground. She was momentarily glad that she'd chosen the black dress. Where was Gabe, though? He was the one who'd invited her here, and now she had to ask for directions to find him? She liked that he was unpredictable, it kept things

35

interesting, but this was ridiculous. She was starting to wish she hadn't agreed to come. This was so not her scene: house parties, alcohol, a bunch of people she didn't know. Parties with her friends usually involved watching movies into the early hours of the morning and eating enough junk food to feel ill.

She was just thinking of going back to Sasha and suggesting they do just that when things got worse. A door at the top of the stairs was swung open, and Gabriel emerged from a bedroom. He was still looking behind him as he stepped out, tugging his shirt down, reaching for a drink that someone handed him. A giggle came from beyond the door, and Jenn joined him on the landing. He turned and saw Eva, who had reached the top of the steps, still holding part of her drink, her other hand on the banister for balance.

He looked straight at her, grinning. "Hey, babe!" He said it as though nothing was wrong, as if this was normal.

His face fell when he saw her expression. She looked at Jenn, who stared back at her, unabashed. Before she knew what she was doing, Eva threw what was left of her vodka and juice at him and ran back down the stairs as quickly as high heels could carry her.

"Eva, wait!" She heard from behind her, but was already out the door and into the night air. She slipped her shoes off and kept running barefoot, feeling like the pounding of her feet on the ground was the only thing keeping her from falling apart.

Sasha

Her vision was a little blurry, and she could feel the blood rushing to her cheeks. She'd had too much to drink. TJ and Eric were playing a game of rock paper scissors that brought them closer and closer to the poolside. The loser of each match not only had to step closer to the pool but also had to drink and she and Jason had been the designated drink providers.

"Rock, paper, scissors!" Eric laughed.

"Scissors beat the... rock!" Eric slurred.

"No, you dumbass!" TJ smacked his friend's hand with the "scissors." Jason handed him another drink and Eric shot it briskly.

"Alright, I'm out!" And he jumped into the pool, clothes and all.

"Wait up!" TJ called and launched himself in too. Sasha laughed and squealed, pelted with water. "Want in?" Jason asked.

"No way!" She laughed, "I'm so drunk, I'll drown!"

"Come on!" Jason jumped in himself as did a few girls who had somehow appeared in bikinis. Sasha got up quickly before he could pull her in. She laughed so hard that it made her dizzy, or maybe it was the alcohol. "I have to go find Eva!" She said.

"Bring her back here!" TJ called.

"And Gabe!" Jason added.

Sasha nodded and headed back into the house. She made her way through the crowd, the buzzing in her head making it easier to cope with the feeling of being crushed. She knew she wasn't thinking straight, and wanted Eva to ground her. She also needed to pee. Sasha headed up the steps, holding onto the banister when the world tipped a little. She took out her phone from her pocket and texted Eva. "Where are you? I'm drunk."

She marched up the stairs to find the bathroom door locked, so she sat down next to it to wait. With a flush, Gen came out. "Oh hey!" Sasha scooped herself up from the floor. "Have you seen Eva?"

"That little bitch? Yeah, I saw her."

"Excuse me?" Sasha shouted indignantly.

"She threw a drink at Gabe and me and then ran out."

"What do you mean ran out? Why?"

"Ask her, not me. I'm not the one throwing drinks at people. Gabe's pissed off too."

Gen swept past her and down the staircase. Sasha had never had an issue with Gen before, she even lent her class notes sometimes, but she was livid. Sasha went into the bathroom and locked the door. When she was done, she looked at herself in the mirror. Round face, smudged makeup, she felt like an imposter. Coming to this party had been a stupid idea. She hardly knew anyone here and the only person she did know had taken off without her. She checked her phone again, her message had still not been read. She felt sober as she marched through the crowded halls to the patio area to tell Jason she was heading out, her desire to be at the party had gone with Eva. The pool was completely full, everyone crushed together like sardines, limbs and heads bobbing up and down, laughter rising.

"Alexandra!"

She turned to see Jason sitting on a pool chair. She walked over and sat on the edge of the chair, close enough to feel a bit flirty, far enough that she wasn't touching him.

"You look bummed." He said. "Find them?"

"I'm fine and no, I didn't."

Jason laughed. "Isn't that girl language for 'watch what you say?'"

"It's human for 'I don't want to talk about it,' not exclusive to girls." She answered, watching everyone splashing around and being silly. She wished she was the sort of person who did silly things like that, but she didn't feel comfortable throwing herself into a pool full of drunk people.

"Anything I can do?"

She sighed. "No. I guess I just don't feel like being at a party."

"Want a lift home?"

She was surprised. "I thought you were having a good time."

"I am, but you're not, and I invited you."

She tried to argue, but he insisted that she wasn't walking home drunk, which was sweet.

"Okay, let's go then." He got up swiftly, stretching. Jason was certainly easy on the eyes. She'd expected him to try and convince her to stay but he'd just accepted what she wanted and was willing to help. It was flattering and novel to have someone pay attention to her like this. Was it possible that Jason actually liked her? She tried to think of a single moment before now where she'd felt anything towards him and came up short. To be fair, she'd never paid him any mind either.

"Are you okay to drive?" She asked.

"I haven't been drinking."

She lifted an eyebrow at him sarcastically.

"I don't drink much. Makes it hard to work out the next morning."

That was admirable. She followed him through the house, trying not to step on anyone's foot and let him lead her to his car, a black jaguar. She had no interest in cars, but their school was full of people who did. Maybe she was just jealous of his fancy life. It wasn't fair to him, he didn't choose to have privilege; he was born into it and made the most of it. When he turned the ignition, the radio blasted hip-hop, and she promptly shut it off.

Jason laughed. "Yeah, I didn't think that was your brand."

"I'm *basic* that way." She agreed.

He pulled out onto the street, and she played with the radio until she found a station she liked, something soft and lyrical. He didn't give her grief about it. She breathed in, clearing her head.

"I'm on Elwood." She said, "corner of Blossom."

He drove responsibly, slowing down gradually and making full stops. She felt safe and glad to be away from the party.

"So Evangeline left?"

"Yeah,she got into a fight with Gabe and ran off without telling me." Sasha said, resentment slipping into her tone. She wished she wasn't always wearing her heart on her sleeve.

"Don't hold it against her. Gabe has that effect on girls."

"Makes them stupid?" Sasha scoffed.

"Makes them feel important."

The fact that her phone was still quiet made her blood boil. She and Eva had gone together, and they should be going home together.

"So you think it's inauthentic?" She asked.

"What?"

"Gabe and the girls. You said he makes them *feel* important, not that they *are* important."

"I didn't say that. I'm sayin' girls choose to chase Gabe; that's not his fault."

"You and Gabe got close fast." She said.

"He's a cool guy."

"What makes him cool?"

Jason shrugged. "Hard to know, but he is."

"So what about me then?" She said.

"What do you mean?"

"Why aren't I cool?"

"Who says you aren't?"

"Oh, come on, Jason."

"You're riding home with the MVP of our school."

Sasha laughed. "The humble MVP"

"Here you go. Home sweet home." He said as they pulled up in front of her house.

Sasha looked over at the small, quiet bungalow. "Thanks, Jason."

"Good night Alexandra."

"It's Sasha."

"Does that mean we're friends?"

She smiled. "Sure." She leaned over and pecked him on the cheek.

"Can we hang out again? When you're not pissed off?"

"I'm always pissed off."

"I don't believe you."

"What are you, twelve?" She teased. He stuck his tongue out at her.

"Bye Jason." She got out and walked up to her front door. She turned and stuck her tongue out at him too. When she shut the door, she felt simultaneously elated and dismayed, a feeling that felt very much like the teenage life promised on TV.

* * *

A few weeks later, she was at a school sports event. She'd never been to one before, and it felt like an upheaval to her identity. The stands were full, the day's heat lingering, mixing with the heat generated by the hundred or so people in blue and white squished up on the bleachers. Their football team was called The Rattlers, and it only now occurred to Sasha that they had chosen a rattlesnake because they lived in a desert. She'd never given any of the school sports any thought before. When Jason invited her to the game, her first instinct was to laugh but then she thought that maybe it was time she tried to live the real high school

39

experience. After all, she'd be in college next year! Besides, it was a sweet sentiment.

As she neared the stands, the music roaring from the loudspeakers, she quickly spotted Jason's family. They were distinctly good-looking. Gwen was on the cheerleading team, so she couldn't see her, but their youngest sister Leanne had just started 7th grade and was sitting proudly between Jason's dad, wearing a tie with the Rattler's gold and red colour and his mom, wearing designer jeans and a Rattler's sweater. She considered approaching them, but it just felt too weird. Were she and Jason dating now? Judging by what had happened to Eva and Gabe, it depended on who you asked.

She'd put in the extra effort of blow-drying her hair and putting on some lipstick, but she still felt self-conscious in the unfamiliar setting as she stood on the sidelines.

"Sasha!" Daphne called down to her, waving. Sasha gratefully climbed up the bleachers to sit with her and Mel. She wiped her sweaty palms on her shorts, relieved.

"What are you doing here?" Mel asked.

"Jason invited me."

Daphne grinned. "Good for you!"

"Yeah, it's um, a lot." Sasha confessed, taking it all in: the illuminated field, the sounds of excitement all around her, the smell of popcorn and sweat.

"It shouldn't be! Jason's a catch." Daphne said encouragingly.

Sasha nodded. She knew Daphne was right, but she wasn't sure she felt it. It was as though she was playing a role: the Girlfriend. She wasn't sure it suited her.

The opposing team came out first, their names a bit fuzzy over the loudspeaker, and Daphne and Mel joined the crowd in booing and calling out quips. It seemed like everyone knew this routine inside and out. Sasha stayed seated, chewing on a piece of gum. When their own team came running onto the field, whooping, their arms raised, she made a point of yelling along with everyone and clapping, then quickly sat back down. There was also a chant about rattlesnakes and poison, which she'd heard chanted in the hallways many times at Saint-Ignatius, but that she'd never learned. She waved slightly and smiled when Jason spotted her in the stands. This was good, right? She was doing what she was supposed to be doing. She shook her head to clear it, trying to get into the spirit of things.

Gwen and Pamela performed with the cheer team with impressive stunts, leaps and fluffy pompoms. It always seemed stupid on television, but in person, it was breathtaking. Their dusty gold costumes shone under the pitch lights. The girls smiled and lifted each other with so much energy that Sasha wished they would keep going instead of the football game.
"I never realized how much work goes into being a cheerleader." She said to Mel.
Daphne leaned in between them. "Forget the cheerleaders. Here come the guys!"

The play started, the whistle went, cheering, clapping. It was hard to pay attention to the game, so she observed people's reactions instead. Sports sure brought out the drama! As she watched the stands, she spotted Gabriel sitting at the front with TJ and Eric. Beside him was Gen, the one from Eric's party. Sasha scowled. As though Gabe felt it, he turned and looked straight at her. She looked away quickly and kept staring at Jason as he ran across the field, his arms in the air, presumably having scored a goal. Eva had been avoidant and mopy since the party, which reinforced her stance on Gabe.

Something soft swiped across the side of her cheek. Gabriel Wells had somehow found his way beside her, sitting between her and Mel, and his long braid had whipped the side of her face as he sat down.
She crossed her arms and moved as far away from him as she could, not far enough.
"What do you want?" She grizzled.
"Is Eva with you?"
"Obviously not." She grunted.
"Bad day?"
"It was fine until you got here."
Mel and Daphne were pointedly not looking at them.
"Whoa there, who pissed in your corn pops?" Gabe retorted.
"Leave me alone, Gabriel."
"Why?"
She turned to look him in the eye. "You cheated on my friend."
"I didn't cheat on her!" He seemed genuinely insulted.
"Oh yeah? Then what do you call sleeping with someone else when you're in a relationship?" People started turning around to look at them. Gabe made placating hand gestures. "Relax."
"You invited her to a party and then hooked up with someone else while you were there." She articulated through gritted teeth.
"It's none of your business."
She watched his hands clench into fists as he looked away.

41

"How is she?" He asked.

"What do you think, Gabe?"

"Can't you get off your high horse and stop treating me like an asshole?"

"That's what you are, asshole." she hissed.

"What did I do to you, specifically?"

She took a deep breath. "Since you got here, I've had to put up with you monopolizing Eva, but she was happy, so I didn't say anything, but when you hurt her and then act as if nothing happened? That makes you an asshole."

They sat silently as the crowd roared around them, Gabriel's hands clutching his knees. Finally, he threw his arms up in exasperation and hopped off the bleachers. Sasha watched him return to the front, Gen leaning on his arm as he sat down next to her. Who did he think he was? She exhaled, trying to focus on the game. She could feel the adrenaline rush through her, making everything feel surreal. She'd read that this was called dissociation, a typical anxiety symptom, but that didn't make her feel any calmer. She gathered up her bag.

"Where are you going?" Daphne asked.

"Home."

"Are you okay?" Mel added.

"Yeah, I don't think sports are my thing."

As she left the game, she heard the cheering of the crowd as they made another goal. She felt bad leaving before seeing Jason but she wasn't in the mood to stare at Gabriel's back all evening. She texted Jason "Sorry, wasn't feeling well. Heading home. You're a winner, win or lose! xox." She still wasn't sure how she felt about him, but the least she could do was show him she cared.

Chapter 5
Expectations

Eva

She awoke to her mother's voice calling her name. Had she slept through her alarm? No, it was only 6:30. Did she have swimming this morning? No, it was Wednesday. She'd stayed up late studying and her mind was still asleep.

"What?" She called, her voice groggy.

"Eva!" She sounded annoyed, making her wince. Her books were strewn all over her nightstand and her mouth felt dry.

Her mom's footsteps on the stairs made her stagger out of bed. Her mom stood in the doorway, looking much more awake than Eva. Her hair was already pulled back in a soft pony tail and she'd changed out of her nightgown into black leggings and a sweater. The floor felt cold under Eva's feet.

"What's going on?" She asked.

"There's a guy on the porch who says he wants to speak to you." Her mom said with an amused expression.

"A guy?"

"Yes, and if you don't want to see him, say so now because daddy is already talking about fetching his gun."

"Oh, crap." Her brain was finally catching up. There was someone at the door for her at six in the morning. Nothing good could come of this.

"Language, Eva!"

"Who is it, though?" They both knew she was stalling, but her mom seemed to be getting an exorbitant amount of pleasure from what she imagined to be the utter mortification on her face.

"That boy with long hair and the expensive car."

"Gabe?"

"He looks like he hasn't slept much."

"Okay, I'm coming." She rubbed her eyes. "Just don't let daddy talk to him, please."

Her mom shook her head, "I can't make any promises sweetheart. She shut the door.

Eva scrambled to find clothes, glancing at herself in the mirror. Her hair looked as though she'd put her finger in a light socket and her freckles stood out against her pale skin. There was no time for this. She pulled her hair into a quick top-knot, trying to flatten it as much as possible, an impossible task without a comb. She pulled a maroon hoodie over her head. Unfortunately, her window didn't reach the front of the house, so there was no way to tell what was happening. She took a swig of the water bottle she'd filled last night and pushed herself out onto the landing. As she descended the wooden stairs, her brother ran past her holding up a superhero. "Boom! Dad's already outside." He warned her. "Your boyfriend might be dead."

"Oh god." She said, quickening her pace, holding onto the banister so as not to slip in her bare feet. Even a kid knew that her dad and the word boyfriend didn't mix. Not that Gabe was her boyfriend anymore.

Her mom was right. Gabriel Wells stood on the front steps with his laces untied, hair loose, wearing a rumpled black t-shirt and black basketball shorts. He looked a hot mess. Her dad was standing before him, leaning back against the doorframe with his arms crossed, making it quite clear whose house this was and who Gabe was messing with - a high-ranking military officer's little girl. Despite being about Gabe's height, her dad gave the impression of someone much taller and stronger.

"Gabe?" Eva shut the door so as not to let the dog out as she stepped out onto the porch. Gabriel's bloodshot eyes lit up when he saw her.

"Eva..." Her name sounded so strange coming from him. Had he ever called her by her name, or had it always been 'Babe' or 'Princess'?

"Gabriel's got something to say." Her father said, keeping his arms crossed, shifting his weight from side to side and nodding at Gabe as though he were a door-to-door salesman.

"Dad, I've got this." She pleaded, embarrassment rising in her stomach.

"I'll be right inside." He turned to Gabe, who stood straighter. "Remember what I said."

"Yes, sir." Gabe sounded off. When her father closed the door, Eva marched past Gabe towards his car and sat in the passenger seat. He let himself into the driver's seat. "Whatever he said, forget it." She started. "My dad thinks he's always at work."

"He *really* cares about you."

"He *really* needs to mind his own business."

"You're his business."

"Gabe," She turned to face him directly, "what the hell are you doing here?"

"I needed to talk to you."

"And it couldn't wait until school? Or at least until I brushed my teeth?"

"I'm sorry. I've been drivin' all night. I was losing my mind. Just hear me out."

"You have five minutes." He looked tired. His dark eyes were deep in their sockets, making them look bigger than usual. To be honest with herself, he looked a lot more like the boy she remembered from when she was little, disheveled and frustrated. What was he hiding? Was he ever going to tell her? Did she owe him an explanation if they were broken up?

"Babe, I didn't mean to hurt you. I didn't think you'd take it that way."

"What way was I supposed to take it?"

"Jenn's nothing to me. None of them are."

"And neither am I."

"No, that's not..." he paused. "You're better."

She laughed. That was the most backhanded compliment she'd ever heard. They were nothing and she was better? He rubbed his face and then ran his fingers through his hair, catching his fingers in the knots. She was mad, but she couldn't help reaching over and undoing one of the knots she could see. It was crazy how easily physical intimacy came when she was with him. He was magnetic.

"I'm better than nothing?" She laughed bitterly.

"No, you're...I'm not good enough for you."

"You can do what you want, Gabe."

"But I want you." That made her feel warm, like sinking into the hot tub in her parent's backyard, like a gulp of hot chocolate on a rainy, cold day...but it wasn't enough.

"You can't have the entire school and me."

She wasn't sure how she felt about him seeing others as "nothing", either. How could he spend so much time with people who meant nothing to him? Was he so callous?

"What do you want me to do?" He asked. It sounded more like a genuine question than an accusation or an ultimatum. Wasn't it obvious what she wanted? She wanted him to be her boyfriend, her real boyfriend, not whatever the hell they were doing, but she couldn't ask that of him. He had to want it too.

"You're the one here at the crack of dawn. What do you want?"

"I want you back. I want to keep hanging out with you while I'm here."

"While you're here?" Why did it always sound like he was on the verge of telling her something else entirely? Where else was he planning to go?

"You mean while we're young?"

"Yeah, I want to spend as much time with you as possible."

"Well, there isn't a whole lot of time between Pamela, Jenn, Genevieve, Lucy, Audrey..." She was counting down on her fingers.

"Okay, I get it." He held up both hands.

"Do you? Really?"

"Yes. So, do you forgive me?"

She looked up at his tired-looking face. "It depends..."

"On what?"

"On what you're promising."

"I won't hook up with anyone else while we're together."

"You won't?"

"I promise. Do you forgive me then?"

"Okay...if you really mean it...I forgive you."

"Can I kiss you now?"

"Not unless you want my dad to shoot you through the window." They both looked up to see the curtain shift in the large bay window. She reached over and squeezed his hand. He pulled her to him and held her a moment, clearly wishing for something more than a hug. She didn't feel one bit self-conscious, even though she hadn't put herself together at all that morning. She pulled away.

"I'm gonna go get dressed. Be right back."

Gabe nodded. They would probably have to stop off at the apartment. He didn't have his uniform with him either, though Eva noted that he didn't seem to care. He stretched and let his shoulders slump, rubbing his eyes. She wondered what exactly he'd been through in the past few days.

She'd grieved, of course, but she'd never imagined he'd take her cold shoulder so hard. Would this be enough? Would he really choose her over all those other girls? Right now, it felt like a weight had been lifted off her chest, and she couldn't wait to catch up on time. He'd asked to kiss her, and she would be more than happy to oblige—as soon as she got herself in order and away from prying eyes.

Sasha

Jason's house was insane. It probably spoke volumes that she kept thinking about how long cleaning would take. She doubted that Jason's family needed to worry about washing the massive windows or dusting the chandeliers. He had led them through the foyer, through the open plan kitchen and living room filled with contemporary art pieces and tastefully arranged furniture, to the backyard, where a beautiful inground pool surrounded by lounging chairs welcomed them.

Sasha tried not to look like a deer in headlights, but she wanted to scream, "You live here?" Gwen and a few of the cheerleaders were already tanning by the poolside, Gwen in a bright yellow bikini that flattered every curve and her two friends in navy one-pieces that she thought might be the school's swimming team uniform. However, she'd never paid any sports team any attention to know. They each had a tall glass in their hands.

Jason brought snacks and put them on the tables near the pool area. Gabe whistled at the girls, and Sasha threw him a dirty look. When Jason had invited her, she'd initially wanted to turn him down. He was sweet, but this was not her scene, as she'd learned at Eric's party. The music and pool all felt like being on stage somehow. Then she considered that if she kept saying no, he would eventually move on. She may not have been a fan of Gabe, but Eva was dating him now, so she would have to get to know him, too, right? Jason was sweet, with his easy demeanor and quick smile. He was so unlike her that she couldn't understand what he saw in her, and part of her wanted to find out.

Jason, TJ and Eric threw their shirts off and canon-balled into the pool. Gabe seemed to be trying to assess Eva's willingness to get into the water. "I'm good babe; you go ahead." Eva told him airily. "Suit yourself!" He said, launching himself after the guys, splashing Gwen and her friends in the process. "Come on, babe! It's not cold once you're in!" He called, taking to the water like a fish. "You coming?" Eva asked as Sasha sat down. Sasha tugged at her summer dress self-consciously. Eva looked over at Gwen. "We really shouldn't be comparing ourselves." "Easy for you to say. You're in a bathing suit at least twice a week." Sasha replied. "Here." Jason handed them both cold drinks, the glasses covered in condensation. "What's in here?" Sasha asked, sniffing it dubiously. It was a little early to drink, wasn't it? "Mojitos. My mom loves them." "Thanks." she said, take a small sip. It was minty and citrusy all at once. Also, most definitely alcoholic. Why did it seem like they were always drinking? Jason notably didn't have a drink. Eva nodded her approval beside her. "Thanks, Jason. My mom makes these too."

Sasha watched the muscles on Jason's back and shook her head. How had she gotten here? At least now she had an excuse not to undress right away. She wasn't usually embarrassed by her body, but next to these Adonises, it was hard to feel entirely confident. They were all sporty - Jason, Eric and TJ played football and basketball. Gabe's shape suggested he worked out a lot too. Gwen and her girls were on the cheerleading squad, and Eva was on the swimming and dance teams. The closest thing Sasha did to sports was walk to school, and even that was because she didn't have a driver's license or a car. Maybe the mojito would help.

She and Eva had finally spoken a little, though they hadn't gotten to spend any time together one on one recently. The red-haired girl was almost always with Gabe now that they were suddenly back together. Sasha still couldn't shake the feeling that Gabe was getting away with murder. Eva told her they'd talked it out, and she wasn't mad anymore, but Sasha was still feeling raw. Gabe hadn't brought up their discussion on the bleachers. The rumours were that Gabe had left the game by himself instead of hanging out with the team afterwards, and that the next day, he had driven in with Eva in the passenger seat.

"Who wants to play, 'never have I ever'?" Gwen suggested.

Gabe laughed. "This again? I always lose!" He was in the pool, the sun playing off his naturally tanned skin.

"We have extra players now. Maybe Sasha's got a really exciting past." TJ joked.

She felt this was a bit juvenile, but as the new person in the group, she decided it was best to play along. The game went pretty quickly as every person said something they'd never done, and those that had done it had to put down a finger. Everyone started with their hands up, setting their drinks down. Sasha put her fingers down for having lived outside of the United States (Jason), speaking a second language (Gwen), kissing a girl (Pam), kissing a boy (Eric), failing a class (Eva), owning a pet (Gabe) when it came to TJ , who said "Never have I ever hooked up with Gabe." Sasha kept her four remaining fingers up and looked at Eva, who was already a little red from the alcohol and glared at TJ. "I'm going to the bathroom." She said and went inside.

Jason turned on his friend. "What the hell, man?"

"What? I thought it'd get a whole bunch of the girls at once!"

Gabe got out of the pool and wrapped a towel around his torso. "I'll be back." His long hair dripped footprints on the stone path to the house.

"What is wrong with you?" Sasha hissed at TJ.

"Jesus, sorry." He said again.

"It's not me you should apologize to."

Sasha got up to follow, but Jason hopped out of the pool to intercept her. "You should let 'em go after her. He'll know what to say." She sat back down, downing most of her mojito. The others went back to chatting while she pressed her nails into the palms of her hands. If Eva left again, she would go home too. If this was what it was like hanging out with Eva's new friends, it wasn't worth it.

She was chatty and loud with her friends, but with this group, it never felt right to speak up. It wasn't the right crowd, and every joke that came to mind seemed too nerdy. Jason tried to get her to join them in the pool, but the best she could do was go and sit with her feet in the water.

Luckily, Eva and Gabe came back soon after. Eva sat beside her, still cradling the same drink.

"Are you okay?" Sasha asked.

Eva nodded. "Yeah, I'm fine. I was just being too sensitive."

Sasha sighed. She couldn't understand how it could be fine.

"Sorry, Eva! I was just being an idiot!" TJ said, swimming up close to them.

"It's fine." Eva, "you're always an idiot." Eva said, without malice.

Sasha shook her head. Gabe and Jason must've told TJ to apologize. Sasha finished her drink and kept quiet. Eva eventually went into the pool, but Sasha got up and went to sit further since she kept getting splashed. Jason kept checking on her, which was sweet, but she just wanted to pull her book out of her bag and read.

A few hours later, Gabe dropped them both off at Eva's, where Sasha was planning to sleep over. He'd invited them to stay the night at Jason's with him and the rest of the gang, but Eva's parents were already expecting them, so they couldn't even have used the excuse of being at Sasha's. Dinner with the Valliants was must better than spending time with Jason's group. Eva's mom was an amazing cook and Sasha devoured every bite of lasagna, glad she didn't have to think about wearing a bathing suit again today. Eva's dad asked them both about school and their plans after graduation, and her brother Matteo dragged them over to watch Pokemon with him. It felt like the old days, before Gabe had shown up. Eva's parents were always a little too present when she was over, nothing like her own parents who gave her all the space she could possibly want, but it was nice anyway. Later, as they curled up on Eva's bed, falling asleep to the radio, Sasha finally got up the courage to pry.

"Do your parents know about Gabe?"

"Mmm, sort of." Eva muttered sleepily.

"What do they think of him?"

"Well, my dad's already threatened him so that's probably a good sign." She smiled.

"It's pretty serious, isn't it?" Sasha asked.

"I guess so."

"You were watching his every move today."

"I'm not like, obsessed or anything.", said Eva quietly.

"You trust him?" Sasha whispered.

Eva lifted her shoulders and let them drop again.

"Why?"

"Because I was to."

Sasha leaned over and gave her friend a side hug.

"I hope you're right. Just don't let him break your heart."

"I think that ship has sailed."

Eva

The final days of school before the winter holidays were luxurious. The hallways were adorned with garlands and wreaths, and the trees along the path to the school were speckled with multicolored sparkling lights. It got chilly but never enough to snow. She wore a thicker jacket and leggings instead of knee socks. There was a buzz of excitement as the days grew shorter and the promise of holidays drew near.

"I'm starving." Sasha whispered as they headed downstairs with their class. It would be their final Christmas mass at school. The chapel was on the opposite side of the school, just below the library.

"Hey, babe." Gabe caught up with them.

"You're supposed to stay with your class Gabe." Sasha hissed at him.

"Is that what Jesus would want, Alexandra?"

Sasha rolled her eyes.

"Okay, kids, settle down." Eva chuckled. Gabe took her hand so they wouldn't separate in the flood of students. His hand was so big that it swallowed hers up. Their fingertips fit into one another like gloves. Even after all these months, her heart beat faster when he was near her. Gabe was right; no one would notice where he sat during mass. They filed into the aisle at the back, the first years in the front looking like babies. She couldn't believe she'd been one of them once upon a time.

Father Paul, the school priest, stood at the pulpit in his Christmas best, in pure white robes. The chapel's stained-glass windows shone with mid-morning sunlight, depicting various biblical scenes, the most significant of which was the one at the center, with Christ on the cross. The nativity scene, complete with wax animals, also stood on stage, though she couldn't make out the details from the back of the room. It smelled of incense, the smoke from candles long extinct, and students. Gabe's palm was clammy.

"Warm in here, huh?" She said.

"If they take any more students, we'll have to have a chapel annex." Sasha answered on her right. She was up against a large Christmas tree, and some branches hung quite close to her head.

Eva squeezed Gabe's hand, and he squeezed back. She remembered the little church he'd lived in when they were kids. She wished they could talk about it, but he looked far away, staring at the stained glass with wide eyes. He didn't remember her, of that she was certain. Maybe that was for the best, not all the memories she had of that time were good, and the end was confusing and awful.

"So, what do you do for Christmas?" she asked him.

"Nothin' much," he said noncommittally. "You?"

"Well, there are full weekends of shopping with my mom, decorating the house and preparing a feast for an army and then the neighbours usually come for Christmas dinner. They have a kid the same age as my brother, so I'll probably be stuck babysitting them both. Then we go to midnight mass, the one and only time we go to church. In the morning, my parents make pancakes, eggs, fruit, eggnog, the works."

He was finally looking at her. "Real American-like."

"Yeah, it's nice, actually."

The side of his mouth rose a little.

"If you don't have any plans, do you want to come over?" she asked.

"I'm headin' to Jason's parent's cottage." He looked disappointed. "Did you want to come to that?"

"My mom would kill me if I missed Christmas!"

In the years between her childhood and this Christmas, she wondered where he'd been. She thought about it throughout the sermon, even as Sasha's stomach whined loudly beside her. She sang along to the prayers and Christmas songs performed by the school choir and band. She was surprised to hear Gabe singing too. She thought he'd think he was too cool.

"Gabe's not a bad singer, huh?" Sasha whispered. Eva agreed.

Sasha

Lunchtime couldn't have come fast enough. She'd helped herself to a few Body of Christ Wafers as they were passed along, but it did very little for her hunger. She'd also forgotten her lunch on the counter this morning. Now that Eva had said she wasn't coming, she felt even more conflicted about the holiday season. Jason had invited her to his parent's cottage too, and, thinking she'd have Eva with her, she'd said yes. Spending the holidays an hour away from home with the popular kids by herself was not her idea of fun, especially since she couldn't drive back if things went awry. She split off from Gabe and Eva to wait in the cafeteria lineup and ran into Mila, playing on a handheld console.

"Mass was so long today; I'm starved." She said.

Her friend laughed, pushing her glasses up and shutting the device. "I thought Pamela would kill you with her gaze when you took three hosts at once."

"I don't know why Pam cares, it's not like she's religious."

"She wears a cross."

"So does Gabe Wells."

"Does he? That's ironic."

"Whatcha doing for the holidays?" Sasha asked, her mind still on the idea of being stuck at a cottage with people like Pamela.

"Family stuff, the usual. You?"

"Jason invited me to go up to his big cottage blowout."

Mila made a face. "Sounds fun. What do they do up there?"

"To heck if I know. There might be snow if they're up on a mountain, so maybe skiing? Hot tubs? Whatever it is popular kids do."

"Sasha, I don't know how to break this to you, but you're dating Jason O'Neil. You're a popular kid."

"I'm dating Jason, but that doesn't mean I want to spend time with him during the holidays."

"Can I be honest?" Mila asked.

Sasha braced herself a little, "I guess so."

"It doesn't sound like you like Jason as much as he likes you. I'm not sure you like Jason at all. You might just like what he represents."

Sasha wanted to argue, but she wasn't sure Mila was wrong. "But if I say I don't want to go, won't he dump me?"

"That would make him a pretty terrible boyfriend."

"And if he doesn't?"

"I don't know."

"Why are you dating someone you don't want to spend time with?"

"He's nice."

"So is Mr. Blunt."

They both burst out laughing. The mere thought of dating their English teacher was enough to prove the point. Sasha had never been more ready for greasy fries.

Chapter 6
Storms

Sasha

Sasha made her way down the steps in relief; she'd had enough chemistry labs to fill a lifetime. Why did Margo insist she needed to be there? Mila said it was because Margo got lonely being the smartest girl in school. Sasha had to agree. She planned to call Eva and ask to hang out this weekend. Eva had apologized about the party, but it just wasn't the same between them. They needed some one on one time to get past all of this. She also wanted to talk to someone about Jason. Mila had been a bit too insightful on that front. She said that Sasha didn't like him as much as she liked who he allowed her to be at school and that she was getting wrapped up in the popularity. Who needed a therapist when they had Mila? She wanted a more positive spin on the situation, and who better to give it than the person dating Jason's best friend?

She was about to go down towards the school gates, cell phone in hand, when she heard the noise coming from the parking lot at the left of the school. She tried to remember if there was some sort of sports event that she'd failed to care about as usual; she wasn't in the mood for more school spirit.

"Hold him up!" Jason's voice, she was certain of that. Figures that he would be anywhere where the action might be. She'd intended to ask him about his wanting to be tutored. He'd mentioned it a week or so ago at lunch but hadn't mentioned payment. She supposed he might just be trying to spend more time with her.. They were in the parking lot, a crowd gathered, and everyone was either standing around or cheering. "What's going on?" She asked a young girl beside her as she stood on her toes, trying to get a glimpse of the show. "Jason's fighting that new kid!" The girl cried. Sasha's stomach dropped.

"Jason's fighting Gabe?"

That seemed pretty irrational, and she'd never seen Jason lose his temper, but they were gathered around where Gabriel usually parked his convertible. She pushed through the throng, trying to see anyone she recognized. When she stumbled to the front of the crowd and halted, someone tried to push her aside to keep filming on their cell phone. She froze.

53

The scene was horrific. She took it in like flashes. Hale, covered in blood, was held up by Eric and TJ. Jason stood above him, screaming something she couldn't hear over the crowd.

She'd never seen Jason like that. Then, when all she'd been able to utter was Jason's name, the tables had suddenly turned. Eric and TJ were thrown to the floor in moments, flipped over onto their backs and now Hale was up and treading slowly and dangerously towards Jason, who had staggered back so as not to get kicked in the face. Hale was smaller than Jason in height and build, but the look in his eyes was petrifying. It wasn't vengeful or angry; it was absent. He grabbed Jason mechanically and hurled him against the pavement with a sickening thud. The crowd made a larger circle; the jeering had stopped.

It was all happening so quickly. Sasha heard herself scream and covered her mouth with her hands. Jason was on the ground, hair sticky with blood, oozing onto the gray of the cement. The punches came hard and rhythmic. Hale wasn't paying him back; he was finishing the job. Eric and TJ had both sat up but neither of them moved forward.

"Hale!" She cried. He couldn't hear her, hyperfocused on Jason. Someone was pulling on the back of her bag, and she turned. It was Eric's brother, "Back up!". He was still holding up his phone. She moved forward towards the fight and someone pulled her back. She pulled her arms free of her backpack and shaking head to toe, crossed the gap of pavement between the crowd and the fight. She fell to her knees, criss-crossing her arms in front of a descending fist. "Hale, stop! You're going to kill him! Please!"

His fist gently touched her forearm. Their faces were so close that she felt his exhale. He let his hands drop to his sides. Looking as though every muscle in his body was aching, he braced himself on his bloody hands and pushed upward, walking away as the crowd parted.

Sasha looked back down at Jason, so close to her. He was unconscious but breathing. She swerved towards Eric and TJ, both of whom were now crawling over to look at Jason. There were very few students left around them. Where had they all gone?
"Don't just sit there! We need help!" she screamed, tears now obscuring her vision. Eric's brother was standing above them, dialing 911.
A million emotions hit her, not the least of which was panic now that the adrenaline was receding. She felt lightheaded, her breaths coming in short bursts like an elephant was sitting on her chest. She turned away

from Jason, just to take a breath, and realized that Hale was holding himself up against the hood of Gabriel's car. She watched him use the side of the car to keep walking until he was on the grass, where he let himself fall to his knees. She looked up again at Eric and TJ, both looking at her as though she had some sort of answer and back down at Jason. She pulled herself off the cement, scraping bits of stone from her knees and went over to Hale.

Crouching beside him, she quietly whispered, "Are you okay?" It sounded like the stupidest question she had ever asked. He was bleeding from his nose, and his breathing came out ragged. She looked him in the eyes to see how alert he was or if he still looked like he might kill someone.

"I'm fine," his voice hoarse and weak as he attempted to stand again, but his body wouldn't allow it. "Don't," she squeaked. He looked up as though she'd somehow gotten hurt. She took his arm and put it over her shoulders, lifting them both off the floor. Slowly rising, she kept one arm around his waist, but she was unsure how hard to hold onto him in case he'd broken something internal and vital.
"Where are you trying to go?" She asked.
"Away from them."

One part of her mind screamed at her for taking the side of the seeming bully, or at least, the winner of the fight. Another just knew that Jason would be taken care of while Hale was alone. Painfully, slowly, she guided their awkward, broken gait behind the gazebo. Her shoulders were beginning to ache, and he didn't seem like he would manage much further, either. They collapsed onto the grass right behind the gazebo, barely a dozen feet away, and she helped him sit up against the gazebo wall, scooching away. All along, she kept a steady flow of words that felt entirely disconnected from the anxiety spiral in her head: "come on, a little further, just a couple more steps, okay, we're doing alright, just breathe, okay? There, this seems like a good place. They can't see you from here."

Anxiety jerked her mind through all of the potential outcomes very quickly. It struck her that this was exactly the sort of situation where you're supposed to get an adult. They both looked up at the sky. Hale turned away from her and heaved. Nothing came up. Fatigue was taking its toll, and he placed his head in his hands, stained red.

"Did I really do that?" he asked. She'd never heard him sound vulnerable before.

Sasha had turned away when he had turned to vomit and kept staring out into the distance at grassy green hills and the rooftops of beautiful suburban homes in the distance. When he spoke to her, the first answer that popped into her head was, "Try to kill Jason in cold blood? Yes.", but she softened as she turned to look at him. He looked awful; it made her heart tense to see it. "That must have been terrible" she chose instead. It was as though he were coming out of a trance, and he seemed as shocked as she was.

"I think it had something to do with getting my exam notes, I don't remember much." He closed his eyes. The sun was peeking out from behind the clouds. His bangs stuck to his forehead with sweat and blood, which trickled down the side of his face, paving rivulets down to his chin. With his eyes closed like that, he looked like he was dying.
"Don't move." She said and got up. She walked around the gazebo, wiping tears as she went, finding her backpack exactly where she'd dropped it in the parking lot.

Jason was still lying on the floor with his two friends around him; Eric's brother was smoking. All who were capable of doing so looked up at her.
"Did you call an ambulance?" She asked.
"Yeah." TJ said. There was an uncomfortably long pause.
"Is he okay?" She tried.
"What do you think, Sasha?" Eric spat.
Her mind was a maelstrom. Of course he wasn't okay! Why did she even ask that? What was she even doing right now? Her tongue stuck to the top of her mouth, she didn't have a comeback.
Grabbing her bag, she turned away and pretended they didn't exist. She could only deal with one broken human at a time. When she sat back in the grass in front of Hale, she tried to shake off thoughts of Jason. Hale's eyes were still closed. "It's me." She said softly like speaking to a cowering animal. She took her water bottle and her spare polo out of her bag.

"Hold still. I just want to wipe some of this off. Tell me if I'm hurting you," she instructed. Dampening the shirt, she waited for approval.

Opening his eyes and nodding his head seemed like an immense effort. She dabbed at the blood, trying not to scrape at the places where it had already dried. The air around them was warming with the returning

56

sunlight. She wasn't sure if she'd made things better or worse, but she kept working anyway. The smell of blood made her nauseous. Once some of the gore was cleared away, she could see his cheek was swelling, as was his eye on the same side.

"They did a number on you. The ambulance is coming"

"No." He croaked.

"What do you mean *no*? You probably have internal bleeding. You need x-rays or stitches or a tub of morphine."

"I can't."

"You have no choice." She said quietly.

"I'm not going to a hospital."

"Then what do you propose?"

"I need to go home."

She took a shaky breath. Insurance? It must be about insurance. They had money, though, didn't they? He wasn't on scholarship like she was. She knew all the other scholarship kids. He and Gabe had an apartment of their own, and that car.

"Hale," she began in an argumentative tone.

He looked at her in silence, his expression saying a million things; fear, regret, pain. All he said out loud was "please".

She sighed, knowing another questionable decision was about to take place on her part.

"For god's sake. How do you usually get home?"

"Walk."

"Is it far?"

"Somewhat."

The path from the school to the street had never seemed longer. She huffed in exasperation.

"What about your parents? Isn't there anyone we can call?"

He shook his head. She supposed she wouldn't want to tell her parents if something like this had happened to her either, but she was running out of options.

"I can call mine if you want. My mom's pretty good in a crisis." She suggested.

"No."

Her mom would automatically drive them to the hospital; he'd already said he didn't want to go there. She looked around, trying to come up with a plan. Her eyes landed on the red Mustang in the parking lot. That meant Gabriel hadn't left the school yet.

"Do you have keys to the red car?"

"No."

"Where's Gabe?"

57

"With your friend, most likely." he answered flatly, an edge to his voice. She wasn't sure why discussing Gabriel annoyed him so much, but he was their last hope for a ride.
"What's his number?" She sighed, holding up her phone.
Hale shrugged. "He never has his phone."
Sasha dialed Eva's number. It rang.
She dialed again. And again. And again.

Eva

They were sprawled out under the shade of a tree, the remains of a picnic shoved into a plastic bag beside them, limbs intertwined. She sat on his lap, their breathing synchronizing as they kissed. "Okay, down, boy," Eva said, pushing his face from hers.
"You're kidding me, right?" Gabe laughed, letting himself fall into the grass with his arms spread out.
"There are kids here." Eva said, pointing at a mother pushing a buggy along the path near them with a slightly older child skipping ahead.
"So?"
"I don't want to traumatize them."
"They should know there are perks to adulthood."
"You're hardly an adult."
"Eh, close enough." He leaned forward again to try and catch her lips. She pushed him back down with her hands on his chest. Her phone went off in her bag.
"Whoops." She climbed off of him and went rummaging in her backpack. It kept ringing as she tried to dig it out from beneath books, makeup, and her gym uniform. It stopped.
"Okay, couldn't have been that important."
"It might've been my mom, Gabe."
"Wondering what my intentions are with her daughter? I think you should let her know they ain't Catholic."
"It's not my mom you need to worry about in that sense."
"Dad has a hunting rifle?"
"Dad is in the military and has much more than a hunting rifle." Eva laughed, finally finding her phone.
"Your dad's a soldier?" She was sure she'd mentioned it before, but he looked surprised somehow.
"Yeah. I'm a military brat. We moved around a lot when I was a kid. We've lived all over the place.Washington, Louisiana, where my mom's from, Santa Fe..."
She searched his face for recognition, but he gave nothing away, as per usual.

"I'm not too worried about your dad." He finally said. Her phone suddenly rang in her hands. They both jumped.

"Oh, it's Sasha." Eva was about to answer when Gabe gently and swiftly pulled it out of her hands.

"Miss Sasha can wait for homework help."

"Gabe!" Eva cried, trying to grab it back as it kept ringing.

He backed up in the grass, holding it up and away from her reach and then rose to his feet to hold it above her head.

"No fair!" Eva laughed, practically climbing up his body to get to it. The ringing stopped.

"Done!" Gabe said, bringing it back down and pulling her into him for another kiss. She relaxed into it, feeling his hand on her back. She could feel herself melting into how perfect this day was.

The phone rang again, squished between them. What was so urgent? She should pick up. She and Sasha had just made up after the debacle at Jason's party. She didn't want her to be mad at her again.

"Hell, no." He said as Eva reached between them to answer. Gabe shoved the phone into his pants.

"There!" He announced.

"Gabe!" Eva cried. The phone rang yet again, this time in a fairly inaccessible place.

"You're busy! That girl needs to catch a hint."

"Gabe, give me back my phone." She demanded, unable to keep the giggle out of her voice.

"Come and get it!"

"I'm not going down your pants in public!"

"But on school property..." He mocked.

"That was a brain fart." She blushed. "She'll start calling your phone soon! Does Sasha have your number?"

"Joke's on her. I don't have one."

"You don't have a cell phone?" That wasn't right. She'd seen him handing it to the other girls at school on that first day. Why was he lying about it?

"I never have it with me. I live in the now."

"Hipster." She shook her head. At least he'd corrected himself.

He shrugged, "Sounds like hipsters are your type."

"Not usually." She answered, as they sat back down in the grass.

The afternoon had been blissful. Things always seemed easy around Gabe, even though her secrets were slowly eating away at her. Was it cowardice? Most likely, but there was something else. Try as she might, this boy was sweeping her off her feet one toe at a time. A big grin spread across her face as they made their way up the stairs to Gabe's apartment.

"Think anyone's home?" she chuckled.

Gabe turned the key. "Who cares?" The smile on his face made Eva's chest swell. She disagreed though. A knock and a monotonous "Gabe, your laundry." tended to ruin the mood. She'd seen Hale at the apartment a few times and he always avoided them like the plague. It made her feel like an intruder.

"Honey, I'm home!" Gabe called gleefully into the living room as they stepped inside. There was a noise. Gabe froze and pushed Eva behind him in one swift motion. She held onto his arm so she didn't fall.

"What's going on?" She cried.

"Quiet!" He hissed.

Sasha glared from the couch, muting the sound of the court show she was watching.

"Welcome home." she replied sarcastically.

Slowly, Gabe removed himself from in front of Eva.

"How did you get in here?" He spat, with more venom than Eva had ever heard from him.

Eva tried to side step him but he stood firmly in front of her.

"Calm down, babe. Sasha? What's going on?"

"Your roommate let me in." Sasha told Gabe, glancing at Eva, fear in her expression.

"That so?" Gabe seemed dubious.

"Where have you been?" Sasha asked in an accusatory tone.

"Sorry I missed your call; someone held my phone hostage. Are you okay?" Eva kept looking up at Gabe, waiting for him to let her move forward. What was he doing? She couldn't piece his reaction together any more than Sasha's. She was desperate to diffuse the sudden, inexplicable tension in the room.

"Peachy," Sasha muttered, still glaring at Gabe.

"I'm gonna ask you one more time: how did you get in here?" Gabe repeated, calmer now but no less threateningly, walking over to the couch. Eva noticed the way he clenched his fists. Sasha, however, seemed not to be catching any of the danger vibes emanating from him. Eva had never seen Gabe react this way, and the emotional whiplash was hard to handle. He was like a wolf circling prey.

"I've been here for more than an hour waiting for you, lovebirds." Sasha said with such animosity that Eva winced.

"What for?" Gabe's eyes swept the room as though expecting other people to be there. Eva looked from her boyfriend to her friend. What the hell was going on?

Sasha shut off the tv and got to her feet, trying to take up more physical space for whatever frustrations she'd been sitting on. "You would know if you answered your calls! Where the hell were you?"

Gabe scoffed, "Who do you think you are?"

Eva could tell this wasn't going to end well. Something had happened while she had been at the park with Gabe, and she hadn't fought hard to call Sasha back. Sasha was temperamental, but she didn't fly off the handle like this for no reason, and what was she doing at Gabe's?

"Sasha, just tell us what's wrong!" Eva cried.

The tall girl bit her lower lip and took a deep breath. "While you guys were out doing your kissy face thing, your friends," she pointed at Gabe, "decided to gang up on Hale and beat him to a bloody pulp!"

"What friends?" Gabe looked as confused as she felt.

"Jason, TJ and Eric!"

"What are you talking about?" Gabe looked baffled.

"I just told you! Do I have to do an interpretive dance?" She stamped her foot, red in the face.

"You could just explain!" he growled at her.

Tears of exasperation sprang to Sasha's brown eyes. She blurted out the story in one breath, "I was coming down from the chemistry lab, and I saw them pinning him down and kicking him and there was blood everywhere!"

Eva gasped. "Is he okay?"

Sasha held up both hands to show she wasn't finished and kept going. "I ran up, and then suddenly they're all on the floor, and Hale's on top of Jason, and he looks like he's the Hulk or something, and everyone is screaming, and then I had to get in there and stop it, and you should have been there instead!" She cried, pointing at Gabe accusingly. "He was waiting for you, and you should have been there!"

"And you", she locked eyes with Eva, "should have picked up your damn phone! We had to walk here because Hale doesn't have a bus pass, and then we had to climb four flights of stairs when he's probably got internal bleeding !" She stomped her foot again, her bravado deflating like a balloon.

"Where is he?" Gabe asked quietly, finally allowing Eva to stand beside him.

"In his room."

Gabe unclenched his fists and closed his eyes for a moment. "You two should go." He said quietly, "I've got it from here."

"I'm not going home, I want answers! You and your roommate show up at our school out of nowhere, and no one knows where you came from." She counted it off on her fingers. "You're living alone, but neither of you have jobs. Hale wouldn't let me call an ambulance. You moved in together, but I never see you hang out, and when I ask him about you, he doesn't seem to know you from Adam. What is the deal with you two?"

"Go home, Alexandra." Gabe repeated, not looking at her.

Part of Eva wanted answers too, but she recognized that she wasn't getting them this way.

"Are you going to take him to a doctor?" Sasha demanded.

Gabe sighed, then took a low toned voice. "You're going to leave of your own volition, or I'll throw you out. Take your pick."

"I'm not leaving."

"Sash, let's go." Eva took her friend's arm and pulled her towards the door, looking back at Gabe.

"Eva, this guy is lying to you." Sasha insisted, turning to her.

"Please Sash." She pleaded. Whatever Gabe was hiding, it was bigger than them.

"This isn't over." Sasha choked out, her voice shaking, then turned on her heel, grabbed her backpack and slammed the door before Eva could follow.

Eva turned to Gabe, standing in the middle of the living room, his face unreadable. She swung the door open to run after Sasha. She knew Sasha was right, there was definitely something off about Hale and Gabe, but even with the little she knew, she couldn't piece together why that would keep them from taking Hale to the hospital. She knew Sasha would cool off and realize that none of this was Gabriel's fault, but in the meantime, she didn't want to lose her friend.

Eva chased her down the street.

"Leave me alone." Sasha exclaimed, tears rolling down her cheeks, "You took his side."

"The phone was my fault, not Gabe's." Eva replied, out of breath.

"He didn't help either."

"Yeah, but you can't hold it against him; he didn't know."

"He just kicked me out of his apartment."

"You freaked him out! You were sitting on his couch when we came in."

"Well, I had to get Hale home."

She was purposely walking fast so Eva had to jog to keep up with her.

"Why are you pissed off at me?"

"Because I needed your help, and as usual, you were off with Gabe. You ditched me at Eric's party, you keep blowing off plans and now you're taking his side even though you know there's something fishy going on and you refuse to tell me what it is. Plus, this time it got someone hurt. What if Hale's really injured? He refuses to go to the hospital!"

"I didn't know! I already said I was sorry." Was Sasha right? Had she been a bad friend these past few months? She'd tried to balance it all, but clearly she was failing. Sasha slowed her pace.

"What were they fighting about?"

"To heck if I know."

"You said Jason's at the hospital?"

"Yeah."

"Sasha, just stop," She held onto her arm. "Talk to me. Why are you freaking out?"

"You're still trying to protect him! He doesn't deserve it. He's toying with you."

"Sasha, you don't even know him."

"I know that it can't be good if he's basically isolating you from your friends and making you keep secrets."

"It's not my secret to tell, and he didn't ask me. Gabe wasn't the one fighting!"

"So there *is* a secret then."

Eva ran the palms of her hands over her face. "Okay, just listen. Do you remember that story I told you about how I used to go to school in a little church with an orphanage in it?"

Sasha stopped walking.

"I guess so."

"Well, I think Gabe was in my class at that church."

It took her a moment to answer, trying to process. "Why didn't you say anything?"

"Because he doesn't know! Or doesn't remember or is pretending not to."

"That's just proof that he's full of it."

"Didn't you just accuse me of not telling you things?"

"That doesn't explain anything and it doesn't excuse you siding with him just now."

Eva started saying that she hadn't but Sasha cut her off.

"We've been friends for years. He's been here for a few months and you're choosing to believe he's got your best interests at heart just because you sort of knew him ten years ago and he hasn't even confirmed that it was him or you think he's pretending not to remember you? We're not going to see eye to eye on this, obviously. I'll see you tomorrow." She shook Eva's arm off and marched in the direction of her house.

Eva pulled out her phone to call Gabe and realized she still didn't have a phone number for him. She considered going back to the apartment and trying to help, but that didn't feel right either. Eva stood on the street corner feeling powerless, then took a deep breath and went home too. Maybe everyone needed some time; she'd just have to sort it all out tomorrow.

Chapter 7
Alignments

Sasha

Sasha hated that Gabe was tearing them apart, but she couldn't stand being lied to repeatedly. She kept going over everything that happened in her head, from the moment she saw the fight to the little Hale had said, to Gabe and Eva's reactions. There was also Jason to worry about. She was quiet over dinner and went to bed early to try and turn off her mind, but all she did was toss and turn all night.

There was still dew on the grass as Sasha made her way up the path to school the next morning. Her hair was still wet too, she hadn't properly dried it that morning. The chill in the air made her tuck her hands into her sleeves. Although she wished she could have stayed home, her mom gave her a dirty look when she suggested it and said it wasn't anyone's fault she went to bed at three a.m. She texted Jason as she walked, "Please tell me you're okay.", the messages were left unread. What kind of girlfriend was she?

Her eyes stinging, she got into the lineup for the coffee machine. It surprised her how many students were already there. Why would anyone come to school so early?

"Hey!" Mila's familiar voice made her jump. She saw her friend sitting at a table reading manga. She waved and left the lineup. Maybe coffee wasn't such a great idea, her hands already felt clammy and cold.

"You're here early!" Sasha said.

"I'm always here early. What are you doing up?"

"I couldn't sleep."

"Why?" Mila tipped her head like a character in one of her manga, making Sasha smile. In the madness that her life had suddenly become, Mila was still Mila. She sat down in front of her. "Guess you haven't heard about everything that happened yesterday?"

"I don't really care about gossip."

Sasha could have kissed her friend in gratitude. She tried to collect her thoughts to explain when she felt something cold and wet running down the back of her shirt from her hair. She turned to find Gwen standing there, tears rolling down her cheeks, Eric standing beside her. She was clutching a large cup in her hands.

"You have a lot of nerve showing up today!" she shouted. Gwen had just thrown iced tea at the back of her head. Mila got up and put her book back in her bag.

"I'm sorry." Sasha stuttered.

"My brother's in the hospital!"

Sasha nodded. Without another word, Gwen stalked off, Eric behind her. Mila put her hand on Sasha's shoulder. "Come on. It's just iced tea." Sasha let herself be led to the girl's bathroom. Mila hugged her and let her cry, not asking any questions. Once she'd calmed down, they went to sit outside. They were right beside the parking lot, where it had all happened. It felt surreal.

"Do you want to talk about it?" Mila asked. She pulled at strands of grass, her glasses catching the light of the sun.

"Are you okay?"

Sasha considered the question a moment. "I'm not the one in the hospital."

"That's a low bar for okay-ness."

"I just don't know if I did the right thing. It felt right at the time, but now I don't know."

"Just because someone throws iced tea at you doesn't mean you did the wrong thing."

Sasha's eyes filled again with gratitude. Both girls turned their heads as the red convertible pulled into the parking lot. Despite being used to it by now, the car still turned heads. They watched Eva exit the passenger side, Gabe from the driver's seat, and Hale from the back.

"Yikes," was all Mila said when she saw Hale. His eye was swollen shut, with deep purple bruising around it, and she could just imagine the cuts on his face when they got closer. The fact that she'd been the one to clean the blood off his face was surreal. He was still virtually a stranger, just a boy from school she'd met just a few months ago. Her throat felt dry.

Gabe and Hale exchanged words she couldn't hear, then Gabe turned to Eva and said something, to which the shorter girl nodded, a familiar expression of understanding on her face. Eva understood when it was time to be serious, it was something Sasha appreciated about her.

"Are you going to go talk to them?" Mila asked.

"Should I?"

Sasha hadn't realized that she'd frozen up, her fingernails making little crescents in the palms of her hands.

"Isn't Hale what all this is about?"

She turned to look at Mila.

"Isn't it about Jason?"

"Not for you." Mila gave her a little nudge, and they started walking toward the car.

Before they reached them, Sasha turned to her friend, "Thank you, you're amazing."

Mila's shoulders rose and fell, "It's almost like I'm an objective observer of your drama with no vested interest."

Sasha managed to choke out a laugh.

Eva

Eva ran forward to meet her friend. Sasha was pale and her eyes were puffy, shadows underneath them, though Eva hadn't slept particularly well herself. Mila stood beside Sasha like a guard. She was a quiet girl and rarely said much to Eva but seemed open with Sasha, maybe because Sasha was such an emotional rollercoaster.

When Gabe had pulled up to pick her up this morning with Hale in the backseat, judging by Gabe's expression, neither of the two was eager to talk.

"Hey!" She started in a friendly tone as she approached the girls.

"Hey, did your boyfriend take him to the hospital like he'd said he would?" Sasha began, sounding hoarse.

"He's okay."

"That's not what I asked, Eva. Are you getting lessons from Gabe on how to be evasive?"

Why was Sasha always taking her frustrations out on her?

"Don't take this out on me." She snapped back.

"Don't you want to get to the bottom of this story?"

"Right now, I just don't want to be late for class."

Sasha huffed.

"We don't need more trouble." Eva suggested, hoping it would be enough for her to drop the subject.

No such luck. Sasha bombarded her with questions the whole way to class. Mila headed in the opposite direction after giving Sasha a quick hug, shrugging her shoulders to Eva.

The truth was that Gabe was finally starting to trust her. How could she push him beyond what he was willing to share? She wished they could talk like they used to.

"Why is this so important to you all of a sudden?!" She finally snapped.

"Because I care about you!"

"Oh yeah, this is totally about me." She spat bitterly.

"What else would it be about?"

"Oh my god, Sash! I'm sorry I wasn't there when you needed me yesterday, but I couldn't have known what happened and neither did Gabe!"

Sasha opened her mouth to argue, then closed it again and stalked off. The distance between them felt like a cavern.

Sasha

Eva had intercepted her in the parking lot before she could speak to Hale. It felt imperative that she speak to him. She had so many questions and Eva wasn't going to answer them, whether because she didn't know or because she didn't want her to know. Where had they come from? Where were their parents? Eva told her Gabe was from New Mexico, but Hale said he was from New York. Where had Hale learned to fight like that? How did he manage to take on Jason, Eric and TJ at the same time? None of it added up.

She was afraid of running into Gwen again too. She'd never really been bullied at school. It wasn't as though she'd been popular, but she'd always smoothly slid under the radar.

Gathering her books, she spotted TJ, clearly retelling whatever happened yesterday. With her arms full and her head down, she quietly walked past the group.

"Then, out of nowhere, he loses his shit," TJ stopped abruptly, and his audience turned to look at her like she'd fallen out of the sky. He looked directly at her as he continued, "the ambulance dude said he was lucky to be alive. He was gonna need stitches, maybe even surgery."

Sasha bit her lip, guilt spreading through her insides like vines. Turning away, she kept walking, her feet like lead. This wasn't going away. A locker slammed beside her just as she reached class, making her jump.

"Are you gonna visit him?" TJ asked, appearing behind her as though he'd teleported.

"I guess so."

"Wow, you really are the worst."

She would've retorted, but he wasn't wrong. What kind of person lets her boyfriend get taken to the hospital and doesn't even call?

She got to class just as the bell rang. The hours wore on like molasses. She got a coffee after the first period just to stay awake and feel jittery through the second period.

"You should really go home." Mila told her as they made their way downstairs from art class.

"I'll see how I feel after lunch." She answered, feeling dizzy. Her friend might be right, but these weren't the problems she could sleep off either. She had to figure out what to do - should she go to the hospital to see Jason? Would he even want to see her?

"Hey!" Eva called from the bottom of the stairs.

"I'm going to the library."

"Books?"

"Nap." She could tell that Eva wanted to talk to her, but she was angry, and letting it go was proving near impossible. She was also angry that she hadn't been able to catch Hale this morning. She wasn't sure what she wanted from him, but she needed to understand what had happened; her memories seemed unreliable. She tried the cafeteria first, then his usual bench by the tennis courts. He was in neither. Sweaty and defeated, she went back to her original plan.

The library was cool and quiet, the librarians chatting under their breath behind the circulation desk. She inhaled the smell of old books and remembered how magical Saint-Ignatius had seemed when she first came here: the beautiful old historical building with its winding staircases and crown moldings. She loved the glossy feel of the floors, the smell of old wood and pine sol, the way the way sound carried easily. The library had really stood out to her, which its large stained-glass window at the center, with rows of mahogany desks and chairs along the walls and tall stacks of books creating nooks for students to gather together. It was practically empty today, which was exactly what she needed. She headed down along the row of desks to find the perfect one to nap behind. Sleep came as soon as she laid her head in her arms.

"Alexandra."
She opened her eyes through the fog of sleep and looked up at a bruised but handsome face.
"Hale?"
She lifted her head and swept the back of her hand over her face, just in case she'd been drooling.
"The bell is about to ring." He said.
It took her a moment to figure out that she hadn't set the alarm. She looked up at the analog clock on the wall. "Oh, crap."
"Sh!" A sharp voice hissed from the circulation desk.
"Thanks. Were you here the whole time?" her voice was gravely from sleep.
"No, I was leaving and saw you."
She pulled her backpack onto one shoulder and stretched her shoulder blades as she rose from her seat. Her hair felt messy in the humidity, and she felt all-around gross, though less exhausted. She also realized how hungry she was, but now there was no time for that. "Thanks, I would have slept through third period." she whispered.
He nodded. They left the library together, and she pulled an apple out of her bag on their way down the stairs. "How are you feeling?" She asked, between big bites.
"Fine."

She was very aware of the time, but she needed an answer. "I actually need to ask you..."

"What?"

"The fight, whose fault was it?"

His brows furrowed. "What do you mean?"

They stopped, students milling past them to their classes, lockers slamming, people laughing, calling to each other. She hesitated. "Did you attack him? Jason. Did he hit you first?"

"Yes."

"Yes, what?"

"He hit first."

"If I hadn't been there,what would've happened?"

"Nothing good." He looked confused, and struggled to maintain eye contact while she searched his face, trying to piece together what might be going on underneath all his silence.

"You're going to need to give me a little more than that. This is important."

"I'm sorry." He said, looking away. The way he jumped straight into an apology made it seem as though he didn't think he was worth defending. She couldn't wrap her head around what made him have such low self-esteem. Now that she'd been to his place, she realized how weird it was for him not to hang out with anyone at school or at home. It must be so lonely. No one deserved that.

"For what?"

He looked up, as though he was apologizing for existing. "I'm not sure." He looked extremely uncomfortable and finally lifted his gaze with an intensity she hadn't seen there before.

"You deserve to have someone on your side, Hale."

She remembered Gwen, Eric and TJ, and it horrified her to think what others might be thinking, but she still felt that she'd made the right choice. He hadn't started the fight. She'd asked him to stop, and he had. The hallways were quiet. The bell rang.

Eva

The wind whipped against Eva's sweater as she made her way down the main road toward home. The clouds cast a gray light over everything. Eva stopped at a street corner to pull the strands of her red hair out of her eyes and get her bearings. Gabe usually drove her home, but he hadn't shown up at four, leaving her to her own devices. After several futile calls to her mom and Shauna, she concluded that she would have to walk home.

After he'd dropped her off at school, she waited for him between classes but he didn't show. Then, at lunch, he was nowhere to be found again. She went out to the parking lot and found that his car was gone as well. She'd had to ask Pamela for his phone number, which was both infuriating and embarrassing. Maybe he'd gone to see Jason at the hospital? When she called, it had rung a number of times until Gabe finally picked up and, without asking who it was, told her to "fuck off" and hung up. She wanted to have faith in him. She wondered if it was misplaced as she walked numbly down the street, avoiding cars and crazed rollerbladers.

She neared a familiar intersection from which she could catch a bus the rest of the way home, but if she crossed the street and caught the one going East, she could get to Gabe's apartment in fifteen minutes. She wasn't sure Gabe deserved her company, but he did owe her an apology and an explanation. There was so much left unsaid between them, and it felt heavy. She waited for the light to turn green and dashed across the street to catch the bus. It began to drizzle just as she got off at his stop. Speed walking, she made it without getting her uniform soaked through. Even now, angry as she was, she was worried about him. Why hadn't he told her he was leaving? She imagined him disappearing as suddenly as he had appeared - vanishing from her life again without a word. She imagined his apartment empty, with all the furniture exactly as it had been before he'd moved in. She knew her life wouldn't go back to normal with him gone either, they were too entrenched. She ran up the stairs and knocked on the door.

There was a long silence, followed by a flat voice. "I didn't order pizza."
"Good! Cause I don't have any!" Eva snarled at the door as it swung open just enough for Gabe and Eva to be face to face but not enough for her to come inside. This wasn't the welcome she'd expected, but the flood of relief that he was here was accompanied by the sting of him not telling her he was leaving for the day. His hair was in disarray, whole strands escaping the lightly woven braid. He was wearing a tight off-white t-shirt.
"Hey, is this a bad time? I tried calling." Eva couldn't keep the edge out of her voice.
"Kind of. Do you need anything?" He asked, looking her up and down.
"No, Gabe, I don't *need* anything!" She growled, her temper flaring. Her mom called this her Scorpio side. "I only dragged my ass here to see if you were okay despite the fact you bitched at me over the phone and stood me up!" She was incredulous at his attitude. Did he not care? Why did she keep falling for this hot and cold bullshit?

"Sorry, Eva, nothin' personal, babe." He let the door open wider. His voice had none of its usual cheerful undertone, just a kind of surrender.

She walked briskly into the apartment, taking a seat on the large green sofa "I'm not like them. Don't treat me like one of your booty calls," she said. "I know you, Gabe. Better than you think." The words had come out rough and raspy, like her tongue and brain had been at war.

"You wouldn't wanna know me if you knew anything about me." He sat heavily beside her. His shoulders were slumped, but he looked up at her defiantly,making him look so much like the little boy she remembered that it was unbearable.

"Gabe, you're being stupid," She said, leaning towards him.

"Eva, this is a terrible idea."

"What is?" She said, hurt.

"Us. I'm going to end up hurting you. I don't want that."

There it was again, him talking to her as though she didn't understand her own heart, as though he was stringing her along and she didn't know any better. It was infuriating but heartbreaking. Did he really think so little of them both? "This is my decision just as much as yours."

He opened his mouth, then changed his mind and exhaled. "I know that."

"Gabe, talk to me. What's going on?"

"I fucked up. I should've been there yesterday. I should've brought my phone."

"How was that your fault?"

"I took your phone too."

"I let you." She said, frustrated. Why was he making this all about him?

"I'm never there when people need me the most." He was looking at the ground; his palms closed into fists. She wondered if they were still talking about Hale. She wondered again how he'd survived the fire at the church when they were kids. He had lived there. Her mom had hidden the newspaper with the names on it, but she'd found it. His name was there. She'd even checked online recently. He'd been announced as dead. Was he there at the time?

She leaned on his shoulder, pressing up against his side. "Gabe,there was nothing you could have done."

"You have no idea what I'm capable of and what I could've done and didn't." He had the same edge to his voice as he had last night when Sasha was here, a side of him he hid from everyone but couldn't keep under wraps forever.

"Gabe, you didn't know. Do you really want to break up?"

He takes a deep breath. "I don't want you to get hurt, that's all."
"You're not going to hurt me." She said.
"Babe, you have no idea, none. I'm not the person you think I am. If
you did, you'd understand why this can't work out."
His tone made Eva wince, but there was no turning back now. The
proverbial can of worms had been opened, and now she had to play for
all the cards.
"You're exactly the person I think you are, Gabe. I can't believe you
don't recognize me."
That caught him off guard. "Look, it's probably been the best couple of
months of my life, but ..." He was starting in on his breakup speech and
it was now or never. He had to know even if this meant it was over
between them.
"This version of you isn't the one I'm talking about," she heaved a heavy
sigh, so many skeletons were about to come tumbling out of the closet.
"I'm talking about the boy I met in Santa Fe back at Saint-Judes," her
heart was pounding. She clasped her sweaty palms together as she peered
into his eyes. She hadn't uttered that name in such a long time.
His eyes widened. She could practically see the words sinking like stones.
"Shit." He whispered and shook his head. His eyebrows narrowed,
"Who are you working for?"
Eva startled, leaning away from him, wide-eyed. "What?"
"I'm not working for anyone! I grew up in Santa Fe, Gabe." she said
calmly, hoping to talk the comprehension into him. "I was in Sister
Martha's class with you!"
Pushing off the couch, Gabe paced to the window, one hand pressed to
his forehead. He looked like he was trying to draw a memory of her
from the back of his mind and failing.
A few times, he cursed under his breath, "You are kidding me." He
mumbled to himself, his face pale and haunted. She was sure he was
running through the same faces, voices, and hallways as her own
memories in his mind: The teachers at the little church, their classmates,
all those who'd perished in the fire.
"How?" He demanded.
"My dad's been in the military since before I was born. We moved
around a lot and were stationed in Santa Fe when I was eight. We stayed
there until just before the...tragedy."
He finally looked back at Eva with wild eyes. "I don't remember you at
all." His voice sounded hoarse, as though he was about to cry.
She had spent so many years trying to forget it all and all the memories
that came attached. Now, they felt as raw and open as the day she had
found out that the church had been destroyed. It was as painful as when

her letter to Lexie was returned with a red stamp indicating she could not locate the recipient.

They called them dead letters, and now here they were: dead letters to each other. "I was blonde back then." she said as she curled herself into a ball on the couch. "I sat two seats behind you, and you would always steal my lunch." she half-smiled at the memory.

That brought an ironic smile to his lips, a ghost of a smile for Gabe, who smiled so freely and frequently. His voice still sounded choked up, as though he was going to cry. "Blond, huh? I don't see it. I stole your lunch?" Unknowingly, he reached for a wooden cross that he wore at his heart and pulled it out from beneath his shirt, gripping its side into the palm of his hand. She'd noticed it before but never thought to ask for its meaning. It instantly made her own silver chain feel heavy and cold against her chest. The weight felt comforting, a grounding force in the chaos. Letting the serene smile of the sisters take her troubles away.

"Every day for a month, my mom made damn good food." She giggled. Suddenly, she remembered having an old school photo in her bag. She'd dug it up months ago from the shoebox under her bed. She knew she'd have to tell him eventually.Quickly, she dug through her bag and found the photo at the bottom. Dozens of smiling faces peered up at her as she ran her fingers over the print. "Here, maybe that'll help if you still think I'm working for someone?" She held out the picture like a piece of rare art. "Gabe,what did you mean by that?"

Letting the cross fall back onto his chest, he held the picture at its corners with trembling fingers. It was as though they'd both risen from the dead but these little faces hadn't. He laughed as tears gathered at the corners of his eyes.
The rain began to pound against the roof, and the wind blew a few droplets through the open balcony door, along with a cold gust. He ran a finger over the faces, memories fleeting behind his irises. He chuckled, he was the only kid in the photo with a scowl.

"Sister Martha made me wear the bow tie and I hated it. I screamed at her but wore it anyway. She was so patient with my tantrums. She said I looked handsome, the other kids didn't think so, and Jamie said I looked like a priest." He stood at the front, having been a pretty short child, and he'd puffed up his cheeks and looked at the camera with an expression of discontent. Right above him, Ryan was holding up bunny ears. On his left was a little girl with blond hair and dark eyes; Eva watched him finally find her in the photo. He looked up from the picture to the girl beside him in complete and utter shock: "T-this is you?"

She nodded her, remembering the dreaded pink dress. Her mother had woken her up early so she could curl her hair and ensure she was presentable.
"It's like looking at a ghost," she said in a small voice. "I'm sorry for bringing this up." She couldn't even imagine how hard this must be for him. Even the good memories seemed to leave scars. "I'm sure they'd be so proud of you. You've grown up to be so different." Her voice came out hoarse and tear ridden.

A tear hit the photograph, and Gabe wiped his face quickly, embarrassed. He shook his head and handed the photo back to Eva. "They wouldn't. They died because of me." He whispered.

The weight of his words crushed the air out of her lungs. How could he blame himself for something completely out of his control? Slowly she forced the air back into her lungs and moved closer to him. The rain splattered angrily against the windows. When had it started to rain? "There was nothing you could have done. You were just a kid." The tears slowly slid down her cheeks.
"I'm sure they wouldn't blame you."
"Course not. They thought I was an angel. But I'm not."
"What happened, Gabe?"
"I wasn't there.They told me to go and get bread from the bakery in town. They said we would have guests. Some bigwig from the military was coming by. By the time I got back, it was over. Everything was gone. I wasn't there when they needed me."

Allowing her to shift closer to him, he looked her in the eyes again, looking for something. "She died in my arms, Sister Martha. She wasn't even thinking about herself; she kept thinking of me. She kept saying that God would bless me and all I could do was sit there. There were sirens and people everywhere, but none of them did anything." Tears rolled down his cheeks, and he swiped them away with the back of his hand.
Again, she felt breathless, like the world had run out of air. "I can remember her voice so clearly sometimes." She whispered, leaning against the back of the sofa, "God loves you, child; no matter where life takes you, remember that God will always love you even when others don't." She closed her eyes, "That was the last thing she said to me before I left."

He smiled at her, a profound sadness in his eyes. "I wish that was what I remembered about her.There was so much to remember that wasn't the end of her life, but I keep thinking back to those last minutes."

They sat silently as Gabe stared at the photo, tears streaming down his face. She'd never seen him cry before. He didn't wipe them away now. He let them fall onto his shirt and gather on his cheeks. His olive skin was flushed. After a long silence of rain battering against the windows, he spoke again.

"How long have you known?"

"I thought I was going crazy at first," She admitted, "But your smile is the same." she placed her head on his shoulder, seeking comfort, "I wasn't sure how to tell you."

He put an arm around her and pulled her closer, so she was lying on top of him, slumped over the hand-rest. He laughed, refreshing and bright after the tears. "Now I feel like a total asshole for earlier."

They were so close that she could feel his tears against her cheek, mixing with her own.

His laughter was such a welcome relief to the harsh tone he had taken with her earlier that she giggled with him, her heart fluttering in her chest. "You should!" She lay her head on his chest, "But I think I can let it slide this one time."

She sighed contentedly, his warmth enveloping her. He lifted her chin to meet him and kissed her gently. His lips were soft and salty. Kissing him back felt like sealing the deal. He held her tight, and she closed her eyes, deepening the kiss as she felt him running a hand up and down her back. Suddenly, they both heard the sound of the key turning in the lock.

Eva groaned, exasperated, "Looks like it's the party crasher." She buried her face in Gabe's chest as Hale walked into the apartment. As she lifted her gaze, she saw him turn to give them a look of disgust, accentuated by the bruises on his face. He soaked through from the rain. It looked as though she hadn't been the only one who'd gotten stood up for a lift home.

Gabe gave his roommate an apologetic wave as he passed. Hale went straight into the washroom, and within a few seconds, they could hear the shower running. Eva sighed.

"He has a timing issue, doesn't he?"

She put the photo safely away in her bag. She still felt raw emotionally but the relief of finally having told Gabe the truth was amazing. Behind that though, questions still lurked: What had Gabe meant when he'd asked who she was working for?

"I gotta tell you somethin' else." Gabe said quietly, glancing down the corridor.

"I'll believe anything at this point."

Maybe he would trust her now that he knew they were connected in many more ways than he could imagine. Maybe he'd finally open up to her.

"I can't be around Jason anymore. What he did..."

Maybe not.

She nodded. "I get it. Hale's your friend."

"He has to be."

"What do you mean?"

"Hale's like me. We're the same - and we have to look out for each other."

She wanted to pry further, but she was still afraid. If she pushed him too far, would he shut her out again?

"I don't care who you hang out with as long as one of them is me." She smiled reassuringly.

He exhaled, looking like he might have said more, but changed his mind.

"Course it'll be you." He finally said.

"Will it? Because it doesn't always feel that way." She confessed.

He sighed. "Babe, things are going to change, ok?"

"I'd like it if we could be more honest with each other." She said, hoping he took that to heart. He didn't have to be the cool guy with her; he just needed to be Gabe. The light had faded during their conversation, a very long day coming to a close. She let the words hang in the air, hoping he would tell her what he was doing here in this tiny town or where he'd been all these years.

"Come on, I'll give you a lift home." he said instead, scooping them off the couch. His voice was lighter.

Eva heard the thunder outside and nodded. She'd kept the secret for months, now she hoped her honesty would help him to be honest back. He was definitely in trouble, and if he could just tell her, maybe they could fix it together.

Chapter 8
Ebbs and Flows

Sasha

It was Friday, two days after the fight, when the intercom requested her presence in the principal's office. They were in the middle of an exceedingly boring math class about charts and all eyes turned to her. With the teacher's approval, she obliged, gathering her things and heading downstairs. What was this about? She knew she had a record for tardiness but it seemed a bit silly to bring it up this far into her last year. As soon as she entered the principal's office, she knew. There sat TJ and Eric alongside two empty chairs. The principal and their guidance counselor stood behind the large mahogany desk. She took a seat as asked, and they all sat in awkward silence. She'd done her best to avoid both Eric and TJ, and she still hadn't spoken to Jason.

There was a confident knock. The principal opened the door for Hale, his face still showing signs from the fight. "Mr. Yu. Thank you for joining us." She pointed to the final chair in the room beside Eric. Sasha tugged at her fingers. The tension in the room could be cut with a knife.

"I don't think we've ever properly met." The woman at the front began, speaking directly to Hale. "I'm Principal Alder. This is our guidance counselor, Mr. Earl." Mr. Earl was a tall man with salt and pepper hair dressed as though he were attending a funeral. Saint-Ignatius was formal, but not to this degree. It added to the feeling of surrealism. "He's here to help us sort out what happened at 5:15 on Wednesday evening in the school parking lot."

Sasha desperately tried to make eye contact with Hale, but he ignored her. "I've heard Eric's side of the story, along with a video which showed part of the fight. It was shared extensively through social media, it seems." She seemed embarrassed to say so. Of course, that was what this would be about, PR. "Thomas Jonathan was about to tell us his story, but we thought we'd wait for you to arrive." She hadn't even known that was what TJ stood for up until now. She was a terrible sleuth, clearly.

TJ started: "It's like Eric said, Mrs. Alder, we were just asking him about a homework assignment, and he started picking a fight. Then he attacked Jason without provocation."

She could feel her pulse rising, biting her lower lip as hard as she could so as not to interrupt.

"Thank you." Mrs. Alder said. "Mr. Yu, anything to say?"

"No." Hale said, resigned, looking only at Mrs. Alder.

"Mr. O'Neil's parents are calling for immediate expulsion if not police action."

She couldn't take it anymore, and her hand shot up: "Mrs. Alder?"

"Yes, Ms..." She seemed to be looking down at her folder on her desk to get her name. "Star..."

"Staraselski." Sasha corrected.

"Did you have something to add?"

"I do, actually." Her sentences came out in a rush. She could feel color jumping to her cheeks. "Eric and TJ are misrepresenting the situation. I saw the whole thing, well, not the beginning of it, but at least the part they're talking about, and from what I saw, they were holding Hale up by his arms for Jason to beat him up, as you can see." She pointed towards Hale. "He threw them off and attacked Jason too, but it was three against one at first." TJ and Eric stared at her, loathingly.

"Gentlemen, anything to say?" The school counselor said calmly, he looked bored with the situation. He was the last person she'd have ever asked for any sort of guidance.

"Jason was just defending himself!" Eric said. "My brother got it all on video!"

"If I understand correctly, Ms.," She did not attempt her family name a second time. "You were the one who broke up the fight?"

"Sort of, I just rushed in and begged them to stop. Not fast enough either."

"That was brave. Why did you do it?"

That caught her aback.

"Because Jason's my boyfriend." She said quietly, looking out the window. This was mortifying.

"So, you were defending Jason."

"Yes."

"You're not defending him now!" TJ cut in, seemingly unable to stay in his seat.

She glanced at him nervously, wondering if she was going to be next in finding herself face down on the asphalt in the parking lot. She continued nonetheless. "Jason, Eric and TJ all ganged up on Hale. Hale hurt Jason really badly. Jason hurt him too. It's not fair that neither of these two gets punished either." She could practically feel Eric and TJ's wrath.

"Mr. Yu? Were you provoked?" the principal insisted.

He nodded, still not looking at her.

"Alright. The punishment will be as follows: Alexandra, you will serve detention after school for one week for throwing yourself in harm's way." She opened her mouth to argue but Mrs. Adler continued.

"You three," She said to the boys, "will serve community service on campus. 10 hours for Eric and Thomas and 20 hours for you, Hale. You will come in during the break when students are at home."

"What's that?" Eric said.

"Cleaning floors, toilets, scrubbing dishes, taking down all the Christmas decorations, preparing the school for reopening, polishing the floors."

"We have cleaning staff for that." TJ muttered under his breath.

"What was that?" The woman demanded.

"Nothing Mrs. Adler."

"Thank you, ma'am." The four of them chorused.

As they waited for the secretary to write them notes to allow them to return to their respective classes, Eric and TJ hissed curses at Hale, but it was obvious they were afraid of him. They stood as far as possible from him in the small office. When they were finally allowed to leave, her anxiety shifted to irritation. This was the stupidest thing she'd ever heard! Why was she being punished when she hadn't done anything? The boys were gone as quickly as possible, but Sasha stood in the hallway, gathering her thoughts and trying to contain her anger.

She slowly made her way back to the stairs, where she found Hale sitting on the steps, looking down at the paper outlining his assignment for his parents.

"Hey," She said. He got up as she approached, "How are you feeling?"

"What do you mean?"

"I mean, are you okay? That was ridiculous, right?"

"I'm fine." She reached out to see the paper and he handed it to her. The part asking for a parent's signature already had a scribble on it. She furrowed her eyebrows. He'd signed it himself, why? She handed it back to him.

"Can't believe I got detention too," she admitted.

"I expected worse,"

"I guess community service isn't so bad,"

"The lightest punishment I've received." He mumbled.

"Will your parents be mad?"

He shrugged, folding the paper in four and sliding it into his pocket, "We should get back to class."

She grabbed his wrist.

"Wait," He looked at her hand in confusion. "Hale, I don't know how else to approach this. Do you want me to leave you alone? Just say so. If you want me to, I will."

He paused, caught aback. She felt the disappointment in her stomach. She'd thrown herself into a fight, and gotten punished for no reason, and now he would say that he wanted nothing to do with her. Could this week get any worse?

"What do you expect from me?" He asked. The question seemed genuine but so odd.

"I just want to be friends."

"Friends?" She thought he might be mocking her, but nothing in his tone or face suggested as much. He seemed completely disoriented by the suggestion. She let go of his wrist and crossed her arms.

"If you want."

"You don't have to do that."

"I want to. Don't you get it? I *want* to be friends if you'll let me."

"I'm not a good friend to have."

"Let me be the judge of that." At least something good could come out of this horrible situation!

"If you insist."

"Okay, see you!" She hurried up the stairs to class before she could get into any more trouble or before she did something stupid like reach out and touch the spot on his cheek where she'd cleaned blood from it on Wednesday. Since the fight, she felt Hale to be someone who desperately needed a hug, but she suspected he might throw her down the stairs if she tried.

Eva

When Gabe said things would change, she wanted to believe him. Would he really choose her and stop fooling around? Was he really going to stop hanging out with the popular kids? Was he even capable of that? Would he finally tell her how he'd ended up at Saint-Ignatius? Thoughts raced through her mind as she threw beach supplies into a big yellow-striped bag: Towel, extra bathing suit, sweater, sunscreen, hair brush, condoms. Just in case. What else did she need? Snacks.

She headed downstairs, where her mom was chopping fruit for her little brother. "Where are you off to?"

"Sasha and I are going to the beach."

"In that fancy red convertible with Gabriel?"

Eva blushed and stuck her nose into the pantry, filling her bag with granola bars and fruit rolls ups. Her mom knew she and Gabe were dating but had been surprisingly cool about it so far. "Can I have a ride in that car?" Matteo asked. He was playing a video game, waiting for his snack. She could hear the sounds of Mario, just like she'd played as a kid.

"It's not mine. I can't just ask for rides."

"What time will you be home?" Her mom chimed in.

"Not late, I promise."

"And you'll keep your phone on this time?"

"Yes." She tried not to be visibly annoyed.

"At some point, you'll have to bring that boy over so we can meet him."

"You've already met him, Mom."

"Six in the morning doesn't count."

"Okay, fine. I'll ask him. Let me know when you're free."

"How about next Friday?"

"Next Friday? Mom..." she groaned.

"Eva, if he's going to be in your life, I want to get to know him."

"We're just hanging out." Why did she need to deal with this at home too? Why was it anyone's business besides hers and Gabe's?

"I'd still like to get to know this boy my daughter is 'hanging out' with."

Eva grabbed a water bottle. "Bye!"

"No *bye* until you agree."

"Okay, I'll ask him, I promise. Can I go now?"

Her mom stepped out into the hallway and pulled her into a quick hug. "Be smart."

Gabe was waiting for her at the corner of the street, just as he'd promised, though she supposed her cover was blown. He was the only one in the car.

"Hey, Princess." He said.

"Hey, babe. I thought you said it was a group thing. Sasha's not going to be happy."

"And we care about this?"

"Babe!"

She'd eased into calling him pet names, which she still couldn't quite get herself to do in public. It felt so easy, so natural between them. She hoped he felt the same way.

They pulled up in front of Sasha's place, where she was sitting outside on the doorstep, wearing a large straw hat for shade. "Hey, Sash!"

Sasha greeted her warmly and waved at Gabe, putting her bag into the back seat and sliding in, "I will admit, this is a very nice car."

"I think that's the nicest thing you've ever told me." Gabe scoffed.

"Oh, excuse me, Fabio, am I the only female who hasn't fallen to her knees before you?"

"Who's Fabio?" Gabe asked.

Eva laughed. "You two are ridiculous."

"So, without stating the obvious here, weren't we going to be a foursome?"

"Kinky." Gabe teased.

"No other takers today." Eva said, batting Gabe in the shoulder.

Sasha sighed and slouched. "Fine."
"Don't you mean 'Thank you for the ride, Gabe?'" He teased.

Eva turned on the radio and drowned them out. Gabe and Sasha had achieved a sibling level of bickering, which was better than the outright hostility they had shown each other before, though she still wished her best friend could just get along with her boyfriend. Gabe was easy to be around for just about everyone; all Sasha had to do was let him. She wondered if Gabe missed Jason and his old friends, but he never mentioned them, so she didn't ask for further details.

Eva and Gabe had been to this beach a few times. It was usually deserted, but today it was full to the brim. Umbrellas of every colour bloomed along the sand, and towels piled with bags created tiny pathways for them to walk through. Parents chased their toddlers, squealing in delight into the shallow waves. Teenagers sunbathed and blasted competing music from tiny speakers.

After smearing themselves with sunblock, Sasha said she would stay with their bags while Eva and Gabe headed straight for the water, trying not to step on anyone. Gabe shirtless was truly a sight to behold. It was funny to think that he worked out so much, he'd never said anything about it, nor had she ever seen him do so. The water was warm on her toes but quickly became cold as she went deeper. The lake was just narrow enough to swim across, with a small dock at the halfway mark. She pushed herself a little further past the initial point of not wanting to be cold and felt completely relaxed, her arms and legs moving in sink without her having to think about them, years of muscle memory kicking in.

"Where'd you learn to swim like that?" Gabe asked, floating beside her.
She laughed. "I love water. Always have. My mom used to drive me to practice at 5 in the morning before school."
"I definitely prefer a pool to the lake, but this is pretty awesome."
"How about you? Where'd you learn to swim?"
"Necessary life skill." He said, "Your mom sounds amazing."
"Speaking of my mom, do you maybe want to drop by the house and meet her sometime? My parents are curious about you." She expected a sour expression, but Gabe took it in stride.
"Yeah, whatever. Why not?"
"Okay, but fair warning, my dad can be a lot."
"I think I can handle an old man."

"My dad's not old, and you'd better not say that to him." She swam around him in circles, enjoying making him spin to look at her. If only they could always stay like this, just the two of them in their own little world, without everyone else's opinions. He didn't seem nervous about meeting her parents at all. Should he be? She tried to imagine Gabe with her parents and Matteo. Gabe was unpredictable, charming when he wanted to be but also secretive.

They swam and talked, kicking against each other's feet, pulling one another along and before they knew it, they'd reached the other side of the lake. She could feel her arm muscles complaining but didn't want to turn back.

"Hungry yet?" He asked.

"Guess so."

"Want to head back?"

"Not yet."

They stepped out through the muck and sat in the shadows of old trees, letting their skin dry in the midday sun, resting before swimming back. She was in the middle of a story when she turned to look at him and realized how close they were sitting to one another, how their knees were touching, the one warm spot on her body at that moment. He kissed her then, and it was like no kiss they'd ever shared - needy, hot, and breathless. She felt them tipping down into the sand and pushed him gently back up. "We should get back."

His eyes opened, and he exhaled as though it took everything in him to stop. He hopped up to his feet and helped her up too. "Alright." He had the decency not to sound too disappointed.

Swimming back was harder, but they were both strong swimmers and picked up the conversation exactly where they'd left off.

It was when they returned to shore that she remembered Sasha, who was at the end of a book and through her third granola bar when they returned to their towels, giving them a look of disdain nearly ranked alongside Hale's sneers. "Welcome back, folks. It's almost time to go home."

They shared what Eva had brought along as snacks, and Sasha went for a short swim before they left. She said she felt cheated otherwise.

Sasha

The first few weeks back at school after the holidays were stressful. Her friends surprised her by both showing their support and simultaneously making themselves scarce. Bullying at their school was a quiet, insidious affair. No one knew what to make of the situation and most people didn't want to be in the line of fire from TJ, Eric or Gwen. She was glad not to be getting any more threats or iced tea thrown at her, but she could feel the shift in how people saw her. There were fewer friendly moments with acquaintances, and far fewer people to talk to all of a sudden. She'd completed her days of detention easily, though her mom had given her a funny look when she had to sign the form she'd been given from the office.

"Putting you-self in harm's way?" She asked, reading it out in her eastern European accent. "What is that?"

"I broke up a fight."

"You were in a fight?"

"No, I stopped the fight."

"Do you need me to get involved?" She asked in Russian.

"No. It's easier just to play along. I'll be out of there in 6 months."

Her mom shook her head and signed. "Stupid."

Sasha couldn't agree more.

As exam time was fast approaching, and many of her friends had signed up for early admission into ivy league universities, even those that wouldn't have cared about what the popular kids thought of her were too busy to hang out. Margo was always nose-deep in a prep book; Daphne and Mel were busy with the numerous sports events on campus, and everyone else was focused on exams, though they insisted nothing was wrong. Mila was steady as always, but was kept busy with a stream of tutors.

Sasha felt Jason's absence not only in his empty seat and the sneering looks from his friends, but in the silence of her text messages. She hadn't realized how much time she'd spent either speaking to Jason or about Jason. Eva and Gabe were even more overtly mushy than usual, so while they welcomed her with open arms, she rarely sat with them for very long.

She knew she should visit Jason in the hospital but kept putting it off. She replayed the fight in her head, trying to figure out who was wrong and right. Maybe they were all wrong. She hung around Hale, trying to make good on her promise to be friends. He was a good listener, or maybe just quiet. The result was the same. His good looks became less of a big deal too. He was just a quiet, awkward guy she'd promised to befriend. He never made much effort but sometimes she felt as though he'd been waiting for her when she arrived during recess. He even

85

humored her and listened to some of her music occasionally, each of them sitting quietly with a headphone in each ear. Spending more time around him felt like piecing together a puzzle. She used to think he was hard to read, but it got easier the more she was around him, like learning a new language. His face spoke volumes even if he didn't voice much. His hands also gave him away, he'd pick at his thumb when he was nervous or irritated and then sooth the same spot with his forefinger when he was calm.

The day that Jason returned to school was the day after football season ended. He appeared in English class on Monday morning, still gorgeous, still full of energy. He'd been gone for three weeks. He seemed to have healed completely. He approached Gabe first, and the two said hi to one another. The interaction felt cold; she'd expected a hug or at least a pat on the back, but all Gabe said was, "Welcome back, man." Hale was focused on his computer, and to her surprise, Jason made no move toward him, not even a glance.

She tried not to stare, but it was impossible, so she put her head down into her arms on the desk until the bell rang. She felt like a coward. Even if she thought Jason had been in the wrong, he was her boyfriend. She should have visited him. Why hadn't she? She thought about it constantly, but never mustered up the courage to go. She lifted her head once Mr. Blunt began lecturing, and Eva hand-gestured, "you ok?" at her in silence. She nodded, but the lump in her throat stayed put. Unable to focus, she pretended to take notes, her pen scratching patterns into her page repeatedly. When the class ended, she began packing her things quietly when she felt someone near her desk. She didn't need to look up to know who it was; his presence was familiar, and the smell of his aftershave was too.

"Sasha." His voice was deep, and light-hearted.
"Hey, Jason. I'm...I'm glad you're back." She managed to look up, feeling her eyes fill with tears. He looked down from his significant height advantage, and she could see from up close that he hadn't quite healed. He looked tired and older somehow. He actually looked more like his dad than he had before - someone serious.
"I missed a lot, I hear." he said.
"I'm really sorry I never came to visit...and I didn't stay with you until the ambulance arrived."
"It's okay, Sasha. You didn't do anything."
"I ...I should have, though." She choked out.

"Yeah, you should've." It wasn't an accusation, but it wasn't forgiveness either, more of an admonition.

"Is this it then? The world's most boring breakup?" He asked. She could see the class emptying, people seeming to sense Jason's wishes. It showed how much he was respected that no one was actively eavesdropping.

"I'm sorry." She said, ashamed, wrapping her arms around herself but continuing to meet his gaze. She felt miserable, but she also didn't want to talk to him about it, mostly because she couldn't explain it to herself, much less this handsome guy who'd been nothing but sweet to her for months.

"Do you like that guy?"

"Who?"

"Gwen says you spend a lot of time with him."

"I'm not dating anyone." It irritated her a little that she refused to use Hale's name, as though Jason thought he was above him.

"Did you stay away because you chose him?"

She paused to think. She definitely felt something for Hale. She felt protective of him, she cared about him, but she wasn't about to share that with Jason.

"No, I didn't."

"Then why'd you stay with him?"

"You...he was alone." She couldn't think of anything else to say. "I'm sorry."

"You've known me for five years."

"You're right, okay? It was a messed-up situation. I didn't handle it right."

"So, you admit you were wrong? That it was a mistake?" She kept gazing into his eyes, trying to see if there was a hint of the connection they once shared. Had there ever been any real connection in the first place? She'd been asking herself whether she'd sided with the wrong person since the fight, and the way he looked at her, calm, cool, collected Jason, made it hard to believe that he would gang up on another student.

"Wasn't the fight a mistake?"

"Considering I lost, probably." He admitted, though his tone held no remorse.

"Why did you do it then?"

He looked up and back at her, as though considering it.

"He just pissed me off. The way he talked to me."

"How did he talk to you?"

"Like he thought he was better than me - and he's not. He's a nobody."

"He's not a nobody just because you've decided he is." She cut in, setting her jaw.

"You just said you were sorry Sasha."

"Yeah, but you should be too."

"I was in a hospital, why should I be the one who's sorry?."

She swiped at the tears in her eyes, anger bubbling up, "You had Eric and TJ holding him up while you punched him. Did you watch the video afterwards? He wasn't even fighting back at first. You looked like you were getting a real kick out of it."

"He broke my nose and three of my ribs."

"Did he throw the first punch?"

"Does that matter?" he didn't raise his voice, "He ran his mouth."

There was silence.She knew they weren't going to see eye to eye on this. She could've done better by him, but there was no way to find common ground about the fight. He wasn't sorry he'd hit Hale, he was sorry he'd lost and that was the crux of it. She could argue with him until she was blue in the face, but it wouldn't change his mind.

"I'm sorry, Jason. I'm glad you're okay." She repeated, looking down at her desk.

"Gabe came to see me," he said.

"I'm not surprised. You guys are close."

"He told me to stay away from Hale."

Sasha knew she must have looked surprised because Jason smirked. "I'm glad you weren't part of that." Why would Gabe do that? He was much closer to Jason than to Hale. The more she knew about those boys, the more questions she had about them. She wanted to ask what more Gabe had said, but it seemed pretty insensitive.

He answered as though he hadn't heard her, "People are sayin' you've been hanging out a lot, you and Gabe."

"What are you implying?" she asked.

"Are you into Gabe now? You didn't like him much when we used to hang out."

"He's Eva's boyfriends, I can't exactly avoid him."

Jason shook his head, as though she'd disappointed him.

"You don't have to speak to me." Packing up what was left of her books, she adjusted her bag on her shoulder, looking up at him again.

"I don't hate you, Sasha."

"Thanks, I'd better go."

The class had emptied, save for Eric and TJ. There was nothing more to say, so they left the class not looking at one another, back to the strangers they had been before. She let him move back to his group once they were out in the hall, and she walked in the opposite direction. He'd been important to her for a short time, and now he was back where he belonged. She wondered if this meant that Gwen, Eric and TJ would stop hating her and then felt selfish for thinking about that. Would she ever be able to think of Jason without guilt? So much for living the full spectrum of the high school experience. She went off to find Margo for their next tedious chemistry lab together. Colleges wouldn't care about her trauma.

By the time she and Margo had finished, her entire body was buzzing with anxiety. She kept replaying the conversation in her mind, wondering what she should have or could have said. It made pretending to be good at chemistry all the harder. She needed to talk to someone. She knew what people probably thought about her. She couldn't avoid the rumors. People said she was obsessed with Hale, that this was some sort of love triangle, it was ludicrous. Then why was Hale the one who sprang to mind as soon as she was alone? She decided to find him. She was sure seeing Jason back was a shock to him too. She found him in one of the dozen places he liked to inhabit during lunches. She'd gotten good at identifying the one he'd most likely be in on any given day. There were multiple factors: The weather, where other classes might be, where extracurriculars were being held, and how close it was to his next class. She shouldn't know his schedule by heart, but she did.

"Hey you." she said, out of breath from climbing the stairs trying and failing to smile.
Nodding at her was all the invitation she needed to sit next to him.
She cut to the chase, "Jason's back and he came right over to talk to me."
"Hm." He shifted his gaze from his screen to her, but didn't comment.
"God, I didn't know what to say to him!" she continued, "Did he come to talk to you?"
"No." He seemed nonplussed, as though she were talking about the weather.
"He's the same Jason but I feel totally different, and I know I should've gone to the hospital to visit or called him more or just made more of an effort, but I just didn't know what to say."
"You have regrets." It was a simple statement, said in a neutral tone.
"Yes, I mean, I do regret not visiting and not being there earlier but, I don't know if I regret what I actually did. I think I should've insisted that we go to the hospital and maybe gotten someone to drive you rather than walking or at least called a taxi, but I just saw this whole other side of Jason that I can't unsee."
"I'm the wrong person to discuss this with." She tried to see if he was annoyed, but he didn't seem any more tense than usual.
"Are you afraid he's going to come after you again? Because it's okay if you are and if you want me to say anything, I think he'd still listen to me. He said he didn't hate me at least."

"You don't need to protect me; I'm not afraid of him or his friends."

"Hale, he's two heads taller and wider than you."

"He's no threat."

"Then what happened when I got into the parking lot that day?" She leaned forward and tried to look into his eyes. There was a long pause in which he refused to look at her. His eyes were the darkest shade of brown, but someone in his lineage must have been mixed race because he had flecks of gray. There was a softness about him, just under the surface. Speaking to him was like trying to hold a butterfly between her fingers. He kept saying he didn't need her help, that there was nothing to worry about, and yet she kept wanting to be near and protect him.

"It doesn't matter." He finally said.

"It matters to me!"

He flinched.

The silence hung between them. She supposed it wasn't any of her business, but she wanted an answer. She'd committed to him, or at least to the idea that he was the one in need of protection, and she wanted to know that she'd made the right choice. She'd often seen herself as the underdog and aligned herself with other underdogs, but she still wasn't entirely sure that was an accurate description of Hale.

"I let them." He confessed in barely a whisper.

Just as quickly, she was on her feet, her arms out in front of her. "What does that mean?"

"Calm down." He didn't roll his eyes but his expression suggested that he thought she was exaggerating.

She pursed her lips and breathed audibly. "Okay, I'm calm." She sat back down.

"They can't hurt me unless I allow them to. You don't need to worry about me, and you shouldn't."

"So you won't "let them" again, right?" She made quotation marks with her fingers.

He nodded.

She fell back onto the bench next to him, bumping up against his knee. "You're never going to let me in on your deal, are you?"

"My deal?"

"Yeah."

"I'm not sure I know what you mean."

"You absolutely know what I mean Hale. Where did you learn to fight like that?"

"I'm not answering that."

She let out another deep exhale.

"You drive me nuts."

"Likewise." He said.

"Okay, well, do you mind the company? I really don't feel like discussing Jason with my friends right now," Her voice was shaky.

He shrugged. "I'm going to study."

"Okay, I'll read then." She pulled a large fantasy novel out of her bag and pulled her legs up on the other side of the bench, propping herself against his shoulder. He shifted to make room for her. He smelled of laundry detergent and his particular scent. It was hard to focus on her book, the conversations she'd just had kept bouncing around in her mind and made her reread the same sentence over and over again.

"Hale?"

"Hm?"

"I like hanging out with you."

He looked over at her as though she'd grown a second head. She could practically see the gears in his head turning, trying to think of an answer. The bell rang. No answer came.

Chapter 9
Questioning Tomorrow

Eva

Gabe lay on the couch reading *The Crow* a black and white comic book Eva had brought over weeks ago that had been on the small table in the living room gathering dust.

"Gabe!"

"What?"

"You said you'd study with me." Eva had sprawled all her meticulously color-coded notes around her on the floor.

"I am!"

"There's nothing in the SATs about comic books."

"You're the one who said I had to read it. This guy has some issues."

"You'd have issues too if your girlfriend was murdered.Great, now I'm distracted again. I agreed to come over because you said you'd study."

"I thought it was 'cause we haven't hung out in weeks, and you missed me desperately."

"Well, we can't all get 90s doing nothing as you can. Come on, the exams are next week, then we can hang out."

"Babe," he whined. "I don't care."

"You should - what will you do when we're done school? Keep living here with Hale?"

He laughed, "I'm not worrying about that right now."

"Well, what do you want to do?"

"Join the circus."

"Gabe,did you even register to take the SATs?"

"I don't need 'em."

"Are you planning to work at McDonald's?"

"What's wrong with that?"

"You're smarter than that. You get perfect grades."

"Grades aren't that important in the real world."

She laughed. "Oh my God, babe, the real world? You have to go to college. What's your career plan?"

He deflected,"What are you going to be, babe?"

"Me? A director maybe, or a producer, or if that doesn't pan out, I guess I'll just teach film or something."

"You're going to film school and you need chemistry, physics and math for that?"

"No, but I need a backup plan in case I need to work before my career takes off. Come on, Gabe. There must be something you're passionate about."

"I'm passionate about hanging out with you."

"Too bad you can't get paid for that."

"That would make me a different kinda boyfriend."

She smacked his knee with her textbook. "Why don't you ever answer a question?"

"I just did!"

"So, you have no idea who you want to be when you grow up? What did you want to be when you were a kid?" Eva often asked about his childhood, and he answered with half-truths and snippets.

"I didn't think about it. I just wanted to be old enough to care for myself and choose my own path."

"And now that you are, you're not picking one. Neither of my parents went to university, and I'm dying to go. You could come with me while you decide."

"I ain't going to university, babe."

"I guess you can join the military like my dad."

"No way, I'd rather die than be a United soldier."

"A little much, don't you think?"

"I'm a little much? Have you read this comic? This crow guy..."

Sasha

Sometimes, Sasha missed being part of a larger group when she spent time with Eva because it lessened the feeling of being the third wheel. Being around Gabe and Eva was fun but also irritating. They always behaved as though they were out on a date and she just happened to be there with them. Eva would tell her jokingly that she was technically the fourth wheel but Hale wasn't a wheel at all. He was his own vehicle altogether and rarely spoke unless spoken to when they were all together.

They would hang out around town or in the apartment, walk on the beach or study. She missed having Eva to herself but was slowly getting used to Gabe being around. They teased each other in the way she teased her older brother, and it almost felt like friendship. It was never a given that Hale would show up to activities and even less of a given that he'd stick around if he did. Sometimes, they would drive an hour away from the apartment, and he'd still take off and make his own way back without them. On Valentine's Day, she saw Jason give a rose to Pamela, which meant that whatever he and Sasha had shared, was now officially over.

That same week, Gabe was swinging by to take herself and Eva to the mall, which meant it was unlikely that Hale would come along. Prom dresses had started cropping into conversations at school, but Sasha still felt like she had time before having to worry about any of that. To her surprise, as the car pulled up, Hale was sitting in the back, leaning up against the door, looking about as casual as Hale could look, his body language still rigid.

For some reason, seeing him in clothes besides his school uniform was still startling. Today, he had a dark gray sweater that looked a little big for his smaller frame and plain black pants that still looked like their uniform. His hair was messy from the wind.

"Hey, hon!" Eva was cheerful today, her hair a freshly dyed shade of fire engine red.

"Gabriel."

"Alexandra."

They got on the road, and Eva and Gabe's voices were drowned out by the radio and the wind.

"I can't believe they managed to drag you to the mall." Sasha laughed, turning to Hale.

"My computer needs a new part." he said, looking annoyed.

"Too much porn?"

"What?" He looked so genuinely confused that she nearly asked him if he didn't know what porn was,but she also didn't want to offend him.

"I was joking. What broke?"

"Gabriel severed the cable for my charger with a chair."

"And you didn't send him to get it himself?"

"I don't trust him."

"Couldn't imagine why." She chuckled. The edge of his mouth lifted just slightly. Finally, something she and Hale agreed on. Her heart felt full, and she cursed herself. Why did she always feel so bubbly and stupid around him? He wasn't flirting with her!

"So, where did you guys get this car?"

"It's Gabriel's."

"Where did he get it?"

"I would rather not ask."

"Not asking isn't my thing."

"I hadn't noticed." He smirked.

Was that a joke? It was the closest to one she'd heard from him. He must be in an exceptionally good mood.

The mall parking lot was full, and they circled for a long time before Gabe veered in front of a van that was trying to back up.

"Gabe!" Sasha exclaimed. "That was dangerous!"

"You snooze, you lose." He chortled.

"Come on, babe." Eva rolled her eyes.

They walked into the mall side by side, Eva and Gabe holding hands, Sasha and Hale lagging behind them, a safe distance apart. Hale looked visibly uncomfortable joining the crowds, his eyes darting to the exits as they walked through the spinning glass doors.

"Anxious?" Sasha asked.

"No, why?"

"You look it."

"There's nothing to be afraid of here."

She didn't want to argue but he certainly didn't look happy anymore. The moment of ease had vanished. The mall was loud and bright, with kids running and yelling around the play area and the LEGO store, seniors lounging in the food court, and teens going store to store with large bags weighing them down. Music blared somewhere overhead.

"Let's go to the pet shop!" Sasha suggested.

"Yes!" Eva agreed.

"I'll meet you back here." Hale said, pointing at the computer hardware store.

"Come on, man!" Gabe tried to convince him, "We'll go there after. We're in no rush."

Hale ignored him and walked off. Sasha sighed. "Come on Sash." Eva beamed at her. "I love the pet store too."

"What about Hale?"

"He'll find us. He does this every time we come here. He just wants the ride and then disappears."

"I'll catch up with you," she said and power walked after Hale, dodging between happy couples and families. She caught up to him in front of the laptop displays, running his fingertips along the keys of the latest Apple product.

"I love those but they're so expensive." She said, glancing up at him.

"I thought you were going to the pet shop."

"I thought I'd keep you company first."

"That's not necessary." He slipped between two people to get to the power cables along the wall and reached up for what he needed. He promptly got in line at the cash register with the item in his hand and one hand in his pocket.

"Are you okay?" She asked, joining him.

"I don't like these places."

"The mall?"

"It's chaotic."

"I know what you mean. I get totally overstimulated."

He looked at her as though she'd identified something on his behalf. "It helps to focus on just a few things at a time." She said, recounting a mantra that worked for her, "Like, five things you can see directly in front of you, four things you can hear, three things you can feel, like your sweater or your socks or your arm against your side, two things you can smell," she inhaled plastic and air freshener, "and one thing you can taste."

He didn't answer.

"I know it sounds lame. It works for me," Sasha shrugged.

He kept looking around. "Have you finished the history paper?" He asked, his eyes coming up to meet hers.

"Yes."

"What was your topic?"

"How ineffectual our government is."

"Controversial."

"Only in the South."

It surprised her that he was so politically minded. "I wrote about healthcare reform, another thing we're not great at here in the South."

"Tell me more."

She did, he focused on her, as though she were an audiobook.

The lineup was fairly long so by the time they got out of the store, Eva and Gabe were waiting for them with small containers of ice cream.

"We didn't know what flavour you wanted." Gabe said.

"There were puppies!" exclaimed Eva, "and this one," she pointed at Gabe, "almost left with one."

"We cannot have a dog." said Hale flatly.

"Can't handle puppy love?" Eva joked.

"I'll wait by the car." He said quietly and stalked off.

"Hale!" Gabe called after him. He turned, and Gabe threw him the car keys. Sasha sighed. "I'll see you guys later, I guess."

"Stay Sash." Eva put her hand on her forearm. "Didn't you say you wanted to look at prom dresses?" Eva asked.

Gabe put a hand on Eva's shoulder. "It's okay, he'll like you being there," he said.

It was like music to Sasha's ears. She wanted to ask him to repeat it because it felt so far from the truth. Despite her best efforts, before the big fight between Jason and Hale and even after, it always felt like she was imposing. Hale never indicated wanting her around and never shared anything that wasn't strictly necessary. Even now, the only reason she knew he was stressed was his body language, alongside the obvious storming off.

Sasha stopped by the ice cream stand before heading out to the car, getting them both soft serve vanilla, the simplest peace offering she could think to buy. Hale was sitting in his spot in the back seat, looking up at the sky as she approached. He turned to look at her instantly. It struck her that he wasn't on his phone like any other teenager would be.

"I got us ice cream." She said, holding up the cup.

"No, thank you."

"Well, I'm not going to eat both, so have as much as you want." She handed it to him and stuck a spoonful in her mouth, savoring it. Hale looked down at it as though it were poison but finally took a tiny pinch off the top and tried it.

"Well?"

"Thank you." He looked surprised by it, reluctantly trying another spoonful.

"So, still mad at Gabe about the wire?"

"No."

"So, what happened back there?"

"He wanted to bring a dog to the apartment when he's never there, and we won't be here forever. It's stupidity."

"Do you like dogs?"

He shrugged. "That doesn't matter."

"So, you're mad that he wanted to commit to something he wasn't going to follow through on?"

"As usual."

"What else did he not follow through on?"

"He acts as though we'll be here forever."

She wanted to ask if he meant Eva, but it felt like overstepping, "If it makes you feel any better." she said, between bites of sweet, melting ice cream, "I think you're right."

"How so?"

"If you decide to bring something like an animal into your life and allow it to bond with you and love you, you don't deserve that love unless you commit to it. It's not love if it's just when it's convenient and fun."

Hale nodded, and they fell silent. Sasha wished he would elaborate, but he didn't seem so inclined. She pulled a new fantasy novel from her backpack and opened it to the front page, creasing it in the middle. "Want to read along? I'm just starting."

"I'm fine."

"Humour me." She leaned onto his side so they were shoulder to shoulder and could both see the page. He didn't argue. "Let me know when you're at the end, and I'll turn the page." He nodded again. This would've been awkward a few months ago, but after weeks of leaning

97

against him on school benches, he'd gotten less tense about it, and she could only fantasize at the idea that he might actually like it. The wind ruffled their hair, the world fell away as she read, and the time went by page by page.

Eva

Gabe and Eva were preparing to head out for dinner at her house. She still couldn't believe he'd accepted to meet her parents again after his last interaction with them, but if she was going to keep spending all of her time with him, she needed them to be on board. There were only so many times she could ask Sasha to pretend she was at her house.

"So, are you going to change?" She asked him, looking Gabe up and down. He was still wearing his school uniform.

"Change to what? It's clean enough."

"You don't want to wear something more comfortable?"

He laughed.

"Princess, do you want me to change to try and impress your parents?" he teased.

"Yes, please." She admitted.

"Your wish is my command." He went into his bedroom and pulled a pair of black pants, a black t-shirt and a black sweater out of a pile that she assumed was clean. He changed in the hallway and threw the uniform on top of the pile. He was the least self-conscious person she'd ever met.

"Who does laundry anyway?" she asked.

"Hale."

"He doesn't mind?"

"He hasn't complained yet. He doesn't fold it though, terrible service." Gabe joked, pulling on a sock.

"Does he fold his?"

"Yup."

He gestured to himself.

"Better?"

"Can I braid your hair?"

He grimaced. "I guess."

Gabe sat on the floor, and Eva perched on the edge of the couch. She ran her fingers through the length of his hair to detangle it quickly, but braiding it was another challenge altogether. It was a completely different texture from hers and kept slipping through her fingers.

"Alright, enough of that." He pulled it into a low ponytail and adjusted a hairband that he kept on his wrist. "How's that?"

"Great," Eva said, admiring him.

Most of the dinner was already on the table when they arrived, but her dad was out back barbecuing, the smell of charcoal wafting in through the patio door. Matteo was sitting at the table with a game console blasting music, eyeing the vegetables warily. Her brother was a level of picky eater usually found in toddlers.

"Hi, mom!" Eva said cheerily. "Hey Teo."

"Hi Mrs. Valliant." Gabe greeted her mom politely.

"Just Val."

"Thank you for inviting me." Gabe said, taking a seat beside her brother.

"Hope you're hungry."

"Very." He said.

Matteo took a moment to look Gabe up and down, pausing his game.

"So you're the guy with the car." He said.

"Matteo!" her mom corrected.

"Gabe with the Car, yeah."

"How come your hair's like that?"

"It's a cultural thing."

Matteo shrugged. "Dad's gonna tease you about it."

"He can try." Gabe laughed, helping himself to chips and dip.

"Don't fill up on that." Her mom said, "A lot of meat is coming this way."

"Don't worry about me. I've always got room."

Her dad, carrying a full plate of burgers, appeared at the patio door. She'd have appreciated him at least asking how Gabe liked his burger, but this was pretty typical of her father: his way or the highway.

"Gee, dad, think another family of five is dropping by?"

"Hi Gabriel, hey kiddo."

Eva went and fetched drinks, wishing there was wine or something. Once everyone's plates were full and Matteo's gaming device was confiscated by her dad, the table fell silent. Her parents had each taken a beer, which they notably hadn't offered to her or Gabe, and he thankfully poured himself a glass of soda and didn't say anything about it.

"So," her father began, "Last year of high school, kind of a funny time to start at a new school."

"Yes, sir." Gabe agreed.

"Why the change?"

"We moved."

Gabe had an uncanny ability to tell the truth while simultaneously dodging the question.

"Military?"

"Not quite."

"And what do your parents do?" Her mom cut in.

"Not much that they share with me," Gabe said, filling his mouth with a bite of burger, clearly buying himself time.

"And where will you be headed next year?" Her mom continued.

Gabe shrugged, swallowing. "Workin'. I know Eva's going to University, pretty great."

"Not you, though?"

"Nah, I've never been great at school."

"Is that right?" Eva's dad made eye contact with her.

"Actually, Gabe's in all the advanced classes. He's great at school."

"Oh, yeah, I'm good at high school, but I'd rather just work."

"You didn't go to university either, dad." Eva cut in, hoping to change the subject.

He chuckled, "maybe I would've if I'd been in all those advanced classes."

"So what sort of work do you want to do then?" he asked.

"Oh my God, dad."

"It's fine, babe." Gabe jumped in. "I've got a job lined up. You don't need to worry about me."

"Can we ask what kind of job?" Eva's mom asked.

"Intel." he chuckled.

"Intel?" Matteo asked, "like spies?"

"Close enough." Gabe shrugged.

Thankfully, Eva's mom shifted the conversation to something she'd read in the paper about some sort of uprising in Washington. Her dad turned his attention to monologuing about anarchists and delinquents, one of his favorite rants. Gabe listened and chewed, allowing Eva to poke him with her foot and mouth, "You okay?" to which he replied by poking her back with his own foot. Matteo caught on to this game and started poking them both underneath the table. Eva was mortified, but Gabe was visibly trying not to laugh in the middle of her father's speech.

By the time dessert came around, they insisted on helping with clearing dishes. Her mom's homemade nanaimo bars, which Matteo and Gabe ate four each, were the perfect way to shift the mood.

"These are amazing, Val." Gabe complimented genuinely.

"Thank you, Gabriel."

"They taste like childhood."

Eva laughed. Of course, Gabe would inadvertently refer to something he'd eaten as a kid but somehow forgot that her mom always packed them in her lunch - easy to grab for a hungry classmate.

"So, how long have you two been dating?" Her mom asked, making Eva choke on her glass of water.

"Uh, a few months, I guess." he shrugged.

"Hey, Gabe?"

"Yeah?"

"Do you wanna go play video games?" Matteo asked.

"That's a great idea." Eva added, coughing.

"If that's okay with you guys." Gabe said, checking in with her parents, which felt completely out of character for him.

"Go right ahead." Her mom smiled, so they scrambled to put their plates into the dishwasher and marched downstairs in a row, like kids heading to the playground. Eva exhaled as soon as she was on the stairs.

Matteo pulled another Nanaimo bar from his pocket and handed half to Gabe. "Congratulations, you survived."

Gabe grinned. "Thanks, buddy."

The next few hours allowed Matteo to show them every video game he owned and only let them each play for about twenty minutes or so. Gabe was endlessly patient. In fact, he seemed delighted by her brother. Eva sat beside him, recovering from that meal.

"So my dad didn't bully you about your hair." Matteo said, still staring at the screen.

"Nah, he was busy worrying about me being poor and dumb." Gabe laughed.

At about 9, her mom descended the stairs and said Matteo had to go to bed. Gabe got up and thanked them for their hospitality. Matteo hugged his new best friend, and Gabe said his goodbyes.

"Thanks for having me. Hope I wasn't too much trouble." Gabe said, grinning at her parents.

"Don't be a stranger." Her dad said.

"It was a pleasure." Her mom was more generous.

Eva walked him to the door and slipped outside onto the doorstep.

"Oh my god, I'm so sorry about them."

"They were great, Babe." His face said something different, though.

"See you tomorrow?" He leaned forward and kissed her lightly on the lips.

"Do you have swimming?"

She sighed. "Yeah."

"I'll be here at 7:30, then."

"Thanks for this."

He kissed her again and got into his car, revving the engine and waving as he backed out of their driveway.

Sasha

The countdown to graduation was on. Instead of focusing on the next steps of her life, letting the bubble of high school burst and emerging on the other side, she decided to throw her best friend a killer surprise birthday party. She, Shauna, Daphne, Mel, the swim team, and the dance team were all planning a big blowout at Eva's house, which she was still shocked Mr. and Mrs. Valliant had agreed to, given their usual overprotective tendencies. Eva was also with her most of the time, which made planning surprises have to be navigated carefully.

It was pouring rain outside, and the girls were huddled on the stairwell finishing up assignments, or at least they were supposed to be, but Eva kept checking her phone, looking morose.

"What's the matter?" Sasha asked.

"Nothing,"

"Okay, well, can you get over your nothing then? We have class in twenty minutes, and I want to get coffee first. Did you finish page 12?"

"What? No, and I don't think there's much chance of that." Her friend held up the empty page.

"Eva, what's going on? Seriously. Are you and Gabe fighting again?"

"No, we're not fighting."

"I know this is about Gabe."

"How do you know?"

Sasha sighed and shut her book. "Because you've been available to hang out, but you're in a terrible mood. What did he do this time?" Of course, she couldn't say, "getting in the way of my birthday planning time."

"He didn't do anything! He's just been weird and distant."

"You mean he's being a jerk."

"Sasha..."

"I know you think he's Prince Charming but Eva, I don't buy his whole "devil may care" thing."

"We went from hanging out daily to radio silence out of nowhere. Maybe it was my parents?"

"Well, if that's the case, he's even worse than I thought."

"You're not helping at all."

"Okay, I'm sorry. I don't think he'd ditch you for no reason, but don't you think he's suspicious?"

"Oh yeah, because your crush is so transparent," she shot back.

Sasha felt the blood rush to her cheeks.

"Me having a crush isn't the same as you having a boyfriend who you're saying isn't holding up his end of the boyfriend bargain."

"I have to go." Eva said, slamming her book shut and walking upstairs.

"Eva! I'm sorry, I didn't mean that."

Her phone went off in her hand. It was a text from Daphne.

"So, is she available that day?" It read. Being stuck in between was so frustrating. She'd been blind to it when she was with Jason, but now that she was on the outside again, the questions and whispers about Eva's relationship were a lot. She didn't understand why everyone else was so invested, except that Gabe had ghosted all of his former friends after the fight at the gazebo, and they were clearly resentful. Eva ignored her apology and kept walking upstairs.

"Y to the date, but what about G? They're fighting."

"Too late, Shauna invited him, and he agreed to play the diversion." Daphne replied.

Sasha sighed. If she didn't apologize to Eva and tell her it wasn't a problem, she would be risking the whole party. The truth was that she did like Gabe a lot of the time, especially now that he wasn't with the popular kids. He was sweet, clever and funny, and he could dish it out as much as he could take it, but she still couldn't shake the feeling that he was always hiding something, and that just didn't sit well with her.

It wasn't that she didn't want Eva to be happy, but not having her under Gabe's spell meant that she could actually see past the Wizard of Oz veil. If she and Eva could just work at this together, they could figure out what was up with Hale and Gabe. She'd found nothing about either of them online, not a social media account nor any reference to past awards or school participation. It was as though they'd come out of thin air. The weirdest part was their presence here - this wasn't exactly a place people moved to for no reason. Their school was fancy but not famous. There had to be a reason.

She sighed and started climbing the stairs, she needed to apologize or risk messing up the party.

She followed behind until she heard Eva's voice speaking to someone at the top of the stairs. She was speaking to Hale, who she could imagine sitting in his favourite spot on the top floor, where almost no one ever went at lunchtime. She knew eavesdropping was wrong, but she wanted to know how this would play out.

She heard Eva greet him, and the silence that followed before the reply.

"Hi?" Hale had that same tone the first time she'd approached him in the cafeteria, confused and just slightly annoyed.

"I need to ask you something." Eva continued. "Do you know what's been going on with Gabe?"

"What do you mean?"

"He's been acting strange or at least, to me, It seems that way. Is there someone else in his life?"

"No, there isn't."

"Really? Then, what's wrong? Is he in trouble?"

"You don't need to worry about him." The boy said in his quiet, low-toned voice.

"I can't *not* worry. Why is he avoiding me?"

"For your own sake."

"Can't you just tell me?"

He sighed, exasperated. "I just did. Don't worry about Gabe."

"Okay, then what about Gabe and me? Should I worry about us as a couple?"

"You don't need to worry about that either."

"What does that mean?"

"Speak to him yourself and find out."

They both sighed this time, a full discussion within their respective exhales.

He'd used those same lines he always used when she tried to pry: For your own sake, for your own safety. He always said that. Why? What was it about those two that he thought should be avoided? Were they drug dealers? Gambling addicts? What else could a teenage boy be? Hearing Hale comforting Eva made her smile to herself. At first, he just seemed rude, but once you got used to him, you could catch the inflections in his voice, the silences that lasted a little longer than others. He always sounded genuine, even when he was being evasive. Picking at the hem of her skirt, she imagined the way Hale must be sitting, his back so straight, his computer open on his lap, his hair falling into his eyes. It had gotten longer since he'd started at school. It always made her want to push it back when they sat together. The bell rang, making Sasha jump. She'd really gotten lost in thought. It was time to hightail it to class with her unfinished assignment.

She texted "Sorry, I didn't mean it." to Eva as she dashed to class and hoped that would suffice.

Chapter 10
Mistakes for Memories

Eva

She was sitting at the kitchen table, her books splayed in front of her as her mom whipped rich, fluffy, pink icing in the mixer. "I can't believe you're turning eighteen." She yelled over the noise of the machine. "Me neither." Her mom handed her a spoonful of icing, which she licked. "Mmm. This is amazing, mama." "Do you remember your first birthday party when we moved here?" "Yeah, I didn't know anybody." She was turning nine, and they'd just moved from Santa Fe. Her brother was just a toddler then. She had wanted to celebrate with her friends in Santa Fe, but her parents had spoken in hushed tones about what had happened after they left. The fire at the old church, the school is completely destroyed.

"And now you're going to be flying off to college!" Her mom chirped. Eva nodded, thinking about the boy she'd unknowingly left behind when she'd moved here, wondering what Gabe's 9th birthday must have been like. As though reading her thoughts, her phone buzzed. Gabe's number appeared. "Oh, sorry, Mom, I have to take this." She turned the phone off and bolted upstairs. "Hold on." She said as Gabe's cheery "Hey babe!" greeted her, as though nothing had happened between them. He was so confusing! After weeks of acting distant and avoiding her altogether, now he calls out of the blue. "Hey, you! Long time no see." "Yeah, sorry about that. I've had a lot goin' on. You free Saturday night?" "Um...yeah I think so. My parents might want me home for dinner though, it's my birthday weekend." "Oh, yeah, no worries. It won't take too long. Want to drop by at about 6?" "That can work." Why did he sound so nervous? "Everything okay?" He hadn't even responded to her telling him it was her birthday. What was going on? "Yeah, can't wait." "Yeah, me too. How have you been?" "Alright, just busy. See you Saturday, babe." With that, he hung up.

When she returned downstairs, her mom placed the bowl of icing in front of her, ready to be licked clean. "You look like you need this." She said. Her mom was the best.

When he opened the door to the apartment, Eva was nervous. She wore her skinny blue jeans, a black tank top and a green hoodie. She'd taken the time to put on makeup and earrings, too, with a matching necklace with a pale green jewel.

His eyes swept over her.

"You look amazing." He said, stepping aside as she set her bag down and sat on the couch.

"Thanks, you're not too bad yourself. I was surprised when you called."

"Surprised? Why?" It wasn't as though she hadn't been here for almost the entire winter break.

"No reason." She said, tucking her hair behind her ear. "So, what did you want to do?"

"I dunno, just hang out."

"Did you want to get pizza or something? I'm starved."

"Nah, I'm not hungry yet." Gabe, not hungry? Another reason to feel suspicious.

"Okay." She couldn't help feeling uncomfortable, unsure what to do. This was her chance, maybe her last chance, to try and win him back, if that's what was happening. "Gabe, we need to talk."

"I actually had something to tell you too."

Her eyes filled with tears suddenly.

"Whoa, babe, what's the matter?" He was at her side instantly, his hands on her shoulders.

"I just...you can't do this."

"Do what?" He sat on the couch and took her hand.

"You can't just break up with me after everything. I thought you were dead after the church burned down, and then I found you here of all places, and now you're just going to leave again."

"Break up with you?" He seemed genuinely surprised. "Eva, why would you think that?"

"You've been avoiding me for weeks!"

His face was inches from hers. "I'm not breaking up with you." He came closer and kissed her instead. She kissed back hard. She didn't want to talk or keep running all the scenarios over in her head of what might be wrong and what the future might hold for them. Right now, she just wanted comfort, to feel safe and wanted and loved. She pushed him back when things were getting intense, which he seemed to have expected. What she did next surprised even her. She got up, her hoody was already on the floor, and her hair was a wild mane around her head. Taking his hand, she pulled him off the couch and into his bedroom, shutting the door. They would be nearly an hour late to her surprise birthday party, but it would be an 18th birthday to remember.

Sasha

It was hot. The grassy field was dotted with groups of students, the buzz of their conversations mingling with those of her friends. She leaned back to stretch and noticed him right away. Hale wasn't like anyone else at school. He walked with purpose, his shoulders back, spine straight. She watched him circle around the whole field, unable to find a shady place to sit that wasn't too close to someone. He was now standing in the parking lot, probably the way he'd stood when the fight had broken out. It was strange how something so violent could happen, and yet no trace of it remained, only the blips of memory that kept pushing against the corners of her mind. The parking lot was full of expensive cars, including Gabe's.

He walked past the car, past a group of kids smoking and chatting, and looked into the gray gazebo. She immediately caught his eye from her spot sitting cross-legged on the floor. She'd cut her hair short over the weekend. It now barely reached her chin. She hoped he'd notice; the other guys at school certainly had.
"Picking up your boo?" Mila teased her.
She shoved her playfully. "Hush! I think he'd actually implode if he heard you."
"Are you going to invite him again?" Daphne asked.
"If you guys don't mind."
"Since when do you care if we mind?" Mila chuckled.
Sasha waved. "Hale! Come sit with us!"

He shook his head and gave a small wave but didn't come over, walking away from the gazebo entrance, back toward the school. Sasha huffed. "I'll see you guys later." She wasn't about to let him return to that stuffy cafeteria.

"Hey! Wait up!" she was jogging after him; her bag's strap was so long that it hit her knees. "Don't make me run; too hot." She ran a hand over her forehead, pushing her hair to the side.
"I was looking for somewhere quiet." He stated.
"No luck for you, everyone's out and about. I know a place if you want."
She beamed.
"It's fine."

"Come on, for god's sake." She turned around and led him across the parking lot and up the hill separating the school grounds from a modern-looking row of houses behind it.

"It's still school property, but no one ever comes up here."

"Why?"

"Because it's like being on a platform. You can't smoke or cheat where everyone can see you."

At the top of the hill, they could see the path down to a gated set of houses with a long stretch of well-kept lawn and squares of vibrant yellow, purple and red flowers. She stopped and turned, pointing to the view of the school grounds below. Because the entire campus was on a slope, they could see all the way to the water to the west and the military base to the north.

"Everything the light touches is our kingdom, Simba!" Sasha exclaimed.

He looked at her quizzically.

"Lion King?"

He shrugged to indicate he had no idea what she was talking about.

"Forget it, you can either sit and watch everyone or just turn that way, trespass on private property a little and pretend you're by yourself." She took her own advice and walked through the flower patch to sit in a temptingly shady spot below one of the large trees. She let her bag fall beside her and tapped the grass beside her. "I used to come here during lunch breaks when we first moved to Atlanta before I met anyone to sit with. The only people I've ever seen here are gardeners."

He sat down and pulled out his laptop, unsure if she would leave now.

"Hang on, before you start typing. I wanted to ask you something."

"Okay." He said, waiting.

She tugged at her fingers and looked at the houses behind the gate. He followed her gaze. It was quiet here, barely a gust of wind.

"So, are you going to prom?" She asked.

He had that look in his eyes again, the same one he had when they were at the mall, overwhelmed and overstimulated; she knew that feeling well.

"Hale?"

"Sorry." He'd clearly missed what she'd said.

"What's wrong?"

"Nothing. What did you say?"

She was unconvinced but decided to carry on, "Prom?"

"What?" He struggled to focus on her, his breath catching before reaching his lungs.

"Never mind. Here." She took a water bottle from her bag and handed it to him. "It's not open. I just bought it." He snapped the cap with a twist and took a long drink. She wondered what was eating at him.

"Sorry, it's not cold. You should try that trick I taught you at the mall."
She could practically see the gears turning, his mind going through a list
of senses. The color returned to his cheeks.
"Thank you." He finally said, still holding the bottle, unsure whether to
return it to her.
She reached up and put her hand on his forehead. He pulled away.
"What are you doing?"
"Just checking if you have a fever. It might just be the heat."
"I'm fine."
"Okay." He didn't seem fine.
He took another long deep breath, about to lift the lid of his laptop, then
stopped. "What did you want to ask?"
"You're not coming to the prom, are you?"
"No."
"Are you sure? You only graduate high school once. No pressure, you
don't have to go with me. I just thought we could all go as a group, you
know, as friends."
"No, thank you."
"You're not going to show up with someone else, are you?" She joked,
hoping it might calm him.
"No, I'm not going."
The fact that she was teasing had gone completely over his head. It
wasn't uncommon for their conversations to go this way. Hale was smart
and sensitive, but he often missed social cues.They'd spent enough time
together that she considered him a friend, or at least a good
acquaintance. She'd seen him getting more and more agitated as the end
of the school year drew near. It was subtle, but he'd get that look of
anxiety more often than usual. She wondered if there was any possibility
of staying in each other's lives after graduation. She'd miss him next year,
she'd never met anyone like him and she wasn't sure she ever would
again. She wanted him to know that she'd gotten attached to him, and it
sounded like she was running out of opportunities to tell him.

"What are you doing after?" She asked.
"After what?"
"After graduation. Next year, I mean."
"Leaving."
She laughed. "Me too. I can't wait to spread my wings. It was great having
someone new to talk to this year. I hope I made your time here a little
less miserable too. I know it was a rough go."
"It wasn't all bad." He admitted.
She smiled.

"Yeah? What were the good parts?" She knew she was fishing for compliments, but she didn't care. The school year was almost over; he wasn't coming to prom. She suspected he liked her, or she hoped he did. Wouldn't it be a waste not to try something?
"I haven't had many friends." He said earnestly.
"You don't exactly put yourself out there."

He held the water bottle back out to her and she pushed it back, their hands touching. Her face was very close to his. Her hair had fallen into her eyes, and she blew upwards to get it out of the way. She was always chewing gum, which she was happy about now. He still hadn't leaned away. Was he inviting this? She could wait but she might be waiting forever. She closed her eyes. Her lips were on his. It was strange, soft, sudden and warm. He closed his eyes too, just for a moment. The world was very quiet. She could hear her own heartbeat.

His eyes flew open, and he leaned back. She opened her eyes too, closing her mouth. She was about to say something; he looked like he might say something too,but he didn't. Instead, he was up on his feet; walking away, back towards the school, still holding the water bottle she'd handed him.

Her legs had turned to jelly. One minute, they were kissing tentatively, and the world was all sunlight behind her eyelids and warmth that bubbled up from her chest; the next, he was gone.
Before she knew it, he'd crested the small hill and vanished from sight. She grabbed her bag and scrambled up, her heart sinking and her eyes blurring with tears. Squinting against the sun, holding her arm up to shield her vision, she got to the top of the little hill and watched him walk back into the school.

How could she have been so stupid? She turned back towards the row of houses, trying to compose herself as something metallic and shiny caught her eye. His laptop. He'd left his bag and everything in it where they'd been sitting. Exasperated, she returned to the shady spot and gathered his things back into his bag, taking deep breaths. She wiped her eyes angrily once everything was packed up and sat back down, holding both bags in her lap. Tears hit the gray of his bag, darkening the fabric.

She shook her head. No, this wasn't okay. He didn't get to leave her crying here. She opened her phone to look at herself in the camera view. Her face was red and blotchy; her fringe was sticking to her forehead, and she had a zit on her left cheek, lovely. That water bottle would've been pretty handy right now. Stupid Hale. She did her best with her shirt, wiping tears and sweat off her face. How was she going to walk back into school? She started looking through Hale's bag, looking for a tissue: Laptop, school books, notebooks, pencils, and a town map with notes on it.

"Weird thing to carry around," she muttered. Did he plan his jogging routes on a paper map? She opened it. There were marks all around the military base where Eva's dad worked. The curiosity almost overturned the feeling of abandonment and mortification. Still no tissues. She refolded the map, her sweaty palms leaving marks on the paper. There was also a moleskin notebook with an elastic around it. She glanced up to the top of the hill before flipping through it. It wasn't a journal nor a schoolbook. She found it full of mathematical equations that meant nothing to her. Finally, at the very bottom of the bag, tissues. She blew her nose, shoved the tissues in her pocket, picked up both bags and headed back to school, struggling under the combined weight. The bell rang just in time for her to stagger into the chemistry lab. Hale looked up at her from his seat, his expression unreadable. She walked in and dropped his bag in front of him. The computer made a loud noise against the table.

"You're welcome." She said, refusing to look at him. Sitting next to him through class was going to be insufferable. Her eyes roved the classroom looking for a seat as the teacher walked in. Mila waved at her but all the seats around her were already taken. The only available spot was the one occupied by Gwen's purse. There was no way she could sit next to Gwen, she'd probably spit on her.
"Alexandra? Sit down please."
The teacher's voice startled her, and she reluctantly slid into her usual seat. Feeling the heat in her cheeks, she opened up her chemistry book to the correct page and stared at it. They were revising for finals but she couldn't concentrate at all.

Was he so disgusted by the idea of kissing her? How could he not have said anything? He'd let her kiss him, closed his eyes, how had she misread the signs so badly? She peeked from the corner of her eye, and caught him looking at her. He flinched. Her heart clenched as she looked away again. When class finally ended, she turned to face him, "It's fine. I don't want to talk about it, okay?"
"You always want to talk."
"Not this time." She picked up her things and walked out.

Eva

The sound of the traffic off the interstate hummed, drowning out Eva's thoughts as she anxiously tapped her fingers against the steering wheel of her mother's tiny blue Mazda. She had no idea how long she had been here in the semi-empty parking lot of a rundown little church, but it felt like hours. She carefully detached her shaking hands from the steering wheel, took a deep breath of humid air, and opened the car door. Every decision that had led her to this moment spun through her head like a nauseating merry-go-round.

She wasn't sure if it was morning sickness again, though the name didn't quite fit her constant desire to throw up or what she was about to do. She had no choice, this would ruin her life. She was going to go to college, get a degree, get a job in film and forget this had ever happened. No one needed to know, and no one else's life needed to be impacted - not her parents, her brother, and definitely not Gabe. She wasn't sure why she'd parked here rather than in the lot behind the Family Planning Center, but she couldn't bring herself to turn left as the GPS had said, and instead, she was here. It wasn't a far walk. The thoughts of someone spotting the car added to the shaking in her knees.

"It's just down the road." She told herself. "One step at a time." Soon, this would all be over, and she could return to her life. It was one mistake, one night, it didn't have to be the deciding factor for the rest of forever. Her phone pinged. Shauna asked whether she'd chosen the dress yet, and Sasha asked if she was free. Not now, guys; I'm making life-altering decisions. Once she'd forced herself out of the car, the dust off the freeway made her cough, but she put one foot in front of the other and walked. Every step was one step closer to freedom.

The waiting room of the clinic smelled of cleaning products. The woman behind the counter asked her to fill out a form, which she did in the tiniest writing she possibly could. She checked off symptoms, allergies, blood type. In the spot where it said "reason for visit," she wrote *abortion* because she couldn't think of what else to write. She handed the papers over to the woman and sat patiently in the world's most uncomfortable plastic chair. The minutes ticked by, and none of the women in the clinic made a sound apart from the occasional sneeze or clearing of throat. The room was filled with tension. Occasionally the bubble of nervous energy would be punctuated by chatter from behind the reception desk. Eva scrolled through her phone in an attempt to distract herself.

Forty-five minutes had passed when a small, plump nurse called her name. Eva followed her into a small, sterile room and barely heard her instructions over her racing heart. As directed, she stripped off her clothes and put on the pale blue hospital gown. A tall, middle-aged man with glasses walked in. "Good afternoon Miss." He said, looking through what looked like the papers she'd filled out. On the final page, he'd crossed out the word abortion and written "pregnancy." She wanted to ball up the paper and throw it at him.

"So, you're in quite the predicament." He sounded far cheerier than she thought was appropriate.

"Um. yes, and I'd like to not be in it anymore."

"Well, we'll see about that."

He rolled out a piece of long paper over a black leather table and had her sit on it. She closed her eyes as he examined her. Having a stranger's fingers on her stomach and elsewhere made her feel small and alone. Soon, it would be over . Soon, he'd tell her what she needed to do next.

"When was your last period?"

"Maybe 5 or 6 weeks ago." She said with complete certainty.

"Not very far."

"That's good, right?"

"Your baby is about 2 millimeters, its heart might have already started to beat, though it won't pick up on an ultrasound for another couple of weeks."

Why was he telling her this? What did that matter?

"The baby?"

"Yes, it's about the size of a strawberry seed."

"A strawberry seed?" She repeated, imagining a tiny little girl with strawberry curls. How big was a strawberry seed anyway? That seemed very small. It made her think of Thumbelina.

He asked her to list her symptoms, which she did as neutrally as possible and seemed futile given that she'd just written them on the paper he was holding. She just wanted to get this over with, not discuss her body and how it was behaving and not strawberry-seed-sized heartbeats.

"Okay then, Evangeline, here are some prenatal vitamins to get you started. Nausea should subside in a few weeks. Still, in the meantime, you really need to take care of yourself, eat properly, no alcohol, no caffeine, no drugs of any sort and that includes cigarettes and no raw fish or meats, in case you're a fan of tartar or sushi. We can pencil you in for an ultrasound in about two weeks if that's okay with you. How's Tuesday, June 12th at 9:30?" He'd walked over to the small desk and computer on the other side of the room and pulled up a calendar on the screen. She would be in English class at that time.

"What? No. I don't want to come back!" She cried. "I just want to get this taken care of right now. Isn't the earlier, the better?"

"I'm sorry?"

"I want an abortion!" She couldn't believe she had to spell it out.

"You live in Georgia, Miss."

"Yeah, so?"

"You cannot legally obtain an abortion here, and even if you could, this isn't a drive-through. You would have had to book an appointment for surgery. You would need someone else with you to drive you back. This isn't a decision that should be taken lightly."

"I'm not taking it lightly! I'm making myself very clear about what I need from you."

"You cannot get a legal abortion anywhere in Georgia."

She wanted to vomit directly onto this man, and if she kept waiting in this room, wearing this ridiculous gown, she just might.

"So, what do I do?"

"Consider giving the baby up for adoption or foster care."

"I don't want to do that either!" Why was he acting so calm about this? Was this the punishment for having slept with Gabe? She knew it was stupid, but it hadn't felt stupid then. It had felt normal, amazing even - but none of that mattered if this was the outcome.

"Perhaps you should have thought of this before you decided to have intercourse." The doctor, or whatever he was, said calmly.

Intercourse. That's what they called it here? A clinical word for a clinical problem has nothing to do with passion and love.

"So, shall I pencil you in for the 12th? Congratulations, by the way."

"Yeah, sure, thanks."

She couldn't think of what else to say. He left soon afterwards. She put her clothes back on, her hands shaking and numb, she stepped back out into the street. The walk back to her car was a blur. She wasn't a smoker but she thought a cigarette might be appropriate right now, except for the fact that it was exactly what she'd just been told not to do. She leaned against the car and looked up to the sky. It was gray. She wanted to pray, but she didn't feel like anyone was listening. The small church stood looking abandoned and derelict, just like she felt. She walked to the mahogany-painted door and slipped inside, surprised to find it warm, with the scent of melting wax and the ghosts of candles-past filling the space. The pews stood empty row by row like a classroom.

Her steps echoed as she walked down the aisle and eased herself into the front, peering up at the statue of Jesus on the altar. Candles flickered around her. She didn't have any money to light one, though she certainly needed a miracle. She closed her eyes with her hands laced together, though no prayer came. Sister Martha would have said that she wasn't alone and that God was with her. She wasn't sure she believed it, but she could sure use the company.

Chapter 11
Travel Plans

Sasha

She and Eva came over to Gabe and Hale's apartment in the late afternoon, both looking worn out. Finals were getting to them. Eva had her mom's car with her, on which she'd started practicing her driving. The joke was on her parents; of course, Eva had been practicing on the Mustang for months. She was pretty good, and much more cautious than Gabe. Currently, Eva was lying with her head on Gabe's lap while they quizzed each other for finals. Gabe said he knew it all already and refused to participate.

Sasha let the book drop. "Am I ever really going to need to know every new government for the last decade? It just sounds like they get worse with every new leader."

Eva chuckled. "The current one's pretty dumb. Hard to compete with that."

"People are sheep," said Gabe. "Rules for everything instead of following a moral compass. It's time for a revolution."

"Those never go very well." Sasha said, shaking her open book at him for emphasis. "Violence, death, destruction. I'll nope out of that, thanks."

Gabe bleated at her. Eva laughed. "That's actually not bad."

"It's because people think like you that we're still where we are. You accept the status quo because it benefits you."

Sasha rolled her eyes. "Oh yeah, because you're changing the world."

Eva sat up suddenly, putting a hand on her chest, looking pale. "You okay?" Gabe asked.

"Yeah, I just haven't been feeling too well lately; it's just stress."

Gabe turned his attention back to Sasha. "I'll make a difference yet."

"Okay, you two! Change of subject." Eva cut them off. "I got my acceptance to USC, so I will be changing the world with a camera in hand. Who's coming with me?"

Sasha laughed. "To California? I got into Mcgill. I'll be in Canada by this time next year, speaking French and eating baguettes and croissants until I explode."

They both turned to Gabe, "I ordered pizza."

"No, wait just a second." Eva stopped them before Sasha could start in on Gabe about his future for the 90th time in the past few weeks. "I have a crazy plan."

"All ears, babe." Gabe said.

116

"I say we go on a road trip before we're all split next year."

"A road trip?" Eva was bouncing a little, her hair falling out of its ponytail. The colour slowly returned to her face, but she still looked a bit green.

"Yeah, we can drive through New Mexico and end up in Cali. We can go to the beach and get all tanned and beautiful before college."

"And whose car will we be taking, pray tell?" Sasha was dubious.

"Well..." Eva turned to Gabe. "I was hoping..."

"You wanna go to California with me?"

"If you're up to it!"

Gabe looked elated. She'd never seen his grin get so broad. "I, yeah-" he stuttered- "that would be the best idea I've ever heard, Babe."

"Perfect!" Eva beamed back at him.

"What about your parents?" Sasha knew how Eva's family was, especially her dad. She hadn't even been allowed to sleep over at her house for the first year of their friendship, and Eva always pretended to be at her place when she stayed at Gabe's. Were they really going to let her drive cross-country with her boyfriend? She supposed they wouldn't have much say in what Eva did when she was away for college, but were they ready to cut the umbilical cord?

"I'll figure it out! They'll let me if it's a group of friends. My parents also took a big road trip after high school, before my dad joined the military."

Sasha smiled, "well if you can convince them."

"And you come."

"What?"

"It'll be amazing!"

"Um, I'm going to have to run this by my folks..." Sasha muttered. She was sure how she felt about it. "And what do we mean by a group of friends?"

"You, me, Gabe and Hale, four people's a group, right?" Eva coaxed.

"Shouldn't you ask somebody?" She turned to Gabe. "An adult of some sort?" She'd always found Gabe and Hale's situation suspicious, but her goodwill towards it went back and forth. It had been easier to ignore when she wasn't angry at Hale, but the fact that Gabe could just take off after graduation without a word with his supposed friend whose parents also didn't need to be asked was beyond weird.

"I'm ready to go. The day after grad then, no later, okay?"

"Thank you, babe! This is going to be amazing!" Eva and Gabe were already celebrating as though it was all set. Gabe put an arm around her friend and pulled her towards him. Eva allowed herself to be pulled onto his lap, but her gaze went to Sasha.

Sasha got up and said she was going to the washroom, heading down the hall, giving them a perfect opportunity to get on with their shenanigans. Gabe and Eva were cute, even though they were a little much. It made her envious, but she did her best not to put that on them. It was no one's fault but her own. She supposed she hadn't lost Hale; he was never hers in the first place. Did she want to visit California with the happy couple,and him? Did she want to let Gabe take Eva across the country alone or stand in the way of their trip? She still didn't really trust him. She stood in front of Hale's bedroom door, right in front of the bathroom door.

He wasn't home, off on one of his mysterious errands. There was so much she still didn't understand. She was certain that whatever secret Hale kept, Gabe was in on it too. She turned the faucet on in the bathroom and shut the door, tip-toeing back into the hall. She listened for footsteps, but she heard Eva giggling in the living room. Heart racing, she turned the doorknob to Hale's room, stepping silently inside and closing the door behind her. She didn't have much time and wasn't sure what she was looking for either.

His laptop was on his desk. She'd only been in this room once before when she'd brought Hale home after the fight with Jason. She could remember hobbling over to the bed, her knees and lower back struggling to hold Hale's weight. She had helped him get on the bed, even though he insisted he didn't need help, and she'd fetched him a glass of water and a Tylenol. She sat next to him until he closed his eyes and then left and sat in the living room, calling Eva repeatedly. The room looked about the same, sparse and white. The bed made crisply and tightly. It was so unlike a teenage boy's room. There were no posters of girls or cars or pictures of family anywhere. There were no curtains either, making it look even barer. She started with the closet, which had neatly hung clothing and an IKEA rack of socks and shoes. It took seconds to sweep through because it was so organized.

She gathered her courage and marched to the small desk, the only furniture besides the bed and nightstand. She opened up a drawer full of papers in file folders. The first folder had what looked like profiles, lists of people's names, height, blood type and other medical information. None of the names were familiar. There were x-rays, test results for various medications she'd never heard of and all sorts of things that made no rational sense for a high schooler to have on their nightstand, but she'd already known Hale was weird. The weirdest part was the fact that some of them had big red, menacing exes on them. As she shut the drawer, she heard a faint metal clang. There was nothing metal in the drawer. She scooped out the papers, set them on the desk, and checked the back. Still nothing. She slid the drawer beneath it, only more of the same strange papers and blueprints to a huge building. What building is this? She wondered. Finally, it dawned on her. This was the base - the one at the center of town. Why did he have blueprints for their military base? She knelt down andpushed her hand back as far as she could into the top drawer. Her finger felt a small hole. Hinging her pointer finger into it, she pulled the wooden bottom of the drawer up and couldn't believe her eyes.

There, lying underneath the false bottom, was a handgun. If she were someone else, she might know what kind, but she'd never taken any interest in weaponry and, in her opinion, nor should anyone else. Why did Hale have a gun? Her hand reached for it to see if it was real. The metal object was heavy. She realized this was exactly how a person might get suspected of a crime if their fingerprints got on the weapon, but she had nothing to wipe it with and had already been here for a long time. What if Gabe or Eva came over to check on her? She put it back and shut the wooden lid on top, quickly packing the folders on top of it and trying to arrange them the way she'd found them. Was Hale some sort of school shooter? Was he contemplating suicide? She went back into the hallway, shutting the door behind her softly. She went into the bathroom, flushed for effect, and then turned off the faucet. Now the idea of California became even scarier,presumably, Hale wouldn't leave that gun behind at the apartment.

When she returned to the couch, Eva and Gabe were practically horizontal and scrambled up, disheveled.
"You okay?" Eva asked.
"Yeah, just hungry." Sasha said, sitting back down on the floor. Her mind was abuzz. The doorbell rang, and the pizza arrived, which distracted her friends from the look on her face. When Hale returned home hours later, grabbed a slice of pizza and went to his bedroom, all she could imagine was him holding that gun in his long fingers.

Eva

The dress still fit perfectly, a cerulean blue taffeta gown with a sweetheart neckline, which looked even better than it did at the store, an unexpected perk considering the circumstances. Her mom walked in with her hands over her mouth, tears in her eyes.

"Eva, you look so beautiful." She swept a golden chain around her neck, clipping it behind her and adjusted a curl. Eva turned to the side, looking down at her stomach. She'd expected it to show somehow, to ruin this night, but if she'd gained a single pound, she certainly didn't see it. Considering how many times she'd thrown up in the past few weeks, it seemed unlikely anyway.

"Thanks, Mom." She said, watching the dress flow down to her toes. She slipped her feet into the pumps her mom had brought in, adjusting the little golden chain on them, popped on some bright red lipstick and smiled at herself in the mirror. Before Gabe arrived, her dad snapped a few pictures, and she dragged her brother in because she knew her parents had been waiting for this day for a long time.

Despite her irritability and short temper, they'd been so understanding for the past few weeks. Even more insane, they'd agreed to her crazy plan to take a road trip to California with her boyfriend and best friend. She wished she could tell them what the trip was really about, but when they'd said yes, all she could do was cry, clinging to them and wishing with all her might that she'd never have to lie to them again. She'd said thank you so often that they'd grown tired of hearing it. The sound of Gabe's car pulling up in the driveway was a blast of heavy metal and brakes. Her parents stepped out onto the lawn with her as the automatic lights showed Gabe waiting for her in the car, wearing his school uniform.

"What is he wearing?" Her mom asked as they stepped out after her. Eva clutched her purse to her as Gabe walked up to meet them.
"Hey babe, you look amazing." He looked the same as he always did, his eyes bright, his smile dazzling, but her mom was right - wasn't he supposed to be in a suit?
"Sir, Ma'am." He smiled at her parents. "Sup Matt?" Matteo waved from the doorway.
"Son." Her dad said, shaking his head. "Come with me."
Gabe's eyes darted to Eva. "Don't worry; you'll be back in one piece."
"Where are you going?" Eva asked, but her father waved her off.
"That's quite the car, isn't it?" Her mom said, walking around the Mustang. "I can't believe anyone lets their 17-year-old drive something like this."
Eva laughed. "Sounds more like you wish Daddy would buy one like this for romantic drives."
"Don't get sassy, missy." her mom said. She had her pose on top of the car for a few more pictures, and Matteo took a turn too. Fifteen minutes

later, her dad emerged from the doorway, followed by a slightly sheepish-looking Gabe.

"Is that?"

"Your dad's best suit? Yeah. He, uh, insisted."

Eva couldn't help but laugh. Gabe looked like he'd returned in time, yet it fits him nicely. "Well?" Her dad demanded.

"Thank you, sir." Gabe said, looking like he was ready to hightail it out of there.

"Come on, Gabe; we'd better get going."

"Hold on!" Her mom had them pose all over again until the camera flash made Eva dizzy, or perhaps it was the lack of food. These days, she felt lightheaded anytime she didn't eat for more than an hour. Pregnancy sucked. "Okay, Mom, we'd better get going."

"Wait, wait." Her mom returned inside with her corsage and a matching flower to pin on Gabriel's vest pocket. They were red roses with baby's breath. Her mom loved roses.

"What did you get these?" She exclaimed.

"Just today. I had to keep them in the fridge."

She hugged her mom again, allowing her to pin the corsage around her wrist. The flower's smell was strong, another bonus due to her condition. Once Gabe's flower had been added, another round of pictures followed.

"Now you can go." Her mom finally said, lowering the camera.

"You sure?" She laughed. Honestly, her feet were already starting to hurt.

"You'll have her home by midnight?" Her dad said to Gabe, looking him straight in the eyes. Gabe nodded and smirked. "11:59."

It was only when they pulled away from the driveway, and Gabe was able to pull the tie away from his neck that Eva could breathe again, letting the cool night air soothe her. It wasn't about the baby; tonight was about her and Gabe and the end of high school, the beginning of the rest of her life.

"Sorry about my parents. They're excited." Eva said.

"Felt like it was their night! It's cool though, and this suit's pretty nice too."

She chuckled. "And the guy in it isn't bad either. I can't believe you wore your uniform."

"Eh, I figured it didn't matter much."

She laughed. "You never cease to amaze me, Gabe."

"It's just one night."

"You know, I thought so too for the longest time, but", she reached for his hand where he it's our night. It's the end of high school. We're not kids anymore. By next year, we'll be done with our first year of college."

He didn't feel like getting into this again, so he simply laughed. "Guess so. I'm more excited about your crazy California plan."

"Yeah, I can't believe my parents went for it. I've never been out of state without them."

"We'll call 'em at every truck stop along the way." She closed her eyes as a wave of nausea hit her. Wasn't this supposed to be morning sickness? Not all-day sickness?

"You alright?" He asked.

"I'm a bit nervous."

"If you reach into the back seat, there's some liquid courage." He watched Eva reach back and pull up a flask. She could smell the rum. It did not help. Eva shook her head. "I'm ok."

"Come on babe; it's the stuff you like."

She put the flask between her lips and pretended to drink. It smelled disgusting.

Everyone was dressed above and beyond their usual level of prestige, with girls in massive ball gowns and full faces of elaborate makeup and guys pulled up in limousines, the likes of which she'd only seen for politicians on television or her father's bigwig coworkers. Drivers stepped out of the front to open doors for the Hollywood versions of their classmates.

Jason, TJ, Eric, Pamela, Gwen, Jenn and Gen exited a stretch SUV, laughing and tipsy. The girls were almost unrecognizable with the amount of bling on them. The guys wore tuxedos that made the one her dad had given Gabe look thrifted. Gabe hopped over the car's hood, opened the door for her, stepped out and waved her arms broadly at Mila, Margo and Sasha, who had just gotten out of Mila's mom's Porsche, each in their own version of decked out. Daphne, Mel, and their friends had also exited a limo, parking a little further.

By the gazebo, a photographer and his assistants set up lights to take pictures of the teens as they arrived. Eva hugged her friends, and Gabe greeted kids from seemingly every grade.

"You know everybody!" Eva remarked. He took her hand, the one with the red rose on it and led her into the fray. They smiled for a few photos, with their friends and one another. They then stopped to snap a few pictures on people's phones.

They entered the gym, which had been transformed: LED lights hung from the ceiling in the dark room, bright pitch lights in different colours showing off a large dance floor. There were tables along the walls with black tablecloths, huge bouquets in the school colours, and candlesticks.

They'd hung a massive poster saying "Congratulations Graduating Class" up near the ceiling, where the ribbons of school teams had always been. The brightly coloured cloth was hung all over the place in patterns. Eva felt tears spring to her eyes.

"You okay, Princess?"

"Just a bit nostalgic."

"Sounds like we need punch."

He went to the lineup of guys waiting to fill tiny plastic cups from a massive pink bowl. There were also tiny sandwiches and cupcakes laid out with the school crest on them. She watched him from afar, seeing Pamela making a beeline for him with Jason on her arm.

She watched him turning to them and inched closer to listen.

"Hey guys. Lookin' fine."

Pamela smiled her big white dental-commercial smile. "Jason had something to say."

Jason nodded, looking uncomfortable. "Listen, man, I'm off to Yale soon and just wanted to say, no hard feelings."

"Same here, man."

"So, you and Eva, huh?" Jason asked, wiggling his eyebrows. "Got tamed?"

Pamela elbowed him in the stomach "Jace!"

"Yeah. Guess that makes two of us." Gabe laughed. He was so much smaller than Jason in height, and yet they had this easy camaraderie from the get-go. If it hadn't been for Gabe, Eva wasn't sure she'd ever even have spoken to Jason.

"Where are you headed next year?"

"No idea. Going to wait to figure it out."

"I'll, uh, miss you, man."

Gabe laughed, and the two boys patted each other on the back. It was definitely a goodbye. He came back to her holding her cup of punch and a cupcake. She accepted the sugar, both in liquid and cupcake form.

"So what does this mean for you and Jason?"

Gabe shrugged, "that it was fun while it lasted."

"Will you keep in touch?"

"Nah, but I appreciate 'em. It was cool to be part of that world for a while."

"You could still be."

"That wasn't really me and I think we all know that. No point holding on to something."

The music was blaring over the loudspeakers, so everyone had to yell over it to be heard. Teachers milled around the room, having pictures taken, and their outfits matched the occasion. After a few speeches and awards, proper food arrived. It was fancy, like everything else, with a bunch of different utensils and napkins, which Eva had to guide Gabe through. The chatter of a hundred teen voices filled the room.

"Wonder if the teachers know the punch is spiked."

Eva paled. "It is?"

"Ohhh yeah, that's not juice."

She set her cup down and gulped down a glass of water.

"You alright?" He asked her.

"Yeah, this is just a bit fancy for my taste." Drinking while pregnant, she was a disaster! "If Gabe knew...", she thought.

"Same, babe, same."

Slowly, the dance floor filled with groups and couples, and the music dipped down to accommodate the dancers. People got drunker and sang along. Gwen became prom queen. "So, will it be weird for the prom king and queen to be siblings?" Mila asked, holding up a tiny potato on her fork.

Margo shrugged. "Gabriel Wells!" the principal announced.

All eyes turned to Gabe as the sound technician spotlighted him.

"The heck?" Gabe said as he got up and took a deep bow, his hair falling past his shoulder. They started blasting some cheesy radio song that Eva surprised herself in knowing all the lyrics to despite her best efforts, "You're the king, babe!"

He was coaxed on stage and stood there to receive a plastic crown. Gwen gave him a dirty look.

"And now, per tradition, the king and queen will share their first dance."

Gabe shook his head and held out a hand. They danced in a circle, Gwen keeping as far from him as possible, a slow song playing on the speakers. It was over in minutes, allowing him to return to his table.

"Congrats, babe!" Eva said as he let himself fall into his chair.

"Glad that's over!" They'd served cake in his absence, and he was happy to shove sugar into his mouth. "So that's prom, huh?"

"That's prom!" Eva agreed. "But the best part of prom is what happens after this ends."

"And what's that?"

"The after-prom beach party."

"That was definitely not on the invite. Sounds way better than this stuffy place."

"You can't say that! You're the king!" Sasha teased him from across the table. Gabe laughed and placed the crown on top of Eva's head instead.

"Now that makes way more sense."

She rolled her eyes but didn't argue. They went back onto the dance floor for a while, but honestly, she was glad when they all filed back into the parking lot. Now, the real party could begin.

Sasha

They could hear the music from the parking lot, a beat she could feel down into her toes. She couldn't wait to throw her shoes off and dance in the sand. She and Mila had matching corsages, and she was never so happy to have gone to an event without a date. By next week, she'd be on the road with Eva, headed for adventure, but tonight it was about the end of a very long year and the last day of stupid high school drama. She'd had some of the punch at prom, but the open road and the huge, velvet sky above made her feel so happy she could burst. They'd dropped Margo off at home since her parents were super religious and overprotective and then followed the instructions sent to the entire senior class to this one spot of sandy beach. Mila wiped her forehead. "I'm about ready to jump into that water."

"We probably could."

They grabbed their towels and headed off to the beach. Most of the grade had already beaten them to it, and the water was filled with shirtless classmates and girls who had foregone the process of taking off their dresses and gone on with full ball gowns. They looked like mermaids, various colours sparkling all around them. The music pulsed through the sand, and a DJ booth set up a few ways from where they stood. The DJ booth naturally formed a dance floor, bodies swaying to pop songs with a low base. She could smell the skunky weight of marijuana in the air, mingling with the various perfumes and colognes on the teens.

They both kicked off their shoes, and their feet left marks in the sand as they walked down to the water, the slight movement of the waves dancing along with the song. When they were on the surf, Sasha uncuffed her corsage of daffodils and sent it floating away on the water. She imagined what it would be like to be here with a date, holding someone's hand, looking out into the night where a lighthouse beacon sent light across the sky in the distance. She closed her eyes and swayed to the music, twirling in the water. At this point, it really didn't matter if she made a fool of herself. Exams were over, she would be moving up to Canada in August, and she'd have a wild adventure on the West Coast to look forward to before that. Life was glorious.

"Hey." A familiar deep voice. She opened her eyes and whipped around, her heart pounding.

"Hey, Jason." He was holding a red plastic cup and wasn't wearing a shirt. His black tux pants were soaked through. "Guess you went swimming?"

He laughed in a way that made her feel like the most important girl in the world. "Yeah, it's not as cold once you're completely in there." His smile was soft. He didn't seem likely to drown her.

"I totally thought you'd win prom king." She said.

"Then I'd have to dance with my sister. Nah, this was fine. Gabe deserved it."

"Really?"

"Yeah, he's a good guy. He's got some issues, but he seemed like he really wanted the popularity."

"Gracious of you." She said though it came out a bit sarcastic. She wondered why he would approach her here, alone. Where was Pamela? Where were all his friends?

"I just wanted to say goodbye."

"Goodbye?"

"I'm off to my dad's alma mater - heard you're headed to McGill."

"You've been asking about me?" She grinned, flattered.

"A little. Also heard you're going to California with Gabe and Hale."

"Mostly Eva, actually; Gabe just happens to have a car."

"And Him?"

She didn't need to ask who he meant. "Seems to come part and parcel with Gabe."

"So why didn't you bring 'em to prom with you?"

"Who?"

"You know who, Alexandra."

"He uh.." she considered telling him a half-truth, that Hale had chosen not to go to prom, which was true, or that she hadn't been able to find a date or that she'd simply wanted to go alone, but Jason was right, this was goodbye, and there was no point in putting up appearances.

"He rejected me."

"What?"

"What's that grin for?" She splashed him a little, though she didn't want to get splashed back.

"I'm in disbelief, really."

"Oh, come on, Jason, you're thrilled."

"A part of me definitely doesn't hate this."

"Nice."

"Sasha, that guy is trouble. He might've done you a favour. He's also an idiot if he thinks he can do better."

She didn't know what to say. Her mouth hung open like a fish. The music suddenly seemed very loud. "Um, thanks, Jason."

"I gotta go check on Pam now, I don't want her to think anything's goin' on. I just wanted to say, I had fun with you; it was a good time, and I want to remember it."

"I had fun with you too." He submerged himself into the water and swam off with confident strides. She sighed deeply and made her way back up to dry land, letting only her feet touch the water.

In the distance, she spotted Gabe and Eva, only their heads visible as they swam out to the dock where some other strong swimmers had gathered. She hoped they'd keep the making out to a minimum when they got on the road next week. Would it feel like this - being alone even though she was with three people? Would she end up wandering around alone all the time while Gabe and Eva were lost in their love bubble, and Hale disappeared or hid from her because his unacknowledged social anxiety got the best of him?

Shaking the melancholy thoughts out of her head, she gathered her skirts and headed to the dance floor. After all, they didn't have dancing on the beach in Montreal.

Chapter 12
The Open Road

Eva

"You have to come." She pleaded.

Sasha sat with her knees up to her chin, sulking. "Ugh, I just can't imagine spending that much time with Hale after everything." They were sitting in Eva's bedroom, maps open on Eva's large desktop computer. They'd been here a million times before, but Eva felt every day leading up to the trip so intensely it hurt. No matter what happened after this trip, she would never feel the same again. She wouldn't be the same girl ever again. Abortions weren't the sort of thing you could just forget about.

"He didn't go to prom though, so it's not like he rejected you and went with someone else."

Sasha rubbed her eyes with her knuckles. "Okay, this is really mortifying, but here it is. I...kissed Hale."

"You and Hale kissed?" Eva often found it hard to bring her problems to the forefront with others. Sasha's moaning about whether or not Hale liked her felt tiny compared to her predicament. Still, there was no way she would be able to choke out that she was pregnant on the heels of this seemingly normal conversation.

"No, I kissed him. He...walked off."

She tried to imagine how this could happen and came up short. "Wait, wait, wait, what do you mean *walked off?*"

"I mean one foot in front of the other in a half jog. He opened his eyes, got up and walked away from me."

"You're kidding."

"I wish." Sasha spread her arms as if to say, *This is embarrassing enough with or without an explanation.*

"And that's why you're going to throw away the road trip of a lifetime? Because you're embarrassed that Hale's an awkward turtle?"

"It doesn't really make me want to spend a month with the guy."

"But I'll be there too! And Gabe. You and I will share a room; we'll have legal drinks in New Mexico, we'll drive through the Sequoia trees in San Francisco."

"Okay, it's not just that." It sounded like they both had secrets.

"There's more? What else did you two do?"

She took a deep breath. Sasha adjusted her sitting position to listen.

"I'll start at the beginning. When I was in the fourth grade, my family moved to New Mexico." Eva began. "My dad had just gotten a big promotion, and, as usual, we followed.So, I started at this new school called Saint-Judes, beside a little church. Some kids that lived at the church also attended Saint-Judes. I didn't get why back then; we were told they were orphans. They were all indigenous, though none of them had indigenous names. One of those kids was Gabe. I remember him because he was such a troublemaker and was always getting into fights."

"Did he have the long hair?"

She smiled wistfully. "Yeah, but it was unruly, messy back then, and loose."

"Was he cute?"

"Not exactly. He was kind of a mess."

"So, you knew Gabe when you were super little? And you never mentioned this to me?"

"Let me finish!"

Sasha made a zipping gesture across her mouth.

"He used to steal my lunch, but I never said anything because he was always in trouble anyway."

"You were a nice kid."

"We moved away before the end of the year - right in the middle of the school year,and I had a best friend in that class, Lexie. I wrote letters to her. She never wrote me back, and I couldn't understand why."

"And she dated Gabe?"

"Oh my god Sasha - hush!"

Her friend smiled and threw away her fictional key.

Eva tried to gather her thoughts. This story wasn't for a casual discussion,she looked away from Sasha so she could focus. "It turns out that only a few days after we moved away, there was a fire at the church in the middle of the day, and it burned down, and so did the school. My parents tried to hide it from me, but as soon as I was old enough to look it up, I found out that all the kids who lived at the church were killed in the fire, and so were the people who took care of them, the priest and some of the nuns."

Sasha was quiet. "Oh my God, Eva, that's awful."

Eva swallowed, feeling the blood rushing to her cheeks as the memory brought on a flood of emotions.

"Yeah, so when I saw Gabe that first day, it was like he'd returned from the dead. I kept thinking maybe I was confused, that it was another guy named Gabe, but then I dug up the old class photo, and there was no mistake, he survived the fire."

"That's crazy."

"His name was listed among those that died."

"And your friend?"

Eva shook her head.

"Were there other survivors?"

"I don't think so."

"How...how did it happen?"

"He has a lot of guilt about being the only one who made it out."

"And you."

"Yeah, but, Sasha, I don't think it's a coincidence that we moved. My dad is in the military. We were living in a military town with a lot of tension around indigenous rights and politics and everything about that fire was super suspicious. How did they not put it out in the middle of the day? All the kids that lived at the church were from different tribes, like Gabe. It's super messed up. I was just a kid, so I didn't know any of this then, but when I start to really look at it now, I don't like what it adds up to."

"You think your dad knew?"

"I don't know if he did, but all the military families suddenly moved at about the same time."

"But why burn down a church?"

"I don't know."

"Have you told Gabe all this?"

"I did except for that last bit. I don't want him to feel even worse,, I don't want him to think of my family that way. The newspapers called it an accident, a tragedy and as far as I know, that's what he thinks it was too."

"So, where did Gabe go after he was living at the church?"

"I don't know. He never talks about it."

"I guess a family must have taken him in?"

"I doubt it. Honestly, there was a lot of prejudice against indigenous kids, still is, I guess, but there were a lot of homeless indigenous people where we lived then."

"You think he was homeless? At that age?"

"It kind of sounds like it, and he's lived all over the place since then."

"So, how did he end up here?"

"He won't say."

"What do you think?"

"I think he has a credit card and enough money to pay for an apartment, but he doesn't have a job. That's odd."

"Yeah, I've been thinking the same thing for a long time now."

"So, where does Hale come into the picture?"

"He only said that they met a little while before moving in together and that they share the rent. He really doesn't tell me much beyond that. He says they're friends, as much as anyone's Hale's friend."

"It still doesn't add up." Sasha huffed.

"Okay, I've told you the story. You said you had something too." She couldn't wait to get off the subject. She hoped this secret was enough. Her other secret seemed unimaginable to divulge.

Sasha seemed to be considering her options.

"Okay, but don't freak out."

"Um. Okay?" That wasn't promising.

"I found a gun in Hale's room."

"What? Way to bury the lead."

"Like, a handgun of some sort, hidden in his drawer - and there was a bunch of other stuff in there too. Bizarre stuff like profiles of people and x-rays and medications- oh, and blueprints and maps. Maps of stuff like the town, and I can't say for sure, but I think it was a blueprint of the base. I looked it up in the library later, and it's about the right shape, not that I know what's inside it."

Eva wasn't sure what to think. She remembered Gabe's reaction when she'd told him she knew him from his childhood, that line of questioning, "Who are you working for?"

"Why did he have all that stuff?" she asked.

"I don't know."

"Did you ask him about it?"

"And tell him I searched his room?"

"Wait a second; you searched his room? How? When?"

"Two weeks ago, when we were at the apartment. I pretended to go to the bathroom when he wasn't home."

"When I was there?"

"Yeah, sorry."

"Why, though? What made you do that?"

"I wanted to know what his deal was."

"Sasha, that's not okay!"

"Neither is having a gun."

"Do you think he'd hurt Gabe? Or himself?"

"I don't think he'd hurt Gabe. He seems to really care about him, honestly."

"And you think he'll bring it with him, is that why you don't want to go?"

"Yeah, it worries me."

"I mean, we're in Georgia, and lots of people own guns. My dad, for one."

"17- year- olds?"

"Maybe it's not his?"

"Then why does he have it?"

There was a long pause where both girls stared at one another.

"I have to go on this trip, Sash."

"I'm worried for you. I don't want anything to happen to you. Can't you just not bring Hale, then?"

"I trust Gabe." She said again. "And for some reason, Hale has to come. I don't understand their connection, but there's something there."

"Then why do you trust him?"

"I just do."

"But he hasn't told you anything!"

"I know, but I think that's why he hasn't told me, because he's trying to protect me from it. Look, I don't know what's going to happen in the future, but right now, we're young, we have this amazing opportunity to have this adventure together before we're on different coasts for the next four years."

Sasha sighed. "My parents, I'll have to convince them."

Eva nodded, grateful. "It's going to be amazing!" She said, hugging her friend.

"I also can't let you go alone...and now you know why."

"Thanks, I really do appreciate it."

They lay back on the bed staring at the ceiling for a moment. They'd lain here together so many times over the years. Eva was going to miss this little gabled room.

"So, even after finding the gun, do you still like Hale?"

"I don't know. He's so frustrating. I'm sure I'll meet guys in college who don't make me feel like I'm jumping through hoops to get their attention."

"You definitely will."

Sasha

She could hear the car before it reached her, the music blaring. Gabe and Eva were in the front with iced coffees while Hale sat sulkily in the back seat. He was frustratingly good-looking in the morning.

After she hugged her mom at the door and shoved her suitcase into what was left of the trunk space (very little), she sat as far away from him as possible and set a giant cooler full of snacks and drinks between them. Gabriel teased her about the number of supplies she'd brought while Eva grabbed herself a snack.

"Your hair looks amazing, Sash." Eva said. She'd dyed it last night, hoping it would give her more courage on this trip and for the photos.

"Thanks!" She peaked at herself in the mirror. The contrast made her look edgier.

"Want one?" She offered Hale a can of soda. He nodded. She wrote his name on it with a large black marker and handed it to him. "It's so we don't get them all mixed up."

"And we're off!" Gabriel announced, hooting and hollering as they got onto the freeway.

Eva had created many mix CDs so she and Eva could sing along, smiling at one another in the rearview. Hale stared at the town silently as the sun rose slowly above them. Leaving before dawn was hard, but it was worth it to beat the traffic. In no time, they'd driven through and past the tiny downtown core, past the beach and further along the 20, headed West.

The houses turned into long deserted landscapes dotted with empty billboards and signs for truck stops. By the time they reached Memphis, hours later, she was getting hungry and said as much. Eva agreed, but Gabe insisted they were making a good time.

"That's entirely against the point of a road trip Gabriel Wells; we're supposed to stop to enjoy the sights!"

"Unless you're planning to sleep in the car, we must make it to our motel."

"Fine, then, can we do a drive-through?" She huffed.

"Baby." Gabe teased but acquiesced.

She didn't speak to Hale much, and he didn't seem to have much to say either. He was either looking out at the road or avoiding her gaze. It was as though they were in class together that day after she'd kissed him. It was going okay, overall. If Hale wanted to be a sourpuss the whole way, that was his choice. Only when they reached Dallas, Texas, things went wrong.

Eva

When she gave her parents huge hugs that morning, Matteo had already gone camping, she could hardly breathe. Was she really doing this? Was she really not going to tell them about the pregnancy? They waved goodbye, made Gabe promise over and over again that he would drive safe, that they would check in and that they would be back in no time at all, and then they were off. She watched them get smaller and smaller until they turned the corner. She felt an immense weight on her chest.

They had to swing by Gabe's apartment to pick up Hale and then Sasha. Even though she knew that what lay ahead would be super hard and painful, it felt glorious to be on the road. Once, they were driving with the wind in their hair, rock music and songs from old musicals blaring and Gabe's hand on her thigh now and again; it tasted like freedom. She was in a Bon Jovi song, coasting down the highway. Gabe looked so happy out here, the sun on his skin, his hair coming loose. He drove recklessly and wanted to stay on the road as much as possible, but they seemed to be making food time.

When they'd been on the road for ten hours, her legs cramped. "Come on, babe, let's stop and grab something to eat." She pleaded. The nausea of the first few weeks of pregnancy had largely passed, but now she was always hungry. She was glad Sasha had packed so many snacks.

It took some convincing, but Gabe finally took an exit ramp.
"Are we going into the city? I'm sure there are some amazing restaurants in Dallas." Sasha said, pulling out her phone and looking for something nearby.
The sun was descending along the horizon as evening began to set in. They could see skyscrapers off in the distance.
"How about here?" Gabe said, already easing into the right lane.
"Do they have vegetarian options?" Sasha cut in, her phone still out, her knees propped against the back of Eva's seat.
"I'm sure they do."
"How? Have you been here before?" Sasha cut in.
"Trust me." Gabe replied, looking a bit nervous. They pulled up in front of a large freestanding building with a pagoda roof.
"Guess we're having Asian food!" Eva cheered. She was mostly glad to be able to stretch her legs.
The restaurant was a buffet, with people meandering up to large tables of steaming buns and rice, serving themselves. They claimed a booth by the window, and Sasha volunteered to stay and save their seats. She was deeply interested in something on her phone. It had been miles and miles since they'd had Wi-Fi access.
She and the guys picked up red plastic trays and split up to fill them. Gabe got himself a large cup of coffee.
"You okay, babe?" She asked him; he'd gotten quieter as the hours passed.
"Yeah, just tired."
"Did you want to switch drivers?"
"Nah, I'm alright."
When they returned to the table, Hale was already sitting there, and Sasha was in the middle of a rant.
"Then why are we here then?"
"Sasha? What's the matter?"
Sasha held up her phone. "We're miles away from the direction we should've taken. Either Gabe doesn't know where he's going, or he's purposely taking us too far south. There's no way we're headed to the hotel we booked."

Eva looked at Gabe, confused. Hale took a bite of his spring roll without a word.

"Oh, relax! The driver gets to decide on the route. There are many hotels around, and I promise you'll be safe and sound."

Sasha looked like she was about to explode. "Gabriel Wells! You agreed to this trip! We had a plan! You can't decide stuff on your own or with your friend here, who clearly knew this was going on. Are you guys going to tell us what's happening right now?"

The tension was almost too much for Eva's stomach to handle. "I'll...I'll be right back..." She said in a choked voice and made a b-line for the nearest bathroom.

Sasha

"Well?" Sasha demanded. The proof was in the pudding.

They were headed in the wrong direction, and neither of the guys wanted to tell her what was happening. On top of everything, Eva was still acting completely bizarre. For months, she had been acting food averse, though that wasn't uncommon going into prom, so she hadn't said anything, but now that the two of them were on the road, she needed Eva's support. They weren't in Kansas anymore. When Eva suddenly disappeared, it was the last straw.

"This is ridiculous. This conversation isn't over." She hopped up and followed her friend. There was something seriously wrong. If this was some stupid bulimia thing. "Don't do anything dumb, Gabe." she called over her shoulder. So much for dinner.

She could hear Gabe asking Hale, "What the hell was that about?"

When she got to the bathroom, Eva was sitting on the yellowing tiled floor, heaving.

"When the hell is this supposed to let up..." She muttered miserably, seemingly to herself. She managed to get herself up with a lot of effort just as Sasha slipped inside.

"Eva, what the actual hell?"

"Sasha?" She said with a slight note of shock in her voice. She had been so rushed that she hadn't seen her friend follow her. "I'm alright, let's get back to the boys."

"Eva. What's this all about? Gabe's all over you all the time! This is no time to get self-conscious. There is something seriously fishy going on right now; we're way off course; we're in the middle of nowhere. How can you think about weight?"

"What are you talking about? You don't seriously think I'm doing this on purpose, do you?" Sasha gestured for her to come back into the washroom. She wanted to show her the map she'd been looking at and get her to confront Gabe about the situation, but seeing how pale her friend had gotten made her reprioritize.

"Hon, I'm not going to judge you here but for my sake, or Gabe's sake, but mostly your own, cut it out! If we were home, I'd be more patient about something like this, but you can't be hurting yourself when we're miles from home and help or even a hospital. You're not even chubby, okay? Not that being chubby would've made this okay."

She took a deep breath, "Sasha, I don't have an eating disorder. Can we drop this?"

"Then what? Why are you puking your guts out when we haven't eaten all day!?" she shouted.

"Sasha, drop it! Please!" She shouted back; she looked cornered.

"No! What is wrong with you?" Both girls were getting teary-eyed in exasperation. Eva tugged at the bottom of her shirt, rubbing her stomach. Sasha bit her tongue.

"I'm pregnant! That's what's fucking wrong with me!" She yelled. As soon the words left her lips, reality shifted. Eva turned away, curling her fingers around the sink, her head bowed. There was a long silence.

"Say something." Eva pleaded, her voice thick.

Sasha forced herself to blink and swallowed thickly. She looked at the ceiling, the sound of her heartbeat beating too quickly in her ears. She felt faint; one more deep breath,"Oh my God," She looked back at Eva, "What're we gonna do?"

"I don't know," Eva answered, turning back to Sasha. "Gabe doesn't even know yet." She could feel her shoulders slump forward a bit. "I haven't been able to tell him."

"How could you keep this to yourself?" She was so upset and confused that she wasn't sure if it was anger or hysteria.

"I know I shouldn't have... I just didn't know what to do. I'm scared, Sasha." She whispered.

Sasha pulled her friend into a hug. "You have to tell Gabe."

"I know, and I will when the time is right," she clung to Sasha as if for dear life, "I've gotten us into a huge mess. I'm so sorry." She managed to mutter through sobs. "I don't know what to do anymore, and I couldn't get rid of it in Atlanta."

"Shhh...it's okay. It's not your fault. You didn't know this was going to happen." She was surprised she wasn't bawling too; she sure felt like it. She waited for Eva to pull herself together.

"We should go. If somebody finds us like this, we'll get in shit" She stood up. "Let's get back to the guys."

"I know this isn't what you want to hear right now, but they're not taking us where they said they were." She showed Eva the map, explaining what she'd found. Eva nodded but said nothing. "I really need you to back me up on this. Either we're going where we said we were going,or we have to return."

"I have to go to California. It's the only place I can resolve this."

It took Sasha a moment to grasp what she meant, but it felt like a kick to the gut when it finally did.

"You mean you want to?"

"What else am I supposed to do?" Eva looked determined, despite all the tears.

They were both red and shaken. Sasha shook her head. "Hon, tell him soon. You don't have the time to stall. I won't say anything, but he has to know. Just eat, okay? You're eating for two."

"I'll tell him soon, I promise" Eva led the way down the corridor towards the dining area, both filled with new anxieties.

Eva

Eva returned on her own while Sasha went to fill her tray. She sat next to Gabe and leaned on his shoulder. "Babe, what's going on with the hotel? Just tell me. Sasha's freaking out. Whatever it is, we'll work it out together."

He glanced out the window. It was already getting dark. "We're not going to California."

She lifted her head off his shoulder and looked him in the eyes, confused. "What?"

"Well, you're going to California. I'm expected somewhere by tomorrow."

"Where?" What the hell was he talking about? Was he about to leave them in the middle of nowhere? She wasn't even insured on the car! She hadn't driven enough to drive across the country alone either!

"I can't tell you."

"Then why did you agree to go on this trip?" She was incredulous. Was Sasha right after all?

"I can't tell you that either, but just know that it's because I care about you."

"Gabe, you're scaring me right now." She hadn't taken a single bite from her plate but took a moment to sip a soda.

"I'm sorry." He said. She wasn't sure which part he was apologizing for.

"Just tell me what's going on before they get back."

"I'll tell you tonight, okay? It's a long story and I can't risk anyone overhearing."

"And you'll tell me the truth?"

"I promise."

She nodded. "Does Hale know?"

"Yes, he's in the same boat. Before he returns, you do need to know that we'll be taking a different car from here. We'll be leaving the Mustang in the parking lot." He spoke quickly. "Act casual when we get to the other car. Hale's moving our luggage to it now."

She nodded. "I'm guessing you can't tell me why?"

"It's not my car."

"I figured." She shrugged. "And will this one be?"

"No."

She nodded. "Let me speak to Sasha then, or your whole con will blow up in your faces." She had to follow through. No matter how scary this was, she had to trust that Gabe knew what he was doing. "I'll be back." She said and went over to the buffet to speak to her friend. "Eva?"

"Yeah?" She turned.

"Thanks." She watched him sipping from her soda.

Chapter 13
Reading Constellations

Sasha

The tiled ceiling had a suspicious-looking coffee-colored stain. Sasha had been wondering what it could be for the past half hour, forcing herself to think of something besides her current predicament. God, she hated the way motel rooms smelled. Why would it be so musty in a room in the middle of the desert? She had to make a decision.

After Eva's big revelation, the world seemed to barely hold onto its axis. Eva asked her, pleading that she trust Gabe, that she pretend that they had driven up to the restaurant in the rust-coloured jalopy that Hale had parked directly in front of the Asian restaurant. It wasn't as though she had much of a choice. The shiny red Mustang was gone. She had so many questions but no way to get answers to them. She knew two things: firstly, Hale and Gabe were criminals of some sort and couldn't be trusted, secondly, her best friend was carrying Gabe's baby. The first thing meant that she and Eva should get as far away as possible from these two guys, as quickly as possible. If Eva needed to go to California, they would have to go alone.

With a deep sigh, she pushed herself onto her elbows and glanced at her suitcase, which now seemed much too small for the journey ahead. She'd packed for a vacation, not a traipse through the middle of nowhere to a state that allowed abortion. Getting up, she found the motel-provided pen and post-its and scribbled a few words to Eva, leaving the paper on the bed. After rereading her message six times and still feeling dissatisfied, she crossed the room, grabbed her suitcase and walked out into the hall. She was leaving, and she would wait and see if Eva wanted to join her. She'd already found out where the nearest bus stop was from the cranky receptionist at the front, and all Eva had to do was meet her there. She would have texted, but her cell phone was out of satellite range. Eva and Gabe had been gone for a few hours, but staying would only lead them further into danger. If Eva didn't show up, she would find a police station and get help, send out an amber alert and find her. She didn't think Gabe would hurt Eva, but she also hadn't expected Hale to have a gun either.

The hallway was dank and quiet, with peeling wallpaper and neon lights making everything look green. Someone was pacing up and down the end of the corridor, and she stopped quickly, recognizing Hale.

"Where are you going?" he asked bluntly into the darkness.

Sasha had the impression of being a teen sneaking out of her room in the middle of the night.

"I'm leaving," she said, unable to keep the challenge out of her tone.

"Leaving?" he repeated, much more angrily than she'd expected. He leaned against the shabby wall, "Where exactly are you going?" Instead of looking at her, he peered down at the gray carpet of the hall.

"Home." she stated firmly.

"You can't," he replied, still not looking at her.

Sasha lifted an eyebrow, not that he could see it in the dim lighting, "Because you're going to stop me?"

He heaved a sigh that seemed to go on forever, "You just can't," he repeated, sounding desperate now. She'd never heard him sound that way before.

"I can do whatever I like. You're not my parent or even my friend, so I don't see where you get authority on where I can go. You're taking us somewhere and I don't want to go. I agreed to a road trip to California. I didn't sign up for this, and I'm going home." With that, she lifted her suitcase off its wheels and attempted to step around him.

In one swift motion, he took hold of her wrist, "There won't be anything for you to go back to." A bitter edge tainted his words.

She froze. Her gaze flicked down to her wrist, then quickly to his shadowed face. "Excuse me?" she mouthed. His hand was cold against her skin. He was trying to scare her, and it was working.

"Don't make me repeat myself." his voice was quiet.

"Well, you'll have to!" she cried, wrenching her hand away as best she could. He held on. She tried not to panic. They both stared at her wrist as though they were both trapped.

"The base is set to explode in four hours." He said it quickly and clearly.

"What kind of an excuse is that? What base? *Our* base? The one in town?" She was livid. How could he expect her to believe something so ludicrous?

"If you don't believe me, then ask Gabe," he said through clenched teeth.

"He's an even bigger liar than you are! Explain again." she growled, enunciating each syllable.

He looked her in the eyes, finally. "You won't believe me either way." Fatigue and frustration reflected on his face, dark circles under his eyes. She was so used to thinking he was handsome, but now all she could think was how unreadable he was, how unpredictable, how violent he'd been with Jason. So many moments between them took on a completely different meaning all of a sudden. There was also the gun, the map she'd found in his bag with the markings around the base... The realization was beginning to trickle through. If he was lying, he was even more twisted than she could imagine. If he wasn't... "How would you know something like that?" She was breathing heavily, her heart racing.

He took a deep breath that looked like it hurt, "I was the one that planted the bombs." The words came rushing out as he exhaled.

The floor had suddenly jumped out from under her. Her vision spun, and she held a hand out against the peeling wallpaper to steady herself. "Why?" She expected anger, but only a numb shock was there at that moment, and a disbelief, a strong desire to disbelieve.

"I was following orders,"

"Orders?" she mumbled. There were tears in her eyes; she hadn't even realized it until they rolled down her cheeks, paving a trail down to her chin. The anger flared inside of her so quickly that it shocked her. Before she was certain of what she was doing, the hand he wasn't holding down had shot out and connected with his cheek with an open palm.

"How could you?" She cried.

He held a hand to his cheek but didn't let go of her arm.

"Stop screaming; you'll wake everyone up," he growled under his breath.

"What do you mean by orders?!" Her entire body shook, making every word ragged and loud enough to echo through the hall.

"Be quiet. People will hear you."

"I hope they do! I hope they call the cops! How can you tell me that and expect me just to stay quiet?" If he was telling the truth, everyone back home was in danger.

"You need to calm yourself."

"I have to do something!"

She let go of her suitcase and tried again to sidestep him in the tiny hallway. Four hours. There was still time. The suitcase landed on the floor with a thud.

"Don't be stupid," he glared, holding tightly, his gaze like a laser. He grabbed hold of her shoulder. She could feel how cold his hands were through her t-shirt. "You're acting like a child."

"I *am* a child, and my family is back there, in case you hadn't thought of that! Now let me go so I can call my mom, and she can get out of there! The base isn't far from my house." How she could be so coherent, she was a little unsure. The panic had receded, but the adrenaline was still as strong. The clear goal of the pay phone in the lobby made everything vivid and lucid.

"I can't let you do that," he said in a steady, assertive voice.
She looked up at him, straight into his eyes, searching. He had to let her
go. There wasn't much time. He was surely strong, but she was
desperate; hopefully, that would be enough. "Let me go, please. If you
ever cared about me at all, even a little bit, or as a favour for getting you
home after the fight with Jason. Whatever this is, it has nothing to do
with my family or friends. They don't deserve any of this." It was all she
had to offer: The memories they'd shared in the past year, the good and
the bad, the idea that he wasn't this kind of person.
He dropped his hands down by his sides. "Fine," he choked out.
"Thank you." She heard herself say through a sob. His face looked the
way it had when she'd helped him to bed back at the apartment and
offered him a glass of water, as if all the strength had been squeezed out
of him.

The hallway seemed much further and dimmer than on the way in. She
reached the lobby in what seemed like an eternity and emptied her
pockets onto the floor. The change clinked in a musical cacophony, and
she fell to her knees to gather the largest coins. She counted out loud to
herself, two, three, three and twenty-five, six dollars. Her fingers
trembled as she slipped coins into the slot and punched in the numbers.
"Please answer.", she thought.

There was a sleepy voice on the other end of the line. She knew she
should be calling the main base, but as he'd put it, she was a child. All
the words caught in her throat as she heard a sleepy series of "Hellos" on
the other end of the line.
"Mama?" Once the first word was out, the words fell like rain, a jumble
of warnings and apologies. Once she thought she'd made some
semblance of sense, she stopped for an answer. "Where are you?" her
mom asked. Anger flared inside her. She told her it didn't matter, that
they had to evacuate, then she hung up. Without questions, she'd have to
listen. If she tried to explain, it would sound even crazier. Next, the main
base number, what number was that? She didn't know. Her phone was
out of range. She dialed Mila, Margo, and anyone she could think of
whose number came to mind. She left voicemails. It felt insane, but there
it was. If Hale had lied, she would have had a lot of explaining to do
when she got home. Evacuate, bombs, danger, she hoped it would be
enough. She needed to call the base. Eva would know! Her dad worked
in the military.
"I have to go find Eva." She said to the looming figure standing in the
hallway. He was watching her make her calls without a word.
"Will you run?" He asked.

"No." He nodded, and she stepped out into the night. As she called Eva's name into the darkness, she realized she hadn't told her mom that she loved her.

Eva

They lay intertwined in the cool grass. Gabe constantly sighed, burying his face in her hair. She'd planned to press him for what was happening but the night was full of stars, and the motel had sprung for a grassy spot near the rather gross-looking pool. They both had secrets, and she still wasn't ready to share hers with Gabe, though Sasha knew now, so it was only a matter of time. She knew Gabe was in trouble and he was bringing her deeper into it, but more than anything, she wanted comfort. She didn't want tomorrow to come, she didn't want to go back to the room to listen to Sasha's theories about what Hale and Gabe were up to. Gabe had started talking, he'd started telling her about a place they were going that he called Headquarters but she'd cut him off. She just wanted a little more time with him before it all imploded. The sun could just stay under the horizon, and the world could turn without them. Her eyes were closed. She gave into other senses, the smell of his shampoo, the grass, and the night, the warmth of his body. Instead of the truth, they'd talked about nothing, they'd laughed, and they'd made out.

It was a euphoric blur. There weren't any words in the dictionary that could describe how she felt.

"Gabe?" she mumbled softly as she ran her fingers over the skin of his shoulders, "you awake?"

"Mmm." he mumbled back, the smile sounding in his voice. "Only if we don't have to move."

"We'll have to move eventually," she giggled as she played with stray strands of his hair. "Otherwise, the cleaning staff will find us."

"I can live with that." he chuckled. "They'd just be jealous."

The door to the motel swung open, and the light poured out into the night, a distant light from their sanctuary beneath the tree.

"Eva!" Sasha called, her voice echoing into the silence.

"Damnit." Gabe muttered.

Eva pushed Gabe off her. "Guess the party's over," she sighed as she sat up to await her friend's arrival. Gabe leaned back on his elbows and looked up at the sky.

"Eva!" Sasha called again, her voice breaking. She spotted them and jogged over, breathless. Looking down, she turned to Gabe. "Did you tell her what you did?"

Gabe didn't look at Sasha, he looked at her instead, "Here it comes." He sounded resigned.

The door of the building shut, and the darkness returned. "Tell me you told her what you did." Sasha demanded, her hands on her hips.

He sat up and put his hand over his eyes, "I was getting to it." he mumbled.

Eva could hear what was being said, but couldn't comprehend it. "He was just about to tell me." She got up, dusting herself off. Gabe remained on the ground.

"Fine then. If you don't tell her, I will." She looked down at Gabe as though she was going to spit at him.

"Come on, Sash." Eva began, reaching for her friend's hand.

"No! He needs to hear it too. They," She pointed at Gabe, "planted bombs in the base, *our* base, the one your dad works in and they're set to go off tonight! You've gotta go call home - right now!"

Gabe gave the panicked girl a miserable look as though to ask her why she had to go and say a thing like that. Eva stared at Sasha, then her boyfriend, her mind trying to catch up.

"Gabe?" She waited for him to deny it, to laugh, to make a joke. None of those things happened. He wouldn't even look at her. He just kept looking up at the sky.

"She's right. You should call home." he said in a small voice. She felt her stomach drop. Gabe reached over and draped his t-shirt over his neck as he sat up. It was starting to dawn on her how they must have looked to Sasha when she'd found them. Shock and embarrassment mixed in the pit of her stomach.

"Eva, please! I called home. We need them to evacuate the town." Sasha pleaded.

It didn't sound real, but Gabe wasn't arguing, wasn't dismissing her, wasn't even telling her they hadn't done it. The eye of the storm, somewhere between laughter and sorrow. In silence, she stood and began walking toward the motel, unsure what to do once she got there. The wind had begun to pick up, throwing strands of red hair into her face. Sasha followed closely behind her and pointed to the pay phone on the wall. Confused, she checked her cell phone, but of course, they were out of range. She felt Sasha placing coins in her hand. She looked up at her friend. Sasha nodded.

With a deep breath, she crossed the room and put the cold, heavy phone to her cheek. The coins clinked as they fell. She dialed her home number "please, dad, come on," she muttered as the phone rang for a minute without a response.

"Hello?" her father's voice rang out accusingly, he hated to be woken up, but his military training made him alert.

"Papa, it's Eva. I don't have long, so please just listen," her voice began to crack as a lump formed in her throat. "There's a bomb on the base, and I need you to get everyone out... I love you" The phone hit the receiver with a thud as she slumped to the floor, the carpet becoming a sea of blues and browns in front of her eyes. She could hear footsteps approaching her. She heard Gabe step forward, seeming to want to comfort her, but Sasha beat him to it, pushing him as she stepped past and slumping to the floor, wrapping her arms around her.

"That's it, that's all we can do." Eva whispered, her head buried in her friend's shoulder.

Sasha nodded, her body shaking, "Can we leave?"

"I don't know, I don't know anything anymore," Eva replied with a ragged breath.

In a daze, she began to look around the room. A bitter taste filled her mouth when her eyes fell on Hale and Gabe, standing next to each other like sentinels by the motel doors. She got off the floor as her blood began rising to the surface like a pot of boiling water.

"My brother is twelve years old! I swear to God, if they die you'll both join them!" With that, she swung the motel doors open and ran into the parking lot, unsure of where she was going but needing to be as far away from this nightmare as she could get at that moment.

Sasha

"Eva!" Sasha and Gabe both called in unison.

"To hell with this." Sasha sighed, heading towards the door.

"Wait." Gabe caught her wrist. "Not this again," she thought. Why did these boys think grabbing hold of her was okay?

"Let me go talk to her, okay? I know we really messed up but don't ruin everything for her and me."

Sasha was about ready to slap him too, just to balance out her night.

"I didn't ruin anything! You did this! Why did you bring us?"

"I tried to tell her."

"But you didn't."

"I brought her to protect her."

"And me?"

"She wouldn't have come without you. Come on, let me fix this."

She gaped at him, incredulous. How could he possibly believe there was anything he could say that would make Eva forgive him? She looked at Hale, staring at the floor in the exact spot where she'd left him earlier. On what planet was this the sort of thing one could forgive?

"Would he hurt her?" She asked Hale.

"Of course, I wouldn't!" Gabe exclaimed, defensive.

Hale shook his head. She sighed. She let Gabriel pass, saying nothing.

145

"Will she forgive him?" Hale asked her as they looked towards the swinging doors.

Sasha looked down at the floor, then back up at Hale, "You know? Probably. We're all so stupid." The tidal wave of emotions had passed. That one hug from Eva made her feel so much less alone.

"Thanks for telling me."

He was standing awkwardly at the opposite end of the room. She wondered how he felt.

"You're welcome," he whispered, careful not to look her in the eyes, "What are you going to do?"

She looked up at the ceiling and yawned, covering her mouth with the back of her hand.

"I guess I can't leave her alone either." She looked for his reaction. How had he put it? Following orders? It sounded like such a pitiful excuse. Her curiosity was coming back, pushing back the disappointment.

"It would make things easier if you came of your own free will."

She let out a tiny laugh. It almost sounded like he wanted her to come.

"I wouldn't be so sure, but I'll take your word for it." His cheek was pink where she'd slapped him.

"Get some rest. I'll wait for Evangeline and Gabriel." His voice was firm but soft in the still air.

"I honestly can't believe it's come to this." He didn't say anything. Since secrets were all coming out, she decided to push her luck. "So where are we going?"

"To a place where you'll have to ask fewer questions, if any."

"Would you have let me leave?"

He was picking at his nail beds with his thumb, "You already know too much."

"I don't feel like I know anything at all, actually."

"Then listen, don't ask questions, argue, or step out of line. These aren't people to trifle with, and if they think you're a risk to the operation, you won't be walking out of there."

She shuddered. "Sounds like a threat."

"The rules apply to everyone, to me even more so."

"Who are these people?"

"Guess you're starting tomorrow then."

"You said I couldn't ask tomorrow."

He stuttered a few words, but stopped, "You'll figure it out on your own, but keep your head down."

"What should I do and say then?"

"Say as little as possible. Do whatever is asked of you, whether you think it makes sense or not. Don't let your feelings get in the way."

"How long will we be there?"

"I don't know."

"You've been there before?"

"Yes."

"And you want to go back?"

"What I want has nothing to do with it."

"Was that gun meant for us?"

"What?" He finally looked up, alarm on his face.

"The gun you have."

He shook his head. "You need to figure things out quieter."

"That doesn't answer my question."

He said nothing. She couldn't think of a follow-up so she went to her next question.

"Am I also going to be "following orders"?"

"Yes."

"Are the beds there comfier than here?"

"I wouldn't count on it."

She let out a small laugh and started back down the hallway to her room, rolling her suitcase behind her, "Good night." She heard him say it back, his voice echoing. The fact that she could sleep that night was a testament to human resilience.

Eva

How could he not have told her and risked leaving her an orphan like himself? Being outside calmed her, the simplicity of a world that didn't care, a world outside of human experiences. She found a tree and sat down beneath it. The ground felt very dry, but the air was humid. She kept thinking of ways to hate Gabe but came up empty. Was she betraying her family by loving him? Was she betraying herself? Most likely, but when he smiled at her, the world stopped. "I'm so sorry Papa, I can't hate him." she thought, peering up at the expanse of sky. She knew there would be no answer, and her father may never answer her questions again, but it comforted her. She was aware that Gabe had followed her. He finally stepped out from the shadows.

"Eva," He started, "I know you're pissed off, and you should be. I tried to tell you."

She straightened up, lifting her gaze to look at his face. She felt the prickle of tears, "I should have listened." She felt a droplet of rain on her cheek. It was an unseasonably rainy Summer, "I should've insisted more. I should've asked more questions. I just wanted to believe something else. I just didn't think...*that*." She couldn't bring herself to articulate anything about bombs or the base.

"Do you still mean what you said? About trusting me?"

She wrapped her arms around herself and stared out towards the parking lot. The past couple of hours had changed everything, "I don't know what I mean anymore," she sobbed, hiding her face from the world that seemed much too harsh.

He got down on his knees in front of her, leaning in close. "Listen, I know I really messed up, but I promise I'll make it up to you. I'd take it all back and bring you home if I could, but I'm asking you, if staying with me is worth to you what keeping you is to me, then I swear I won't let you down again. I don't have anything else to give." He looked like he was crying too, but it was probably just the rain. She felt it soaking her shoulders and hair. The tree didn't have much coverage. Hadn't he planned to leave her behind? Had the offer changed? She wiped the tears from her eyes so she could see Gabe clearly. He was definitely crying, and not making any attempts to hide it. She wanted to throw her arms around him. It would be easier to comfort one another than to talk. "The truth is, Gabe, you can't do anything to change what you've done." Her breathing was slow and hoarse from crying. "You put my family in danger...like they were nothing." The rain was drizzling now, but the cold droplets helped her to speak clearly. "The other thing is I'm in love with you."

He didn't seem to know how to respond so she continued, "I need you, so just tell me you love me, and I'll go with you, wherever it may be." He couldn't possibly understand all of the implications. If he was targeting military bases, he must somehow be part of the resistance, though he was way too young. She'd never come into contact with it, but it was on the news every now and again, people disliking the current government, not liking how much of a role the military played in civil issues, the way minority groups were treated. It always felt so far away. Maybe she was just naive. She put her hand on her stomach. He had no idea what he was getting himself into, but that seemed fair since neither did she.

"I," he stuttered. The rain stuck his bangs to his forehead and drenched his shoulders. "I don't deserve you." He hadn't said he loved her this time, but he'd said it so many times before, and she wanted so much to believe him. She held her finger to his lips. "Don't."

His eyes softened. He put on his token grin. He swiped her finger away with one hand and used the other to pull her closer, their breath visible in the suddenly chill night air. She snuggled in closer, her head on his shoulder. "We should go in, it's getting wet out here." he said.

148

If they went inside, they would have to face the facts, that he'd done something unforgivable, and that she was hiding a secret that could still end it all. "Or we can stay here." A small sigh escaped her lips.

"Tempting," he said, nibbling at her ear, his breathing warm and teasing against her neck. "But I'd rather you be warm." And with that, he put both arms under her and picked her up as though she weighed nothing at all.

She giggled as he carried her, bridal style, back to the motel, "Take me away Casanova."

They wouldn't be sharing a room tonight, as they'd split the rooms by gender. She wished he'd never let her go. As they came into the lobby, Hale was standing by the pay phone. Gabe set Eva down, but kept hold of her hand. He and Gabe exchanged looks.
"She's coming with us." Gabe said.
Hale nodded, then went down the hallway and into his room.
Eva turned back to Gabe.
"See you in the morning babe." She kissed him goodbye and went to her room. Sasha was already asleep, so she curled up into a ball on the bed, trying to forget everything and closed her eyes.

PART II:
UNDER THE SURFACE

Chapter 1
Descending

Eva

Eva and Gabe sat in the back of the car for a change. They were driving off road through the dunes and the shocks on the old car could barely handle it. They'd driven for six hours straight and the desert stretched on in all directions except for the massive fence in the distance - their destination. Gabe's head kept hitting up against the roof of the car despite his seatbelt, and Eva had sprawled across the remaining seat, nauseous.

This was, undoubtedly, a bad idea, but her instincts and, perhaps, an unwarranted optimism also told her that they'd scrape by and find a way. As he and Eva exchanged sweet nothings, she couldn't help thinking back to that first day he'd found her at lunchtime. How could she have imagined that it would lead to this? Masked figures carrying semi-automatic weapons opened the giant barbed wire fence in the middle of the desert to let them through. They waved for them to keep going, Hale seemed to know exactly where they needed to go.

The ground swallowed them up, a car-sized elevator bringing them down to the compound, silence falling between them. Eva's eyes were wide as they watched the sun disappearing above them.
The sky had disappeared far above. The slow movement downwards felt endless. She held Gabe's hand and breathed. The walls opened up to glass panes on all sides. They were now above a huge gray space filled with people scurrying around in various shades of black and gray clothing. She put her hand over her stomach. Everything she had said to Gabe was true, but there was much more to it than just love. Eva's decisions weren't just for her now; they could never be just for her again. Sometime soon, another life would be involved, and she needed Gabe to get on board with that. She would need him all the more now that she didn't know when to see her family again. Soon, she would have to tell him.

She'd been to a military base before, many times. This place was not that. It looked like a warehouse, full of equipment and people in lab coats. There didn't seem to be any rhyme or reason, but everyone seemed very busy. A few people looked up to stare at them as though their arrival was important. Before long, everyone was staring, and she sat up to stare back.

"Gabe?"

"Babe?"

"What is this place?"

"Welcome to Headquarters; you're now a terrorist to some, freedom fighter to others."

Sasha

It might have been the emotional exhaustion from the previous day or the knowledge that now that they'd crossed the gate, the next steps were entirely outside her control but despite the terrifying revelations of the previous day, she had yet to have a panic attack. Hale, on the other hand, gripped the steering wheel so hard that his knuckles had gone white. The knowledge of how heavy everyone's burdens were - Eva's pregnancy, Hale and Gabe's mysterious cause, maybe she'd gotten off easier than the others. She hoped her family and friends were safe back home; she hoped she'd get to see them again someday, or at least to call them.

Instead of the powerlessness she'd felt sitting on the motel floor yesterday, she was gathering her resources, ready to finally uncover what these boys had been hiding all this time. Eva and Gabe had gone quiet in the back seat. She glanced back at them, holding one another. She looked over at Hale, her unlikely companion. She had told him she wanted to be friends, and he'd warned her that it wasn't a good idea. She'd kissed him, and he'd clarified that was an even worse idea. He'd told her what he had done so she could save her family. So much had happened between them in the short time that they'd known each other, yet she barely knew him. She reached out her hand and put it on top of his on the steering wheel.

"Hey, don't freak out. We're all in this mess together now. We're just going to have to look out for each other."

The elevator stopped. Hale unlocked the doors and stepped out.

"Stay here." Gabe said to Eva, "I'll come get you when it's safe."

He pecked her on the lips and scrambled out, closing the door behind him.

Sasha swung the door open and stepped out. They were at the center of the warehouse - it wasn't as though the car was going to protect them. Eva followed, scrambling behind her. Whoever was going to decide her fate today, she wanted to look them in the eye.

Hale's footsteps echoed to the high ceiling of the hanger. People stopped on metal stairwells, overpasses and catwalks above their heads. Hale threw Gabe his duffel bag, and he slung it over his shoulder, pulling the girl's luggage out next and leaving it on the car roof. It didn't take long to notice their welcoming party: An old man, a tall woman with long dark hair and a shorter man wearing a lab coat.

"You're late." The old man said by way of greeting as he approached the car. He'd probably been tall in his youth but was now folded forward. It was hard to place his age, but wisps of white hair stuck out in all directions like Einstein. He didn't seem intimidating, but the silence around them spoke volumes.

"We completed the mission, though, and we got all the intel and some." Gabe said, stepping forward. He stuck out his hand. "Gabriel Wells, at your service."

The man stared at him over thick glasses, pale watery blue eyes seizing him up above a large, straight nose. He didn't take the outstretched hand.

"With some complications, it seems." He turned away from Gabe. "Hale, who are these children?"

Hale was standing directly behind Gabe. Gabe put his hand back in his pocket and looked around. "He's scared, and he's doing a bad job of covering it." Sasha thought. Gabe locked eyes with a few people, who all quickly looked away. He was trying to gain their sympathy, to see if anyone here would protest if things turned sour. This place was bizarre.

"They're here to join the cause." Hale said monotonously.

The man laughed, a sound like sandpaper, deep and eerie. "Is that so?"

"Yes, Sir." Eva said, approaching Sasha and standing beside her. Gabe gave her a warning glance. Eva looked the man straight in the eye, unflinching. Sasha gaped. She supposed Eva didn't get the same lecture as she had in the lobby of that motel.

"I'll do whatever I have to." Eva repeated, her voice steady. Sasha wiped her clammy hands on her shirt. She was trembling, though whether from fear or the air conditioning, she wasn't sure.

The man considered Eva, then nodded slowly. "And what if you don't?" He turned to Hale rather than Eva like she wasn't worth acknowledging. Hale was staring at the ground like a dog being scolded for chewing up a shoe. Sasha immediately loathed the man.

"I'll take responsibility for them." Gabe said quickly. "I'll make sure they stay in line." Hale was still silent. Why wasn't he stepping up too?

"And will *you* stay in line?" The man asked Gabe. "Socrates insists you're well trained. I have yet to see proof of that."

Gabe smirked. "You don't know me yet."

"I know enough." He croaked. "These girls will work; there are no idle hands here. If they step out of line, you will pay. If they're in the way, they will be eliminated. There are no empty rooms, so you can keep them both in yours, Gabriel Wells. They are not to wander around and make themselves a nuisance. They will be given work tomorrow and they will get it done. We're on a tight deadline, and lives are on the line. You can drop them off at the laundry rooms at seven tomorrow, it's one place they aren't likely to cause damage. You will report for training immediately afterwards," the old man's voice was slow and steady, with a cadence she recognized; he spoke like Hale, "You'll receive your schedule tonight. Hale, welcome back."

"Happy to be home." Hale answered, as though the man hadn't just threatened them all.

Hale led the way up three flights of stairs, Gabe carrying Eva's suitcases and his small duffle bag, while Sasha dragged her suitcase behind them.

"Who was that?" She heard Eva asking. Every sound carried in this place.

"Pythagorus. He's the leader of the rebellion."

"He looks like a substitute teacher." Eva replied.

"He has the sense of humour of one too." Gabe chuckled. "He's got quite the reputation. They say he's ruthless, doesn't give a rat's ass about anyone, ready to chuck you into the fire if you're in the way. He used to be a pretty high-ranking military strategist, even worked for Interpol, if you can believe it. You did good back there babe." He put his arm around her shoulders.

"My dad brought his bosses over all the time until he became the boss. I kind of wonder if he knows him."

The floor they needed was just a long metal platform on the side of the warehouse with doors along the wall. It was like the bridge of a ship in a sci-fi movie, like hanging above a parking garage, the fiberglass steps rattling as they walked.

"What's the idea with the giant room?" Sasha asked, out of breath from carrying her overly large luggage, looking down as people milled about below.

"They build weapons, big weapons." Gabe replied.

Hale stopped and pointed them to a door, which Gabe opened with his usual dramatics.

"Here we are! Home sweet home!" He chirped, clicking the light on. The room was anything but welcoming. Barely big enough for the single bed that had been pushed to the corner, it also offered a tiny desk with a gray lamp, gray linoleum floor and gray walls. Sasha hauled in her suitcase, "Well, this is cozy."

Hale walked past them, opened the next door, and promptly closed it behind him.

"Guess that's his room." Sasha said, sitting on her suitcase.

"Doesn't this feel like being back at the apartment?" Eva laughed. "Now Hale's going to go shower."

She could hear the sound of water through the left wall as though on cue. A door on that side of the room suggested they also got an en suite, if one could call it that. Gabe swung the door open to what looked like a converted closet with a toilet, sink and standing shower.

"I think I'll shower too." Sasha said. She stared at herself in the tiny mirror. Her face was red from the sun, contrasted against the dark hair-dye she'd chosen for the trip. The lighting was horrendously unflattering. She went over what she knew: Gabe and Hale were part of a rebel group with an underground facility in the middle of the desert. They were under the reign of that old man - Pythagorus. It explained some things: Why they were so physically strong, why they didn't seem to care about grades, why they were able to live on their own, why they'd blown up the base. The larger context was blurry but she understood that tomorrow she would be part of this somehow, contributing to a cause she hardly understood.

In the meantime, she'd be sharing a room with Gabe and Eva, who couldn't keep their hands off each other. The idea of sleeping in the same room as them was somehow more oppressive than the rest of the madness. As she stepped into the shower, unable to get the water warm enough, she realized that either Gabe and Hale would have to share a room, or she would have to choose the lesser of evils, for the sake of sleep.

Eva

Gabe and Eva climbed into the tiny bed as Sasha disappeared into the washroom.

"You okay, babe?" Gabe asked her.

"Yeah, I think so."

"You don't need to pretend if you're not."

"It's fine. I can manage."

"And now we get to spend every night together."

Eva nodded, her thoughts racing. She needed to tell him about the pregnancy, but even she didn't want to think about it right now. The possibility of terminating it had slipped through her fingers; she would need to figure out her next steps. How long would she be able to hide it?

What would happen when she couldn't anymore? She cuddled up to Gabe and closed her eyes.

Sasha emerged from the shower in a sweater and pajama pants, her hair wrapped in her beach towel. Eva pushed Gabe off of her. "Sorry."

"It's fine, ignore me." Sasha said, zipping up her luggage and going to the door, pulling the towel off her head as she went.

"Where are you going?" Eva asked quickly.

"Well, I can't exactly share a room with you two, can I?" Eva looked apologetic. "Gabe and Hale can share a room. You can stay here with me!"

"Don't go wandering around." Gabe warned her. "You're not in Kansas anymore, Dorothy."

"Thanks for your concern." She huffed and rolled her suitcase out into the hall.

Eva leapt from the bed to follow. "Hon, come back. Where are you going to go? He said there were no rooms. This place is super dangerous."

"I'm going to stay with Hale."

"Are you sure?" Eva grimaced.

"If he agrees."

Eva sighed deeply. "You don't have to."

"Yes, I do. Now please close the door."

She marched to Hale's door and knocked.

Sasha

She was angry, but more importantly, she wanted answers. He didn't answer at first, so she called out his name once, twice, then for a third time a little louder.. His hair was still damp from the shower when he opened the door in shorts and a sleeveless black shirt. Both Eva and Sasha were still standing in the hall.

"Hi." said Sasha.

"Yes?"

"This is a bit awkward but, can I, " He patiently waited for her to finish her sentence, "Stay here?"

He looked completely caught off guard. "You want to stay here?" He turned to look towards Eva, who was standing in the doorway, looking guilt-ridden.

"She doesn't have to." Eva said.

They stood awkwardly until he stepped aside and allowed her to come in. She waved at Eva, giving her a small smile as if to say, "This is fine; go back to what you were doing."

As soon as she was inside, they stood in front of one another, unsure of what to do next.

"I'll take the floor. I just don't want to deal with them being all mushy all the time."

"You can't sleep on the floor." He retorted.

"Well, there aren't many options, are there? It's only weird if we make it weird."

He looked around like another bed might slide out from a trap door. He stepped aside and let her roll her suitcase further into the room. The lamp on the desk was on but it failed to illuminate the room.

"Were you asleep?" She asked, glancing over at the too-small bed. The covers were pulled back.

"No." He sat back on the bed, and she set her suitcase beside the desk in the corner, identical to the one next door, where Hale's laptop was already charging. There was also a small dresser in the room, and she could see he'd taken the time to unpack his few belongings. The room smelled of soap and slightly stale air, a bit like an airplane.

"Just resting?" Sasha asked, to fill the silence.

"It's been a long day."

"Tell me about it." Sasha agreed, letting herself slide down onto her suitcase.

"Go on.I know it's physically debilitating for you not to ask questions."

She raised an eyebrow at him. This was almost teasing, and it made her wonder where they were at in their friendship. He wasn't wrong. She was dying to know everything, "So this is...headquarters."

"Yes."

"Of a rebel group trying to do what?"

"Change things."

"Start a war?"

"The war is already underway."

"So you're a terrorist organization?" She wasn't choosing her words carefully; she knew that.

"Define terrorist."

She sighed. "I've read about other attacks in the papers and seen them on tv. I always imagined that it was done by other sorts of people. Not people like you. It was always this far-away event that happened in little towns around the country, tragic events that no one could control. What do all these people call themselves?" She gestured broadly.

"A rebellion."

"And your role?"

"A soldier."

"Okay. So that guy, Pythagorus, like the mathematician, he's the boss."

"He and four others."

"Where are the other four?"

"At other bases like this one."

159

"So they give the orders, and you and everyone else carry them out."
He nodded, the dark circles under his eyes evident in the unnatural light.
"And what happens if you disagree?"
"That's not up to me. There's a bigger picture."
"And what picture is that?"
"Nothing changes unless you make sacrifices."
"Okay, so he sent you to our school from here."
"To learn more about what your government was up to at the base, yes."
"And he might send you out again whenever?"
"Yes, I must always be ready."
"When you go, can we leave too?"
"No. You won't be sent out on missions. You'll stay here."
"For how long?"
He shrugged, looking away.
"Hale!" She exclaimed.
"I don't decide."
"Well, can you try? I don't want to be here until I die!"
He nodded. "I understand."
"And you believe in this," She struggled to find a word that wasn't offensive, "cause?"
He nodded again.
"You think it's worth living in a place like this, following orders, putting yourself and others in harm's way."
"Yes."
"You're not trying to convince me."
"Why would I?"
"Because it matters to you enough to give up everything."
"I didn't have much to give up." He seemed resigned to the notion.
"Okay, but you believe this is more important than your life, choices, and everyone you care about."
"I'm a soldier. Do you know what that is?"
"A pawn in a game, it seems."
"We're more cogs in a big machine. There are things that only I can do."
"Like what?"
"That's confidential."
She sighed, rubbing her eyes. She felt mentally, physically and emotionally drained.
"Okay, practical question: Where and what do we eat?"
"Downstairs in the cafeteria. Breakfast is at 7, lunch at 1, dinner at 6."
She groaned. "Every day?"
He didn't respond, but a subtle look of sarcasm crossed his features.
"How's the food?"
"Eatable."

"And what's my role here?"

"To make yourself useful."

"And yours?"

"The same, but more."

"Are you higher up in the hierarchy here?" She indicated a ladder with her hands, "Can you ask for things from Pythagorus? He seems to like you."

"No, I don't get special requests."

"What's his first name?"

"Who?"

"Pythagorus."

"I don't know." He shrugged, as though it was a silly question.

"How long have you known him?"

He thought about it, "10 years or so."

"And you never asked for his first name?"

"He doesn't use his real name, like many here."

She grimaced. "Is Hale *your* real name?"

"It might as well be."

"Oh my God, what does that mean? This is a yes or no question."

"I don't have any other names."

Sasha massaged her temples with her fingertips. "Why do you make this so difficult?"

"I don't intend to."

"So what happens after the war? Do you all disband and walk off into the sunset?"

"Don't be naive, there's no after the war for most people here."

"That's bleak."

"You asked."

She shook her head. "And you believe in this? You want to be part of this rebellion to cause a war, and there's no after the war? What are you trying to change, exactly?"

"How much time have you spent away from that little town?"

"I'm not a total idiot, Hale; I know there are oppressed people and poverty out there and a million other problems. Is that what you're fighting for though?"

"Enough questions for tonight." He said, shutting her down.

She grumbled and dug her hands into her eye sockets. They could still hear Eva and Gabe's light-hearted voices through the wall.

"I'm going to sleep. I start training at five tomorrow. You're not tired?"

"I'm wired." She answered in a huff, though she knew she was exhausted. Crossing the room, she took a book out of her bag. He shifted to make room for her, and she moved the pillow over to the wall.

"Scoot over so I can read."

He did as he was told and lay back down, facing the wall. She lay down, facing the opposite direction, propping her head up on her elbow and holding her book flat on the bed. It was hard to read in the dim lighting, but it was better than nothing. Before she knew it, her head was down on the page. It would take weeks for it to stop feeling awkward to sleep beside each other, but when it did, neither of them could identify when or how.

Chapter 2
Dusk and Dawn

Eva

Contrary to what she initially believed of Gabe, he was not a morning person. When left to his own devices, he slept until 9 or even 10. For the same sadistic reasons that she suspected motivated every part of the training on the base, however, Old Man Petri Dish (her nickname for Pythagorus) made it clear that the non-existent hour of 5 am would now replace the concept of morning. It was warm under the blanket, and Gabe was even warmer and sweet-smelling where she lay in bliss against his chest, their legs intertwined. Then, the alarm. He groaned slightly and buried his face in her hair. The alarm clock had been set a few feet from them to encourage him to move.

"Too early, five more minutes," Gabe muttered, putting his face flat into the pillow.
"You gonna get that?" She whispered with a slight giggle. The alarm shrieked louder and louder, demanding attention. She wrapped herself tighter around him, not wanting him to leave her arms.
Gabe turned his head and opened one eye tentatively and focused on her. He smiled groggily, preparing to gather his energy to get through the day. With a final squeeze and an inhale, he pushed himself up and upright, stretching his arms out extravagantly.
"All right, I'm up!" He put the blanket back over Eva and crossed the room to the screeching cell phone on the desk. At some point during the night, he'd lost the piece of string that kept his braid in place so it cascaded gloriously behind him. He smacked down on the alarm and sighed in relief, quite loudly, at the silence afterwards.

Eva laughed. With a soft smile, she propped herself on her pillow and gathered the excess blanket underneath her chin, watching him. "Morning, babe." She sighed, followed by a much-needed stretch.

He answered the greeting with a great yawn, "Mornin' to you too. How'm I s'posed to leave you when you're lookin' at me like that?" he laughed, with another yawn. Finding a new hair tie on the table, he quickly pulled his hair up with a swift and practiced motion.

"Looking at you like what? I'm innocent." She could feel the lids of her eyes start to grow heavy again. As the days turned to weeks, they got used to life on the base. They were given daily chores around the large compound that took up every hour of every day, to the point that she hardly saw the hours go by. They were up early, regardless of the day of the week. The only reprieve was Gabe, his kisses first thing in the morning and last thing at the end of the night. Gabe waved her over at mealtimes, pulling her into conversations about a future together where they could be happy, go to concerts, go to the beach, see movies, and live normal lives. He hadn't spoken about any of that when they were dating at school, but now he spoke about them as a couple with such conviction that it melted her completely. He even joked about children.

There were also the people on the base. Most were in their 30s and 40s and were excited to meet a new face. Some of them had been here for months but most for years. Their stories gave her something to think about beyond her secret. There were people from military families, people without the means to go to university who chose to come here instead. The common denominator was that they all believed they were working towards a better world. The hows and whys were a bit fuzzy to most of them, but that was familiar to her with military families. Her dad was never forthcoming about the particulars of his missions either.

There was Stella, the weapons specialist who met her combustion engineer husband at MIT and joked that their catchphrase as a couple was "burn it." There were the tattooed cafeteria men and women who spoke a language all their own and joked that Eva was the Belle to Gabe's Beast. The cleaning staff occasionally doubled as security guards and knew everything about everyone. There were also the techs who wandered around with tablets and refused to speak to anyone but sometimes spoke to Eva or Sasha, the least useful members of the staff. There was a slew of medical personnel, nurses, doctors, and scientists. There were people of all nationalities, religious backgrounds and affiliations.

Gabe learned people's names and personalities quickly. He was unflinchingly chatty and friendly with almost everybody. He was like a butterfly, flitting between flowers. He asked her if she minded as she had at school, but she said now made her feel safer. They were in less danger if people liked them, right? The compound ran like a well-oiled machine, with deliveries coming down the giant elevator once a week on different days and times.

Much to Eva's dismay, there was no communication in or out of the base. It truly was a bunker, and they were all the equivalent of mole people, though it seemed to be a volunteer position. The only time they had together was in the late evenings.

Most evenings, she and Sasha were back before the guys, giving them the opportunity to talk. They would sit on the bed and wait for the guys to return, finding solace in the familiarity of having each other nearby.

"Do you ever wonder why there are no kids here?" Sasha asked one night. "With so many people, some of them married to each other, things will happen."

"I guess there's access to contraception?" Eva suggested, hoping not to explore the possibilities.

"I think it's more than that, maybe they're not allowed?" Sasha said.

"Change of topic, please." Eva requested, playing with the edge of her ponytail nervously.

"Bored of my theories? Well, here's some gossip: I think I have a date." Eva sat up straight. "A date?"

"Yeah, I mean, we can't exactly go for a romantic stroll on the beach or see a movie, but he invited me to sit with him at lunch tomorrow for coffee."

"Who?"

"Mike from the ES team? 'Experimental Substances', I think. He brought down a giant box of pipettes for me to wash, and we chatted." Eva looked worried. "We're supposed to lay low."

"He's nice. It's just a bit of fun. I mean, the last date I went on was with Jason."

Jason felt like a million years ago to Eva, maybe Sasha was right.

"Just be careful I guess, what's he like? " She said.

"Honestly, I don't know. He seemed to like me, though."

"Can't wait to hear all about it!"

"Don't get too excited, it's not like I have anywhere to bring him." She gestured at the room. As though on cue, the door flew open and Gabe walked in. Eva sprung up to greet him, and Sasha waved her goodbye and headed to her own room.

Sasha

Every morning at exactly four o'clock, she felt Hale was up. The fact that the alarm next door would only go off at five was irrelevant. They both lay in bed, side by side. The silence wasn't unpleasant, but she could feel how tense he was beside her. Eventually, he would get up and turn off the alarm that hadn't had the chance to ring and headed to the shower, the sound of his footsteps barely making a sound while gathering his clothes on the way. She didn't like speaking in the morning, and he didn't like speaking at all, so it seemed fitting.

She always dozed while he was in the shower but left off pretending to be asleep when he would come back out, fully dressed. The room's darkness didn't hinder him in the least, and he gathered his gun and bullet clips for target practice. She could see the water droplets slide down his face from his freshly washed hair. He brushed the drops from his cheek and went to the door, but as he passed the bed, he stopped. "You're awake." He said quietly.

"Good morning to you too." she answered, peering upwards and wiggling her foot absent-mindedly.

"Did I wake you?"

"No. I always wake up with you."

"I've noticed." He stated, "It isn't necessary."

She shrugged, one-shouldered, lying on the other arm. "I know, I just like doing it. Do you mind?"

"I'll see you in a couple of hours." His voice trailed off as he headed for the door. Sasha nodded, uttering a soft "good luck" to his retreating form. It was inevitable that seeing him first thing in the morning and his being the last person she saw before going to sleep would make her feel closer to him, wasn't it?

Mike was tall and fair, with a ginger beard and broad shoulders. His eyes were the pale blue of a morning sky. They'd just gone through the initial introductions of where they were from and what they'd studied or planned to study when the situation's absurdity slipped into the conversation.

They were sitting at the cafeteria with their trays, Sasha shivering slightly in a short skirt and t-shirt, Mike in a pair of slacks and what looked like a varsity jacket.

"So, what brings you down here?" He asked.

"Kidnapping." She semi-joked.

He laughed incredulously. "What?"

"I was supposed to be going on a trip to California, the trip of a lifetime actually, my senior year, end of a high school trip with my best friend and instead, I ended up here."

"Your best friend's the little red-haired girl?"

"Yeah, Eva."

"I have to tell you, that doesn't make a lick of sense." He had a slight accent that made the ends of his sentences rise. It suited him like he was born to ride a wave.

"I understand that Gabe didn't want Eva to be there when he blew up our town." She looked down at her fingernails, picking at her cuticle, "I was just collateral."

He shook his head. She wondered how old he was.

"It sounds pretty crazy to me too. What about you?"

"I graduated in mech tech and bio-med and then got recruited. I was analyzing medical data in a lab. Socrates found me and offered me something I couldn't refuse."

"And what's that?"

"Money. Lots and lots of it."

"Is everyone here paid?"

"The techs all are, I think, except the higher-ups. The experiments aren't; I don't think."

"Experiments?"

"Like Gabe and the guy you came in with. They're here for the rebellion, pure and simple, maybe for the room and board. I don't think you can pay anyone enough to go through what they do." He said it matter of factly, then seemed to realize he'd said too much and lowered his tone. "Sorry, I got a bit carried away."

"So they're not like everyone else here?"

"Guess that's no secret. Everyone here works with them and around them."

"Just the two of them?"

Mike seemed to backpedal. "Yeah, they've got a different status than the rest of us."

"And there are others?"

He nodded, poking at his dessert. He looked around to see if anyone was paying attention to them. Sasha wondered what happened to people who spoke out of turn here. If she was to believe Hale, nothing good. Still, her curiosity always got the better of her.

"I haven't met any others." She said.

"You will, probably. It depends how long you stay."

"What makes someone an experiment?"

"Genetics, I guess, predispositions to handling things the rest of us couldn't." He said quietly.

"How do they know about their genetics or predispositions or whatever?"

"That's a question for Pythagorus or Socrates, but I don't think they will answer." He shook his head. His eyes darted around the room.

"So, how do I get paid too?" She chuckled to lighten the mood. She'd backed him into a corner, though he was the one who had run his mouth.

"Find yourself a skill."

She laughed. "Wanna teach me to be a scientist?"

"What did you want to study?"

"Literature, maybe the arts."

He smiled. "How old are you again?"

"Old enough." She shrugged. She was Hale and Gabe's age as far as she knew, and that didn't stop everyone here from acting as though they were fungi in petri dishes. Why would her age matter?

He shrugged his jacket off his shoulders and handed it to her. "You look cold."

"Thanks. I packed for California." She let him put it over her shoulders. It smelled masculine and clean.

"Any chance of a second date?" He asked. "Maybe something where I don't upset you?"

People had started to leave, and she realized their time was up. This was the dating world in the headquarters of a rebel base.

"You didn't upset me. I appreciate you telling me the truth. It means a lot to me."

"So, is that a yes?"

"Sure." She agreed. "Not like I'm doing much else around here."

He laughed, and it was the sound of sunshine. "I had a nice time Alexandra."

"Sasha." She corrected him. "Bye, Mike."

Chapter 3
Experimentation

Eva

They'd been playing a card game called bullshit, the three of them killing time late into the night. Sasha and Gabe bantered at each other like siblings, each competing for Eva's attention. It almost felt normal: enthusiastically throwing cards on the bed, shouting, laughing, teasing each other. Somehow, it descended into cards down Gabe's sleeve, which evolved into him without a shirt and quickly yet predictably concluded with Gabe pulling Eva towards him and kissing her.

"I'm done. Too much bullshit for me." Sasha resigned scathingly, tossing her cards down. She stomped out, slamming their door shut behind her.

Eva pulled away from Gabe just in time to hear the door close.

"Babe, we've got to stop doing that. It isn't fair to Sasha," She said gently, doing a horrible job of concealing a smile as they kissed.

His eyes flickered open long enough to take a peek at her face, their noses inches from each other. "How's it not fair, babe? Ain't ya heard the old expression, all's fair in love and war?"

She shook her head slightly. "It's like we're flaunting it." She sighed heavily and wrapped her arms around his waist. "I'm just saying that we should cool it when other people are around." She couldn't help but grin at him, which undermined her statements quite a bit.

He laughed aloud. "I am flaunting it! Flaunting you!" He pulled her completely against his torso and finally unlatched her bra, placing small kisses along her neck as a distraction. If they kept talking about Sasha, it was going to kill the mood. She tasted sweet, soft and warm.

"I'm serious, babe," She said. "I wanna try and make things as bearable as possible for all of us. We don't need to make them more uncomfortable." She closed her eyes and allowed herself to enjoy the kisses.

He ended his chain of kisses down by her collarbone. "All right," he finally complied, propping himself up and pushing her hair behind her ear. "What d'you wanna change? I ain't tarin' your clothes off and tossin' 'em at 'er. Ain't she with Mike from mechanics anyway?"

"They've had coffee a few times, but they aren't dating, and it was SE...or something, experimental substances? Besides, I'm positive that she's into Hale. She denies it, but I've seen how she looks at him."

He scoffed, stroking her side absent-mindedly. "Alexandra's got her quirks, but she ain't crazy. Hale's never going to let that happen."

"I don't think it's crazy for her to have a thing for him." She said softly. "Although, I doubt Hale would ever make a move on her. He's just not that perceptive."

"Or maybe he just ain't into this kinda thing." Gabe noted.

"Maybe," She gazed up at the ceiling thoughtfully. "There's only one way to find out."

He rolled over to invade her line of vision. "Whatcha cookin' up there, babe?"

"I think we should see if we can get them together." She smiled, fairly proud of herself.

"How?" He didn't drop the cynicism in his tone. He kept planting kisses on her lips, brief but taunting, a drop of pleasure.

"I'll talk to Sasha, and you'll see if Hale can be coaxed out of his shell."

"Switch roles?" He laughed, obviously feeling he'd drawn the short end of the stick.

"Not a chance." She said playfully. "Hale would never listen to a word I said."

"Fine, fine. Whatever you want, Princess. Are we done talking about other people yet?"

"Yup." She said in a pleased tone. With a slight stretch, she lay back in a more comfortable position.

Sasha

Loneliness. It was the middle of the night, with nothing but the humming of the pipes and air conditioning to keep her company. Mike was nice, and Eva was important, but all of this hurt; it ached under her rib cage throughout the day, but tonight, it was all too much. She sobbed as quietly as she could, but the more she allowed herself to think about her predicament, the more it hurt.

"Is everything alright?" Hale said quietly as he sat up.

She jumped and inhaled, startled. She'd been so caught up in feeling miserable that she forgot Hale was even there. She hadn't meant to wake him up. She swallowed thickly before answering, "It's nothing." It came out muffled and thoroughly unconvincing.

"It doesn't appear that way." He said a little more forcefully.

She sat up, pulling her knees to her stomach and wrapping her arms around them, eyes open to stare into the blank canvas of the dark room.

"I just—" she stuttered, "I hate how cold it is here, and I miss Mila, and I miss my cat and my bed and every morning it's the same thing with nothing to look forward to and nothing to wake up to and I miss sunlight and open windows and sky-I miss sky and-" She had to inhale because speaking with one's nose blocked was proving difficult "and I miss my mom." The thought of her mother brought on a whole new wave of tears. "God, I'm so pathetic," she sobbed.

He was quiet for a moment, then promptly tossed the blankets off himself and stood up in a single motion. "You aren't pathetic. Take a walk with me," He braced himself against the wall and stepped towards the door.

She shivered a little and apprehensively staggered to her feet: "Where are we going?"

"The third floor." He said as he stepped out into the hall. The dim emergency lights flickered slightly, giving the narrow space an eerie feel. He paused on the staircase, "This way."

She followed, a little dazed, at first at a distance, eventually deciding that she was more scared of her surroundings than of Hale. She rubbed her fingers over her shoulders and forearms. They entered a stock room she hadn't been to before, thick with dust and full to the brim with packing crates. Carefully, he navigated his way around the obstacles and she followed. A blue-tinged light brightened the further they got into the room until finally, they were met with a massive round window way above, giving way to a dark desert sky filled with pinpricks of light. In the distance, the moon hung suspended amongst thousands of stars. Dust was rising and swirling, seeming sentient.

She struggled to squeeze between crates, following the iridescent and steady light, so different from the artificial bulbs in the rest of the compound. She finally stumbled over the last crate and coughed a little, looking up. Her breath caught. Standing in the illuminated circle, she wanted to float upwards and press her fingers to what she imagined to be cool glass, devouring the sight. She sat on the floor, craning her neck upwards, gazing up for what seemed like forever.

"This is what I wanted to show you." She heard Hale say cautiously. She tore her gaze from the window and saw him leaning against the wall, watching her from a distance.

With a small nod, she uttered, "Thank you. It's amazing."

He'd made it better. The weight inside her had lessened.

"You're welcome, we should be heading back, though; being caught here would not end well,"

She got up but stayed in the circle, "Already?" It was eerily quiet, amplifying their voices.

He nodded. "Yes, guards patrol the area." He motioned for her to follow.

With one last glance, she turned away, though she needn't go far since the crates created such a narrow area. She emulated his steps to navigate the room. As they reached the door, he turned to check that she was keeping up, and she felt a pang in her chest. Without letting herself think about it, she lifted her arms and hugged him. She felt so grateful all of a sudden, that he wanted to share this with her, that he cared enough to make her feel better.

"What is this for?" He said, frozen.

She let go, taking a step back, unsure. "It's a hug. It doesn't need an explanation."

"If you say so." He said calmly, looking away. "Shall we?" He had the slightest hint of a smirk, like he'd played out some complex plan. Beaming at him, she let him lead the way, keeping close, down the steps and through the hallway, pausing now and again to ensure there weren't any guards in the vicinity. The emergency lights were still on. She tried to hold onto that moment, to cement it in her mind as they walked. He glanced at her with a strange expression.

"Here," he said when they reached their door. She heard the exhaustion in his voice as he swung open the door. "Are you okay now?" he asked. "You aren't usually quiet."

"Just tired," she smiled sheepishly and took her spot on the bed, turning the pillow over to the dry side. Lying down, she mumbled, "good night." with half-open lids.

"Good night." He said softly, lying beside her. He pulled the covers over them both.

Eva

Training picked up slowly and took a hard left to impossible for Gabe. They wanted him to start something he called "simulation training" and insisted he was already way behind. He would need to be in top physical condition to start; they'd said, since it would put such a massive strain on everything else.

"You should write to Socrates. Tell him you didn't sign up for this." She told him one night, as he rubbed the soreness out of his legs.

"Pythagorus calls the shots here, and if I write to Socrates, it'll just paint me as weak," he told her. He said it didn't matter. He said he would exceed expectations. He said men like them always had low expectations for people like himself. She admired his commitment, but she worried.

It was a few weeks into that training when he returned to the room hours after midnight, holding a bloody tissue to his face. He looked like he was struggling to stay on his feet.

"Sorry, I'm late." He said by way of greeting.

She and Sasha had been sitting on the bed chatting, worrying, Sasha cross-legged, leaning against Eva. Her friend had been in the middle of a long rant about the cold, it was one they all heard from her often. Sasha stopped and put her hand over her mouth.

"Gabe! Are you alright?" Sasha grabbed her hand and squeezed it.

"Yeah no worries babe, just bleedin',", he managed with a smirk. "Tough day on the job and all that."

He almost looked drunk, staggering into the room.

He sat at the edge of the bed, to avoid staining the sheets and leaned his head back to try and get the blood to coagulate. "How're you two?"

"Shocked," Sasha replied, "You sure you're okay?"

"Never seen a nosebleed before?" Gabe teased.

Sasha swallowed thickly and let go of Eva's hand, "You should probably lie down," She climbed off the bed and headed for the door. "Call us if it's something serious."

"Will do." Eva said, scooting over to make room. Gabe leaned back and sprawled out on the bed, his head on Eva's lap. Dark eyes glanced upwards.

"I'm alright; it'll stop when it's ready. Pretty nasty, huh?"

"Luckily, I'm not the squeamish type." That wasn't entirely true. Right now, she could smell the combination of copper blood and sweat on him. She runs her fingers through the loose strands of hair around his forehead.

"It's some stupid simulation they got me on. They've got their balls in a twist that I can't handle it." His n's sound like m's, and his d's sound like b's as he tried to swallow and breathe simultaneously. He leans towards the soft touch of her fingers, ready to fall asleep right then and there.

"You'll just have to prove those dickwads wrong then, won't you?" A small mischievous grin creeps across her lips, but she's sure it isn't convincing.

He mirrors the smile, twitching his nose a tad as he finds that the blood has finally stopped flowing. The shadow of a smile vanishes as some other thought crosses his mind. "I dunno, babe, I'd rather throw in the towel and function like a fucken human being. I'm not sure anyone can get through this and keep their minds intact. I think I'm a good soldier without it. I don't like them messing with my brain like that."

"What do you mean?" Her voice is nearly a whisper. She knows it's supposed to be confidential, but how was she meant to help him if she didn't even know what these "simulations" were?

He closes his eyes, as though reliving something, "It ain't that I can't do it, I could probably get to where they want me to be, but I wouldn't come out of it the same. That thing's made for somebody who ain't got no regrets. Physical pain, no problem, but this is some twisted mindfuck and," he trails off. "Sorry, babe, I don't wanna freak you out."

"It's okay; I can handle it." She tries to sound strong, but she's not being entirely truthful. She wants him to reassure her that he can handle anything. She knows who he fights for, the demons of his past. When she was alone with those memories, those people seemed like myths, as though she'd made them up, but the fact that he could see them too, remember their voices, remember them as real people, it made them real, it made their deaths real too.

He inhales, swallows, and exhales. "I don't wanna let them down, or you." He opens his eyes again and they're bloodshot. He's searching for comfort and salvation. The guilt feels like it's going to swallow him whole tonight.

"You won't. I know you won't." She says with conviction. She leans in and plants a soft kiss on his lips. He lifts his head a little to meet her halfway.

"Thanks, babe. You always know just what to say." He pulls himself up, wanting more but he's too tired to follow through. She lets him sleep, but her worries keep her up. There would never be a good time to tell him her secret, but she was running out of time.

Sasha

The door to the adjoining room closed firmly behind Sasha, and she let out a sigh. The sight of blood always made her queasy. She startled at the unexpected light in the room, the screen from a laptop casting a glow, shadows playing across the sparse furniture and the edges of a familiar face.

"Oh my god Hale, you scared me! I didn't know you were back."

Most of the conversation across the wall is audible, save for Eva's whispers which come through as mumbled.

"Welcome back," he says.

"Thanks. Guess you heard what's going on next door?" She crosses the room and sits in front of her suitcase to dig around for her pajamas.

He nods, "Some." His voice is steady but fatigued. "How are they?" He continues to gaze at his computer screen. She sighs, sitting on her knees

on the ground. "Gabe came back looking like hell and with his nose bleeding. I'm guessing you guys don't have the same training schedule?"
"No, we train separately." He states calmly, "Though when I heard where he was going for afternoon training, I knew it wouldn't be easy."
"What did they do to him?"
"I assume they had him do a simulation designed to make us more efficient. It's a very involved procedure." He turns his chair around to face her and meets her steady gaze.
She can't help showing her disdain. What an empty answer. "How involved exactly?"
"Extremely, the electrodes send electrical impulses to the brain, which can be excruciatingly painful. They try to isolate the part of the brain responsible for memory. Sometimes, it's like watching your life being played out in front of you. Other times, just nightmares. Once you've moved past that, they focus on situations you might face in battle."
She takes in the information, looking down at her hands in thought. Their training was strange. She didn't think reliving her life in flashes would make her nose bleed. There was more to it than that.

"Why did it hurt him so much?"
"Perhaps he didn't like what he saw. The images you have in your brain affect you physiologically. You can't make strategic or objective decisions in a fight if you allow your feelings to get in the way." He says softly. He rubs his left temple as though warding off a headache. She snaps out of her thoughts, and looks up sharply with the realization: He knows all this because he's lived it. She suddenly feels terribly guilty; How could she have been so insensitive?
"Is there anything else you'd like to know?" He asks.
"I'm sorry. I didn't mean to pry."
"It's fine." He says flatly. He looks agitated, his hands gripping his knees.
"It's something he'll adjust to, right? I mean, it's not insurmountable."
She wants him to talk about it, even though she knows he doesn't want to - was that what he dreamt of at night? Was this part of what she'd seen when he fought Jason? That "turning off your feelings" thing?
"It does take time, but I'm sure he'll manage." He nods slightly as if convincing himself. "He's more capable than I was."
His confirmation hit like a stab to the chest. She stays quiet and still, afraid he might not say anything more if she exhales too quickly.
"I was much younger when I started simulations, it got easier." She knew he'd never told anyone this before; the candor surprised her. She'd lived with him long enough to read his moods. It was subtle, but he gave himself away just like anyone else. Right now, he looked afraid.
"How likely are they to stop if it gets too much?"

He fidgets in his seat, "Not likely; it's not how Pythagorus operates."
She nods, trying not to cry. "Is it over now? You don't have to do it
anymore?" She's biting her lower lip, digging her nails into the palms of
her hands.
"Not in the same way that Gabe does. Look, we should change the
subject if it upsets you."
"It doesn't upset me! It makes me angry! I hate what they do here!" she
exclaims, tears welling up in her eyes, which she brushes away with her
sleeve. "It doesn't mean I don't want to know. You shouldn't have had to
go through that! You definitely shouldn't have had to when you were
"younger" she adds finger quotes on the word, "You shouldn't have to
do any of this!"
"We do what we have to in order to end this war." He says, trying to
calm her down. "We both accept that."
"The war doesn't even have to happen!"
"It's happening right now. Just because you lived in an isolated little
town, it doesn't mean the rest of the country had it the same as you. I've
seen it for myself. Your government is corrupt, and we're responsible for
bringing peace."
She sighs and drags the palms of her hands over her face. "I know you
believe in this, okay? It doesn't make it any easier. I'm not okay with your
sacrifice." She gets up from the floor and sits on the bed.
"Call it what you will." He says and joins her on the bed. "Let's get some
rest."

She snaps off her bra from under her shirt and tosses it atop her suitcase
in agreement. This might have embarrassed them both a few months
ago, but now it felt companionable. They found their respective positions
on the small bed, each carrying their anxieties.
"Can I ask you something?" She says into the dark.
"I suppose." He answers sleepily.
"Why do you feel responsible for anything having to do with the war?
You didn't start it. You're no more responsible than anybody else.
We're not even old enough to vote. What do you do it all for?" She
yawns mid-sentence, covering her mouth with the back of her hand.
"It's the only thing I've ever strived for." He answers, "I'd always wanted
to be a soldier."
"Why?"
"The man who cared for me as a child was a soldier. I wanted to be like
him."
"Your father, you mean?"
"No, I don't think that's what he was."
"Did he work for Pythagorus too?"

"No, we didn't live in a base. He lived alone with me."

"And did he want you to be a soldier too?"

"I don't know what he wanted. He died before I was old enough to ask. He would go on missions and tell me he'd be back. Pythagorus found me at the apartment when he didn't come back; he offered me somewhere to go and something to do, so I did, and that's what I've been doing since."

She wished she were more awake. This was everything she'd ever wanted to know about him; she had so many more questions. Who was his mother? Who was his father if it wasn't the man who cared for him when he was little? Who was the man? How did Pythagorus find him or even know to find him? She didn't ask any of her questions. There would be other opportunities, she hoped. He'd shared so much with her tonight. "You're worth more than that, you know." she mumbled blearily.

Chapter 4
Games, Narcotics and Neurotransmitters

Eva

It was barely 7 o clock one evening when Gabe suddenly bounded into Sasha's room with more energy than he'd had in weeks. The door was open, and the girls had been sharing grievances. He pounced loudly and clumsily through the door and onto the bed with a "CHARGE!" landing precisely on top of Eva.

Sasha had been sitting with a pillow propped up against the wall to lean on and rubbing cream into her fingers. She squeaked and jumped off the bed in one terrified rabbit-like motion, slipped on the metal floor, and landed on her butt, "Gabe!"
"Why hello there." he chuckled, looking down at a wide-eyed Eva.
"Hi, babe!" Eva said in a shocked tone. She wrapped her arms around his warm frame and pulled him closer. "You're back early." She couldn't help but be pleased, regardless of Sasha's annoyance. She had so little time with Gabe these days.

Hale appeared in the hallway. "Hello," he said stoically, closing the door behind him.
Still sitting on the floor, Sasha looked up with a smile, her mood instantly brightening. "Hey!" She chirped brightly. "Are you guys playing hookie?"
"I was given the evening off. I assume Gabe was as well."
Eva pulled away from Gabe, who'd been planting little kisses down her neckline, a little breathless. "So how'd you escape from the claws of Dr.Evil?" Eva inquired.
"With undeniable charm and brilliant choreography." Gabe snickered. He lifted himself, tossing his hair over his shoulder. He leaned back against the wall where Sasha's pillow was still propped and made himself comfortable. He kicked his shoes off; each shoe landed with a dull thud.
Sasha got up in a huff. "Okay, you two, make room; that's my bed you're hogging!"
"Finders keepers." Gabe laughed, "round here, if you want territory, you gotta claim it as your own."
"How colonial of you." Sasha teased. "Whatever! We've got time today. What are we doing with it?"
"Well, dunno about you. We're never bored." Gabe teased, "I ain't had a day off since we left school, and that wasn't s'posed to be time off either.

What's there to do around here?" He was looking at Hale as though there was any chance he'd be helpful in this.

"If it's entertainment you're looking for, you won't find it," The tall boy stated factually.

Eva moved closer to Gabe. "Here Sasha, come claim some space."

Taking a spot on the bed, Sasha said, "We should play a game."

"Sure, whatever you say ladies." said Gabe.

"Not Never Have I Ever." Sasha suggested, remembering the last time they'd played that game, in another life at Jason O'Neil's house.

"Something fun." Gabe responded..

"A gentleman and a scholar." Sasha muttered. "Okay Eva, your pick."

"I was going to suggest "guess the lie," but maybe truth or dare?" Eva said.

Hale sat in the only chair in the room and shook his head, bemused.

"And what do I get when I win?" Gabe inquired.

"How do you win truth or dare?" Sasha sighed.

Eva giggled, "You don't win. The point is to answer the questions honestly if you pick the truth, and do whatever dare the other person throws at you." She cracked her knuckles.

"You in?" Sasha asked Hale, looking happier than she'd seen her in a long time.

"I don't suppose you're giving me a choice, are you?" He said in a somewhat defeated tone.

"Nope! It'll be fun, don't look so miserable. Truth or dare, Gabe?"

"And I can't win?" Gabe insisted teasingly.

"If you do the dare or tell the truth, you win." Eva said helpfully.

"Then I already won."

"Gabe, pick one!" Eva laughed.

He looked up dramatically. "Man, what a choice. Can I buy a vowel?"

"Gabe!" Sasha chided. "Just play!"

"Dare."

"Argh! I was thinking of a Truth."

"Did she lose yet?" Gabe mocked.

"Fine, I dare you to stand on your hands for 5 minutes."

"That's easy." he shrugged. "What do I get if I do it?"

"Nothing. That's not the point."

"Come on babe, everyone likes a reward." He directed the latter at Eva.

With that, he got up, gave himself a little momentum and stood easily on his hands against the further wall. Upside down, he cocked his head to the side. "Now what?"

Eva burst out laughing. "You stay there for five minutes, and then you get to ask someone else a question."

"Fine! Hale, I dare you to outstand me!" Gabe challenged.

Sasha giggled, covering her mouth. "You must first ask him 'truth or dare?'."

"Truths are for cowards!" Gabe announced, tapping his socked foot against the wall behind him.

"Fine." To Eva's surprise, Hale muttered and took his place on the wall next to Gabe. He flipped himself upside down easily.

"You look like bats." Eva said with a laugh.

Sasha took this opportunity to take Gabe's spot on the bed.

"Hey! Babe, that's gotta be against the rules."

"Claiming my territory Gabe." Sasha said.

"Of course, you are a white girl!"

Eva often felt that they competed for her attention, and as flattering as that was, it also came with guilt. "So you guys now have to stand there until one of you gives up. Your turn Hale."

Hale just scowled.

"What'll it be, Sasha?"

"Dare I guess? Can't have the guys showing us up." She said, laughing. "But I can't stand on my hands at all."

"Don't go easy on her." Gabe suggested, changing from one hand to the other to ease the muscles in each arm.

Hale's mop of dark hair made him look like he'd been electrocuted. He looked to be thinking of a dare. "Go and take something from the laundry room."

"Ummm, okay." Sasha shrugged. "Eva, tape this. I don't want to miss the finale." She said, running out. Meanwhile, Gabe reached for Hale's elbow, carefully poking at him.

"I suggest you stop trying to cheat," Hale stated, the closest thing she'd ever heard to him whining.

Sasha returned quickly, triumphantly holding a pillow. Coming back inside, she cracked up in the doorway. "I can't believe they're still standing!"

"I wouldn't call this standing. I swear to God, man, give up already! I'm losing brain cells." Gabe retorted.

"Eva, Truth or Dare?" Sasha asked, tossing the pillow to her.

"Dare!" Eva said enthusiastically. She straightened herself up.

"We can come to an agreement at any time," Hale said.

"Mmm, dance the spice girls dance from your grade 8 recital and sing it too. Upside-down performance coming right up, guys."

"Okay, what kind of agreement? You got nothing riding on this; I'm getting a favor tonight. I can also annoy you till you cave. I know a lot of songs that never end." Gabe tried.

"Wannabe or Spice up your life?" Eva asked, smirking.

"Wannabe of course." Sasha snickered.

"Bow out now, and I won't shoot you later." Hale growled in Gabe's direction.

Gabe scoffed. "Yeah, with the same gun I got; see who draws first, cowboy."

"Guys shut up; Eva's gonna sing." Sasha quipped.

Eva shook her head, "I wouldn't call what I'm about to do singing." She sighed and started swaying her hips and singing the lyrics to the best of her ability. After a few minutes of shaking her butt and singing the dumbest lyrics ever invented, she stopped. "Alright, boys, new round, you can stop now." She smiled at Gabe. "Babe, truth or dare?"

"Hell no, he's gotta put his feet down first. Dare, obviously, but man, not that again."

Sasha laughed, "I think it was a good idea."

"Give it up, boys." Eva sighed. "Truth or dare, babe?" She repeated.

"This is ridiculous; we both go down on three," Hale scoffed impatiently.

Gabe shrugged, which was strange when his shoulders were preparing to give up. Sasha had fished her camera out of her bag and snapped a picture.

"What happened to the count of 3?" Gabe asked, with a whine in his voice.

"1, 2, 3?" Sasha counted.

On three, Hale lowered himself down and took his place in the chair.

"The winner by 5 seconds!" Gabe crowed his victory and stood right side up, flexing his shoulders.

"Okay, back to business. Truth or dare?"

"Dare," Gabe repeated, then stopped suddenly as he ran his hand over his upper lip, his fingers smeared in blood. "All your fault Alexandra."

Hale stood. "I think this game's gone on long enough."

"Way to kill the mood, buddy. It's just a nosebleed." Gabe shrugged. Sasha looked apologetic.

"Guess we better head out." Sighed Eva as she scrambled off the bed. "See you guys later." Gabe was quick to follow. Tonight, they might even have time just to talk. She'd missed that, just lying beside him, no exhaustion, no plans to concoct, no proximity of death. She wanted to keep talking about their beach house. "Night, you two. Don't get too gloomy without us." Gabe took Eva's hand on the way out the door and twirled her around for a kiss in the hall.

Sasha

Hale sighed as he watched them leave. "What was the point of all of that?" He questioned.

"Well, it was supposed to be fun." Sasha said, slumping down in the bed. The room was nearly silent, laughter still resonating in the hall. "I'm sorry we dragged you into it, and I'm sorry if I added to Gabe's situation."

"There's no need to apologize. I suppose the point of those kinds of activities escapes me."

She shook her head. "What would you rather spend your night off doing? Standing on your hands, isn't it I guess, I can't even get myself upside down you know." She stretched her hands upwards to make a point of it, the remnants of her good mood remaining.

He smirked slightly, "I suppose not. Did you have something in mind?"

She laughed lightly; that was the closest to innuendo a conversation between them could get, and she wasn't even sure he knew it was how it sounded to her. "Anything that can get you to relax is fine by me. Gabe wanted a massage. Does that sound relaxing, or would you just be uncomfortable?"

"I wouldn't know."

Sasha clapped enthusiastically. "You have to sit down first."

He sat down on the bed. "Now what?"

She perched behind him and put her hands on his shoulders. "Now you close your eyes, trust me, and tell me to go up or down if I'm missing something. Don't be tense. It's not helping." She said after a few seconds.

He closed his eyes as instructed and let his shoulders drop slightly.

She rubbed his neck and shoulders with her thumbs, glad that he was turned away from her. She knew she was blushing furiously.

"How's that?" She asked, smiling.

"That's fine," He said. When she was done, she wrapped her arms around his neck. "There. You're about 3.5 percent less of a grouch. Now if I do that every day for the rest of your life, you may figure out what a game is."

He scoffed but kept his eyes closed. "Doubtful."

That night, she was jolted awake with an elbow to the ribs. Her bedmate was thrashing around, muttering something that sounded vaguely like a foreign language. She could see his eyes darting behind his eyelids. He looked in pain.

"Hale, hey, wake up." She put a hand on his shoulder, sitting up. He was burning hot to the touch.

He bolted upright, eyes wide and panicked, breathing like he'd run a marathon. It took him a few moments before all the data was retrieved. "What?" He whispered in a strained voice, his right hand still grasping the bed frame.

"You were dreaming." Sasha uttered in a hush, looking at him with concern. Shaken and disoriented, he moved her hand off of him. The sheets were bunched up in a pile around him. He extracted himself from the fabric and tossed half over the other side of the bed.

He sat upright, "How did you know?"

"You weren't speaking English." she answered. She kept a steady gaze on his face, trying to decipher his thoughts. The blanket was damp with sweat.

"I wasn't speaking English?" He questioned. He slumped down, scanning the ceiling tiles in the darkness, taking deep gulps of air.

"What scared you so much?" She kept observing him while his breathing stabilized.

"Something I did a long time ago," He said, his voice regaining its usual tone. "It's nothing; get some rest." He said softly and closed his eyes again.

"Hale, " She lay back down facing him. "It's not nothing. You might feel better if you talked about it." He shrank back from her, but they were already in such close proximity that there wasn't too far to go.

The words came out slowly. "Sometimes I don't think you realize what I am, what I'm supposed to be training to do."

"What do you mean?"

"I'm a killer." He let the words fill the empty spaces in the room. "Not all of the people I've killed deserved to die." His hands balled into fists.

"I know that already. Did you have a choice?"

"Perhaps I had a choice in some way, but it seems more likely that this path chose me."

"But you wouldn't kill, " she paused on the word for a moment, "someone who you don't think deserves it." It came out as a statement more so than a question. "If you could choose." Was she asking him if he was a sociopath? A psychopath? There were definitely enough red flags that should've been going off in her head that weren't. She laid her hand over his fist.

"If I could choose what?" He slipped his hand from underneath hers, placing it directly beside it.

"If you had a choice, you wouldn't kill anybody." she reaffirmed.

"No, I wouldn't," he answered with a heavy voice. She wanted to believe he was someone better than he thought he was, that he was like the boys she'd dated or been friends with in her hometown. "Now, can we get some rest?"

"You know you're still a kid, Hale. You could have a different life."

"No, I can't. There's a lot about me you don't know, and I'm not a kid."

"I might if you told me." She muttered under her breath. "And the fact that you're offended at being called a kid rather than a killer is beyond messed up."

"Good night Sasha."

"Sweet dreams," she let out, keeping her eyes open and tucking the bottom of her half of the blanket under her feet. She was still awake as he dozed off.

Eva

The sound of dozens of washers and dryers spinning their loads in a chorus of tumbles made it hard to hold a conversation. On the bright side, this was the warmest place in the compound, where the pipes that heated the maze of hallways and the massive hanger above it criss-crossed over the high ceiling and the machines whirred day and night to keep up with demand. Sasha emptied another bag of clothing and sheets into a machine and let her hands drop to her sides, rubbing her shoulders.

"This is the job that never ends," Sasha sang loudly, her voice echoing in the large space over to her friend in the next aisle of washers. Eva knew that Sasha didn't hate laundry as much as she hated regular inventory, but whining was something of a sport to her. It filled the silence that often fell between them these days. They both have a lot on their minds.

"And it goes on and on, my friend!" Eva replied.

"I didn't even know we had this many people in this catacomb." Sasha shuts the lid with conviction and crosses over to the next row of washers, propping herself up against the machine next to Eva.

"Is that the last of it?"

Eva chuckles. "Well, we're out of washers, so if it isn't, whoever tossed their shit late isn't getting it today. At least it stopped smelling like dirty men in here." Indeed, the room now smelled of soap, which Eva greatly appreciated. Finally, a smell that didn't make her gag. She hadn't actually thrown up as often as she would've expected, but she was in a constant state of unease.

"I'll go check, I guess." Sasha crosses the room to the laundry shoot on the far wall, pausing to put her weight on the heavy lever. The door lifts with a jolt, and with a wet smack, a bundle of white cloth smeared in red falls to the cement floor. Sasha jumps, backing away from it. "What the hell?" she squeaks, backing up into a machine with her hand over her mouth. Suddenly, the room seems to drop by 10 degrees. "That's a lot of blood." She stutters the obvious, eyes wide.

The stench is almost too much to handle, but Eva approaches slowly, "There's so much of it, what's going on up there?" She takes shallow breaths through her mouth. Sasha stops grimacing and looks away, turning to Eva. "I dunno, but I've got a terrible feeling." She grabs her friend's hand and leads the way to the stairs.

"Please don't be them. Please don't be them. Please don't be them." Eva's thoughts repeat like a mantra. In a mad dash, they stumble down the stairs to the main floor, the sounds of shuffling feet somewhere above them warning them that they aren't the only ones in a panic. They skid to a halt at the top of the stairs. "Where do we go?" Eva cries through ragged breaths.

There are footsteps down the hall, they stop a few feet away. Eva looks up at the tall, red-haired figure, a pleasant face with a worried expression. "Alexandra, Evangeline, what are you two doing here?" The tension in his voice is obvious.

"Mike!" Sasha cries, relieved. She dashes up for a hug. "What's going on?" She asks. She steps back to stand beside Eva and grabs her hand.

"We got a ton of blood down in the laundry room." Eva says, her voice still shaky, her words coming out too quickly. He looked down at his feet.

"There's been an accident." He says deliberately, "Someone was shot." Eva's body feels completely numb. "Do you know where Gabe and Hale are?"

Mike shakes his head.

Sasha scowls at him. "It's funny how everyone in the facility picks up the same mannerisms. You all look down at the floor when you're lying. Please, Mike, tell us whatever you know." She pleads, her hand gripping Eva's.

"I heard that one of the experiments shot one of the guys from the electrical unit," he sighed heavily. "There was some kind of fight going on before that. The shot was what broke it up." The numbness gives way to fear as Eva holds on to Sasha's hand for dear life.

"What about Gabe?"

"He was part of the fight." Sasha nods. "Thanks, Mike. We're gonna go find out what's going on."

Tugging her friend behind her, Sasha bolts past him and up the next flight of stairs. Eva tears her gaze away from Mike's stern face and follows on shaky legs.

"If they're answering to Pythagorus, we can't see them. If Mike's right, they'd be in the medical wing." Sasha reasons aloud, "Let's go check the rooms first."

Eva nods. She tells herself this is no time to fall apart, but of course, telling yourself that never actually keeps you from falling apart. Their feet pound the metal steps and their breathing prevents any more conversation and they finally reach their desired floor. Their sweaty hands let go of one another as each girl reaches for her own door. Sasha turns the knob to her room first with a quick flick of her wrist, and it jams.

"It's locked?!"

The rooms are never locked. Eva tries her own door, it opens. The light is on. She dashes into the room but is greeted by silence. She runs back into the hallway.

"Sasha. I'm going to check the med wing."

Sasha hesitates. "Wait!" She pounds on her door. "Hello!"

"You wait here then." Eva says, turning to make her way down the hall. "I'll be back in a bit." She doesn't look back. She rounds the corner and bumps into someone's chest. Mike puts out both arms to catch her before she can hit the floor. "Whoa, you alright?"

"I'm going to the medical wing. Gabe is there, isn't he?" Mike nods. Her heart nearly jumps out of her chest.

"Sasha's door is locked." she states. "It doesn't lock from the inside." Mike holds up his set of keys. "I'll take care of it."

Eva can't think of Sasha right now, she needs to find Gabe.

"Thanks Mike."

Sasha

Sasha had sunk to her knees by the door, her forehead on its metal frame. She hears the footsteps before she sees him and looks up; Mike again, holding a set of keys. He really was her hero.

"These should work." With a soft click, the door unlocks. Mike asks her gently if she wants him to stay. She hesitates. The room is dark. Why lock an empty room? As she gets up off the floor, she squints through the pillar of light cast from the hallway, terrified by what she might find.

"They probably just locked him in there to calm him down." Mike says. Sasha grimaces.

"Thanks Mike, I'll take it from here." She can't help the bitterness in her tone.

He nods and slips the keys back in his pocket. "I wasn't here, okay?" She nods, her heart racing.

She slips into the dark room, her fingers on the lightswitch. "Hello?" she tries again into the silence. She hears a shuffling on the floor and just about trips on Hale.

"I'm here."

"Hale? Are you okay?" She doesn't turn the lights on but gets down on the floor instead while her eyes adjust. There's a trickle of light from beneath the door. She can see his outline sitting against the wall on the floor, his legs up into his abdomen.

"I'm fine," he says in a tired voice.

She sits beside him on the ground tentatively.

"Where's Gabe?"

"They probably took him to the fourth floor." He's struggling with his words and takes a moment to rub his eyes. She lifts her hand to his shoulder. She's looking directly into his face, what she can make of it in the darkness.

"Why was there blood?" she says it softly, trying to keep her voice steady.

"They wanted Gabe to try the serum again, for the simulations. I just wanted them to stop." Sasha's heart sinks further into the pit of her stomach.

"How did you end up back here?" She crawls over to sit beside him against the wall, reaching her arm around his shoulders, hesitantly offering comfort.

"I don't know." He answers honestly. "I was knocked unconscious." He breathes deeply. "I must have been brought here after that." He rubs the back of his head, "I was easy to knock out."

"What do you feel?" She asks.

"Guilty, how else should I feel?" His temper burns just under the surface.

"You shot somebody?" She always wants to see the good in him; she understands that it was to protect Gabe, which meant he was as powerless as she is but it's still a hard pill to swallow.

"Yes, and it didn't help in the end." She can hear the regret in his words.

"There was nothing you could do, Hale."

"It wasn't good enough."

"Stop thinking it was your fault." she says bitterly, the fear replaced by a bite in her tone.

"I could have stopped it."

"By doing what? Killing every person in the room?"

"If I knew it would make a difference, I would have." He says under his breath.

She sighs. "I'm just glad you're okay." She lets her arm drop to her side.

"How did you find out?" He asks.

"The bloody towels and clothes came down in the laundry chute. We ran up here, and Mike opened the door for me. You were locked in, by the way. He thinks you're dangerous, Pythagorus."
"I don't blame him." He says calmly.
She leans forward and looks him in the eye. "Please stop. You did what you thought you needed to do for a friend. Try to understand that this is beyond your control. Do you hear me? And if you plan to blame anyone, Pythagorus should be your primary candidate. Listen to me: You don't have to be here. You don't have to keep doing this. We can find a way out. These people don't care about you or Gabe. Look at how they're treating you!"
"There's no other way."
"Is this really what you want?"
"What I want is irrelevant."
She groans. They sit in silence. She opens her mouth several times but can't think what to say.
"You're exhausted." She finally says.
He nods slightly. He gets up and lets himself slump down on the bed, facing the wall, scooting back to make room. She lies beside him and curls up, burying her face in the back of his shirt. She matches his breathing. She dozes but struggles to sleep.

Eva

The halls seemed to pass by in a sea of gray and white. She barely knew where she was going, but the adrenaline in her veins pushed her forward. She darted up the flights of stairs and took a sharp right as soon as she reached the top. She stood before the door with a white and red sign above it, "Medical." It read ominously. Sliding through the door and closing it behind her, she inched her way inside the room. There were rows of tarped segments to create rooms for patients, but only one further into the room had personnel working. Underneath the rows of halogen lights, she could make out the sound of voices but couldn't make out what they were saying.

"Clara! Get her out of here!"A man's voice shouted. She hadn't made it two steps into the room when a tall woman in nurse's scrubs with dark hair pulled tightly into a bun intercepted her. Behind her, the flurry of activity, beeping, footsteps, talking. She was sure Gabe was back there.
"Do you have authorization?" said the woman, hands on her hips.
"I'm looking for Gabriel Wells," Eva said. There's so much activity in the room that she can barely think, let alone breathe or speak. To her left, there's a body with a white sheet over it. The fact that Clara ignores it completely suggests it isn't Gabe.

"You aren't allowed here."

"Let me see him!" She cries out in desperation, "Please!" She lunges forward.

Clara grabs the smaller girl by the shoulders and pushes her back. "You can't go there; you must leave." She says it authoritatively, but she's not much bigger than Eva.

"Kevin!" Clara calls to someone behind her. Kevin looks up, his masked face unfamiliar to Eva. Had she ever seen him in the cafeteria?

"Get her out of here Clara! She'll just get in the way!"

"I need to see him!" Eva begs. She hadn't told him about the baby - what if she never had the chance? What if this was her last chance to see him? With all her strength, she attempts to escape the nurse's hold on her. The tears start to flow as she struggles.

The woman's features soften. She's quite pretty now that Eva can see her. "Please, Miss, there's really nothing you can do for him right now. Let them do what they can." she attempts to reason with her. Before she knows what's happening, Kevin crosses the room in four long strides and shoves the tear-stricken girl forcefully back through the door as though she were nothing more than a child.

"Make sure she doesn't come back in!" he instructs Clara harshly, obviously irritated at her incompetence. Clara follows Eva through the door and slams it shut, flustered.

"I told you to listen!" she lets out her frustration.

The adrenaline is the only thing keeping her from falling into a heap on the floor. "What was I supposed to do?" She screams, but her voice is choked with tears. "I need to see him."

"Well, there isn't much to see!" Clara cries. Visibly uncomfortable, the older woman sets herself against the door and stares at Eva's torso rather than her face.

"Oh Jesus Christ and Mary above!" she exclaims. Wide-eyed, she lifts her gaze at the crying girl. Eva gasps, looking down at herself. She hadn't noticed that her sweater was unzipped, and now she was left to explain the obvious bump located just above her hips.She fumbles, "Please don't say anything." She looks the nurse in the eyes and hopes to find compassion there.

"Is he the father?" Clara asks, shaking her head.

She can manage a nod, wiping her face with her sleeve. She places one hand gently over her stomach. At least she could protect someone.

"Clear!" There's a shout from behind the door, and Clara looks ready to jump out of her skin. She pulls a packaged box of tissues from her pocket and opens it, holding it out. "Come on Miss." She tries to guide her by the shoulders towards the stairs; her accent sounds like home. "I don't know if it would help but I think you should know that it will be impossible to hide soon. You'll need to find a way to leave this facility." It was like being calmly led away from a burning building with a loved one inside.

"I know." She says softly. She looks back toward where Gabe is being treated. Everything inside her screams not to leave, but she forces her body to move toward the steps. Clara leads her down one floor and goes back upstairs. "I won't say anything." She tells her. Eva runs. She needs to get away from the horrible scene. In a matter of moments, she arrives back in the familiar hallway where she'd left Sasha. The lights in the corridor are dim. Her own room is still empty, and Sasha's door is closed. She knocks.

"Who's there?" Sasha calls out, fear in her voice. She can hear Sasha approach the door.

"Sasha, It's me." Eva shakily replies. She can see Sasha trying to twist the doorknob, to no avail.

"The door is locked. Did you find Gabe?"

"He's in the med wing." Eva whispers. There's no disguising the distress in her voice. "They won't let me see him." Eva sinks to the floor, leaning her forehead on the cold metal of the door.

"Did they say anything?" Sasha says softly.

"No, they kept telling me to leave. They had him hooked up to so many machines."

Eva sees Sasha's slide underneath the door as the sobs rise to her throat. She wants to cling to the other girl. It's the first time they cry so audibly; just to cross the barrier between them, like in a prison cell. They intertwine their fingers under the door.

"Someone's coming," Eva says, fear in her voice.

"Is it Mike?" Sasha answers hopefully, her voice thick. "He has the keys."

"I'm not sure, I'd better go." Reluctantly, she releases her grasp and stands. "I'll see you in the morning." She says solemnly. When a nightmare comes true, what can you say?

She stands in front of the door momentarily, then goes into the room she shared with Gabe just this morning. She shuts the door behind her and makes her way to the bed, curling up in a little ball. "Please be okay... Please." She whispers into the blackness, "I need you."

Chapter 5
Prayers to Father Time

Eva

The doors had been unlocked when they woke up the next morning. Hale had gone off to training as though nothing had happened. Eva couldn't bring herself to go about her day as usual, so she and Sasha had spent the hours curled up against each other, taking turns crying, trying to figure out a solution.

She could feel the blood pounding in her head. She crumpled under the weight of it all and resigned herself to becoming a puddle of mush in her best friend's lap.

"You have to tell him. As soon as he's better, you have to." Sasha said.

She whispered in a choked voice. "If I get the chance."

"He'll know what to do. He's not afraid of Pythagorus."

"Neither am I!" She exclaimed, indignant.

"Maybe we should be," Sasha mutters.

They heard the doorknob turning, and both sprang up from the bed.

In the doorway stood Gabe, wearing a hospital gown, his hair in all directions, his eyes sunken in, scratches and bruises on his arms, but there he was nonetheless.

"Hey, Princess." He smiled. Eva ran to him, nearly knocking him off his feet. He smelled of hospital, but she didn't care. He was here. He was alive.

"It's gonna be okay." He said.

"You scared us to death Gabe. Don't you ever do that again." Sasha said, smiling.

Eva, shaking all over, looked into Gabe's face. There would never be a good time. She just needed to rip the bandaid. "Gabe,there's something I really need to talk to you about."

"Good luck, hon." Sasha said, realizing this was her cue to exit. She put her hand on Eva's shoulder on her way out, and slipped out the door.

The words seemed to stick in her throat like adhesive. Gabe led her to the bed and they both sat down. Eva couldn't seem to stop crying. She tried, but her throat felt like it was closing up.

"Hey, hey." He tried to soothe her, "I'm fine." He held her until she calmed down, then went over to the desk, handed her a box of tissues. While she tried to get herself to speak, he went to the small chest of drawers and pulled on a black t-shirt and boxers.

191

"I'm okay," he repeated, "you don't need to worry. It wasn't as bad as it seemed, and they probably won't try it again. They'll adjust the dose. I'm sorry; I didn't mean to scare you."

She kept shaking her head, trying to gather her words. "Babe, I have something to tell you."

Gabe smirked defensively. "There ever been something good from that start?"

"Please." She sobbed.

"Okay, I'm listening. What is it?"

Eva took a steadying breath and began."I haven't been feeling like myself since we've gotten here." She paused, "There's no easy way to say this, I'm pregnant." She looked him straight in the eyes.

There was a deafening silence in which Eva could have sworn that the world had stopped turning and that they were now in a black hole, and her heart might have stopped. "You're..." he stopped and stuttered, tried again, " that's... amazing!" The sudden smile that spread across his face is shocking with the circles under his eyes and the bruises on him. The planet returned to its axis. There was blood in her veins, there was air in the room, there was life.

"Amazing?" The relief that washed over her felt like the pull of a bungee cord at the end of a freefall. She tossed her head back a moment. "You're crazy!"

"You're pregnant?" He repeated, just to be sure.

She wasn't sure what she'd expected, but this was definitely not it. More tears sprang to her eyes. "Yeah, we're having a baby, Gabe." She said, something close to a smile finding its way to her face.

He laughed, "Holy hell, we're having a baby! I'm gonna be a dad?" She pulled her shirt up and placed his hand on it.

"See?"

"You sure?"

She giggled, emotional whiplash making her feel unhinged. "I'm sure," she said, placing her hand over his, "You sure you're up for this?"

"I haven't got a clue in the world, but I'm sure as hell gonna try."

He leaned forward across the tiny life they'd made and kissed her, deep and longing, demanding and reassuring. She looked at him rather sheepishly and heaved a small sigh. "I was scared that you wouldn't want this. I was afraid I wouldn't even get the chance to tell you."

"Why wouldn't I?" He bent down again to kiss the path the tears had streaked down her cheeks. He kissed her eye last, laughing as he did and making her bangs move in the breeze of his breathing.

"Guess we don't need to worry 'bout much else then, huh?" She laughed.

"Well, I don't think we could have a bigger situation on our hands."

She smiled up at him. "I guess I just didn't want to be the one to tie you down, actually, that's a lie; I just didn't want to do it like this. You've never given me the impression that you wanted to settle down."

He grimaced, scrunching up the edges of his mouth. "You had me tied up way before this ever came along."

"Likewise." She mumbled contentedly. He left her reluctantly to take a shower, but she soon appeared in the doorway. They talked as they got clean, pretending it would be okay.

Sasha

Sasha was back late that day, trying to do everything on their chore list so that she and Eva didn't get into trouble. She found Hale already in the room, deep into some sort of assignment on his computer. She came in and shut the door.

"How was it today?"

"Fine."

"Did you get hauled into Pythagorus' office?"

"How did you know?"

"I asked around about 'Experiment 1'. What did he say?"

"I'm not supposed to lose control like that."

He seemed tired but better than yesterday. The devastation and guilt seemed to have been shoved to the back of his mind, like so many of his emotions. She gave him a tiny, pathetic smile, feeling her pulse quicken a little at seeing him-her pulse really did not need any more quickening today. She walked across to him.

"Gabe's back; he's okay."

He nodded as though he already knew.

"I think you should know, in case Gabe doesn't tell you," he barely glanced up. "Hale, I need you to listen right now."

Their interactions were so odd sometimes. He'd made it quite clear that nothing romantic could happen between them and even gone so far as to say they couldn't be friends, but she felt such intimacy with him. Besides, there was Mike...but it wasn't Mike whose breath she fell asleep beside, and it wasn't Mike she thought of first thing when she woke up in the morning.

"I'm listening."

She hadn't realized how long she must have paused. "Eva is pregnant."

He looked confused, as though he'd never heard the word before.

"Hale?"

"Why?"

"What?"

"She can't be."

193

"She is."

Silence hung between them. He nodded, then looked back at the keyboard and continued to type.

"What are you doing?"

"Catching up on work I didn't do yesterday."

"Are you serious right now?" He was exasperating!

He looked up at her like he had when she blew up about something trivial back in high school.

"What are you asking?" He asked calmly.

"What are we going to do?"

"Gabe needs to figure out how to get her out of here. We aren't going to do anything."

"Can't you speak to Pythagorus?"

"If I say a word, it's over. Keep your head down. Nothing good will come of this."

"What about a baby? A baby is going to come of this!" She said it in a hushed tone. God forbid Eva and Gabe heard them.

Hale shook his head. "I'll speak to Gabriel. I've made the mistake of asking for favours before, it didn't end well."

He didn't elaborate. For the first time in a long time, Sasha wished she was in the room next door.

Chapter 6
Footholds

Sasha

About a week after Gabe's time in the medical wing, Sasha and Mike sat on the stairwell for another impromptu not-quite date. He'd gotten a few snacks from the kitchens, and she was delighted to spend some time away from the tension back in her room. Work was done for the day - hours and hours of scrubbing floors and bathrooms.

"So you're over what happened last week?"

"I don't know that I'll ever get over it, to be honest with you."

"I'm glad Gabe's alright."

"Me too. It's messed up what they make them do, isn't it?"

He shrugged, his ginger hair falling into his eyes. He needed a haircut. They all did.

"Don't you think so?" Sasha continued.

"I just do my job."

"How much longer is your contract?"

"Not a whole lot longer, actually. I will probably get sent to another base in the next few months. There's work to be done with weaponry elsewhere."

"What?" She gasped.

"Yeah, this place isn't going to be here for much longer."

"How do you just drop that in so casually?" Did that mean they'd also be send elsewhere? Did that mean they could finally leave? Maybe she and Eva could get out of here after all!

"I thought you knew. I thought everyone did."

"I didn't! Hale and Gabe didn't, as far as I know."

"Gabe's still got a lot of training ahead of 'em."

"And Hale?"

Mike made a face.

"What?"

"Can I ask you something sort of personal?"

"What?"

"Are you in love with him?"

Sasha nearly choked on her chip. "Excuse me? I thought you said, *sort of personal.*"

"You seem to talk about 'em a lot."

She got up from her seat, spinning around to look at Mike. "He's my roommate."

"But he's more than that, isn't he?"

She didn't know what to say. She was sure she was bright red. "Mike, you're reading this wrong. We share a room. He's my friend. I care about him. Honestly, I'm surprised by how little everyone else does. I know he's not the easiest person to get along with sometimes, but considering his role here, shouldn't you also be invested in his well-being?"

"You're dodging the question."

"What was the question?"

"Are you in love with him?"

She ran both hands over her face and sat back down, her face buried in her forearms.

"I don't know how to answer that." She mumbled.

"It's okay."

"I'm sorry." She wasn't even sure what she was apologizing for - was he right? Did it even matter?

"It's okay. Just be careful."

He got up.

She looked up. "Where are you going?"

"Back to work."

As he began to walk away, she realized she was still wearing his sweater and quickly slipped it off her shoulders, following him with it.

"Wait!"

He stopped a few steps down. "It's okay, keep the sweater. It suits you."

She let him go, waiting for her knees to stop shaking. Hadn't she given Hale every indication that she wanted to be with him? Hadn't he been clear that he wasn't interested? It felt as though she was just making the same mistake time and time again.

Eva

It was Wednesday, though every day was much the same here. Weekends were meaningless. Eva was the first to arrive in the cafeteria. Nothing looked appetizing, but she loaded up her tray nonetheless. Having finally let the cat out of the bag was a relief, but it didn't lessen the physical and psychological weight of the situation. She was still the only one among them whose body was changing to something she didn't recognize, though now that she was hearing more about Gabe and Hale's training, she wasn't entirely convinced that was true. She kept hearing about "the serum" and "simulations" and none of it sounded promising.

Gabe arrived first, and she was glad. Being alone with Hale always made her uneasy. She felt bad for him having to grow up in a place like this, and she didn't like how people on the base avoided him, but she understood why. The long silences were awkward at best. She'd asked

Sasha about her obvious crush on him, and her friend couldn't even attempt to deny it, but that wasn't the point. If Gabe couldn't get Hale on board, Sasha's feelings wouldn't matter.

"Where's Sasha?" She asked when Gabe and Hale joined her.

"She's off with Mike." Gabe said.

She looked around. "Is she? I thought they'd sort of broken up."

Gabe shrugged. "I didn't know if they were together, but I don't see him. Where else would she be?"

"She's angry with me." Hale admitted, poking at his food with his fork.

"What did you do?" Eva demanded.

"What Gabe told me to do." He set the fork down, running his hand through his hair, his shoulders slumped.

Eva turned to Gabe, "What did you tell him?"

Gabe lifted both hands up as though she'd pointed a weapon at him, "Just that she liked him."

Hale sighed, his face suddenly tired. He straightened and rose from his seat, taking his tray with him, his food untouched. He cleared his tray into the bin and stacked his plate neatly as they'd all been assigned to do.

"Hey, where are you going?"Gabe called after him, but Hale ignored him. Gabe huffed.

"What did you say?" Eva repeated.

"That he should make a move, why is everyone pissed off at me? Wasn't this your idea?"

"My idea, not my execution." Eva sighed. "Whatever he did, it didn't go well." She bit her lower lip anxiously. She returned to the room after lunch to find Sasha still in bed, wrapped in a bundle of blankets, her hair damp from the shower and her pillow damp from tears.

"Sash, it's me, are you up?"

"Not yet." came a muffled response.

Eva walked across the darkened room and perched on the side of the bed. "Are you okay?" She said softly.

Sasha sat up, looking miserable. Her hair hung in heavy curtains around her cheeks. She rubbed her bloodshot eyes and went over to the desk where her contact lenses lay in their container. She was wearing leggings and an oversized sweater.

"That's a new shirt."

"It's Mike's."

"Gabe said you guys broke up."

With some difficulty, her friend popped the lenses in and sat back down on the bed. Eva looked away. It squicked her out a little to watch someone putting their fingers in their eyes.

"Not exactly. He basically told me I'm in love with Hale."

"What did you say?"

"I couldn't really argue."

"Oh, hon. Breakups are hard. You can't skip work, though. You know how they are here."

"Well, no one's come to check on me so far, so maybe they don't care." Her voice was hoarse.

"Seriously, are you okay?" Eva tried again, concerned. Sasha sat stiffly, not letting her get closer.

"Yeah, just tired. Guess we should get to work." Sasha said, swallowing hard.

"Duty calls." Eva agreed, trying to lighten the mood. She got up and walked towards the door.

"We're on inventory today."

"Sixth floor then." Sasha got up and put her hand up to brace herself against the wall, taking a deep breath before following Eva out the door, trying to find her footing.

The hallways were quiet, most people already at their respective posts. Sasha lagged behind her on the stairs, looking somber. Eva watched, concerned.

"I hate stairs." the taller girl let out.

"Stairs suck." Eva agreed, unsure what else to say.

They arrived at one of the larger rooms of the compound, filled with packing crates of dried goods and essentials. "You take that side, and I'll take this side?" Eva said, motioning to the wooden crates.

Sasha stopped in the doorway and sniffled, then put her hand over her mouth. Still standing in the doorway, she covered her face with her hands and let out a deep, heart-wrenching sob.

"Sasha, hey, it's okay," Eva ran to her, wide-eyed, placing her hands on her friend's shoulders, "have a seat." She said gently and guided her to one of the crates. Sasha slid to the floor with her back against the large container, tucking her legs beneath her and continued to cry. Eva had never seen her shut down like this and it frightened her. There had been plenty of opportunities for a meltdown in the past few months, so what had triggered this one?

"It's okay, just take a deep breath." She said slowly and sat down on the floor too, though it wasn't the most comfortable with the extra weight she was not carrying in the front. Sometimes, it felt more like she was carrying it on her back. "I wanna help, but you'll have to tell me what's wrong first."

Between sobs, Sasha stuttered, "If someone does something and it's not okay, but you don't tell them it's not okay, is it your fault?" She wiped her face with her sleeve.

"What are you talking about?" Eva asked, perturbed.

Sasha shook her head, "You're going to freak out."

"I won't, I promise." She swept her hand over her chest.

Looking down, the dark-haired girl dug her nails into her palms. "I don't know how to say this: last night," She shut her eyes. "He and I." she stopped.

"Did something happen with Mike?"

"It wasn't Mike." she grit her teeth as she said it.

"Something happened with you and Hale?"

She nodded vigorously, clearly trying to get herself under control.

"You guys didn't hook up? Did you?" She asked carefully.

"Sort of?" She let out a little laugh between sobs.

"How do you sort of hook up?" Eva was glad she'd stopped crying so hard but she was no less confused. Had she broken up with Mike and gone straight to Hale? Was this regret?

"I mean, it happened." Sasha still wasn't meeting Eva's gaze. She kept covering her eyes with her arm or looking at her knees.

"You don't seem happy about it." She stated the obvious, trying to get to the heart of the matter.

Sasha laughed bitterly, glancing up at Eva for the first time. "What gave it away?"

"The tears were a pretty good sign. So what happened? I would think you'd be happy. You do like him, right?" She asked softly.

"What do you mean happy? What's wrong with you?!" She snapped back, suddenly furious.

"Nothing's wrong with me! I'm trying to help you, and you won't tell me what happened!" Eva yelled, feeling helpless. "I wouldn't have thought sleeping with him would be such a bad thing."

She lowered her voice. "He didn't hurt you, did he?"

"He didn't mean to." Sasha whispered, shame on her face.

"Sasha, if he hurts you, I swear to God I'll-" She cried in disbelief.

"You can't say anything! He didn't know, okay?"

"What do you mean he didn't know?" She couldn't understand why she was defending him.

"He just didn't! I don't even know why he did that in the first place. I mean, it's not like it was going there at all. He'd made it clear he didn't see me that way back at school."

"Maybe he changed his mind? I don't know Sash. Are you alright? That's all I care about," She inched closer to her friend and placed her hand on her knee.

"I thought I was alright while it was happening, but then it just felt wrong afterwards, like we were these two strangers who just happened to be in the same bed by accident. I don't know if I can face him." She adjusted her position so she wasn't curled up in a little ball anymore.

Eva hugged her friend, "Look, you didn't do anything wrong. You know that, right?"

"Did he?"

"Given how he's made you feel, I think he did a lot wrong. Maybe we should switch rooms again."

"But then you'll have to tell Gabe, and I don't want Hale to feel..." she sniffled.

"To feel what?"

"I don't want him to think it was wrong."

"But it was wrong!"

"I don't want him to think he's horrible."

"But isn't he?"

"No, he's not; he's really not. He just has no idea what he's doing, and I wonder if maybe he really does like me back."

"Are you okay with sharing a room with him? I'd much rather keep you safe and deal with the awkwardness later." She knew Gabe would hate this plan.

"He didn't mean to; he's not like that. I'm just being an idiot." She decisively rose from the floor and dusted off her clothes. "I just need to talk to him somehow."

Eva got up as well. "You'll tell me, right?" She was confused, but Sasha seemed much better.

"I won't let it happen again unless I'm sure I can handle it, I guess."

"He just went for it?" Eva couldn't help but be shocked. "I've heard of bad communication skills, but this is something else." She shook her head in disbelief.

Beet red, Sasha nodded.

Eva sighed. "Alright, I won't say anything, but if you need anything, just tell me." She started working on her side of the room while Sasha started on hers, trying to process everything she had just learned.

"You know you skipped lunch, right?" She called.

"I'm sure I didn't miss anything good."

Eva agreed. "You can say that again!"

"Well, don't forget you have to eat for two." Her friend reminded her.

"I'm well aware." She said, patting her belly lightly.

They continued to work, both carrying burdens too heavy for their shoulders.

Sasha

She entered her room and shut the door. She'd tried to spend as much time as possible with Gabe and Eva, but when they fell asleep, it was either head back here or sleep on their floor. The past few nights, she'd chosen the floor. Gabe bombarded her with questions, but Eva protected her. Today, she was ready to face him.

Silence had become a permanent fixture between her and Hale since that night. It had only been a few days, but it felt much longer. In all the confusion and resentment, she missed him. Maybe Mike had been right; maybe her feelings were misplaced. He stood up from the desk and turned to face her when she came inside.

"You're back." He said factually.

She nodded her agreement without so much as a glance. Pulling her pajamas on quickly, she sat on the floor to fish for an elastic in her bag. Her hair was getting too long.

"You still aren't speaking to me," He sounded frustrated. "Did I upset you?"

She shook her head, still not looking at him, but she felt jumpy. Maybe she wasn't ready for this conversation, there was still time to return to the other room after all. She found the elastic under the bed instead of in her bag and pulled her hair back, tugging out strands to frame her face as she always did before bed.

"I can't fix anything if you refuse to speak to me." He said, annoyance escalating in his voice.

"I'm not refusing." She finally said, lifting her gaze to him.

"Would you mind telling me why you've been avoiding me?"

"Because I don't know what to say." She felt like crying, again.

"What do you mean?" He looked genuinely bewildered.

"Just drop it, please." She got up from the floor and sat on the bed.

"Fine, I'm done trying to correct the situation when you don't want to." He shut off his computer and took his spot on the bed.

She stayed seated, looking down at her lap. "'Correcting the situation' is a weird way to put it."

"How else would I put it?"

"How about we speak in 'I' for a change? How would you put it?"

"If you would tell me what you're upset about, maybe *I* would put it differently."

"Don't pretend you don't know. You wouldn't be here if you were an idiot." His face betrayed him this time; he looked hurt.

"I want you to tell me." His voice was harsh.

"Well, I don't want to say it!" she cried, pulling her knees up to her stomach and hugging them against her. "For once, you're the one who won't like what you hear."

"We can't continue like this, so you need to tell me what I did wrong."

"What do you think you did right?"

"Apparently nothing. When you're ready to stop attacking me, we can talk."

"I wasn't attacking you." She said in a small voice. "I'm tired of this too. I hate being afraid of you. I hate avoiding you. It's making this place feel even colder than it already is. I didn't mean it like that, I just don't understand what that was about." Her voice got quieter and quieter, and the final words came out in a whisper, audible only because of the silence.

"You're afraid of me?"

"I know you didn't mean to hurt me." She closed her eyes.

"I hadn't realized that I had hurt you. You should have stopped me." He said, fatigue in his tone.

"I couldn't. I mean, I could have, I just didn't want to say anything to scare you off. I just didn't think it was something you wanted until it was happening and then I didn't know what to do or say."

"If you were uncomfortable, you should have told me." The full spectrum of what they were talking about was hard to navigate.

"What would you have done if I'd told you anything? You would've pulled away and pretended there was nothing there, that you don't have any desires. Tell me that isn't true."

"You're right, but it wasn't meant to be just about my desires." The last word caught in his throat. He looked as uncomfortable as she felt. This was all so foreign. Did other couples (were they a couple?) have discussions like this?

"I'm sorry. I wish I could just give you that without strings attached, and I tried. I'm all mixed up. I just don't see that kind of action as something that's just physical."

"I wouldn't have done it if I had just seen it as purely physical. I care about you." He said. It looked difficult for him to formulate the words. She practically gasped.

"And I love you, but you know that already. Everyone knows that, apparently."

"Everyone but me." He answered. There was another silence. She wanted to reach out to him, but was she allowed? She slipped her hand across the bedsheet and put her hand on his, as she'd done many times before.

He looked down at their hands.

"You love me?" He asked.

"Yes, and everyone knows it: Eva, Gabe, Mike. You're the last one to figure it out."

"Pythagorus can't know."

"That's what you're worried about?"

"I'll do my best to keep you safe, but we can't let this leave the room."

"Why can Gabe kiss Eva in the middle of a full cafeteria, and I can't even talk to you outside this room? You're a human being, and should be allowed to act like one." She huffed.

The rules were always different for Gabe, and it drove her crazy. Mike had said that Hale had been here the longest; didn't Pythagorus care about him?

"It was a risk Gabe was willing to take. I'm not willing to take that risk."

She sighed. "Fine, we'll do it your way. What am I allowed to do then?" Her heart was still hammering, but it felt like they'd crossed over a rickety bridge to reach something akin to solid ground.

He looked relieved. "We can speak, but no physical contact outside of the room."

"Okay." Sasha lay down, elbow beneath her head. "Are you okay with this? You're not just doing this because you feel guilty, right?"

"No." He said softly, his voice deep and rough. "I do feel guilty that I hurt you. In the future, I'd prefer for you to tell me that I've done something wrong, please."

"I'll try." She answered. He'd said "in the future, as though he finally imagined one and wanted her to be in it. He lay down beside her. His face was so close. He'd closed his eyes, the day's training getting to him. She scooted forward until they were nose to nose. Gingerly, she closed her eyes and kissed him lightly. She'd done this just above the school once, and he'd pushed her away. At first, he froze, but tentatively, he reciprocated, and it felt as though she'd waited for this since the first time she saw him, the first time he'd let her be near him willingly. They kissed for a long time, and she tentatively ran her hands through his hair, as she'd always dreamed of doing. He didn't try anything but allowed himself to put a hand on her lower back.

When she pulled away, smirking, "Next time you try what happened that time, start with that."

He looked surprised but pleased, the fragility of the moment hung in the air, and she was afraid to break it by speaking up.

"Alright." He agreed. "Good night."

"I love you." She whispered into the dark and it felt amazing to say.

Chapter 7
Nature vs. Nurture

Eva

They lay in the afterglow, waiting for their breathing to readjust; the blanket tugged over them to conserve heat. Eva was satisfied. For once, the clock wasn't her nemesis. Gabe yawned, moving a hand carefully over the bump of her stomach beneath the covers.

"How much do you know about babies?" Eva asked.

"Not much." Gabe confessed. "I've been to some baptisms when I lived at the Church. It smelled of incense, and there were always lots of people, and the kid would get an extra set of parents, just in case; sounds like a pretty good idea."

"Were you baptized?"

"I think we all had to be to live at the church, but I don't remember much about it. It was kind of dumb. We all lined up, and they did it to all of us in a row - just put water on our heads and said a bunch of Latin. I also think dunking something so small in cold water can't be good for it, but the priest just laughed when I told him that. What about you? You're Catholic, right?"

She lifted her chin off of his chest, "Born and raised, but you know that, of course. Remember my mom?" She smiled. "I did confirmation and everything. I wish I could show you pictures. I looked like a wedding cake." She said, tucking the sheets around herself.

"We don't have a priest around, is that going to be a problem? I never considered you religious, but if it's a thing you care about, maybe we can figure something out? Maybe there's a religious person here on the base?" He was uncomfortable with the subject, and she couldn't figure out why.

"You're babbling, babe. What are you asking?"

"I mean, namin's a big deal for Catholic people, right?"

"Sort of."

"It's not like God and I have the best relationship to start with, and I wasn't sure why it would matter, but religion means so much to so many people and if it means something to you, I want to know about it. I don't know enough about my culture to be able to teach the kid about it, and I want him to feel, I dunno, like he belongs somewhere."

She couldn't help but chuckle. "I'm not really religious, babe. I probably should be considering the way I was raised.Names are a big deal in general, though. It doesn't have to be about religion. Have you thought of any you like?"

His breathing made her rise and fall where she lay on his chest. He put his hands behind his head, stretching, fingers laced, and looked up at the ceiling.

"When I lived on the streets, we had kids with all sorts of names. There was one called Wimp and a girl we called Poke. It was cool for them to be short and easy to yell. The ones who remembered their parents were easy to find; Jessica, Andrey. Nobody would pick themselves a name that long. Sorry, I dunno what's with me tonight, babe. How'd your parents pick Evangeline?"

She snickered excitedly and sat up. "They wanted to name me Kayla, but the nurse who cared for me after I was born had a thick accent and completely butchered the name, according to my mom anyway." Thinking of her mom made her feel warm inside. "My mom was too hormonal to think of anything, so my dad suggested the name Evangeline, and it stuck." She pushed her bangs out of her eyes with a flick of her hand. "I've been Evangeline Catherine ever since, not exactly anything dramatic but the name fits, though Eva's trendier."
Gabe quirked a brow. "Why Catherine?"
"My great-grandmother was named Catherine. My mom was really close to her."
She sighed a little. She missed them.
Gabe was still deep in thought, "Somethin' short and sweet that you can call across a big open space is good." He smirked. "If we're gonna have that beach house, we gotta have an easy name to call. So your dad just got hit upside the head with it? He didn't even think about it before?"
"I guess so, I can't say that I ever asked him." She let out a small yawn. "What about you?"
"I had a native name once but I don't remember it. We were a whole gang of us, but I did have a friend that died whose name I liked, Max. I think he named himself too, or maybe it was his real name, I dunno." He was looking at the far wall, lost in memories. "When he died, it was like he just fell asleep, I kept imagining he'd just wake up and laugh at me for cryin' so hard. He was like that; he made jokes all the time. He was the nicest kid, at least to me."
"Max Wells, that's got a ring to it." She tilted his face back towards his. "If we have a boy, I think that's what we should call him." The more she thought of it, the more she liked it.

His eyes went wide, snapping straight back into reality and at her. He pushed himself up on his elbows. "Are you sure? It's your kid too and I know you have brothers and probably grandfathers and great grandfathers and whatever else...uncles, cousins, great uncles, great cousins? Names all over the damn map."

She laughed, "Stop, Babe, I like it."

"That'd be perfect."

She rubbed her right hand over the baby bump. "The little one seems to like it too." She smiled as she received a small tap near her lower rib cage.

He leaned forward, "Hey, lil man, ya hear that? We got a name for ya'. No on-the-spot namin' for you kid, this one's a keeper." He put his hands on her sides and his face close to her stomach. He kissed the spot below her belly button and sat back up, pulling her close and pulling the blanket back over them.

Sasha

It had been a few weeks since the conversation. Their nights were different now.

Gabe and Eva had started spending more time in the room she shared with Hale, which should have been unacceptable to Hale, but he accepted it. It was the four of them in his room tonight. Sasha's bed was occupied, her pillow was occupied. She watched the happy couple doing the occupying. They were so open. Sasha was sitting at the edge of the bed, comfortable around Gabe and Eva. She looked at Hale, sitting at the desk.

"She's been using my internal organs as a soccer ball." Eva winced slightly.

"Well, he's gotta start practicin' good and early. If you're gonna survive out here in the world, lil man, you've got to be a good runner. The first thing to learn." Gabe laughed, resting his head on Eva's stomach momentarily. There was so much pride on his face.

"I can't believe you guys are debating gender." Sasha chimed in.

"Boy or girl, we're gonna grow their hair out." Gabe commented.

Eva yawned. "Okay, I'm exhausted."

"Same."

"Goodnight, guys."

The happy couple filed out, waving, and she could see Hale's shoulders lower. Sasha had told him what was done was done, but of course, that was far from the end of the debate. Hale hadn't and didn't approve of the pregnancy, and told her that they were risking everything by going through with it. She constantly worried about Eva. She knew they wouldn't be able to hide the pregnancy much longer, and she couldn't get a clear answer from either Gabe or Hale about what would happen. Eva had said that a nurse in the medical wing knew, but she'd shooed her away. Did that mean the medical team would take it on? What would happen if there were any sort of complications? Gabe discussed a future for himself and Eva, but Hale gave Sasha no such assurances. The fact that he seemed so relieved when they left suggested to her that he was struggling with the same worries.

"They're a lot, huh?"

"Indeed."

"Can I ask you something?"

"You always do." His tone was almost affectionate.

"What happens when Pythagorus finds out about the baby?"

Hale looked at door. "I'm unsure, I've been trying not to think about it."

"Maybe speak to Pythagorus?"

"No."

"What if I speak to him? I don't think he really knows or cares that I exist. Maybe he'll listen."

His eyes grew wide. "You can't do that. You would need something to bargain."

"Like what?"

"She should have said something before we arrived here." Hale said, not answering her question.

"But she didn't, and I didn't."

"You knew?"

"Believe it or not, I don't run my mouth constantly."

"I didn't say that."

"We're not going to be able to keep our heads in the sand much longer. You're saying I don't have a bargaining chip, and that's true, but you do. Mike says the whole rebellion is more invested in you than in anyone. You're their masterpiece or something. If you go to Pythagorus and say you'll quit if he doesn't let Eva go, he'll have to listen to you or, better yet, both you and Gabe. That way, he won't have anyone else, so he'll have to do as you say."

"He has others, and he can always train someone else."

"He's been training you since you were little. He doesn't have time to do it all over again, and you said he's super proud, right? He seems like someone who doesn't like to be wrong."

"No one likes to be wrong."

"Okay, he won't admit in front of his entire crew that he was wrong about your loyalty. He's going to do as you ask."

"He's already forgiven me for so many mistakes. I can't afford another one."

"Hale, what about Eva?" She was getting more and more frustrated. Why wouldn't he see reason?

"It isn't going to end the way you think it is, even if I did as you said."

"I stuck my neck out for you, remember? I told the principal that you weren't at fault with Jason."

"If I say a single word, it's over for all of you. They might keep me alive because, as you say, Pythagorus is a proud man, but he won't allow insubordination."

"And you'll keep doing his bidding if he kills us all?"

He had the decency to look hurt. "This isn't about Pythagorus. It's about what needs to be done."

"But we need a way out, and you're not helping."

"I'm limited."

She let herself fall back onto the bed. "You're limited because you let yourself."

"I'm sorry."

She groaned. "I'm going to figure something out."

"Please be careful."

She let it go. He was trapped, and getting angry with him wouldn't change that. She could tell he was uneasy when they got into bed and snuggled up.

"What's going on in your head?" She asked.

"That I shouldn't have let this happen."

She pulled away.

"This as in us?"

"I tried to warn you."

"Hale, I do not regret this, okay? I don't regret you."

Knowing what she now knew, it probably only served to make him feel more guilty, but she didn't know what else to say or do, so they fell asleep with that notion in mind and continued their days of endless toil and their nights of trying to find a little light in the darkness.

Chapter 8
The Best Laid Plans

Eva

It wasn't long before the watermelon inside her was becoming unbearable. The stairs became progressively more difficult. She was constantly tired, and she wanted to stay in the room and pile blankets on top of herself. Unfortunately, that wasn't an option. Pythagorus had said they would work, so they did, or more specifically, Sasha did. She was working double time to make up for Eva's inability to lift anything. Certain ways of turning her body were impossible, while others shot pain down her left leg. The excitement was turning to dread.

She didn't have a crib, stroller, diapers, baby clothes, toys, formula...anything! She knew they couldn't simply ride a positive attitude into tomorrow anymore. They needed a plan - but Gabe's schedule was insane, starting at five in the morning and ending at 10 or 11 at night. It felt intentional - like they were stealing him from her. She was also growing restless, sick to death of the hallways, rooms, laundry, and cafeteria. She wanted grassy parks, a beachfront and the wind in her hair.

"Eva?" Sasha's voice outside the bathroom door.
She wiped the tears away and splashed cold water on her face.
"Coming!"
"Ready to go?"
"Ready!" She chirped.
Sasha kept looking at her stomach. Everyone did.
"I wanted to show you something," Sasha said.
"Don't we have to get to work?"
"Yeah, we will; it'll just be a minute."
Curiosity peaked, and she followed her friend to a room they'd been in dozens of times. It was dusty and full of boxes. She scrambled to follow, legs and knees aching.
"Seriously, Sash, I'm trying to keep my head down...if we're late..."
She stopped in a batch of sunlight. Sunlight. She hadn't seen sunlight in months. She peered in absolute awe at a large window she'd never seen before.
"There's more," Sasha whispered. Her voice came from up above. She had stacked many boxes up to the ceiling and was sitting up at the top. The climb didn't appeal to Eva at all; just the window was enough. Then, her friend was pushing up against the ceiling, and with the sound of a

manhole cover being lifted, she had pushed a circle of ceiling aside and was holding onto what looked like a rusty wrung.

"Where does it go?" Eva asked, looking dubious.

"Up, for a very long time."

Eva rested her hands on her stomach, feeling queasy. Glancing at the door, Sasha quickly shut the ceiling trap again and climbed down.

"How did you find it?"

"I come up here to think sometimes. Hale showed me the window."

"Does he know there's an exit?" She pointed upwards.

"I don't think so. He would've escaped had he known, wouldn't he?"

"Have you mentioned it to him?"

"No, but tonight, let's stop waiting for a way out. Let's make a plan. You speak to Gabe; I'll convince Hale."

Eva peered upwards, wondering if she could fit herself through there and what it would take to keep climbing. Either way, she needed Gabe. Even if they got out on the other side, they would still be in the middle of the desert with no way to get back to civilization.

"What if he doesn't want to go?" Eva worried. If Gabe didn't agree to go, she couldn't either. Would that mean losing her best friend? Would Sasha leave without her?

"Why wouldn't he?"

"If Hale says he's not coming, are you?"

"Oh, he's coming."

"Are you sure?"

Sometimes Sasha's naivete surprised her. She was so practical in so many ways, but when it came to Hale, it was always like this. She wondered if the same could be said about her. Eva looked out the window again, the idea of freedom making her heart flutter in her chest, which made the baby kick.

"What's up?" Sasha asked.

"She's excited." They referred to the baby as "she", though they had no confirmation. Gabe insisted it was a boy. They hugged, Sasha careful not to squish her around the stomach.

"This'll work, right?" Sasha whispered.

"Crazier things have happened." Eva agreed, not wanting to dim the moment, hoping against all hope that this could be the answer.

Sasha

She caught Hale directly after target practice, unable to contain her excitement.

"Alexandra?" She was sitting along his route from the hangar.

"I'm sorry. I know you said nothing outside the room, but this couldn't wait."

He went pale. "What's wrong?"

"No! Dummy! This is good news. Come on!"

She grabbed his hand, and he tore it from her grasp. "No holding hands."

"Fine, just follow. If we get intercepted, I'm going to the blue room."

"The blue room?"

"The storage room you showed me."

He looked frustrated. "I can't be late. Can't this wait?"

"Please?"

"Quickly."

She led him to the porthole in the ceiling of the storage room, hoping his reaction would be similar to Eva's. She remembered him leading her here so vividly all of a sudden. Shifting the panel on the ceiling, she pointed up.

"This is just an air shaft, an emergency exit for whenever this base would be terminated. "

"Are you listening to me? There's a way out of here! We can go, all four of us. Eva can have her baby in a hospital, and we can go to college and escape."

"I'm not going anywhere. Get down before someone sees you."

She shut the ceiling panel and climbed back down to face him, standing in the light from the window. He stood away from the sun.

"Why not? Haven't you done enough here? Haven't you suffered enough?"

"I have nowhere to go."

"You can come with me. I'm sure your grades were amazing, we can get you a scholarship, a loan, and you can go to university. It doesn't even have to be with me. You can choose where you want to go. If money's a hang-up, you can go to community college or just get a regular job. You're brilliant. You won't have trouble finding something to do. You can't honestly think all those guys we went to school with have a better chance at success than you do."

He stood speechless.

She clasped her hands together and pleaded, "What do I need to do? Fall to my knees in front of you? Come on, Hale, this is your chance. I know this is hard, I know change is scary, but do you really want to stay here by yourself?" She reached for his hands, but he crossed them and stepped back.

"There's a war."

"There's always a war. Since as far as I can remember, something is going on in the world where people are suffering, but it doesn't have to be you."

"War comes whether you like it or not. You can stand aside and ignore it if it suits you. You're being selfish." He looked at her like he'd looked at Gabe in the mall for wanting to buy a puppy.

"Are you hearing yourself right now? You don't have to do this! Do you *want* to do this?"

"Calm down."

"I'm perfectly calm!"

"I can't."

"It won't be like high school. You never need to go back to high school again. They treat you like trash here, worse than that, they treat you like you're an inanimate object, like you're one of the fancy weapons they're building."

"I can't leave." He said finally, "This is what I'm supposed to do. This is my purpose."

She gently placed a hand on his face. "You don't have to be who they want you to be."

"How many times must I repeat myself?"

He must have gotten used to seeing her cry because he left without a word. She peered through the window longingly. Would this be where they parted ways forever? She supposed she'd never really believed he would choose her, but it still stung.

Eva

When Gabe returned from training, Eva was ready.

"Sasha thinks we should leave." she started, like peeling off a bandaid.

Gabe rubbed his eyes, veins running through them from exhaustion.

"Where?"

"To the nearest city with a hospital so I'm not giving birth in the medical wing."

Gabe let himself fall onto the bed.

She continued. "I'm sure we'd be okay. We could just get back on the road and drive. If we find my dad, they can hide us, and you won't have to worry about being tracked down."

"Babe," He looked at her, the weight of the world on his shoulders. "I can't just leave. I've been working towards this for years. I've been taking these crazy drugs to try and be what they need me to be so that we win the war and change things in this country. They depend on me."

"And what about me?" She cried. "I'm depending on you!" She reached over and put both of his hands on her stomach. "We are depending on you."

"Princess, aren't we in this together?"

"Are you serious right now, Gabe?"

"I'm not abandoning you. I'm asking you to stay."

"That's a death sentence! This isn't about us anymore. It's about the baby, and this is no place for a baby to grow up. We have nothing. We don't even know how long we're going to be here. If I'm going to wait for you, I need to be somewhere safe, don't I?"

He was struggling to find words. He was used to flying by the seat of his pants, but that wouldn't work this time.

"I'll think of something. You trust me, right?"

"I want to." She said, emotion choking her.

"I won't let you down."

Sasha

Sasha could keep being angry with Hale, but what was the point? She'd seen the sort of place that produced someone like him. She knew that she'd put her heart on the line towards someone who could not love her back or offer her what she needed, but he'd done his best, hadn't he? He'd given her more than she ever thought he could - and she hoped that he'd feel it had been worthwhile now that they were at what felt like the end of their journey. Eva asked her to give her a few more days to get things figured out with Gabe, and she agreed to that too. She had a plan in her mind, and that was better than nothing. Hale came back from training later and later every night. She would stay up and wait for him.

It was past midnight this time when Sasha felt the light shift in the hallway from her peripheral vision. She knew he was there, but she took the time to finish her page, then yawned.

"Welcome back" she said, sitting up and stretching, dog-earring the corner of her book. She was on her fourth reread.

"Thanks." He put away the few items he'd come in with and gathered up fresh clothes.

"You okay?" she asked.

"Just tired."

"They're really ramping up your training, aren't they?"

He nodded. He was walking on eggshells around her. She remembered the days of finding sharing a room awkward, but now it felt perfectly normal, if a little tense given his mood. It had been a long road for them to get here. He went to shower and returned smelling of soap. It was getting so late and she wanted to go to sleep, but she could tell he wanted to talk. He sat on the edge of the bed.

Trying to keep her eyes open, she propped a pillow against the wall.

"We need to speak.", he stated.

"Never a good start, but okay,"

"I hope it will be."

"Okay, I'm listening."

"Gabriel found a way out for you." She sat up straighter, biting her lip.
"And Eva?"
"Yes."
"What's the plan?" Her eyes widened.
"You'll receive help from the outside. Others are training like us who have more freedom than we do. You'll meet them; they'll take you somewhere safe."
"What about you?"
"I'll be here until I'm needed elsewhere."
"So, that'll be the end?"
"What do you mean?"
"For us, will that be the end?" She wrapped her arms around herself.
The silence stretched a little too long. She nodded as though he'd answered. He turned off the light as she scooted over to make room for him on the bed. They'd been lying in the dark with their eyes closed, turned away from each other for a few minutes when she spoke again. She said it to the wall so she hoped he could hear her clearly. She hoped he'd remember every word.

"If you change your mind, I don't want it to be over. I'll go because Eva needs me, but if you can, come find me afterwards or during or whenever." He turned towards her and she did the same, they were face to face in the darkness. She wanted to remember the outline of his face and the expression on it when she finished her monologue. "I don't care if it's days, months, or years, come and find me. I'll welcome you with open arms. If you ask yourself if the offer still stands, even if it feels weird and awkward, it does. It will always stand. If you want to, I'd like to be in your life. I won't be waiting around for you, but my door will always be open. Could you promise me that at least, that you'll remember that door is there?"

He nodded, his eyes wide. There was no more talking. There were other ways to express what they felt. He had gotten better at those, and she was grateful for it.

Eva

She burst into tears when he told her the plan. It was unexpected for them both and Gabe instantly wrapped his arms around her as her entire body shook with sobs that echoed through the empty, dark hallways.

"It's okay, babe; you'll be fine. You'll both be fine. Khalil's an amazing guy, and he's got connections all over the place, and he'll take you somewhere super safe and comfortable, and he'll get you set up, and you'll just wait for me, okay? You'll wait, and I'll come for you, and we can raise this kid together! We can go to the beach, and we can go to theme parks, and we can sit on the balcony at night and drink cheap beer and listen to whatever you want and..." he was babbling, trying to comfort her, but all she heard was goodbye, goodbye, goodbye.

When she finally managed to stop, apologetically wiping tears off Gabe's sweater, she lifted a finger to his lips. "Stop."
He did, exhaling, his dark eyes shining.
"Don't make me promises. I can't take it. I'll wait for you. I'll wait and do my best, but please, please, please, be careful and don't let them change you into someone else. You're enough for me Gabe. You're amazing. I'll wait for you and I'll be okay." She needed to believe that.
"I'll see you when you're done." She wished she could keep him with her. She didn't want to face any of this alone, but she knew that the tighter she held on, the faster he would slip through her fingers.

She wished Gabe could have spent the next few days alone with her, making up for all the time they would be apart, but of course, that would be painfully suspicious. This was already the sort of plan that would only succeed because it was mutually beneficial to himself and the higher-ups. Gabe had greatly improved in simulations in recent weeks, so the lab techs even gave him high fives. He needed to get them all on his side. The plan was disgusting in its simplicity: climb up the air shaft, get to the surface, find something with wheels to get to the gate, and meet Remi and Khalil.

On her way to the cafeteria later that week, someone suddenly pulled her into a room, hand over her mouth. She didn't even have time to scream. "Evangeline, it's okay. It's me." It was Mike, Sasha's boyfriend or ex-boyfriend or whatever.
"Oh my god, Mike, I could've gone into early labor!"she cried, waiting for her pulse to settle.
"Sorry, I needed to speak to you - have you thought this through?"
"Thought what through?"
"Your plan."
"I don't know what you're talking about."
She tried to sidestep him, but Mike was significantly taller and broader. "You can't do this alone."
"Are you threatening me or...?" She looked him dead in the eye like she'd faced Pythagorus that first day.
"No, it's an offer. There are people here who can help you."
She put her hands on her stomach, taking a wide step back.

"Help me how?"

"When is the exchange?"

"23h00"

"I'll set off an alarm."

"That's risky."

"Not for me."

"Won't they know it's you?"

"Not necessarily and I won't be alone."

"Who else?" she asked, feeling dizzy. The more people were involved, the more room there was for error, and who could she trust here? When Gabe and Hale needed help, she hadn't seen anyone step up. Based on their stories, they were hardly seen as human beings.

"Clara."

"Who?"

"The nurse."

Oh, she'd forgotten about her. She had been kind at a time when no one else had been.

"I don't want anyone else to get hurt because of us." she said.

"It's a choice. Aren't you getting hurt because of them?"

"You can say their names Mike." she corrected him, though she thought maybe she shouldn't have given that he was offering to help her. He didn't respond to her sassy response.

"One thing, though." He said.

"What?"

"Sasha."

"Yeah?"

"Don't let her be the sacrifice for your happy ending."

She nodded, surprised to find they'd somehow managed to find a small community for themselves in the least likely of places. If they could make it in a military compound full of rebels, maybe they could survive out there on their own.

"I wouldn't sacrifice my friend. You're a good guy Mike."

His eyes softened, "Good luck."

She headed back to her room. There wasn't much time left.

Chapter 9
Gasping for Air

Sasha

On the final morning before the escape, Hale gathered his things and Sasha lay quietly on the bed, watching him get ready.

"I want you to stay." He said it so quietly that it felt like she'd dreamt it. He wasn't looking at her. He was staring into his sock drawer: Matching sets of white socks in perfect order.

"I wish you'd come with me." She replied.

"I can't."

"I know, and I can't stay."

"I know."

"Can you come back early tonight?"

"I can't."

"Have a good day." She pushed herself from the bed and wrapped her arms around his neck. She stood on tiptoe to kiss him and he held her as though she were porcelain. When he left, she climbed back into bed.

By that evening, she'd chewed her nails to the quick and gone to pee more times than she could count. Nothing could have prepared her for trying to sneak out of a rebel base in the middle of the desert under cover of night. She'd dressed for the occasion: Black leggings, a black t-shirt and a black sweater. In a fight or flight situation, she generally felt flight, but at this moment, it was more like freeze. Her fingertips and toes felt as though they might fall off as all her blood went to her vital organs. She'd finally stopped pacing and decided to sit on her suitcase.

Eva came in, backpack on her back, her hands resting on her stomach.

"Ready?" She said, seeming almost excited.

"Not at all," Sasha admitted.

Eva looked ready, as though she was off on an adventure. Her face was all determination and courage, the opposite of what Sasha felt. They both checked the time on their phones. The guys were late. Sasha wished she could simply call Hale and Gabe. That was one reason returning to civilization would be nice - cell phone reception, though she still wouldn't be able to call them. She remembered that Gabe never carried his phone back at school, maybe it was because he was used to places like this.

"One more time, we're going up the shoot in the storage room," Sasha said.

"Yes."

"And we're sure there's a way up from there?"

"Gabe says there is. I just hope I fit." Eva replied, pointed down at what seemed like a tiny belly to Sasha but probably seemed huge to Eva.

Many things happened at once. The sound of sirens began to blare, like a hundred simultaneous fire alarms. The lights flickered and then died. Sasha covered her ears, falling to her knees on the floor. She couldn't see anything in the darkness but shut her eyes anyway. She felt a hand on hers. She opened her eyes, it was Eva's hand.

"Come on!" Eva was shouting, a flashlight in her other hand. There were lights out in the hallway, green fluorescent emergency lights but all they did was add to the surreality of the moment. She scrambled to her feet, adjusting her backpack. There were footsteps and voices out in the hall.

Where the hell were Hale and Gabe? Weren't they supposed to lead them out of here? Eva led the way. Down below, people seemed to be at their stations, knowing what to do. Hundreds of conversations, people making sure the foundations were solid, that there wasn't a breach, that they weren't under attack. As they'd discussed, they took the stairs up to the third floor.

Pythagorus' voice boomed over the loudspeaker. "There is no imminent danger. Remain at your stations."

"What about the guys? Do we wait for them?" Sasha cried over the sirens.

"Maybe this was them!" Eva yelled back.

In the chaos, no one was paying them any mind. As they barreled down the hallway of the third floor, Sasha remembered following Hale here through a lens of tears, and her heart ached. Would she ever see him again? Would he be alive to find her? Eva turned the doorknob and froze.

"It's locked." She squeaked.

"What do you mean, locked?"

"I mean, it won't open!"

Sasha tried it. It was jammed.

"We need to find Mike! He has keys!" As they whirled around, they realized they were running out of time. Sasha's backpack felt immensely heavy. She wished she'd brought the luggage she'd had in the car. There was a crashing sound on the other side of the locked door, and it swung open. A tall, dark-skinned young man in dark, skin-tight clothing stood there, squinting.

"Are you Evangeline?" He asked, a slight French accent recognizable in his voice.

She could only point at Eva, hoping he wasn't asking to know who to murder.

"Yes, who's asking?" Eva said bravely.

The man grabbed Eva by the shoulders and pulled her into the room swiftly, Sasha following. He shut the door. The window illuminated the room, the stars seemingly miles overhead. The sirens had stopped, and the lights flickered, casting eerie shadows in the dimly lit room, hurting her eyes.

"That's our cue." He pointed at a rope hanging from the hatch she had been so excited to find when they'd come up with this crazy idea.

"Who are you?" Sasha finally found her voice, stepping in front of Eva protectively.

"My name is Remi. Gabriel Wells said you needed a way out. We'd better go quickly, you're late. Once Pythagorus realizes there was a breach, this facility won't be here much longer." He spoke softly but authoritatively. It helped that he was the most attractive person Sasha had ever seen.

"Start climbing." He said. "Khalil is up above waiting. I don't want him to get caught."

Eva came out of shock quicker. She handed Remi her backpack and climbed up into the darkness. When she found a foothold, her climb was faster. Sasha's whole body shook as she watched Remi, carrying their luggage, follow Eva up the rope and through the hatch. The alarm had stopped. She could hear scurrying feet in the hallway right outside the door. Remi's voice came from somewhere in the abyss, but she couldn't peel her feet off the ground. She could still hear Eva's steps steadily on each metal foothold. It wasn't a quick climb, and probably not easy for someone with a baby belly. She wasn't even sure if the dark or the height scared her more. She had to remind herself to keep breathing. She decided to forget the rope and climbed up the boxes.

The door burst open, and three guards crashed into the room. "Hands up!" Each was holding a gun pointed directly at her. Sasha knew she was out of time. She slammed the metal hatch shut, turning the metal knob to lock it. They would know where Eva had gone, but it might buy her a moment. She didn't get the chance to comply with the order. She heard the gunshot sound like a firework going off in her head; felt the boxes giving way underneath her, then everything went black.

Eva

Eva heard a clang from below as Remi shut the hatch beneath them, leaving them in darkness, save for a light way above in the distance.

"Sasha?" She called out.

219

The sounds below had disappeared. All she could hear was her own breathing.

"Keep going!" Remi called from below her.

"Almost there!" a soft, masculine voice came from above.

"You going to get me from this hell, Khalil?" Remi's voice carried from below. She kept climbing until someone was helping Eva up and out.

"Gabe and Hale sure are lucky to have friends, aren't they?" Khalil, presumably, called down. "My religion doesn't believe in hell anyway." He added.

A hand appeared in the darkness and pulled her up. A young man barely taller than herself helped her onto solid ground. The sand felt strange underfoot after so much time underground. She wasn't exactly sure how long it had been, but it seemed like forever. It was definitely less than nine months. The air was sweet and dry; the sky was endless above.

"Thank you." She said, as she straightened and turned as Remi climbed up and out from behind them and sealed the hatch.

"Where's Sasha?" She cried.

"She bought us time." Remi said calmly. "Come."

"What do you mean? We have to go back!" She leapt towards the hatch, but strong arms appeared behind her. Remi lifted her as though she were a child. "We don't have time for this."

"Please," the other young man said, with compassion in his voice. "Rescue missions don't always turn out the way you expect. If we don't leave now, we'll all be caught. You have to think of yourself and your baby now." She let herself be set back down. The desert was silent.

The stranger directed her towards a helicopter, which stood out like a sore thumb against the landscape. The mast wasn't rotating, so it was clearly off. Feeling numb, she marched over to it without breaking into a proper run. She wasn't sure she could trust her legs. This was it. She was getting out of here. Gabe was gone, and so was Sasha. Who knew what Pythagorus would do to her for trying to escape? Would Gabe be able to save her too? She climbed up the ladder into the helicopter and found herself a seat. It was small, and the idea of rising into the air in it wasn't the least bit appealing, but what choice did she have?

Remi climbed on board and helped strap her in, setting her backpack, and Sasha's beside her. "Excuse me." He said politely. He handed her a helmet with headphones attached.

"Thank you." She said, her voice sounding far away, lost in the shock of what had just happened.

"Come on, Khalil!" Remi called. His friend climbed in, and some sort of exchange about who was driving took place in a language foreign to her, perhaps Arabic or Hebrew. She didn't know enough of either to guess.

Khalil climbed into the driver's seat. He turned and gave her a thumbs-up. Slowly and loudly, they lifted off into the night sky. Eva looked out to the horizon, one hand on her stomach, feeling world-weary. From the corner of her eye, she noticed that Remi and Khalil were holding hands. She wondered momentarily if that made the ride more dangerous, whether driving a helicopter was the sort of thing one should do with both hands. Still, then exhaustion settled in as the adrenaline receded, and she couldn't the tears that rolled down her face. She'd abandoned Sasha, who'd been with her through everything. What if she was dead? She cried silently, her arms wrapped around herself, the wind blowing all around her. Just like when she was a child driving for hours with her parents, her body adjusted to the movement, and somehow, exhaustion overtook her, and before she knew it, she was asleep.

Sasha

She awoke with a searing pain in her side, shooting down her leg and eclipsing everything else. She cried out and opened her eyes. She was in the medical wing. She knew it instinctively like she knew that Eva was gone. The physical pain was enough to distract her, but the loss was what made her eyes fill.

"Hey!" With difficulty, she turned to find Gabe, of all people, sitting beside the bed. His face was a blur through her tears. His voice was a little too high, a little too enthusiastic.

"Did they make it?" She coughed out.

"Yeah, she's okay."

"The facility was compromised. Hale's on a mission right now. He'll probably be back, but I don't know if they'll let him in here."

"What about you?"

"I've still got some training to do."

"Where's Eva?"

"If I knew, they'd find a way to get it out of me. I don't know."

She leaned back and stared at the ceiling, waiting for some level of consciousness to subside, but no such luck. "Everything hurts."

"I know."

"I'm scared." She choked on the sudden understanding of what she'd done.

"Don't be." Gabe said, which was far from reassuring. "Just focus on getting better."

"You're not going to leave, too, are you?"

"I may not have a choice soon. I made a deal with Pythagorus, and there's no turning back."

"A deal?" She turned to look at him. His hair was pulled into a ponytail and he sat with his elbows on his knees, fingers interlaced in front of him. He looked tired, though she guessed she must look worse. She glanced over at the IV drip in her arm and the bruises from where other IV drips must have been inserted. It made her sick to look at so she focused on Gabe. He took a deep breath before answering in a level voice.

"That he'll leave Eva alone if I complete my training as he sees fit and do everything they ask of me."

"What about me?" Sasha choked out. Her mouth felt like it was full of sand. Was this it? She was trapped here by herself? The heart monitor beside her beeped quicker. Stupid machinery. She didn't need Gabe knowing how afraid she was.

"I don't have any advice. Remi and Khalil were my only channel out of here."

"They didn't kill me."

"True, they must think you'll be useful."

She scoffed, and it sent a wave of pain down her body. "No scoffing," she thought.

There was a silence filled with beeping machines.

"Gabe?"

"I'll try and get you back to Eva. She needs you."

"She needs you too."

Gabe turned away, staring at the heart monitor. By the expression on his face, she'd hit a nerve. Good, that had been her intention. It was great that he'd been so excited about the prospect of being a father when Eva had told him she was pregnant, but it didn't seem like being an active part of that child's life was on the table, and they were way past the point of filtering their words to one another. If you couldn't be honest in a hospital bed, where could you be?

"You're pretty bossy for someone who's just woken up." Gabe deflected.

"How long was I out?"

"A few days."

"A few days? Jesus Christ, that's a long time. No wonder I'm in pain."

"Well, that and you got shot."

"I got shot?" She remembered the sound of the gun and the lightning bolt of pain, but somehow hadn't put two and two together. She remembered holding the gun she'd found in Hale's room that day in Atlanta. She hadn't regretted coming here, despite how difficult it had been. For the first time, she wondered what might've happened had she just said no to the trip, if she'd seen the red flags and bowed out. It wasn't a helpful thought. She felt a hand on her shoulder.

"Which is why you should take it easy. You're fine, or you will be anyway." Gabe said gently.

"Not like I have much choice in the matter," She muttered and looked up at the ceiling, her head spinning. He put his hand back in his lap.

She wanted to ask if Hale had come to see her. She wanted her mom more than anything else in the world, but she also wanted to be unconscious.

"Can you please get me some water or a Tylenol or something?" she asked.

"Yeah, I'll go find a nurse."

She turned to look at him. He looked as exhausted as she felt.

"Gabe?"

"Yeah?"

"Am I going to be okay?"

"Yeah, you got pretty lucky."

He wasn't wrong. Eva was safe; she'd come out of it alive, and neither Gabe nor Hale were blamed for the escape, it could've been worse.A nurse came in and adjusted something on her arm. The woman was unfamiliar and didn't say anything. She closed her eyes. She hoped things would be better when she woke up; this wasn't a reality worth opening her eyes to see.

Chapter 10
Back to Reality

Eva

She turned to Khalil in utter disbelief. She stood at the center of an empty apartment, dingey, derelict and smelling of second hand smoke. She clutched a burner phone that Khalil said she could use to contact him anytime: a stack of cash and a credit card.

"You can't be serious."

"I know it isn't much."

"Khal, I can't stay here by myself!"

It had been less than twenty-four hours since the escape and she missed Gabe and Sasha so much that it was physically debilitating. Having landed in an isolated area of the desert, Remi dropped her off with Khalil to drive to the city. Khalil was kind and attentive to her needs. He spoke only when she wanted to and offered her tissues when she cried, which was near constant. He didn't ask anything of her and reassured her that everything would be okay. When they drove past a sign welcoming them to New Mexico, she couldn't even fathom how she'd gotten there. The radio buzzed to life once they were near civilization, and she'd reached for her phone, but Khalil had asked her not to so they wouldn't be tracked. When they pulled up in front of an apartment building, she was sure they were just making a stop over...but now she knew differently.

"You need somewhere where Pythagorus won't find you."

"I'm pregnant!"

"There's a hospital nearby. You have money, and if you need more, just use that phone, and I'll wire you as much as you need."

"Please, you can't leave me here! Just take me back to the base, take me to wherever you're going, or just take me to my family. I can't do this alone." She pleaded. She'd never felt so broken in her life. She'd always prided herself on being independent, strong, but this was too much. She was so far from home, and if she called her parents and told them what had happened, she'd have to face that night again - that horrible night when she'd called them to warn them to evacuate. Had she reached them in time? Were they even out there? Khalil put his hands on her shoulders and looked her straight in the eyes.

"Evangeline, listen to me. This is the only way Gabe can take care of you right now. He needs you to stay here and stay alive. He needs you to wait. When he can, he'll come to find you." His eyes had speckles of green in them.

"Why can't I stay with you?"

"Because I'm like Gabe."

"You're an experiment..." she whispered.

He gave her a sad smile. "I kind of wish they'd just call us soldiers."

"So you're training like he is."

"Yes, and that means I can't stay here. The war has begun. I'm needed, but Gabe said you were the most important person in his life, and I told him I'd help. This is the only way I know how."

She could keep arguing, but she knew there was no point. This was the next chapter in her life, and she had a lot to figure out.

Sasha

When she emerged from the medical wing, she realized how much time had passed. She was still healing, still felt aches and pains around her abdomen, shots of pain down her leg, occasionally in her neck, but she could move around, and that was enough for now. She let herself cry when she returned to her and Hale's room. All his stuff was gone, but the bed was still there, so she wrapped herself in as many blankets as she could find and wallowed.

The next morning, a guard came with a list of things to do as though nothing had happened. Her task was to complete the last of the packing in the facility. There wasn't much left to do: The place was practically empty. The cafeteria, once filled with techs, was terribly quiet at mealtimes. She wandered the halls like a ghost, not wanting to raise her eyes at anyone.

Gabe returned to the room late every night, and she heard his door open and shut, but she felt no desire to seek him out. She knew he was probably the only person who could understand her numb powerlessness, but she couldn't bring herself to look into his eyes and ask questions. She still had so many, of course: Where was Hale? Where was Eva? Who were the young men who'd come to save them? Where was everyone going that the facility had emptied? What would happen to her next? Everything was gone, all the stuff she'd brought from the surface. She washed the same clothes repeatedly until she finally got fed up and simply took some clean scrubs from the laundry room. It wasn't as though anyone was going to ask her for them. On one of those nights when she lay in bed staring at the ceiling, she heard familiar voices next door.

"We had a deal, Gabe."

"I did what I could."

"Clearly, it wasn't enough."

"What do you want me to do? I sold my soul to the devil now. My hands are tied."

"So she's collateral damage to your story, then."

"Listen, man; I didn't plan this. I didn't want this, but I've used every chip I had, so all I can do is tow the line and hope it's enough."

"Enough? You caused this!"

"Mike, if you plan to get her out of here, be my guest. Pythagorus has control over my family. If I step out of line, it's over for them. You got something to say? Go say it to him."

"And what do you think happens to me then?"

"Same as me."

"Actually, no. I'm a tech. You're an experiment. I'm a number to him, completely disposable. You're like a needle in a haystack, and you're days from deployment. What does it hurt you to try and save a girl you chose to bring here?"

"I didn't..." Gabe sounds defensive, but he's out of breath too.

She lifts herself off the bed and walks into the hallway. The door to Gabe's room is shut but the doorknob turns easily in her hand.

"Mike?" From the doorway, she sees them standing face to face, close enough for a fight. Both have their hands clenched into fists but no one is throwing punches. Mike is about a head taller than Gabe, but Gabriel's never one to back down. Both men jump and turn towards her. She isn't sure what she could say to communicate how grateful she feels to this guy who owes her nothing and yet steps in to help her at every turn.

Mike steps back from Gabe, "Sasha! I'm glad you're up."

She smiles at him, "Thank you for what you're trying to do, but Gabe's right. There's nothing he can do. We tried to escape, and only one of us got out. We can't try that again."

"This facility's going to be empty soon, where will you go?", he asks.

"Home, I hope." She says, her heart filling with hope.

"And how do you think you'll get there?"

She shrugs. She has no idea. "Or I'll find Eva. I hope she isn't alone, wherever she is."

"You still want to go find Eva?" Gabe looks up, surprised.

"Jesus Christ, Gabriel, just because you and Hale have the loyalty of a dead possum doesn't mean the rest of us are broken."

Mike turns back to Gabe as though he has the answers. Gabe exhales, closing bloodshot eyes. "Okay, Mike, I'll find a way for you to contact Khalil. When they shut this place down, take her to Eva. You know I can't."

"You know that means my time here is over too."

"That's your choice."

Sasha's eyes fill with tears. "Really?"

Mike pats her on the shoulder. "I guess we have a plan." She jumps into his arms, desperate for comfort. Gabe keeps sitting there and watching with the sullen eyes she was used to seeing on Hale.

Eva

When there was nothing to do, she knew to keep busy. If she let herself dwell on her predicament, there would be no way to get up daily. When Khalil left, Eva got to work on the apartment, as much as she could when moving around was becoming more and more challenging. She painted one room pink, which changed the smell from nicotine to paint, which helped. She put duct tape over the broken window in the bathroom, which helped too. There was no way to get a bed into the apartment, so she bought a used mattress from a guy down the hall willing to haul it over for an extra 20$. She wasn't sure how far Khalil's money would get her, but she tried to be frugal. She stocked the cupboards with non-perishables and treated herself to vegetables and fruit when she found them on sale. She knew she probably needed extra vitamins for pregnancy, but all that seemed less important than getting back on her feet.

She was going to survive this, no matter what. She'd come from a long line of survivors. She often considered calling home from a pay phone, but she couldn't bring herself to do it in case the line wasn't connected. The possibility seemed more appealing than the reality.

The war began on a Monday at 1:30 in the afternoon. She was more pregnant than she thought possible that day and had bought herself a soda at a bar down the street to use their bathroom, leaving her groceries by the bar in the hopes that the barkeeper would keep an eye on them. When she'd emerged from the bathroom, gagging from the stale, alcohol-scented air of the place, everyone's eyes were glued to the television screen mounted on the wall for sports games. The volume was at its maximum, making the sound come in staticky and ominous. Someone was sitting on the bar stool where she'd left her bags, so she had no choice but to stand and watch alongside everyone else. The flummoxed newscaster was trying to get his facts straight from the

227

teleprompter: There had been several explosions around the country, in key cities - New York, Washington, Texas, Los Angeles, and Miami. A declaration of war had been sent from a rebel group in a computerized voice. Their demands were the resignation of the current leadership. It all felt incredibly far away. She knew this was coming, yet it felt so far from her current situation that she felt numb. All this meant was that Gabe wouldn't be returning anytime soon.

She waited for the bar to clear so that she could access her groceries, but once it was empty, all she could do was sit down and put her head in her hands.

She heard the smack of glass on the table in front of her. "Probably not great for the baby, but it takes the edge off." The old barkeep said. An amber liquid is sitting in front of her in a slightly dirty glass. She considers it. Her lips hadn't touched alcohol since prom, which felt like a million years ago now.

"How old are ya'?" The man asks. He's quite ugly, with leathery skin and tired eyes.

"Old enough." She mutters and brings the glass to her mouth. Even the smell of it is enough to steer clear. She sets it back down. "Thanks, but no thanks."

"Your loss." He says and downs the glass in one shot.

She focuses on him. Wars mean different things for different people, and she wonders what it means for this man with his squalid little bar in a rundown part of a rundown city.

"I need a job." She says. It's the logical next step, isn't it?

He looks down at her stomach. "I don't think you can do much around here."

"So you have work?"

"I have..." he gestures at the back of the room. She turns around to look at a stage cast in the shadows. There are polls there. Oh. That sort of work.

"I can dance. I used to be on my school team."

He looks suspicious, as though she's putting on a gimmick.

"How bout you wait until you figure out this," he points at her stomach "situation." If you're still lookin' for that kinda work afterwards, you can come back here."

"Really?"

"Yeah, why not?"

"So you're the owner?"

"Yeah, they call me Benny."

"Angel." She says. It's her favourite character from RENT. She doesn't want this Benny guy to know her real name. She isn't even sure who she is anymore. Maybe she really is Angel now, just a downtrodden, vie boheme girl with no prospects or future. She shakes off the dark thoughts and takes her groceries.

"Thanks, Benny."

"Be safe, Angel." He says it with a mocking smirk.

Sasha

Mike made good on his promise. She desperately wanted to know what it had cost him, but she was never allowed to ask. Gabe took her to the surface in the terrifying elevator, though not as terrifying as the hole Eva had climbed to escape, so she supposed she should be grateful. He kept his hands in his pockets as though their time as friends had been deleted now that Eva was gone.

"Where's Mike?" She asked.

"I don't know. He went to see Pythagorus, and now he's no longer here. You do the math."

"Gabriel! This isn't math! This is rocket science but with bombs!"

"What do you want me to say?" Gabe asked, looking upwards as the walls slid past them.

"Something comforting!"

He finally meets her gaze. They're about the same height." Keep Eva safe until the war ends."

"What about Mike?"

"I don't know about Mike, and before you ask, you're getting another of your wishes."

The elevator stops, and she sees the beat up jalopy they'd driven in on. Behind the wheel, to her great surprise, is Hale. Blinded by the sunlight, she calls his name and runs to the car. She expects him to get out and embrace her, but he stays put, his hands on the wheel. Gabe walks over through the sandy dunes.

"Aren't you coming?" Sasha asks Gabe.

He shakes his head as he walks up to the car and opens the door for her. She slides into the passenger seat. It's boiling hot. Hale stays impassive as Gabe shuts the door for her.

"Did you get the coordinates?" Gabe asks, walking up to Hale's side of the car.

Hale nods. She buckles in. She watches the boys exchange meaningful looks. She wonders if they're being watched. She wants to say goodbye properly, but she doesn't want to get them into any more trouble. The little car brings them out into the desert, chugging along with great difficulty. She has so much to say, but all the words are stuck in her throat.

"Are you okay?" Hale asks, keeping his eyes on the road.

"No, I'm really not."

"Are you hurt?"

"Define hurt."

"In pain, injured."

"Is anyone ever okay after being shot?"

"I was."

"Could've fooled me." She mutters. He'd never told her about being shot before, but it didn't surprise her anymore. It seemed he'd been through a myriad of terrible experiences for a seventeen year old, if that was even his age. He sighs, his hands clutching the wheel. She can feel the car slowing down, and he pulls over. There's no road, so it seems irrelevant where they stop. He takes a deep breath and turns to her.

"I'm sorry about everything that happened to you since we met."

"And that's why you took this gig, driving me away?"

"No, Pythagorus knew I'd get it done, or he believed so."

"Get what done?"

"Get rid of you." Her heart drops into her stomach. She doesn't really believe he could do such a thing, but Hale was always set on "following orders". Why had they healed her just to get rid of her again?

"He expects you to..."

"We're going to drive. I'm going to bring you to Eva. You're going to make yourself invisible."

"Hale, why don't you disappear with us? It would be easier together."

He shakes his head, as he always does when she goes down this line of questioning. It hits differently when she considers he's been given orders to get rid of her, again, though it's more personal this time.

She reaches for his hand on the steering wheel, and this time he lets his hand drop to hers. He lets her hold his hand for a long while as they return on the road, even when their hands get clammy. They pull over only once for a bathroom break, stock up on food at a gas station, and he trusts her to stay in the car while he pays, then they keep driving. When the desert gets dark, they pull over and fill up on junk food: chips, twinkies, salted nuts, pretzels, until they're full but dissatisfied. She has a million questions, as usual, but she knows he isn't likely to give her any answers. She climbs into the backseat to sleep and beckons him to join her. He does, and the familiarity of his heartbeat feels like home in the immense desert landscape. Being in love felt like a mistake. It was supposed to be glorious and exciting, but it was all heartache and grasping for someone in the darkness who couldn't give you what you needed in the light. She didn't want it to always be like this, but she was willing to express it one last time. She knew he didn't expect to survive his youth, but she was planning to survive - and she was planning to remember.

PART III:
ON THE OTHER SIDE OF THE WAR

Chapter 1
Stranded at the Edge of the Universe

Eva

She became a mother the way one falls off a cliff into cold water. The tiny being born underneath her heart entered the world in a regular hospital room with a dozen other birthing mothers. She'd waddled herself to the hospital alone, knowing it was coming. At first, they tried to refuse her, to say she didn't have the right cards, or she wasn't far enough along or that it was "ghost contractions." She didn't listen. According to her, either they would put her in a bed or they would let her give birth in their parking lot. They didn't call her bluff.

There were so many nurses and doctors that she lost track, and she didn't care about their names anyway, only that they could release the pressure in her abdomen and stop the pain. She didn't argue with anything they suggested, which she later wondered about, but she was so used to having no control in her own life that it felt natural that these so-called experts would figure it out if she couldn't. The only moment that snapped easily into her mind, later on, was the first moment of seeing her daughter: a perfect tiny human covered in white film peering up at her with Gabe's eyes, Gabe's lips, and Gabe's eyelashes. It made all of the pain in her body disappear for a moment - she was a part of him and her, an impossible shake-up of DNA between two people who were fated for one another.

Within seconds of being placed on her chest, the baby screamed, and she wouldn't stop until somewhere close to her first birthday. Eva laughed. Of course, she'd be loud, just like Gabe. She was so beautiful - but spiky and tough, like a Rose. Rosalie Clara Wells was what she named her, Clara for the nurse on the base, Wells for Gabe and Rosie just for her. She wrote Gabe's name on the birth certificate even though he wasn't there to sign. She stayed in the hospital for as long as they would let her, charging each day to Khalil's credit card, hoping against all odds that Khal would check where the payments were coming out of and it would bring Gabe to her, but most of her mind was occupied by Rose; feeding Rose, changing Rose, providing adequate care for Rose. Everything was about Rose now. Every breath, every decision, every step. It would all be for Rose.

235

Sasha

"Evangeline lives in apartment 402." Hale told her as they pulled up in front of a derelict apartment complex.

"Here? You're leaving me here? It looks like termites holding hands."

She took a deep breath and gathered her courage. She couldn't believe they'd hooked up on the road. What sort of person was she turning into? Hale had looked at the scar on her side closely but said nothing. He neither denied nor confirmed her suspicions about what might've happened to Mike either. She reached for the door handle, then turned back to Hale.

"So this is it."

He nodded.

"See you on the other side of the war?"

"I can't promise anything."

"You're clinging to the idea of dying, huh?"

"It's likely."

"Your version of the world sounds a little too easy."

He looked at her quizzically.

"You think you can go through life without connections and then die. You think you don't need to risk yourself emotionally because you will just risk yourself physically," She waited for him to confirm or deny, but he did neither, "well, that's pretty cowardly, in my opinion. You show up in my life, you change everything, and now you're planning just to vanish again, and you can't even promise me you'll try and come back. You won't even offer me a shred of hope. You're sending me in *there*, with nothing and you won't even tell me you'll look out for me?"

"I have as little control over the situation as you do."

She turns to him fully, trying to memorize his face, how his hair falls into his eyes, how the sunlight, what little there is, picks up the slight color in his eyes or plays on his skin.

"Then just tell me what you want." She asks him.

"What I want?"

"Yes, on the other side of the war, when there's no one left to fight. What do you want?"

They sat there in silence.

"Okay, well, think about that." She put her hand on his cheek, and he flinched but didn't pull away. She unbuckled her seat belt and leaned forward, kissing him gently on the lips. She stepped out of the car and walked to the building. There was nothing more she could say. She wanted to see him happy, but she couldn't make him, and he wasn't ready for promises or ultimatums, so she had to stop thinking about him and start thinking about herself now - herself and Eva.

He waited for her to be inside before pulling away, and she sank to her knees once the car was out of her line of sight. God, how was she ever going to do this? All she had with her was a small bag of belongings, not even the ones she'd brought along to California: all of those things had vanished with Eva and that guy, Remi. She didn't know her way around; she had no money or job. She didn't even have any ID!

At least she was finally somewhere with reception; she noted as she turned on her cell phone. Those little bars were like a lifeline. Scooping herself off the ground, she went to the list of names that listed the occupants of the apartments. All of them were blank. This was the sort of place where you needed to know who you were looking for, she dialed 402. No answer. She redialed it, but nothing. An older woman with a small cart opened the door to the lobby with great difficulty, and Sasha peeled herself away from her attempts to help her get the cart through the door.

"Where you goin'?" The woman asked her in the voice of a thousand cigarettes.
"Apartment 402? My friend lives here. Evangeline."
The woman looked her up and down as though assessing whether she could enter the disgusting building.
"You two had better not start takin' clients in. I've been here for 12 years, and we've had it pretty quiet. Once girls like you start showin' up, there's always trouble that follows. Keep your nose clean."
Sasha blushed, realizing what the woman meant.
"Oh, we're not..."
"Yeah, yeah." the woman's hand was birdlike as she turned the key in the lock, which allowed them both to push the door open far enough for her to drag her things inside. Sasha found herself hauling the woman's bags up to the fourth floor too, as it turned out she was in 405.
"I'm Sasha, by the way."
"Sounds like that sort of name, yeah." The woman huffed, not offering her own name in return.
When the woman had shut her door, Sasha returned to the door of 402. There was no doorbell on this level. She knocked gently, then hard.
"Eva!" She called. She was sure the woman was listening in from her own apartment, but if she didn't have anywhere to stay, she really was in trouble.
"Who's there?" A familiar voice called from behind the door. Tears sprang into her eyes. "Eva! It's me! It's Sasha! Open up!"
She could hear several locks being unlatched, followed by a cry - a child's cry.

Could it be?
Eva opened the door. Her hair in a pile at the top of her head. From inside the apartment, the cry continued. Eva put her hands over her mouth, her face crumbling. Tears gathered at the corners of her eyes too. Sasha wrapped her arms around Eva, whose head reached to her chin, and they sank to the floor together in a heap. She sobbed and felt her friend sobbing into her too, her shirt getting wet. Every time one of them felt they were done, the other's cries would just get them started all over again. Eva finally pulled away from the hug. "I have to go check on Rose."
Rose? Who was Rose? The cries from inside the apartment became the only thing Sasha could hear. She followed Eva into the tiny apartment, sparsely furnished and poorly lit. She shut the door behind her and watched Eva go straight for the living room, where she crouched on the floor in front of her old suitcase. She scooped a bundle of blankets from inside, and the bundle screamed all the louder.
"Sorry, she's just hungry. Give me a second."
Eva turned away towards the window, adjusted her shirt, then pulled a blanket from the couch and swept it over herself and the now quieter bundle of blankets.
Sasha let herself slide onto the couch, which creaked underneath her, trying to process what was in front of her.
Eva didn't look up at her just yet, then tugged her shirt back up and lifted the baby, sweeping the same towel over her shoulder and patting the tiny child on the back. When she was done, she spun around and presented her to Sasha in the crook of her arm.
"Rosie," she said, "meet your auntie Sasha."
Gabriel Wells' eyes peered up from the tiny, squished face of the little girl, still red from the earlier crying and screaming.
"Oh Eva...she's beautiful," was all Sasha could muster.

Eva

Having Sasha back was a lifeline, a buoy in the storm of what her life had become. Despite having no experience with kids, she jumped into parenthood like Rose was her own. Sasha wasn't one for getting up early, so she took the late night shift, pacing the apartment with Rose in her arms for hours. She would go out and buy groceries with Khalil's credit card and added formula to the mix. At first, she'd wanted to argue, but she was so grateful for the help that she couldn't bring herself to care. Any break from constantly meeting this tiny being's needs was more than welcome. The war raged somewhere far away, but their tiny part of the world seemed untouched, until it was.

The first thing to go was the phones. No matter where she went in the apartment, she couldn't pick up the signal; she then tried out on the balcony, and so did the rest of the neighbourhood. She could see neighbours walking around with their phones over their heads.

Then, it was the credit card. Sasha walked in looking sour and slammed the piece of plastic on their tiny kitchen table.

"No luck. I tried ten stores. This thing is over. Stores are putting up hand-drawn signs saying "Cash only.""

Eva got up off the couch cradling Rose in the crook of her arm. She'd just finished feeding and was sleepy and warm. Her tiny baby fingers were curled around a strand of Eva's hair, which hurt, just a little but not enough for her to try and extract them.

"So what's the plan then?"

"We take inventory, and we figure out how to make money."

"Well, Benny at the bar did say I could come work once Rose was born."

Sasha made a face. "That grimy bar on the corner? That place is terrifying."

"It's a bar." she shrugged. She didn't want to voice what it was that Benny suggested she do at the bar.

"Okay, it's a start. If you could go see him soon, that would be great. Who knows how long any of these places will be open, right?"

"Yeah..."

"I'll probably need to find something too."

"I'm sure you will. Do you want me to ask Benny too?"

"I don't know, someone always has to be home, right?"

Eva nodded, feeling her shoulders sag. She was so tired already, and she could barely imagine working on top of that.

"Wish we had a library nearby so I could print out some CVs...though I don't know what I'd put on it." Sasha sighed, sinking onto one of the two chairs. They really should've filled their kitchen when they still had the credit card.

"I don't think anyone around here expects a CV."

Sasha rubbed the bridge of her nose.

"Okay, I'll start making a list of what we have."

"Sash, we'll figure it out." Her voice shook as she said it.

"Will we? Because I'm beginning to feel like we should've taken that credit card and hightailed it back home the minute we got here." Eva let herself sink into the other chair, hoping Sasha wouldn't get any louder.

"Take a deep breath, hon. We can't do anything if we panic."

"We can't do anything anyway!"

She knew better than to tell her friend to calm down. No one ever calmed down from being told to, but she wished she could say something helpful. She knew she could figure out how to survive, and she assumed Sasha would too, but who would they be on the other side of that survival? The worst had happened, hadn't it? She'd had the baby. She'd lost Gabe. It all felt so foggy these days; perhaps that was what recovery looked like, but she couldn't bring up the righteous rage that Sasha seemed to be bringing to the table. Sasha's hand clutched the credit card as though she intended to snap it in half.

"This is such bullshit!"

"Yes, it is."

"How could they do this to us?"

"Who?" She knew exactly who, but part of coping was to see the situation honestly.

"Hale and Gabe!"

"You think this is their fault?"

Sasha slammed her fist on the table. "Of course it is! If we hadn't met them, we'd be in college by now, building our futures instead of being stuck in this hell hole!"

Eva cradled Rose in her arms.

"Do you really wish we'd never met them?"

Sasha slumped in her chair. "I...I just wish things had turned out differently."

"If I hadn't met Gabe, there would be no Rose."

"There could be - just not in a crappy apartment with no money."

"Sasha..." Eva held Rose out to the taller girl, the terrible lighting in the kitchen accentuating the dark circles under her friend's eyes.

Sasha took Rose to her chest and let the tears fall, wiping them with her sleeve.

"I'm really glad you're here, by the way. Being here by myself was honestly the worst."

"And being on the base without you was the worst too." Sasha smiled, shaking her head. "God, I just want to cry all the time these days."

"No judgment here." Eva laughed in agreement.

"And I'm nauseous all the time."

Eva shrugged, it was an all too familiar experience for her. "Been there, done that, bought the t-shirt. But hey! I got this bundle out of it." Rose, uncaring about the world falling apart around her, gave a big yawn and wriggled around in the towel they'd used as a blanket to wrap around her.

"She's pretty cute, isn't she?" Eva said, looking into her daughter's squished little face admiringly.

"Well, at least you know you and Gabe make cute babies."

Eva chuckled. "Is that like a compensation prize? What if we made hideous babies?"

"Then blame Gabe."

Eva laughed. She was glad Sasha had calmed down, just in time for Rose to wake up and start to fuss. Sasha got up to go change her on the living room floor.

Eva watched her friend go, grateful, tired. They'd figure it out, wouldn't they?

Chapter 2
Sacrifices We Knew We Were Making

Sasha

The streets around their apartment were always bustling, though not with the sorts of people she would usually want to be around. From the minute the sun went down, there were women standing on street corners in various stages of undress, getting picked up by cars that roared, with lights installed underneath them like stars.

Once Eva began her job at the bar, nighttimes became all the harder - she would walk her friend to work so that she didn't have to go alone, carrying Rose, and then return to the apartment to sleep in stops and starts until it was time to go and meet her again. She searched high and low for daytime work so that they could switch over with Rose, but anyone who'd had a job before the war clung to it tooth and claw. Eva continuously told her she didn't need her to walk her, but Sasha felt protective now that they were all relying on Eva's salary.

On one of those walks back, one of the girls she crossed daily waved her over. She was wearing a short flannel skirt that looked a lot like her school uniform back at Saint-Ignatius, torn fishnet stockings, and some impressive heels. Her tank top was tight and more than anything, she looked cold. Sasha clutched Rose closer to her chest and walked over. The girl's hair stood around her head like a halo of curls. She was beautiful, though not as young as Sasha had assumed from a distance.

"So you were lookin' for work?" The girl began without skipping a beat. Her voice had the lilt that everyone in this town seemed to have. Her iridescent eye shadow picked up the sparkle of the lights around them.
"How did you know?"
"People around here talk a lot."
"Not to me." Sasha confessed.
The woman swayed a little in her stilettos.
"We've got a room on the East side, by the garage."
Sasha wasn't sure where that was, but she was finally catching onto the sort of work the woman was alluding to.
"Is it safe?"
"Sweetheart, nothing's safe around here, but being hungry's worse than being safe."
"Why would you help me?"

"Oh, a commission from finding new girls, and that's a mighty cute baby you've got there. I know what it takes to raise a child here. I've got three me-self."

"You have three kids?"

"Don't go soundin' so surprised."

"Okay, theoretically, and I'm not agreeing to anything...how would I get this sort of...work?" Her mind was practically screaming at this point. She was rolling down a hill of red flags.

"You'll need an interview."

"With who?"

"Who d'you think?"

She couldn't even get the word out. She imagined the sorts of men that interviewed for this kind of work, which made her nauseous, though that was a near-constant state these days.

"So d'you want me to ask 'em?"

"I guess so..." She imagined her parents and their shocked expressions if they ever found out about this...but how could they?

"Um, can it be during the day?"

"You figure it out with your own clients...he just gets a cut."

"Thanks..." Sasha mumbled.

"Name's Yvette." The woman said.

"Alexandra." Sasha said. "I'd better...get this one home..."

Her feet felt like they were led as she returned to the apartment. Every step was burdensome. As soon as she locked the door behind her, she slid to the ground, her hands shaking so hard she was afraid she'd drop Rose. What had she just agreed to? She wasn't that sort of person! A voice at the back of her head told her, "What sort of person? The kind that survives?" She knew it was right. Rose began to cry, and she was forced to get herself up off the floor and tend to her needs: heat up the bottle, test it out on her wrist, feed the fussy little one, change her, bathe her, swaddle her up again and sink back onto the couch. It was dark outside, and the sounds of the night filled the empty space: sirens, dogs barking, babies crying, and drunk people out on the street. What was she going to tell Eva?

Eva

Work at the bar wasn't as hard as it seemed. It was physically demanding, but if she was honest, it wasn't so different from the combination of a dance team and swimming. Underwear was like wearing a bathing suit, and the dancing portion mostly involved a lot of posing. Plus, she'd been on the dance team at school for years. The other girls were welcoming and warm. Many wore elaborate makeup, and she suspected some weren't biologically women, but that didn't matter. They lived in their own little world, and she was now one of them, so they welcomed her with open arms. She went by "Angel." It was comfortable to slide into that alter ego rather than using her real identity. Benny treated them equally like garbage, so they banded together and mocked him behind his back. The women offered tips and tricks and warned her about difficult clients. She made a fair bit per night and walked home with it stuffed in her shoes. She brought spare clothes so as not to attract attention to herself when Sasha came to meet her in the mornings. Despite the ickiness factor, she found it easy to dissociate from the experience when she wasn't working.

She was happy to come home with enough money to buy formula and necessities. When they began getting letters from the landlord about rent, which she assumed Khalil must have been covering up to that point, she found that they had just enough to get by. Rose was growing fast, and her bright blond hair was darkening into a dark brown, though the curls remained. Her eyes were still bright blue, and she wondered how long they would stay that way. She was starting to babble, just a bit, as though dying to make her opinion heard. Sasha was an awesome co-parent, delighting in her every syllable and never showing a hint of jealousy. In the beginning, Sasha was always home, but she'd started going out more during the day, which she hoped she was using to look for work. She was only ever out a few hours at a time, but when she asked about it, her friend would shrug and say, "no luck."

It was many weeks before she learned the truth. She was heading out the door with a newly acquired baby stroller, which Sasha insisted that they needed and hauling it down the stairs when she ran into Sasha, who was standing in the lobby in an outfit she was sure one of the girls from the bar had lent her last week.
"Sash?"
Sasha jumped. "Oh my god Eva! You scared me to death!"
"What are you doing?"
"Oh, just waiting for a lift."
"From who?"
"A friend." Sasha had gone completely red, folding her arms as though she wanted to sink through the floor.
Eva was so sick and tired of everyone lying to her. She'd dealt with Gabe hiding everything for months, and now she would deal with it with Sasha too?
"Come on, hon, what's going on?"
"I found a job." Sasha coughed out.

As two and two added up, Eva clung to the edge of the stroller to hold herself up.

"You're..."

"You don't need to say it, okay? I know."

"Sash, this is dangerous!"

"I know." They locked eyes just as a white car pulled up in front of the apartment. "I have to go." Eva reached her hand out, and Sasha grasped it and gave it a supportive squeeze. "I'll be back soon."

She disappeared into the car. Eva stood in the lobby in disbelief. She hauled the stroller back up to the apartment and locked the door.

Sasha returned, as promised and went straight into the shower. There were still a few hours before Eva had to go to work, a time during which she usually slept, but they needed to have this conversation, didn't they?

When Sasha came back, wet hair sticking to her face, Mike's old hoody wrapped around her, she sat down on the couch beside her and looked her straight in the face.

"Go ahead, whatever you have to say, I'm ready for it."

Eva's heart broke. Did Sasha really think she could judge her? She shifted over on the couch and wrapped her arms around her friend.

"Thank you."

"What?"

"I'm going to worry myself sick every time you do that."

Sasha pulled two hundred dollars out of her pocket. "Maybe having savings will help."

"Are you, okay though?"

"Um, yeah, sort of."

"Are you safe?"

"Not really, my boss is this crazy gross guy who I think is in charge of all the girls around here, and he's honestly terrifying, but the clients are usually okay. It's super gross, obviously, but..."

"As long as you don't think about it?"

"Yeah."

"Okay."

They sat together in silence, thinking about one another's situation, until Rose began to cry in the next room. Eva jumped up to fetch her. The days of idle chatting about the future in Gabe and Hale's apartment seemed so far away now.

Sasha

The months slid by, the days blending into each other as they tag-teamed parenting and work. The awkwardness around discussing the particulars of their new jobs fell away as they found more and more in common. They each had regulars, clients they hated, and clients they were afraid of. Her pimp, known only as *D,* was discussed as easily as Eva discussing Benny. Both men had immense power over their lives, and both would've made the world a better place by falling straight off it. The days themselves felt immensely long, but the passage of time could be marked through Rose's little milestones: her first time propping herself up on her stomach and trying to move forward, her first baby tooth poking out from her gums, the first time she made a sound that sounded similar enough to a word that Sasha wanted to run to the bar and tell Eva all about it.

With their current earnings, they could slowly fill the apartment with baby things: a crib, a changing table, toys, teethers, and pacifiers. They stocked the pantry and the fridge. They even found a day to pay an elderly woman on the third floor to watch Rose for a few hours when their schedules didn't intercept. Every day was filled with anxiety, but they found one another at the end of a shift or an encounter, and it felt normal for a few minutes. She often felt disconnected from her body - as though she was just a brain in a meat suit. It somehow helped with what she had to do, and it allowed her to feel sane when she went from a trashy girl being picked up by a creepy stranger to mom-on-duty.

It was a rare treat when she and Eva were home long enough to go to the store together. The closest pharmacy was surprisingly far, so they caught the bus with Rose in her new stroller and headed off to stock up on supplies: soaps, baby powder, diapers, shampoo, conditioner, pain medication, moisturizers and all of the other goodies she once took for granted. With Sasha operating the grocery cart and Eva driving the stroller, they walked down the aisles looking at sales. Eva stopped in front of the colorful section of birth control and sighed.
"Ah, the aisle I probably should've stocked up on before turning 18." She laughed.
Sasha grabbed the largest and least expensive pack and threw it into the cart. "I'd argue the fault was mostly Gabe's."
"Well, we used protection up until my birthday."
"That's good. Then what happened?"
"We got carried away when he played decoy for my birthday party."
"Oh god, no wonder you were so late."
Eva blushed. The fact that she was still a little embarrassed by the conversation reminded Sasha how young they still were, despite playing house. Rose had somehow gotten ahold of a box of cookies and was gnawing happily on the plastic.
"Guess we're buying cookies," Sasha sighed. Rose wasn't quite at solid foods, but she was getting close. She'd finally grown enough hair that Eva

could put it into a tiny ponytail at the top of her head. Sasha looked up to read the signs above them to see if she could buy a little bow.

Eva had moved down the aisle to the feminine hygiene products.

"Hey, Sash. We haven't bought any of this stuff for a while...how have you been uh...?"

Sasha thought about it. She legitimately couldn't remember having her period since arriving at the apartment. Between the stress of her job and how she'd felt about her body, she figured it had just vanished for survival purposes.

"It hasn't really been an issue, but we should buy some just in case. What about you?"

"Did you know you don't get your period when breastfeeding?"

"Really?"

"Yeah, the girls at the bar told me. Stuff I wish I'd learned in health class."

"Well, maybe my body's responding in commiseration." Sasha joked, a little uneasy. That feeling of nausea was coming back. She put her hand on her stomach in fear.

"Um, hon, do you use protection with all the clients?"

"I try." She needed to sit down, but there was nowhere to sit, so she let herself down on the floor.

"Sasha?" Eva was beside her, hand on her shoulder.

"I'm okay; I just need a second." She took a few deep breaths, waiting for the wave to pass. She knew people were staring at them, but it was all too much for a moment. Eva handed her a water bottle, which she opened quickly and guzzled down.

"I'm okay." She got back up. "I think we should get a pregnancy test..." she whispered, her cheeks burning and her heart racing.

There wasn't enough air in the world to fill her lungs at the moment. She clutched the water bottle, which they still had to pay for, flooded with a memory. She remembered handing Hale a water bottle on a hot summer. It had been so beautiful: the flowers around them, the school grounds below, having him close to her, even though they were nothing then. They were less than nothing now; he was gone, making her no promises, leaving only the memories of stolen moments together. He never confirmed his feelings beyond "I care about you," and he'd only ever expressed himself physically.

Now, there was only herself and Eva. He was fighting his war, and she was fighting her own. She and Eva were the real soldiers on the front lines, two girls trying to survive in an unforgiving world with a tiny baby. They remained quiet as they paid for everything and dragged themselves back on the bus. Eva would have to go to work when they returned, and she would be home with Rose. The pregnancy test lay among the many other purchases, like a bomb waiting to blow up what was left of their lives.

Chapter 3
Birthing a World

Eva

She couldn't stop thinking about it all through her shift, though she could do the choreography in her sleep at this point. Benny snapped at her for being distracted, but she told him to piss up a rope. He was used to the girls snapping back at him, but Eva was still getting used to it. She'd always been taught to be polite.

"What's eatin' you, Angel?" Stella asked her when she came off stage. She was smoking in the backroom while stuffing extra tissue paper into her bra. Her tall blond wig was magnificently piled up on her head.

"I'm worried about my friend."

"Alexandra? You should be. I'd never deal with D. No amount of money is worth that."

"Well, that's part of it, but I'm worried she might be pregnant."

Stella picked up a tube of dark lipstick off the dusty table and applied it to her bottom lip in the mirror. "Oh, that's not so bad. It'll give her a bit of a break."

"What do you mean?" She couldn't imagine maternity leave being offered on the streets.

"She's young. D'll just up his cut on the other side. Happens all the time."

Eva found herself speechless. The way people were so nonchalant about things like this here never ceased to amaze her. She imagined having this same conversation with anyone she knew back home: her mom, friends, or even a teacher. The idea of there being another child seemed unimaginable. She'd had to live through so many unlikely scenarios recently that some part of her had given up on predicting what might happen next. It wasn't exactly a "que sera, sera," but more of the feeling of being on a canoe without a paddle: all she could do was brace herself and hope she didn't end up in the water.

When she exited the bar, Sasha wasn't at her usual spot waiting for her. That was when she knew, they'd hit the rapids.

Her feet hurt, but she power-walked as quickly as she could down the streets, feeling the darkness creeping inside her while the sun rose, illuminating the streets in their grime and soot.

She wished she were tall enough to take the stairs two at a time. As she reached their apartment door, the dread had solidly settled in her stomach. This was exactly like coming back to the rooms at the end of the day on the base, except that there was no Gabe. Gabe was the only person who'd delighted in her pregnancy. She wondered if he'd feel the same about Sasha because she was sure now.

She heard Rose's familiar cry from inside and heard the bathroom door open. She heard Sasha cooing to settle her and then return to the living room. The walls were paper thin in this building. She turned the key in the lock, then the second one. When she stepped inside, Sasha was sitting on the ground in the living room; tears dry on her face. Her eyes were puffy as she looked up.

"Welcome home." She said.

"Oh hon..." Eva sank to the floor beside her. "It'll be okay."

"Will it?" Her voice sounded hollow and exhausted.

"It will. I didn't think it could be either, but it's all turned out okay, hasn't it?"

"I know, but this isn't the same. This is who knows whose baby I've been going through the list in my head, making me sick."

"What if it's Hale's?" She whispered, kneeling by her friend.

"What if it isn't?"

"So what do you want to do, honey? I'll support you no matter what you decide."

"I don't know...I don't know!"

"Sh..."

There was a small sound from the other room; Rose was an incredibly light sleeper. It was a wonder that they could do anything when she was down for her nap. Eva tried to imagine a second one in the house, another crying mouth to feed, another creature that needed them both 24/7 when all they had to offer was snippets of energy and warmth.

"What about Rose?"

"What about her? We would figure it out. We always have."

"We're hanging by a string here. We don't have anything to offer a child."

"We have us. We're doing fine with Rose."

Sasha stayed quiet. Eva continued. "Just know that I'll be here, and if it's not Hale's, then it's not, but it's not the baby's fault that we had to do what we did. It's not yours either. You don't have to do anything you don't want to do."

Sasha nodded and picked herself up off the floor just in time for Rose to cry out again.

"Sorry," Eva bolted to tend to her daughter. Sasha crawled to the couch and pulled herself up onto it. Eva returned with Rose this time and sat beside her, looking up at the bleak, gray sky beyond the tiny window. Eva wished she could see foliage or stars or anything that could make her feel less like a statistic waiting to happen in a cold, unfeeling city.

"She really looks like him, " Sasha said. They said it a lot and often broke any awkward silences.

"Oh, I don't know. I think she's got a lot of me in 'er." Eva cooed, inhaling above Rose's head.

"She's perfect. Why would we want another one?"

"Say that again when she wakes us up at 4 am."

"Then we would have two waking us up."

"I guess we'd already be up."

"Why do you want this?"

"I don't. I'm just playing devil's advocate."

Eva paused.

"Okay, maybe I do a little. I just think it would be something else we could share. Two mamas, two babies - but I wouldn't want you to do anything if you aren't ready."

"Were you ready?"

"Hell to the no."

A long silence followed. A pregnant silence.

"I guess..." Sasha wouldn't lift her gaze at Eva. She just stared at Rose as though trying to imagine a second one.

"It'll even be better now. We have all the stuff we need, and you can just give them all of Rose's stuff so we don't have to buy anything really, and you'll get a break from work. I'm sure it'll work out. We'll figure it out together like we always do."

"But I don't want to carry any of my client's kids. What if they make some sort of claim on it or I don't know. I've just been sitting here, thinking about it all, and it just seems hopeless..." her voice was barely a whisper.

"Hon," she reached over, putting her only free hand on Sasha's forearm. "It'll be ours. You and me. We'll raise it with Rose, and love him or her like crazy. You're going to be an amazing mom. Look at how you are with Rose! I know we can do this...if you want to."

Sasha nodded, looking pale and small.

"We should call the clinic today and get you seen."

Sasha nodded, her arms wrapped around herself. Eva scooted over to sit beside her, leaning forward to rest her head on her shoulder.

"You and me against the world, okay?"

The storm inside Eva didn't subside, but she kept it quietly inside, just like Sasha would've done for her.

Sasha

She did all the scans and took all the vitamins, but she knew the hardest part: She had to face D. He ran his business from an apartment building on Main Street. She'd only been there once before for her "interview," which lasted all ten minutes. He was a broad man, clean shaven and bald. The bouncers knew every girl who worked for him, so getting an appointment wasn't difficult, but standing in the hallway waiting for the conversation certainly was. It was dark and covered in graffiti, the smell of cigars, cigarettes and body odor lingering permanently. There was also nowhere to sit, so she simply stood there, inhaling and clutching her bag. She'd brought as much cash as possible and felt entirely unsafe with it on her person. She wished she could bring Eva, but someone had to stay home with Rose.

"Let her in!" The room was dark as she stepped inside, with a naked lightbulb up above and a lava lamp in the corner. There was a white couch in front of the desk, which she chose not to sit in. She didn't need to think about what happened on that couch.

"Well, well, well, if it isn't my little dove." The man grumbled, hardly looking up from his phone.

"Hi, I have something important to tell you." She wanted just to spit it out, but she also wanted to throw up on his desk.

"I'll be the judge of that."

She sighed. She wanted to roll her eyes. A few months ago, she would have. Now, she knew the stakes. She remembered Hale and how he'd told her to keep her mouth shut, never to argue with Pythagorus. D was the same: a man with more power over her life than anyone should be allowed to have. She hated these men who had the power to make every decision and chose to harm at every turn. To be fair, she owed him her life or her salary, yet she still hated him. She would've killed him if she had to, or so she told herself. She didn't have that loyalty that Hale seemed to have towards Pythagorus. That must come from years of isolation. It was ironic that now that she was so far away from him, she was finally coming to understand him: Living in fear, in survival mode, made you meek, made you quiet.

Righteous anger rose inside her, overtaking the fear.

"I'm pregnant."
He glanced up at her.
"You don't look it."
"I am. I took a pregnancy test."
"Sounds expensive." he went back to scrolling on his phone.

"So what's the protocol?"

"Protocol?" He chuckled. "You pay me up front for whatever work you're not doing, and then you keep paying me when you have the little bastard. You owe me for whatever your clients ain't getting."

She took out the wad of cash in her purse and put it on the table. The two men by the door kept their eyes on her, presumably checking whether she had a weapon in her bag. D set down his phone and swiped the cash. He counted it, licking the tip of his dirty ringed finger.

"That's fine for now. You'll work another month and make as much as you can before you show, then come back as soon as possible. I know where you live, so no funny business."

She nodded and turned on her heel. The bouncer at the front barred her way.

"What?"

"I didn't hear you thank the boss."

She turned around and choked out a "thank you."

The bouncer moved, and she bolted.

Running felt good, so she kept running, past the apartment and to the park. It was deserted at this time of day. It was prime naptime for babies, and kids would probably be in school. Only a pack of teenagers smoking was visible to her. She sat on the swings and sobbed, kicking against the ground to get herself up and higher off the ground. She wished the swing could take her far away from her situation, to the past, or the distant future, anywhere but here.

Eva

Without Sasha's paycheck, things were harder. She heard about the war approaching, but she saw it only on the empty shelves of stores. She hoped Gabe was okay. It was easier to worry about him or Sasha than herself. Benny's business wasn't doing as well, so she had to add a second job to her schedule, which meant less time with Rose, which she hated, but it was her turn to take care of Sasha's needs now.

The sun had set hours ago, but the neon lights of the strip made the streets glow as brightly as midday. Eva hated the garish colours, noise pollution and general chaos of the downtown core where her second job brought her. This city was a far cry from her suburban upbringing, and it always made her feel overwhelmed. Her pale skin shone fluorescent blue and pink as she turned off the main strip onto a smaller side street. A few blocks south lay her destination; a dive bar called "The 69".

On the outside, it looked like any other bar. However, this particular bar was known for serving some rather unsavoury folks. The patronage consisted mainly of drug dealers and petty criminals. They frequented this establishment to conduct business and watch the dancers perform in tiny sequined thongs.

In the distance, Eva could make out the towering silhouette of Jimmy, one of the bouncers hired around the time she had started dancing.

"Where the hell ya been?" he said with a slight smirk as she approached the club. His short brown hair was slick with sweat, and clung slightly to the tan skin around his temples. His honey-coloured eyes were glowing with mischief. He would almost be attractive if his nose weren't bent at an odd angle. Eva assumed a fistfight had caused this, but she had never bothered to ask him.

"Bite me" she hissed. She was in no mood for banter tonight. Rose had thrown up all over her as she was about to leave, and the bus had been twenty minutes late.

"Ain't you a salty one," Jimmy said with a smirk as he took a drag from his cigarette, seemingly enjoying the look of annoyance on Eva's face. He let the smoke billow from between his lips and handed the cigarette to Eva. She glared at him but plucked it from between his giant fingers. She quickly inhaled and returned it to the towering hulk of a human standing before her.

"Gotta go," she said exhaling a tiny cloud of smoke. She turned down the alleyway next to the club and disappeared into one of the side doors.

"Good Talk," Jimmy said with a slight chuckle. His broad shoulders leaned against the brick wall.

The girls here were less welcoming, too, like extensions of their surroundings. Today, the backroom had the radio blasting. Eva came in and found her mirror, starting on her look. The radio announcer was telling about another explosion in San Francisco. She listened as they listed names and numbers. She listened for news of her dad, who she knew would've been deployed for sure. The rebel group had made asks; the government hadn't negotiated, and the capital city was divided. There were riots and political debates. All she cared about was whether the people she loved were okay, so she listened for her father's name or rank as she powdered her skin and applied layers of mascara and eyeliner.

"So you been readin' the statements from these philosophers?"

Eva turned to eavesdrop on her fellow dancers.

"I ain't got time for that!"

"They're like ghosts." The other woman said, her long blond wig blocking her face. She had a newspaper open on her table. "They write bout the way those rich folks live while we down here scrapin' by. They say it's time to take power back for people like us."

"You gonna strike?"

"If it comes to our city, why not? What've I got to lose?"

"Your life."

"It ain't much of a life, is it?" The other woman stretched. They were up before Eva, so she could glance down at the paper when they left. There was an article by a certain "Aristotle." She flipped through the paper some more. The opinions section was full of responses to the previous week's article from Pythagorus. Her breath caught. Her father had always said that wars weren't only fought on the battlefield; now she understood what he meant. While Khalil, Remi, Gabe and Hale were out there on the front lines, the philosophers worked on the people's minds.

She sighed. The second woman wasn't wrong; she had a job to do. What could she possibly do for Gabe right now? Nothing. He wasn't here. She would keep him alive in their lives for Rose, though. She would tell her all about her daddy and how much he loved her, and she would make sure that if she ever met him, she would know that the war tore him away and that he would never choose to leave them. She had her own words as weapons; they didn't need to be in the newspapers.

Sasha

She named her son Ichigo. She didn't know any Japanese, but Hale had said he was half-Japanese, and she wanted so much for her son to be Hale's that she named him in defiance of the alternative. She read that it meant "Little Guardian" but found out later that it actually meant strawberry, according to a woman she met at a supermarket who said she was raised in Japan. She didn't care. It suited him to a T. He was born on a blistering hot summer night in July and came into the world quietly. It took the nurse a moment to get him to cry out, and even then, he wasn't keen on continuing. Sasha was completely exhausted and numb from the epidural, but she burst into tears instantly when she saw him. He was so perfect that it broke her heart to know he would have to exist in such an imperfect world. She refused to let any of the nurses carry him off to clean him, so they only did so when she fell asleep and placed him into a bassinet beside her bed.

She woke up to two familiar voices: Eva and Rose. Rose, 18 months, was at the point where she constantly mumbled her thoughts, only some of them understandable, and could manage quite a distance on her tiny legs, so Eva placed her into the bassinet and took a million pictures with her phone. She couldn't send the photos anywhere, but Sasha was still endlessly grateful.

"How are you holding up?" Eva asked.

"Not to be repeated." Sasha laughed.

"He's adorable, isn't he? Sticking with Ichigo?"

"Yup, look at him."

Eva agreed that it was the perfect name and repeated it to Rose enough times that she pieced together "Baby Go," which became Ichigo's name until he was old enough to complain about it. She wrote Hale's name on the paperwork with absolute certainty. She hoped it was biologically true, but it didn't matter at the end of the day. She was here because of Hale. If she was honest with herself, he was the reason she got into that car two years ago, and the idea that she would have a shot at raising his son felt as though their story had come full circle. She looked into that little boy's eyes and drowned in them. She vowed that those eyes would never see what Hale's had, not as long as she was still breathing. A new life, a new chance, and a new compass to her otherwise untethered existence.

When she returned to work mere weeks later, it was with a heart so full and a body so numb and changed that she wondered if her clients would accept her. Surprisingly, they couldn't care less. She fell back into her old role as though it were an unwashed sock found underneath the bed. It still fits fine, and it allowed her to start paying off her debt to D. Eva kept working at both bars but rearranged her schedule because Sasha made more per hour. They scrimped and saved on themselves, but at least they knew there would always be food on the table now.

Eva

Rose had started talking early, just as the first flowers of Spring began to appear between the cracks in the sidewalk and the days began to lengthen. Her babbling had become something akin to language. Her first word, unsurprisingly, was "mine." It was declared far and wide about everything and anything. Forks were mine, mommy was mine, auntie Sawa was mine, and of course, *Go* was mine.

Ichigo's first word came much later, to the point that Sasha and Eva had begun to wonder if something was wrong with him. He was nearly three and hardly made any noise besides giggling. He occasionally cried, though never nearly at the pitch Rose had achieved. His crying was quieter, a crumpled sort of sound with tiny squeaks. He came when called, listened intently and would tidy up the few toys they had when asked. He followed Rose around happily and listened to her endless stories. When asked for his name, he would turn to his mother or aunt or, most often, Rose to answer for him.

As much as it worried Sasha, there was something incredibly sweet about how Ichigo expressed himself despite it all. He pointed at things he wanted; he tapped you on the leg if he wanted your attention, and he would point towards the bathroom if he wanted to try potty training. If Rose grabbed a toy from him, he would repeatedly tap her on the shoulder in hopes that she would return it. A temper tantrum from Ichigo involved sitting on the floor looking sullen and refusing to get up. Every time she looked at him, she felt her insides melt. He looked so much like Hale, a tiny, quiet, but incredibly sweet version of a man she'd realized she hardly knew, much less understood. It felt like they'd reset the clock on a life so tainted with trauma and pain, as though they could rebuild a lost childhood.

They tried to be patient about the language, though they discussed it endlessly. Eva would try to coax words from him, "And which cup would you like then? Blue or green?" Ichigo would point. "Can you say, please?" He would nod but said nothing. Between their schedules, the exhaustion of their work, the stress of the news and the endless scramble for money, there wasn't much more room to work on linguistics.

It happened at the park, with Eva trying to strap Ichigo into the swing. She'd had a long night as the dark circles under her eyes gave away. Rose was sitting in the sandbox, digging a hole. Ichigo's eyes followed her every move. "Woe!" He stretched his little arms out. "Whoa? You wanna go?"

"Woe!" He repeated, sounding alarmed.
"You don't want to swing?"
"Wose!"
"Woes?"
She whipped around to see Rose walking off with a man in a gray jacket.
"Rose!"
"Wose! Wose!"

Eva launched forward, leaving Ichigo swinging and screaming. "Rose! Hey! Where do you think you're going with my daughter?"

Rose turned around smiling and dropped the man's hand. The man turned and ran, large boots pounding the sand and the pavement.

Eva grabbed Rose and pressed her to her, stumbling back towards the swing.

She set Rose down, looking out in the direction the man had gone.

"Mommy?"

"Who was that?!"

"A magician."

"Rosie..."

"What wong mommy?"

Eva was shaking; Ichigo had quieted down and wiggled his legs in the swing.

"Wose!"

"He said my name!"

Eva pulled Ichigo out of the swing and took both children home - how would she tell Sasha how her son had said his first word?

Chapter 4
The Big Bang

Eva

The newspapers and television were all claiming the same thing: That the war was nearing its end. She'd lost track of the particulars over the years. Still after mobilizations, conscriptions, attacks, declarations from the rebels and the existing government, speeches about democracy and five different voting attempts that she couldn't participate in because she still didn't have a legitimate passport, it seemed as though the rebels and the newly appointed government officials were finding common ground, or something like that. When you were an "exotic" dancer at a bar with two kids under five, it didn't really matter. The exotic part was new, a bit of a gimmick which required her to dye her hair a bright red monthly, but Benny was willing to pay for it, so she didn't complain.

She preferred to keep busy. She didn't have the brain space to worry about her dad, brother, or even Gabe. When her head hit a pillow, she was unconscious, and the minute her eyes opened, there were kids to deal with and Sasha to touch base with, and now, she had to get Rose registered for school, which was surprisingly difficult. For some insane reason, the school wanted not only Rose's birth certificate, but hers and Gabe's - hers had either been destroyed by Gabe and Hale when they blew up their military town five years ago or it was with her mother, who she couldn't reach out to without confessing everything that had happened. If Gabe had ever had a birth certificate, it would've gone down with the church where he'd lived as a child.

She hadn't heard anything from Gabe since their last moments back on the base in the desert. She knew Khalil was still looking out for her. Now and again, a package would arrive with gifts for her and Rose, gifts with cash stuffed into pockets. There were also postcards occasionally from the strangest places possible: one from Alaska, one from Licking, Missouri, and one from a small island near Hawaii. Of course, there was no real information in any of them, he couldn't tell her what the rebels were doing, but she looked forward to them regardless. She wished Gabe would do the same - at least to tell her he was alive! There had been so many times that she'd watched a rebel plane be shot down on television, or a rebel base be exposed where she would wonder: was this it? Was this Gabe's death? Or Hale's? If Khalil could keep in touch, why couldn't Gabe?

She was still committed to keeping the idea of "Daddy" alive for Rose. She surprised herself by having so many stories to share. There were stories from their childhoods where Gabe was a mischievous little troublemaker, and so many from their time in high school where they went for ice cream, made elaborate breakfasts at his apartment, or went to the beach, and then there were stories about Daddy the Soldier, the one who was taken away from them to fight for a better world. Rose loved these tales, as did Ichigo. Gabe had become something of a superhero in their minds. She wasn't sure why she'd gone in this direction, but Sasha was supportive, which was funny because she and Gabe spent most of their friendship squabbling. Sasha rarely brought up Hale especially around the kids, even though Ichigo looked more and more like his father every day. She assumed it was her way of protecting herself emotionally, which she understood. Sasha's job took so much out of her that she didn't need the extra burden.

It was mere days before Ichigo's birthday when all hell broke loose.

Eva was walking to the bar by herself for a day shift. Benny had started getting lunchtime clients, mostly soldiers, and Sasha was home that day with both kids. Her mind was on Rose's school registration when she heard it: It sounded like fireworks. She turned to see smoke off in the distance. She cursed, spinning to see where she could go. People were running past her; cars tore down the street. Whatever was coming, it wasn't good. The bar wasn't too far, so she began to run towards it. She yanked at the door, to no avail. She could hear more gunfire, not too far now. She couldn't seem to get enough air. She banged both fists against the door. "Benny! Benny, it's me! It's Angel! Open the door!" Still nothing. She dipped into an alleyway and wove between garbage cans to get to a smaller street. When she emerged, there was a grocery store on the other side - all glass, all broken.

There was chaos around her, people running and screaming, kids crying, and car alarms going off. Her every sense was overwhelmed. She looked down the street at a huge plume of smoke. She was running out of time to take cover. She didn't want to climb through a smashed window, so she tried the door, which was jammed shut. There were others taking cover inside, but none moved towards the door. She could see people shoving food into their bags, and emptying shelves. She could see people in military garb running down the street now; it was shockingly familiar to her, reminding her instantly of her dad. Her dad wasn't here, though,; theseinsurgents were looking for something ,and she needed to get out of their way. Giving up on the door, she took a running leap through one of the broken windows just as a car sped across the sidewalk where she'd just been.

She fell hard and clambered up, gritting her teeth through the pain in her elbow where it had hit the ground, tucking herself behind one of the cash registers. A man was going from register to register with a crowbar, popping them open like a soda can and emptying their contents. She pressed herself into the side of the table, trying to make herself as small as possible. There were boots in front of her and dirty jeans. She heard the cash register above her being pried open, the man with the crowbar grunting as he pulled cash out, and coins clattering to the ground. The man bent down to pick up the coins, and she could smell his breath, alcohol strong on his breath. She tried to shrink. He turned to look straight at her. "Ain't you that girl from the 69?" His teeth were gray. "Watcha doin' under there?" He grabbed her by the ankle and pulled her out. She screamed. He was muttering something, but she couldn't hear him; all she could think of was getting as far from him as possible. He was trying to clutch his money bag and grab her at the same time, and his dirty hands grabbed indiscriminately as her body. Shrieking, she kicked off the side of the register and clambered back up on her hands and knees.

Her arm hurt, the air was filled with smoke, and she could now hear explosions somewhere outside. There was nowhere to go. She needed to get back to the apartment.Through her watery eyes, she spotted the big red exit sign. Crawling towards it seemed slow, but she eventually reached it and got up on her knees to push the door. The alarm went off, shockingher that it was still connected. The smoke billowed out from inside the store into the street, and she pulled herself outside, coughing and sputtering, trying to push as much air as possible into her lungs. Her eyes stung, and she tried to stagger upright. It didn't happen. She lay back against the stucco of the building and tried to peer up at the sky. Her eyes closed.

Sasha

"Mommy, look!" Ichigo pointed outside as tanks rolled down the street.
"So cool!" Rose agreed, climbing onto the back of the couch to get a better look.
Sasha was trying to get her heart rate down to a reasonable level so she could deal with the kids. The radio was on, declaring that the war was over. How were there tanks rolling down the street? The whole building shook as though it would come crumbling on top of them. There was

gunfire like fireworks blasting just below. God, wasn't this what they'd been running from all this time? Wasn't this exactly what she'd been promised would never happen?

"Get away from the windows!" she shouted at the kids, both bouncing with frenetic energy. She wished she had curtains. She went to the single bedroom, pulled the sheets off the bed, then went into the kitchen and pulled the tape from a drawer. Standing precariously on the radiator, she taped the sheets over the window, which did nothing to stop the kids from peeking outside. Ever alert to her moods, Ichigo put her hand on hers once she'd stepped off the radiator. "It's okay mommy; we're not scared."

She wanted to cry. This wasn't unusual for her, but there was never a good time and right now, she really did need to keep it together.
"Auntie Sasha?" Rose said, finally pulling herself away from the window.
"Yes, Rosie?"
"I'm hungry."
"We just had lunch."
She shrugged. "but all this noise is making me hungry!" her little voice rang through the apartment like a bell.
That didn't make any sense, but who was she to argue with a five-year-old who wanted to stress eat? She sighed and went to the kitchen. Ichigo followed like a little shadow until Rose called him over to keep watching Armageddon play out just below their apartment.

Rose and Ichigo were like night and day: Rose all sunshine and rainbows, outgoing and sassy. She laughed as loudly as she cried, and her temper was a sight to behold. Ichigo was a quiet summer night, soft-spoken and tentative. He didn't like being alone while Rose was ready to take off down the street and take on the world if you just turned your attention away from her for a moment. As she began making peanut butter and jelly sandwiches, she thought about how differently she loved them. All of the things that had irritated her in Gabe she found adorable in Rose, even her surprisingly dark sense of humour for a five-year-old. Her love for Ichigo was raw and desperate. She wanted to protect him from everything and keep him away from the world outside because he was pure. While Rose constantly asked, "why? how? when? where?" Ichigo would quietly listen and draw his own conclusions. Sometimes she worried about what was going on in his little head, but then he'd curl up next to her on the couch, sliding his tiny hand into hers, and her heart would ache so hard she thought it might implode inside her.

There was a crashing sound as the front door was kicked entirely off its hinges. Sasha screamed, holding the butter knife still covered in peanut butter in front of her. She heard the kids scream one room over. A man was standing in the doorway, dressed in black head to toe, a black hat with holes cut out for his orifices covering his face. She could only guess that he was a man based on his build; the rest of the assumption came from the weapon in his hand.

"Down on the floor!" he roared. Sasha, her back against the sink, did as she was told.

"Take whatever you want!" She cried. There was nothing here to steal anyway. "I have cash!"

"Then get it," he hissed.

"Okay, okay. I'm just going to get up and go to the bedroom and get it, okay?"

She slowly got back up from her knees, clutching the butter knife as though it made any difference. He stepped further into the house, his boots tracking dirt on the floor. She couldn't even begin to guess his age.

"Auntie Sasha?" Rose's voice from the living room. Sasha's whole body was so full of adrenaline that she was practically laser-focused on the man, but she suddenly realized how quickly this could deteriorate. She could hear little footsteps in the hallway.

"It's...it's okay, Rose, just stay behind the couch with Ichigo, okay?"

"Who is that man?" Rose was in the hallway now, holding Ichigo's hand. Why didn't she just listen? This wasn't the time for questions! The man was distracted, turning to look at the kids. This was her chance, but if she made any sudden movements, he could shoot.

I'll just go get the money, alright?" But I have to just put the kids in there."

"You go and get the money" he turned the gun towards Rose, whose eyes widened. Ichigo made a squeaking sound and tried to pull Rose back. "We'll just wait here."

The whole building was shaking; she only knew what he was saying because that gun was the only thing that existed at that moment.

Sasha felt hot tears on her face as she stepped into the kitchen doorway, the bedroom was just to her left, but the kids were in the hallway to the right, and the assailant was blocking the front door.

"Please..." she held both hands up, dropping the butter knife on the floor with a clatter. His gaze went down to the floor, and in that split second, Sasha saw her chance and threw herself into his knees. She knew she couldn't take him, but you fight like it when you're backed into a corner. His body came down on top of hers. She heard the gunshot, and both kids screamed for her.

He tried to scramble back up, but she had a firm grip around his knees. From the floor, she whipped around to look for the kids, still standing there, both still standing, Rose crying hysterically, Ichigo reaching down to pick something up.

"Ichigo! Run! Go find Auntie Eva!" He picked up whatever was on the floor and tugged at Rose's hand towards the door. Sasha lost sight of them as the man quickly got the advantage, and she found herself on her back, staring up at him, his weight on her abdomen. She clawed at his mask. If she was going down, she wasn't doing it quietly, especially if the kids were out of harm's way. He slapped her hard across the face, making her ears ring and her nose gushed blood. She breathed in through her nose, trying to grab at his hands. Why couldn't he have just let her get the money? She hoped he'd knock her out before whatever was about to follow.

That was when she heard it. Another gunshot. She squeezed her eyes shut, expecting pain. There was no new pain, but the person above her had stopped struggling. She opened her eyes. She wished she hadn't. He was staring at her in shock. The foam was gathering around the hole in the mask around his mouth. With a scream, she pushed him off and pulled herself out from underneath him, the disgust and terror enough to keep her moving further and further back. She tore her gaze from the spasming body before her and looked up to a tiny girl in the stairwell, pulling herself up using the rusty banister.

"Auntie Sasha? I scratched my elbow." Rose held up her elbow towards her, the gun lying on the floor where she must've dropped it when she'd saved her life.

Sasha pulled herself up and stepped over the body, scooping Rose up and pressing her to her chest like she had when she was just a baby.

"Thank you, Rosie." She choked.

"That was scary."

"Yes, it was. Where's Ichigo?"

"He ran as you said."

Sasha nodded. "Okay, let's go find him."

"I can walk, you know." She said, wriggling, so Sasha set the brave little girl down and held her hand as they made their way down the stairs.

She knew she should go back into the apartment and get money or at least a coat, but she couldn't bring herself back inside at that moment, not when someone was actively dying on her floor.

She needed to find Ichigo and Eva, and then they'd figure out what to do next. They'd come here with nothing, and she wasn't afraid of that anymore.

Chapter 5
Finding Friends & Strangers

Eva

She opened her eyes somewhere that was not an alleyway. She was somewhere indoors, on a squeaky makeshift bed, and the place was filled to the brim with people. Her arm was bandaged up in a sling. It still hurt. She sat up slowly. All around her, others were lying on the same army-style beds: seniors, children, and full families. Only some seemed injured, which suggested this wasn't a pop-up hospital. They seemed to be in a warehouse. It was noisy and smelled of mothballs and too many unwashed bodies in one place. She got up, trying to identify someone responsible.

She wandered between rows and rows of people, her mind finally catching up with what had happened. She needed to get home. Sasha would be losing her mind when she didn't come home. She wished she had a phone for the millionth time. At the end of one of the aisles, she spotted women handing out juice boxes and granola bars.

"Um, excuse me?" Her voice came out hoarse.

The woman handed her a juice box and granola bar into her good hand and shooed her away.

She awkwardly balanced it in one hand and tried again.

"Thanks, but I need to know where I am."

"The Federation has set up these camps for civilians. If you're looking for family members, please head to the door for the list of those identified." She pointed towards the other end of the large space. "Um, why are they here?"

"Who?"

"The military."

"Rebels were hiding in the city."

"Oh, great. Thanks." She muttered. She was used to these sorts of baffling answers from her father and the media. Now, having seen what that entailed, it was enough to make her blood boil.

Eva walked where she'd been told, taking in the other victims of this meaningless and endless conflict and finally faced an annoyed looking soldier.

"Hi, I'm Evangeline Valliant. You can put me on that list as a survivor. I'm looking for Alexandra Straselski."

The man flipped pages on his sheet and tsk-tsked.

"No, nothing here bout her."

"Rosalie Wells and Ichigo Yu, kids ages 5 and 4."

He kept flipping his endless paper.

"No, sorry, miss."

"Thank you. If they come looking for me, you have me on that list?"

He scribbled her name down.

"You can log my exit as right now."

"You're leaving? It's not safe out there. There are still rioters, insurgents, and fires. Rebels are running the streets."

"This isn't my first rodeo; I'll manage."

He stepped out of the way and allowed her to enter a dystopian world.

She coughed. He hadn't been kidding. There was ash in the wind, which instantly burned her eyes. She covered her face with her sweater, using her good arm. She wished she had a map; this wasn't a part of the city with which she was familiar. A dusty SUV pulled up beside her, and she stood back defensively.

"You lookin' for somewhere safe miss?"

"I'm looking to get back to the East side."

"Everyone's been evacuated on the East side. Your family will be at a shelter!"

"Can you at least drop me off somewhere close to the East side?"

The man checked with the driver, an older woman, who nodded, and he hopped down to help her get in, which was surprisingly hard with the sling."

As soon as she was in the car, she popped open her juice box and downed it.

"I'm Charlie." He said.

"Angel." Eva said. She didn't know why she wasn't ready to share her real name, but Angel seemed tougher. Angel was someone who could handle this.

"This here's my wife, Emma."

"Nice to meet ya, hon!" Emma called.

"Are you looking for somebody too?"

"Our mechanics." Charlie said. "The garage's a safe place to be right now, better than any of these shelters. I wanna make sure my guys find their way home."

Eva didn't own a car and hadn't had any need for a garage, but Charlie and Emma seemed incredibly sweet. They were actually not heading in the direction she'd needed at all, but after hearing her story, they went straight to the apartment.

"Here." Charlie handed her a piece of paper with his number scrawled on it. "That's my phone, if it's still workin'. Gimme a call and let me know if you find your kids. We'll keep an eye out for 'em."

"Be safe, hon!"

She got out of the car teary-eyed with gratefulness. It was amazing to know there were still good people in the world. She took the stairs to the apartment as quickly as she could, ignoring her pain and hunger. The site that greeted her was a dead body in the front doorway. She cursed, tiptoeing inside and having a look around. They weren't there. She found the beginnings of a peanut butter and jelly sandwich in the kitchen. No weapon on the man either...she grabbed the money from her bedroom and scribbled a note to Sasha, leaving it in the kitchen.

"I'm safe. I'm looking for you. If you come back, stay here." - EV

With some difficulty, she locked the door to the apartment which had been kicked off its hinges. She hoped it would deter others from ransacking what was left inside or squatting in it. She couldn't move the dead body, but that was Future-Eva's problem.

Sasha

They looked everywhere. They went to the park, the school, up and down the streets, everywhere she could possibly imagine that Ichigo might go. She called his name with increasing desperation, but it was like screaming into the void. Rose joined her in the screaming but quickly tired and sat down on the floor stubbornly. With a sigh, Sasha lifted her and kept going. Rose complained about being hungry, but nothing was open. They returned to the house and searched the corridors and stairwells. All the apartments were empty now, and she made sure to quickly walk by theirs, unwilling to face what had just happened. Rose had killed a man, but there was no time to dwell.

Exhausted, they went back outside. The streets were chaotic. Between the tanks rolling by, the smoke in the air, and what looked like shredded paper flying past them, their neighborhood had been transformed into a sepia war photograph. The smoke in the air made her eyes water so she took off her sweater and crouched in front of Rose to wrap it over her nose and mouth. The last thing she needed was for the little girl to inhale all this.

"Maybe Ichigo's with my mom." Rose suggested, as she tightened the sweater. Her big brown eyes looked like Eva's, though the consensus had always been that she looked like Gabe. She'd recently swapped from "mommy" to "mom," which was jarring.

"Maybe Rosie."

"Maybe at Benny's?" Rose said. Sasha hated the idea of walking far in this mess, but it wasn't as though they had any other recourse. Rose could be right, maybe Eva really had found Ichigo. He had to be okay, she had to believe that. They began the trek to Eva's work, passing stores with broken windows and men walking around with large guns. She kept her eyes down and walked, thanking her anxiety for the tunnel vision. It wasn't often that a panic attack was the appropriate response to a situation, but she'd finally found it. Rose's eyes were wide and she constantly turned to look around so Sasha held her little hand tightly.

She'd never allowed Rose to enter the bar, and Rose had it in her head that she absolutely wanted in. Sasha lifted the little girl back into her arms, dreading what they were about to see. Just as they got to the door, Benny came lumbering down the alleyway along the side of the building. She'd never spoken to him in all the years that Eva had worked here, but she'd know his pockmarked face anywhere.
"Benny! Is Angel here?" He stopped and looked at Rose, who'd pivoted in her arms to look at him, making her all the heavier.
"Wow, so that's the kid."
Sasha exhaled, adjusting her aching arms. "Yes, this is Rose, and she'd like to see her mommy."
The man grimaced, dry lips cracking.
"I sent her to the shelter down on 92nd and Main."
"That's quite the distance." Sasha sighed.
"They had a caravan driving by for injured civilians."
"Injured?"
He shrugged his large shoulders, looking like a sack of potatoes.
"Have you seen a little boy? Four years old, Asian, answers to Ichigo?" Sasha asked.
"I ain't a GPS." Benny barked.
Sasha sighed. "Okay, thank you."
She turned and began walking again.
"Rosie, do you think you can walk for a while?"
Rose made a disgruntled face but allowed her to set her down.
"I'm hungry."
"Me too, Rosie."
That was not the answer the little girl wanted. "But I'm hungry."
"I know."
"Who's Angel?"
Sasha tried to inhale, but it just made her lungs tense and caught her in a coughing fit.
Unfortunately, Rose was determined.
"Who's Angel, Auntie Sasha?"
"That's just the name your mommy uses at work."
"Why?"

"Because she's a performer, so she has a fake name for when she's on stage."

"Aren't angels dead?" Rose asked. Sasha knew there must be a million thoughts going on in that little head but she didn't have it in her to process any of this with her right at that moment.

"Come on Rosie, talking will make you feel more tired."

They walked in silence. It wasn't long before Rose complained that her feet hurt, so Sasha scooped her up again. By the time they'd reached the Main, she was ready to collapse, and Rose had somehow fallen asleep. She wasn't sure if this was a sign of childhood resilience or trauma, maybe it was the same thing.

There was a large United flag on the door of a large warehouse which she concluded must be the shelter Benny had mentioned. She knocked with her whole fist. The metal door nearly knocked her over as it opened outwards.

"Come in." The man grumbled. She let herself inside, and Rose instantly jolted awake as the door slammed shut behind them. Sasha got to her knees and set the wriggling child down on her feet, taking the sweater off her face. Sasha rubbed the length of her arms, trying to regain circulation.

"Where are we?" Rose asked, looking around.

"Somewhere safe." Sasha answered.

"Name?" The man who'd let them in was dressed in a dark green uniform, covered in soot. Bald and broad, he loomed over them both with a clipboard.

"Alexandra Staraselski and Rosalie Wells." Sasha answered tensely, keeping her eyes on Rose in case she got it into her head to dash into the warehouse. Rows of cots ran up and down the large space, with other shelter-seekers on them.

The man had her respell her name four times over the din of all of the conversations around them, in every language and tone.

"They're giving out food over there!" Rose cried in delight.

"Wait, Rose." She held her by the elbow.

"Let go!" Rose cried, exhaustion finally taking over her little body. She melted down into a full-on temper tantrum, not that it made any difference with the number of other screaming kids in the space. She held tight, trying to be patient, she wasn't about to lose both kids.

She tried to get the man to hear her over Rose.

"We're looking for Evangeline Valliant and Ichigo Yu!"

The man went through his list.

"Valliant, yes. She was here, but she left."

"Where?"

"Maybe the next shelter."

It was something to go on at least.

"Thank you sir. And Ichigo? He's four, with dark hair, and dark eyes. Wearing a blue jacket, I think."

"No, but children are harder to track if they don't speak up."

"Is the next shelter nearby?"

"Not on foot."

Sasha sighed. There was another knock on the door. Another family. Another person looking for sanctuary. She picked up a screaming and kicking Rose and walked towards where food was being distributed. There were bowls of instant soup, which she took gratefully and carried over to an available cot. She poured water over the noodles and handed the cup to Rose. It wasn't even remotely warm but Rose settled in to sip at hers, still sniffling.

"I wanna go home." The little girl mumbled.

"Me too." She wanted to offer playfulness and hope but had no idea what to do next. Eva was her compass in everything for the past five years. What was she going to do from here? How was she supposed to take care of Rose all by herself? How was she going to find Ichigo? They would stay here and regroup. When it was safe, she would go back to the apartment and try to search again. There was no time for despair.

Eva

It had been more than forty-eight hours. She'd searched all of the shelters she could reach by foot. She ate from convenience stores, used gas station bathrooms and hoped against all odds that this wasn't the end. She was so tired. Her feet felt numb at the end of the day, and she'd have to pull off her shoes and run them to get the circulation back. She couldn't even imagine what she looked like, but none mattered until she found them. Things had died down on the streets. She saw fewer soldiers now. There were also fewer cars. She'd circled back and was closer to home again, unsure of where to turn next. It was the middle of the afternoon, but the park was empty, save for a few homeless people sleeping on the benches. She wished she could be pushing Ichigo and Rose on the swings. Someone had tied all of the metal chains together. The swings looked incredibly sad. There was a crowbar lying by the slide. She went over and picked it up. She tried to pry the metal apart by walking over to the sad swings.

"Need help, babe?"

She jumped, spinning around with the crowbar up in the air.

It couldn't be.

It couldn't.

Just across the park, at the foot of where the sand began, stood a very dirty-looking, dressed in a military uniform that definitely didn't belong to him, stood Gabriel Wells. He was broader in the shoulder, no taller, but he was so unmistakably himself that the familiar feeling of him returning from the dead hit her so hard that her knees shook. She was still clutching the crowbar while her other hand held onto the swingset for stability. It shook, and so did she.

"Babe?"

"Gabe..." she wasn't one to cry easily; that was Sasha's forte, but seeing him like a poltergeist in the middle of this desolate landscape that had once been her sanctuary was too much. She smudged the dust on her hand with her tears.

He approached cautiously, taking the crowbar out of her hand. He was wearing one of those giant guns she'd seen on the other soldiers.

"Did you switch sides?" she asked.

"No, just needed a change of clothes." He said, putting his arms around her.

"How did you find me?"

He stepped back and pointed behind him at another familiar face. Khalil waved, a sad smile on his handsome face. He was wearing the same outfit as Gabe and carrying the same weapon.

"Khal said we'd find you around here somewhere. We thought we'd have to wait for the government to clear out, but we found a way into the city beyond the blockade."

She nodded to Khal, her words still trying to find their way to her lips.

"Can I get a hug now?" Gabe said, his arms still open to her.

"God, Gabe." She sunk into him and he wrapped his arms around her. He was both familiar and foreign. She'd had so many chances to find someone else since she came here, but of course, she'd never accepted anything. Her role had been Rose's mom, or Sasha's friend, or Ichigo's auntie. When she was Angel, her role was to tease. He felt and smelled like home after you've been away for a long time like she could put down her baggage at his feet, and he would help to put the pieces back in their right places. They held each other for a long time. She let go first.

"You have to help me."

"Anything." Every line of his face was familiar. His long hair was braided back and shoved into his jacket.

"I've lost Sasha. She's got Rose and Ichigo."

"I saw her picture."

"Sasha's?"

"Rosalie Erin Wells." The man smiled, and she saw how much she resembled Rose, but also how much she resembled her.

"Where did you see the picture?"

"You submitted one to her school."

"You looked up her school records?"

"Of course! I had to see my daughter."

"She's crazy about you."

"She doesn't even know me."

"Oh, she does. Ichigo does too."

Gabe looked confused.

"Your new boyfriend?"

"What? No! Ichigo is Sasha's son. Hale's son." This all felt like a dream. Worlds were colliding; parallel universes were melting into one another. Gabe's eyebrows disappeared beneath the shorter strands of hair that fell into his face. "Huh, wonder how he'll handle that one." He smirked.

"Now he can stop lording our miracle over me."

"I'll be in the car!" Khal called, heading back towards the road. She'd nearly forgotten he was there but felt all the more grateful. Khalil had been her anchor in the storm, a bridge between her old world and this one.

"We've got transportation." She grinned, her heart feeling like it was climbing back from the deepest depths of her or defrosting.

"Okay, can I have a kiss before we go?"

She nodded. It wasn't like him to ask, but she appreciated it.

He kissed her, and her insides fluttered in a way she didn't think was possible for her anymore. It was a quick kiss, but it felt like no time had passed, like they could go back to a time when she hadn't had the weight of adulthood on her shoulders, and no little humans to care for, when it was just her and Gabe, two kids in love. She didn't even want to know what Gabe had been through since she'd last seen him on the base.

He put his arm around her and handed her back the crowbar. "Come on."

They headed in the direction Khalil had gone.

Khal got down from the driver's seat and hugged her too.

"It's so good to see you, Eva."

"Thanks for all the support Khal. I live for your postcards."

"I'm sorry I couldn't do more for you both."

"Where's Remi?"

"Making sure Pythagorus thinks we're nowhere near here." Khalil smiled. Just the mention of Remi's name lit up his features.

"Where's Hale?"

"He's at your apartment, checking for you."

"I've already been there."

She settled into the passenger seat. It was so nice to be with them, not to be alone. Khalil handed her a cold ham and cheese wrap in plastic and a bottle of water. She accepted the food as they drove off.

"Guess we'd better go tell him that." Gabe agreed.

"No, I need to recheck the shelters. Just call him."

"Okay." Gabe texted while Khal drove them back to the first shelter she'd been at. "I've tried this one already."

"It's where I saw her name listed," she said, eating quickly, barely tasting the food. She wasn't going to enjoy anything until she found her family. They pulled up in front of the shelter, and she scrambled out, Gabe at her heels. The soldier at the front rechecked her name and confirmed Sasha and Rose's names. Her heart was beating so hard that she barely heard him. She was so close. She started walking through the aisles, checking every bed. Were they here? Was it possible that they'd been this close the whole time? Every minute felt like hours as she made the rounds one aisle at a time. Every child with a hood on or curled under a blanket could be her, but wasn't.

"Hey, babe!" Gabe's voice from across the shelter.

"Mommy!" Rose's little voice.

People hushed them, but just a few aisles away from her stood Gabe, with Rose sitting on his shoulders, her little hands cupped around her mouth to project her voice into the massive space.

Her knees felt weak as she jumped over one of the empty cots, tripping and bumping her knees and thighs. Gabe carefully maneuvered towards her, trying to ensure Rose was still balanced on his neck as she wriggled and reached for Eva. He scooped her over her head and handed her to Eva as soon as she was close enough, and Eva sank to the ground in a heap with her daughter, burying her face in her tangled locks of unkept hair. Rose clung to her for dear life, and Eva did the same. She may never let go. Rose's tiny body shook as she cried like a big kid, quietly but heavily. Eva's heart broke into a million pieces. She'd vowed to protect her, and she'd failed. As she extracted herself from the floor, still holding Rose like a toddler, the little girl's legs wrapped around her torso.

Gabe stood by, smiling at them.

"How did you...?" She choked out, using her sleeve to wipe her face.

"She really looks like you, babe, but actually, she found me first. She popped out of nowhere and asked if I was her daddy."

Rose turned to look at him, twisting to stay glued to Eva's chest. "You think I wouldn't know my daddy?"

Gabe laughed. "Of course you would, baby girl."

Eva let go of Rose for a second to pull Gabe to them. Their little unit was reunited. The last time she could do this, Rose was still part of her, just a dream.

She heard the sound of something breaking. She turned to see Sasha, two bowls of soup broken on the floor before her.

"Look Auntie Sasha! I found them!" Rose declared proudly.

Sasha looked down at the mess of soup and porcelain on the floor and stepped over it. "Oh my god Eva!" She hugged the two of them, then turned to Gabe.

"Gabriel Wells." She shook her head. "You really do have nine lives, don't you?"

Gabe chuckled. "Yeah, Hell doesn't want me."

"You look older."

"Right back at ya'."

"Oh, come here!" Sasha pulled Gabe into an awkward hug too.

Eva looked around the room.

"Where's the little man hiding?"

Sasha's face fell. "Ichigo's not with you?"

Eva shook her head. "I thought you had both kids."

Sasha looked stricken.

"It's a long story, I was just really hoping..." Tears sprung to her eyes. "It was all my fault. I don't know where he is. I figured he'd eventually end up here..."

Eva set Rose down so she could hug her friend. "It's okay; it's okay. We'll find him. We've got a car and food and money now. We'll find him." Sasha's hands were shaking, but she nodded. Eva took her hand and Rose's and led the way back toward the exit.

Sasha

The wind was full of dust outside, and she got a mouthful of hair as they stepped out into the waning light. She was caught by a coughing fit and let go of Eva's hand. When she finally recovered, she could see Gabe climbing into the front of a jeep with Rose on his lap. Rose was peppering him with questions, which he seemed thrilled to answer. Eva waited for her on the stairs. She followed her into the car, her heart still stuck in her throat.

"This is Khalil, our guardian angel," Eva said, introducing the driver. "He's the one who brought me here the first time."

"I thought it was Mr. Hotty."

"Oh, that's Remi. He and Khal work together."

"It's a pleasure to meet you." The young man in the driver's seat said, twisting around in his seat to shake her hand.

"It's nice to meet you." He had a blush on his cheeks, dark eyes and dark hair. He was handsome in his own right, but the part that she noticed was the softness of his gaze. This was the guy who sent them postcards and money. This was the guy who had saved Eva in their failed escape. He was definitely trustworthy, more so than Gabe.

She wanted so much to ask about Hale but didn't dare. The fact that no one had mentioned him scared her. She couldn't think about that right now. She had to find Ichigo. Eva was reunited with her family, but she was still here alone and now that Eva had Gabe...she had no idea what that meant for her, for them. Eva was beside her, watching Gabe interact with Rose. He was a natural like he'd been around her his whole life.

"So, where are we going?" She finally coughed out.

"We have to go pick up Hale. He hasn't been answering, but I've got a tracker on him." Khalil said gently, meeting her gaze in the rearview mirror.

"Hale? Hale's here?"

"He's here for you." Khalil said softly.

"Who's Hale? That's a funny name." Rose asked, using Gabe as a jungle gym to poke her head between the seats to look at her and Eva. Her little cheeks were still dusty, but she looked back to her old self. Unphased by what had happened to them. Unphased by what she'd had to do...

"Ichigo's dad." Eva clarified, squeezing Sasha's hand.

"Ichigo has a dad?"

"Everyone has a dad, Rosie." Eva said, pushing her daughter's hair back behind her ear. "Now sit down safely." She added sternly.

Gabe flipped Rose around into a bear hug, which she accepted, giggling.

Khalil drove silently, avoiding large bits of metal, holes in the road, pedestrians, and cars flipped over or simply left in the middle of the road. He seemed comfortable enough navigating the disaster that was their neighborhood. Gabe and Rose's voices filled the car, but she wasn't listening. Her mind was racing. She couldn't help feeling immensely jealous. Why didn't she deserve that too? It would never be like that. It would never be Hale and Ichigo like that, would it? She missed Ichigo so much she could hardly breathe. She'd had Rose to focus on before, but now she felt deeply, profoundly alone.

She watched the landscape passing by as they drove. It was both familiar and completely changed. Wrapping her arms around herself, she cried silently, letting the roar of the engine and the rubble cover the sound. What if they didn't find him? What would she do? The horrible things that might've happened to her tiny boy spiraled through her mind like bees, blocking out everything else.

The car slowed and stopped, Khalil cutting the engine.

Eva was shaking her shoulder. "Sasha! Hey!"

She looked up at her smiling face, confused.

"Look!"

Sasha lifted her head to see Rose running through the park towards a tall, familiar figure and a smaller one, who peeked out from behind the adult and began to run towards her calling her name in the distinctly familiar voice of her son. Eva was already outside too, as Sasha tried to get her limbs to cooperate enough to wrench the door open. She tumbled out of the jeep and scrambled up, though her legs felt like jello.

Rose and Ichigo knocked each other down to the floor, giggling, Rose landing on top. Rose's hands were on Ichigo's cheeks. "We thought you was dead!" She declared, squishing his face between her palms.

Sasha approached them slowly, standing just above until Ichigo finally noticed her and sat up.

"Mommy!" He reached up his little hands towards her as he'd done as a toddler before he'd learned to speak. Rose was about to intervene, not having gotten her fill of reuniting, but Eva had scooped her up into her arms with a "c'mere Rosie."

Sasha got down on her knees and pressed his small frame to her.

"Are you okay?" She whispered.

She could feel him nodding. "Don't worry. A man found me."

Sasha opened her eyes, staring at the ground and looked up at Hale, standing just far enough to give them some space. She would've known him anywhere, the way he stood awkwardly, the way his hair fell into his eyes, the way he folded his arms as if he didn't know what to do with them. He wore all black, including a beanie and a scarf covering his mouth. He looked taller somehow, broader, though still lean. He had a cut just above his left eye. Flashbacks of high school flooded her as she sat on the ground cradling her son - their son. They were like two identical droplets of water. They locked eyes, and she got up off the ground, still holding Ichigo.

"Hey." She said.

"I guess you know him?"

The laugh that burst from her was both a surprise and a retort.

"What do you mean?"

"He called you, mommy."

She couldn't find the words for the follow-up.

"Where did you find him?"

"In your apartment. He was hiding in the closet."

She nodded, wanting to scream at him. Why was he being so terse?

"Thank you." She managed. Years of longing, waiting, and hoping, and this was the reunion? This was how he greeted his son and his...she wasn't sure what they were exactly. It was just like the base, a secret love affair, forbidden, but no one was here to forbid anything. The world had come undone at the seams, and they all lived in the cracks. Why didn't he embrace her? Why wasn't he holding their child like Gabe had held Rose? Why was she always chasing after someone who would never be able to express what she needed?

Anger swelled inside her.

"You're welcome. I promised him we'd find you. I just didn't know..."

"Didn't know what?" He looked confused by her change in tone.

"I didn't know it was you we were looking for."

"Then what were you looking for in my apartment?"

"You, but I didn't know that the boy was yours."

"Oh my god Hale! He's yours too!" She cried. She held Ichigo harder, her heartbeat roaring in her ears. Hale's face gave nothing away, but his eyes widened.

There was an explosion somewhere in the distance, and it felt apt. It was the world expressing her rage.

She felt a hand on her shoulder and whipped around, breathing heavily.

"Come on." It was Eva, holding Rose. "Let's go home."

She nodded and turned away from Hale, adjusting Ichigo's weight.

"I can walk, mommy. I just walked a lot, a lot. We went everywhere."

"I know you can, sweetie. I just want to carry you, if that's okay."

She felt little hands on her face. "It's okay; you don't have to cry."

"I know, but I want to. I'm just so happy we found you."

"The man said crying doesn't fix anything."

"It makes me feel better." She sniffled, climbing back into the car. How dare Hale give her son advice about crying? Ichigo nodded. "Me too."

"Was he kind to you?" Ichigo looked up as Hale climbed in. She'd hoped he'd take the front seat or just...walk.

Her little boy nodded, putting his head down on her chest. "Yeah..." he mumbled and yawned, warm breath against her chest.

Sasha scooted them both to the middle seat as Eva got in beside her with Rose.Hale kept his gaze out the window, but she could sense him glancing down at Ichigo and her in turn. She looked up, and he looked away. The fact that he hadn't instantly made the connection was typical of Hale, but it still upset her. Was he really that dense? Rose sprawled out further so she was half on top of her, and to her surprise, both kids were soon fast asleep.

Eva

When they pulled up in front of their apartment building, she was surprised and grateful that it was still standing. Some identical gray brick 6-story complexes hadn't been so lucky. Gabe opened the door for her and gently lifted Rose out of her arms, then helped her down. Her arm ached. She'd forgotten all about her injury, desperate to hold her child. Now, she was feeling the consequence.

"Thanks, babe." She whispered. Rose's eyes shot open as soon as Gabe started walking.

"Mommy?"

277

"I'm right here, Rosie." She said, keeping apace. Hale had climbed out and was speaking to Khalil by the car. Sasha, holding Ichigo's hand, was right behind her. She turned to check on them.

"You okay, Ichigo?" He nodded, reaching out for a hug, which she gave happily.

"I missed you, Auntie Eva." He said in his small voice. "That's Rose's daddy, isn't it?"

"Yes, it is."

"He's just like your stories!"

"Of course." She grinned.

"Is he living with us now? Will he sleep in the living room?"

"I don't know yet. Let's just get home and get settled in, okay?"

He glanced back to look at Hale, then up at Sasha.

"Mommy, are you mad at the man for taking me?"

Sasha looked like she was about to break, so Eva answered instead.

"No, your mom's just tired. We were all worried about you, and glad you're safe."

He nodded, seeming to understand that he needed to be brave for them. He held out his little hand to her, so they went up the stairs together. Gabe had already carried Rose upstairs and was waiting by the door. She was gleefully telling him everything she could think of her school, her friends, her favourite colour, how she didn't like it when mommy worked at night...

Eva released Ichigo's hand and dashed up to unlock the door. The last thing she needed right now was to deal with Gabe's reaction to her career path.

"Here we are." She said, opening the door.

There was a puddle of blood in the hallway.

"He disappeared!" Rose exclaimed.

"Who?" Gabe asked.

"The man who tried to hurt auntie Sasha." she paused, her little 5-year-old brain looking for the right words. "Is he dead?"

Gabe stepped over the gore. "Probably; how about you show me your bedroom, huh? You said you had some cool toys in there."

He turned to look at Eva for a moment, shrugging his shoulders. Gabe was handling all this much better than anyone else, it seemed. She entered the kitchen, fetched a mop and bucket, and then tried the faucet. To her surprise, there was still running water, hot water, no less! She went into the bathroom and filled the bucket, adding dish soap. She hoped she could get the smell out.

"Here." She jumped at the unfamiliar voice.

Hale stood in the hallway with a container of vinegar from her kitchen.

She tried to lift the bucket and winced. She'd really done a number on her body.

"Move aside." Hale stepped around her in the tiny washroom and lifted the bucket out of the tub. She did as told and stood in the hallway, listening to Rose's little voice from the bedroom. Where had Sasha and Ichigo gone?

"You're not needed here." Hale told her, walking into the hall with the mop, full bucket, and the container of vinegar.

"I live here." Eva retorted. She remembered Hale being somewhat rude, but this was another level.

He set the bucket down, spilling a few bubbles onto the floor and poured vinegar onto the puddle of blood. Still holding the mop, he looked at her impatiently. "You're needed in the hall." He said, clarifying. That was when she finally heard the sounds of distress from outside the apartment. As Hale began scrubbing the floor, a scene as unlikely as the rest of the past week, she stepped outside to find Ichigo with his arms and legs wrapped around the banister, sobbing hysterically in a way she'd never seen from him, even as a toddler. His little face was red as a tomato, and Sasha sat beside him, rubbing his back, trying desperately to coax him upstairs.

"Hey, what's going on?"

She walked down a few steps to be able to face them both and sat down on a dusty step.

"He's scared to come inside." Sasha said, tears streaming down her cheeks. "He must've been there long, just waiting for us to find him." Both mother and son were at a loss, and Eva's heart squeezed in her chest.

"Ichigo," She said, putting her hand on his shoe and squeezing it. It was covered in mud. "Can you use your words? Can you tell me what you're scared of, and we can make the scary thing disappear?" She spoke slowly and softly, so he would need to stop screaming to hear her. It was so much easier to respond to Ichigo than to Rose. Rose was willful, stubborn and surprisingly strong, whereas Ichigo's feelings were like deep water; she just needed to skim the surface for her words to ripple down.

"I don't know." He whispered between shaky breaths.

"That's okay. Why don't you just let go." She touched his little fist, and he released the banister. He turned back to Sasha and reached out to wipe his mother's tears again, grimy fingers making patterns on her cheeks. Sasha closed her eyes and let him.

"Are you ready to come up now?" Sasha said, her voice shaking. He nodded and let her scoop him back up into her arms. Sasha turned to Eva.

"How did you...?" Eva shrugged. She didn't know how she'd done it either. By the time they'd gotten upstairs, the mop and bucket were gone, and so was the dark puddle. The floor was glistening clean, and Hale sat on the couch, watching them come inside with his arms crossed. They could all hear Gabe and Rose playing something that sounded like pirates in the other room. There were many happy cries of "argh" and "matey." Ichigo, who had been clinging to Sasha's neck with his eyes shut tight, opened them. "What's Rose up to?"

"Why don't you go find out?" Sasha said, setting him down.

"You won't go again?" The question was directed at them both.

"Why don't we both go." Eva agreed. She was exhausted, but she wanted to watch Gabe play with Rose, and if it could make Ichigo feel better too, all the better. She entered the room to find her long lost lover with a scarf over his eye as an eye patch pretending to row himself and Rose with the bed as a boat.

"Sharks!" Rose cried as they came inside. "Quick Ichigo! Quick mom! Up here!" She threw them a frisbee as a buoy and Eva pretended to use it to bring them to safety, joining Gabe on the bed and pulling Ichigo along. Gabe took the opportunity to pull her into a hug, grinning from ear to ear, the years melting off them both. It was like the base: he was her lifeboat, and their lives were eternal storms.

Chapter 6
How Many More Goodbyes

Sasha

She let Ichigo head towards the sounds of joy in the next room. She needed to speak to Hale. She knew he wasn't like Gabe, that he couldn't just express how he felt and make her feel welcome, but she needed to know where they stood. Was this him coming back? Had he moved on?

"Hey, room for one more?" She asked, as though they were back on a bench at their old high school.

"It's your couch." He said. He had his phone in his hand. "Khalil will return with food."

"Thanks for, well, for everything. Thanks for saving Ichigo and thanks for cleaning the um..."

"I got rid of the body. Ichigo wouldn't pass the doorway otherwise."

"Thank you. Did you really not know he was yours?"

"How could I?"

"Because he looks exactly like you."

"Lots of people look like me."

"Considering you lived in rooms without mirrors, I don't think you're the best judge of that."

"The base had mirrors."

"Are you seriously going to argue about this?"

He sighed.

"I didn't mean to argue. I don't know what to say."

"How are you feeling?" She tried to get him to make eye contact, but that had always been challenging, even more so now.

"Fine..."

"He's an amazing little boy. I'm sure you'll love him; everyone who meets him does. He's sweet and thoughtful and so kind. He's actually pretty quiet for his age, and he's brilliant."

"I know."

"Was it hard?"

"What?"

"Taking care of him for those few days."

"No, it was just strange."

"Strange?"

"It was all so familiar."

She waited for him to continue, a skill she'd learned when they were on the base. Sometimes, it paid off.

"I was alone in an apartment too, for a long time, waiting for the man who raised me to come back. That's how Pythagorus found me, but Pythagorus knew what to do with me right away. I didn't know what to do. I couldn't take him back anywhere, and I couldn't take him with me. I wanted to leave him at the nearest shelter, but he said he didn't want to. It's good that he's yours." This was a much longer response than she'd expected. It was the sort of answer she used to only get in the dead of night when he was too tired to have his guard up. His walls seemed frayed around the ages, but she'd had the time to build some walls too. She used to treasure these little snippets of his past and hold them in her heart like fragile little birds, cherishing the fact that he'd shared something with her that she knew he'd never shared with anyone. Now, it just wasn't enough anymore. She expected more from him; she expected him to give more, offer more, and want to be here.

"Are you still not getting this? He's ours. You're not "the man who found him."" She used her fingers to make air quotes. "You're his father. You're not Pythagorus."

"I don't want him to be like me." He said, looking down at his hands.

She put her hand on his. "I do. I don't want him to live the hard things you lived through, but I'd like him to be like you. I was hoping you'd see some of the things I see in you by now, but even if you don't, I still see them. You're a good person, Hale. You saved him, brought him home, and now you can choose what to do. You don't have to do what they tell you to do anymore."

"The war's not over."

"Isn't it? What more is there to do?"

"Nothing I can share." He didn't pull his hand away.

"Pythagorus got what he wanted, didn't he? And you're still here. Isn't it time to stop fighting now?"

He shook his head. She understood that the war in his head would probably never be over, and now she wondered if the war in hers would ever be over, either. She wanted him to stay, but she didn't need him if he didn't want to, not the way she had in the past. The realization hit her like a ton of bricks. She and Eva had made a life here. It wasn't the life she would've imagined for herself, but it was a life nonetheless. She used to be so afraid to lose him, for him to pull away from her, but what did she really have to lose now?

"Don't you ever wonder what it would've been like to know your biological parents?"

"They're dead."

"Did you ever wonder about them?"

"Only what I remember."

"Well, he's going to remember you now. He's met you. If you want to be in his life, you can. You don't even have to be with me to do it. I'm not trying to add to the list of people trying to make you into something or someone. I'm just saying that if you want to be in his life, this is your chance, and even if you're not in his life, you're still his father. You made him. You and I did."

"And you want that?"

"I want you to be happy, that's it. I'm not expecting anything else from you anymore unless you're willing and able to give it. I don't want to live in this peripheral secret part of your world. I want you to make a choice. Someday, I will find out where my parents went, and I will introduce him to his grandparents. I will find a job that isn't what I'm doing now. You do what you want, but know that I'm here, and your son is too. Unless I'm dead, which I hope you'd be informed of somehow, I will make sure Ichigo grows up differently. You deserved better than you got Hale, and he deserves more than anything he could have if I stayed here."

His hand balled up into a fist. She couldn't begin to imagine what he was feeling. There was a knock on the door.

She sprang up to look into the peephole to find Khalil cradling what looked like mountains of takeout containers. She opened the door and was greeted with the smell of an entire takeout Chinese menu. Her stomach growled as she took some from his hands and headed to the kitchen.

"Oh my god! Where did you go?"

"I drove around and found a place willing to take my money."

"Dinner's on!" She called, and the kids came rushing into the room. Eva appeared behind them and ushered them back to the bathroom to wash their hands.

"Hallelujah!" Gabe's cheerful voice boomed in the small kitchen, "I'm starved."

She opened their cabinets and pulled out every bowl and plate they had. They'd never had so many people in the apartment at once.

Eva served the kids and let them sit at the table surrounded by the feast with Gabe, who had piled so much food on his plate that Sasha wondered when he'd last eaten. Dumplings, chicken, duck, seafood, noodles, rice, fried vegetables, beef, spring rolls, egg rolls, there was something for every taste and soda to wash it all down with.

Khalil was more polite in his serving, and Hale stood awkwardly in the doorway leading to the kitchen until she handed him a plate too. There was nowhere for them to sit, so Rose ended up on Gabe's lap by her own request, and Eva pulled Ichigo up on hers, leaving two chairs for three people. Hale took his plate to the living room and sat on the couch.

"So, what's the plan from here?" Sasha asked, turning to Khalil, who seemed to be leading this expedition.

"I'll leave you with enough money for the next while. I have to get back to the mission tonight."

"Tonight?" It was already getting dark outside, and she'd just met him!

"Unfortunately." Khalil shrugged apologetically.

"Gabe?" Eva bit her lower lip.

"I can stay until tomorrow but..."

"You're leaving tomorrow?" Rose looked up, devastated in the way only a preschooler could express.

"Can't you stay a bit longer, uncle Gabe?" Ichigo chimed in politely. It was shocking to hear how quickly Gabe had slipped from a stranger to Uncle Gabe.

Gabe laughed. "You guys are too much. I'll be back, okay? I'll be back as soon as I can."

Eva shook her head and took a bite of her egg roll. She looked up at Sasha, and knew exactly what her friend was thinking: "Don't make promises you can't keep."

Eva

Khalil left at about nine and said he'd meet the guys back at their agreed-upon location. There were hugs and an exchange of cash. It surprised Eva how quickly and easily she trusted Khalil. She hardly knew anything about him, but she knew he was someone she would know and trust for the rest of her life. The kids and Sasha seemed to know it too.

Bedtime stretched on forever. Rosie came out of the room a hundred times, and she and Sasha took turns picking her up and placing her back into bed. Ichigo stayed in bed but cried every time Rose left. She knew she should just curl up with them, but there was no way she was missing the chance to speak to Gabe. Rose's trauma would still be there tomorrow.

It was just the four of them in the living room. Hale and Sasha sat on opposite ends of the couch, looking like an awkward teen couple on their first date. She and Gabe were on the floor, with him half sprawled on top of her. It was uncanny - as though the past half-decade had never happened. Gabe's hair was full of ash and dust, but she couldn't bring herself to care.

"So what's the plan, guys?" Sasha asked.

"There are still a few loose ends to tie up, and then I plan to vanish off Socrates' radar forever." Gabe said, yawning. "I'll probably try and get as much of the serum off of him as I can first, though, or at least blow up what's left. No way should they get to keep that crap."

"And then what?" Sasha pried.

"Then I'll come find you again." Gabe grinned, addressing Eva. "I promised Rose I'd be here when she starts first grade."

"You, Gabe Wells, are too much." Eva couldn't help smiling. She bent down and kissed him, their lips upside down.

"And you?" Sasha turned to Hale.

"I don't know."

"Lovely. Well, on that note, I'm off to shower. We don't really have more beds, so you guys can rock paper scissors for the couch." Sasha got up tensely and headed for the bedroom to find pyjamas.

"Come on, man!" Gabe hissed at his friend, sitting up.

Hale glared.

"You're just leaving it like that?"

Still silence.

Eva got up. "I need a smoke."

"You don't smoke, babe."

"I'm full of surprises. Come on, Gabe."

Eva retrieved a pack of cigarettes from the fridge, keeping them out of the hands of the kids, and led Gabe onto the balcony. It was narrow and gave a great view of the neighboring building's bricks. The city was wide awake, still roaring from the day's disasters. She lit her cigarette, holding her hand over it to block out the wind, inhaled the smoke and handed it to Gabe. He shook his head.

"Lot's happened, hasn't it, Princess?"

"You can say that again."

He put his arms around her torso, his chest to her back, and she leaned into him.

"I think the last time I was this tired was when Rose was born."

"I should've been there."

"Yeah, that's true." She elbowed him a little. He inhaled smoke and exhaled it again.

"I wish you wouldn't smoke."

"That's a bit hypocritical of you."

"Fair."

"Not as nice a view as your old place, huh?"

"Looks alright to me." He said, kissing the top of her head.

"So, were you serious back there? You're planning to come back?"

"I'll do everything I can to make it back here. You've been on your own long enough."

"Could you actually do me a favour before you come back? Could you find my family? I just want to know that they're okay."

"I will. I'll send you their info."

"I missed you."

"Same, babe."

"I was starting to think you forgot about us."

"Nah, I just...I kinda thought you'd move on, that you might be better off without me."

"I could've."

"Why didn't you?"

"I've never been like that. I wasn't looking for anything. It was either right or it wasn't. Were you with anybody all this time?"

"Not the way I was with you but..."

It stung, but not the way it might've before. It wasn't the same, and he was honest with her, and he was here.

"Did you think of me?"

"Every day."

"So this isn't goodbye, is it?"

"More like a 'see you later.'"

She smiled. The wind blew the smell of smoke from the street up at them. Their cigarette had turned to ash.

"Did you want to go in?" she asked him.

"Nah, let's just stay out here for a while unless you're cold."

"Not with you around." she giggled.

They sat on the ground in each other's arms, finding the flow of conversation again and the ease they'd once had.

Sasha

She returned to the living room carrying pillows and blankets, feeling a million times better after the warmth of the water. Her hair soaked her shoulders and dripped onto the floor, but that didn't bother Sasha. The kids were fast asleep when she checked on them, curled up against one another sweetly. Hale was still sitting on the couch as she arranged makeshift sleeping arrangements on the floor of the living room; Gabe and Eva were smoking on the balcony.

"I have a question."

"You always do." He picked at a scab on his thumb.

"Have you ever wondered where you really came from?"

"What do you mean?"

"I mean, before Pythagorus, before the man you said you were waiting for at the apartment.Who were your real parents?"

"How would I know that?"

"Wouldn't Pythagorus know?"

"How?"

"How did he know you were in the apartment in the first place?"

"I don't understand what you're insinuating. Speak clearly; I'm too tired for riddles."

She sat down cross-legged on the ground. "No need to be a dickhead about it."

"I didn't know I was."

"Okay, hear me out. I've thought about this a lot. You told me that the man never came back. You said he went off on missions and would always come back, but you didn't know who he worked for. Pythagorus gave you the option of being a soldier like you wanted. How did he know to offer you that? How did he know there was a child he could find and manipulate in there? Just for a moment, don't you think it's possible that he created that situation?"

Hale sighed. "You're still not making sense."

"Actually no, I'm making perfect sense. I think Pythagorus knew exactly who you were and where because he's the reason no one else came looking for you. You said the man was a soldier just like you; there's no such thing as a freelance soldier. The man would leave you alone in the apartment to go on so-called missions. For who? It wasn't the government. He wasn't in the CIA. Pythagorus was probably his boss or someone connected to him, and he wanted someone for that serum you said they had you test out, and he wanted a kid who would be compliant and listen. The war is about to end; time you stopped listening to him and started looking for answers. You'll have accomplished your big goal, and until you dig up who you are, you'll never know where you're going. Was the man Asian?"

"What?"

"You said you were Japanese."

"Pythagorus said I was half Japanese. No, the man was American, I think."

"You come from somewhere, Hale."

"What does it matter?" She could see him covering up his anger, the color in his cheeks giving it away. In the past, she had never wanted to anger him, but now what did she have to lose? She wanted so much for him, but he wanted so little for himself. She would have all of him, or she would have none. She was tired of these games of truth or dare.

"If you'd asked me five years ago, I'd have agreed, but I take one look at Ichigo, and I can see my history, future, and yours. I think you've been lied to, a lot, and I think you owe it to yourself to go and find the truth."

He scowled at her. "Anything else you want to say?"

"I'm glad you're okay. I...don't regret loving you the way I did. It was crazy and stupid, and I wish I'd at least tried to listen to your warnings, but I'm glad I met you."

He brought himself down from the couch and onto the floor.

"Can we get some rest now?" He said.

She nodded. "Did you want to go shower first?"

He shook his head. "Do I smell?"

She laughed. "You smell like you. I don't care; you can shower tomorrow before you leave."

They curled up back to back on the floor. Tomorrow, they would repeat their goodbyes.

Tomorrow was Ichigo's birthday.

Around midnight, she woke up to find Gabe and Eva asleep on the couch. It was a wonder that they could fit together up there. The perks of Gabe not being exceptionally tall, she supposed. Hale was asleep too. She adjusted the covers on top of him, imagining how tired he must be. He scowled in his sleep, a pretty typical expression for him. She supposed she wasn't exactly rainbows and lollipops either. She could hear the kids whispering in the next room, their tiny high-pitched voices carrying across the hallway. She wondered what sort of impact the past few days would have on their little psyches. They'd both met their fathers for the first time. They'd already been through so much, and they were so little. How was she going to fix that? How was she going to undo it?

"What's wrong?" Hale whispered. He'd always been an incredibly light sleeper. The room wasn't nearly dark enough for proper sleep.

"Nothing. Go back to sleep. I was just listening for the kids."

He opened his eyes and looked at her.

"It's strange."

"What is?"

"Kids."

"I'll bet someone listened for you once upon a time."

His eyebrows went up, as though the idea was absurd.

She smiled and pushed his bangs up from his eyes. "At least, I hope so."

She lay back down again. She listened until he went back to sleep.

Eva

Staying strong for everybody was just too much. It was morning. She'd made her signature pancakes while Sasha got the kids dressed and brushed their teeth. Both of the guys looked more like themselves now that they'd showered. Gabe's hair was still wet, so he'd braided it and put it up. Sasha and Hale had done the dishes while Gabe entertained the kids. It had started with Rose trying to impress him by doing a cartwheel and had turned into each kid taking turns walking around on their hands with Gabe holding them by their ankles. She wasn't surprised that Rose was into the rough housing, but Ichigo wasn't usually one for this sort of thing. Rose then convinced Gabe to assist them in bouncing on the bed.

She would usually have stopped it a long time ago, but seeing the kids so genuinely happy was so good that she allowed it.

Hale came into the room like a shadow.

"We should go." He said.

"No! Come on, daddy! We're still playing!" Rose appealed to Gabe, clinging to his leg.

Gabe sighed. "Hale's right, baby girl; I've gotta get going. I'll be back before you know it."

He pulled her into a big bear hug and ruffled Ichigo's hair before climbing out of bed and following Hale to the hallway. Eva followed Rose, still protesting.

"This isn't fair!"

"I know, Rosie."

Sasha was already standing there, her arms wrapped around herself. Ichigo took Rose's hand, seeing how distressed she was, but she pushed him away.

"Daddy! Why don't you just stay?" She cried. She pulled at Gabe's arm. "Tell him you want him to stay, mommy!" She screamed at Eva.

Gabe got down on one knee and let her scream into his chest until he finally got up with her in his arms. He went to hand her to Eva, but Rose kicked off again, and Sasha stepped in and took her. "That's enough now, Rosie." The screaming didn't subside, but Sasha held firmly.

Hale opened the door, and Gabe stepped up to Eva. She looked up at him and allowed him to kiss her.

"She's tough, isn't she?" He said.

"Like you." Eva agreed.

"No, like you."

They hugged one last time.

"Bye, Gabe! Bye Hale!" Sasha was still gripping Rose, who was desperately trying to reach for the door. Ichigo stood quietly, holding the door open. He gave a little wave to both men. They watched them descend the stairs until Eva closed the door and put the top lock on so Sasha could let go of Rose. Rose ran to the door, pulled at the lock, and kicked her little foot against it and screamed.

"Rosie, calm down, baby." Eva tried to find the right words to soothe her daughter.

"This isn't fair! You didn't do anything!" She accused her mom and ran to the bedroom. Eva was glad they hadn't gone downstairs. This was hard enough as it was. Both women looked down at Ichigo, who pulled at Eva's hand.

"Can I have a snack?"

Eva deflated. "That sounds like a good idea. Go to the living room, and I'll bring you something."

"Want me to go after Rose?" Sasha said, rubbing her eye.

"No, let's give her a minute."

Both women entered the kitchen; Sasha heated water in a pot on the stove. She always drank tea when she didn't know what else to do.

"How did it end with you two?" She asked.

"He said he'd be back soon. He said he had some loose ends to tie up." Eva whispered, so that Ichigo couldn't hear her in the living room.

"Do you believe him?"

Eva sighed, cutting the crusts off a jam sandwich. "Don't I always?"

"Well, you don't have to. You've had five years to mull it over at this point."

Eva looked to Sasha, her confidante, her best friend, her sister in arms. She knew this was coming from a good place; she was trying to protect her. She rubs her arm, feeling its ache. She wished she could rub her brain instead.

"Why not believe him? He came back this time, didn't he?"

"Yeah, with Khalil, our benefactor."

"Khal's just a hopeless romantic."

"He's not alone."

"Like I said, why not? It won't hurt anybody to hope he comes back, right?"

Sasha rolled her eyes.

"Are you forgetting that Rose is having a full-on meltdown over there?"

She paused. "I wouldn't blame Gabe for that. A lot's happened."

Sasha filled herself a mug of hot water and put a tea bag into it, turning off the stovetop.

"I know, and you probably need to know."

"Hold that thought." Eva went over and gave Ichigo his sandwich. He'd found a book to flip through in the meantime and was happily sitting on the couch, the image of a perfect kid.

"Thank you." He said in his tiny voice. He'd always been quiet, but she hoped this wasn't an indicator of his future. As hard as Rose's outbursts were, they reminded her of her little brother. Ichigo's silence, not so much.

"You okay?"

He nodded, entranced by the trucks in his book.

She returned to the kitchen. "Okay, I'm listening." She sat in front of Sasha, who had gone paler than usual.

"On the day everything went boom...that man broke in, and I tried to hold him off; I told the kids to run, but Rose...well, you know Rose, she's always been like that, hasn't she? She always just does her own thing. Ichigo ran downstairs and that's how I lost him but Rose...she didn't listen to me. I'm so sorry, Eva; I really did my best to protect them both, but..."

"Sasha." She put her hand on her friend's forearm. "Just tell me."

"I had a knife; the guy came at me, I dropped the knife...Rose grabbed it and she..."

"And she what?"

"She took him down."

"The man lying in the hallway?"

"Yes."

"Rose?"

"Yes."

"And then?"

"Then we ran. I didn't wait to see if he was dead; I just got us both out of here."

It was Sasha's turn to put her arm around Eva as she felt her throat tighten. Her mind had gone blank. She waited to feel something beyond the numbness.

"I'm sorry. I'm really sorry."

Eva extracted herself from Sasha's hug and walked to the bedroom. Rose was lying on the bed, her face buried in a pillow. She'd pulled her socks off, leaving them on the ground, and rolled herself up in her comforter.

"Rosie? Baby, you okay?"

A pink wet face turned to her. "Why'd he have to leave? He knows it would hurt my feelings."

"I know. I wish he could stay too."

She sat gently on the edge of the bed. Rose's temper tantrum was done; now she was just a little ball of sadness.

"Who's going to protect us?"

"I hear you were really strong yourself."

Rose cast her eyes down; her eyelashes were enviable.

"Auntie Sasha told you."

"Mm-hm. That must've been scary."

"Are you mad?"

"Mad? Of course not."

"But it's wrong, isn't it?"

Jesus, she thought, trying to find the words.

"You were protecting someone you love."

"It didn't feel good."

"I know, and I hope you never have to do anything like that again."

Rose crawled onto Eva's lap, her thumb in her mouth like a toddler.

"So I'm not bad?"

"No, sweetheart, you're perfect, don't ever think otherwise." Eva reassured her, running her fingers through the tangles in her long auburn hair, the texture of her own, though a darker shade.

"Can you braid my hair?"

She didn't bother fetching the comb; just ran her fingers through her daughter's hair a few times and split it into three parts as smoothly as she could. It wouldn't be the best braid, but it would do.

When Rose was calm, she took her to the living room and gave both kids a juice box.

Sasha was still in the kitchen, standing at the window.

"Is she okay?" She asked as Eva came into the room.

"I think so, are you?"

"No, I don't think I am."

"What did you and Hale end up talking about?"

"He didn't make any promises."

"That sounds like Hale."

"That's the whole problem, isn't it? I thought he'd have missed me; I thought if he was coming back, it was because something had changed. He met Ichigo and didn't even realize he was his."

Eva sighed. "He might learn and grow, but he's still Hale. It's why you like him, isn't it?"

Sasha shook her head. "I don't like him for being emotionally stunted."

"You don't owe him anything, you know. You can move on if you want. It was a crisis; they came to help.They know they're the reason we're in this mess."

"They're in a mess too. I just want him to give himself a chance. Do you remember that time we went to the mall?"

"Which one?"

"That time when he needed a cable for his computer."

"Vaguely." If she was honest, she rarely allowed herself to visit those memories. That was before, when there was room for daydreaming of a different future. She didn't want to get hung up on what could've been. She remembered going to the mall with Gabe, but not much about Hale being there.

"I basically convinced him to be my friend after the whole thing with Jason, and over time, I saw it - Hale's just so scared. He never gives himself a chance to let his guard down, which hasn't changed. When we were at the mall that day, I saw him looking for the exits; I saw him getting totally overwhelmed by the crowds. He's always inches away from a panic attack. He grew up in places like that base; he was isolated and neglected and taught that there was nothing else for him. I just wanted him to leave room for something else. I don't know what it could possibly take to show him what life could be."

Eva chewed on her lower lip thoughtfully. "You've been thinking about this a lot."

"Yeah, I can't help it."

"Maybe he just needs time." Eva said.

Sasha nodded. "You and I have each other though, to work through things."

"And Hale has Gabe and Khalil, even if he pretends he doesn't. He's not alone."

"What's Gabe going to do with Hale's trauma?"

"That's not Gabe's responsibility. He has his own demons." Eva said, leaning against the windowsill.

"Don't we all?" Sasha sighed.

There wasn't much else to say. The day beckoned and the kids needed activities to fill it. They could already hear them squabbling. The fact that they were all exhausted didn't bode well.

Chapter 7
Relativity of Time

Sasha

Eva was right. They all needed time, and so did their little neighborhood. It took months for things to reopen, though her particular line of work was always in demand. More young soldiers were in the streets, far from home and happy to spend their cash on companionship. She went out to work while Eva stayed home. Schools were still closed.

Her mind was adrift, constantly imagining Hale everywhere, especially in places where she didn't want to see him. It made her loathe her work in a way she hadn't before. She felt the bitterness spreading inside her, a shadow cast over everything. She couldn't push it away any more than she could stop the nightmares. Eva saw it too, patiently trying to fill in where she could. When school finally opened and Rose could see other kids, Eva spent the days with Ichigo, trying to give him the undivided attention that Sasha couldn't manage. She knew she should do better as a parent, but she was bone tired to the depths of her soul. She started a new stash of cash in their mattress and waited; every dollar felt like a cry into the void.

When Benny's bar finally opened, Eva had to return to work, which meant she was often on pickup duty. Ichigo was happiest when Rose emerged from the school gates, bursting with stories about her friends and enemies, teachers who'd slighted her and every other little kindergartener's drama. Ichigo was happy to listen to her every word as they walked home hand in hand while Sasha carried Rose's backpack and lunchbox. She would walk them to the park near home for a little while before convincing them to come home. They finally had a TV, so she let them watch whatever was on while she made dinner - something easy and quick that could be microwaved quickly when Eva returned.

Months passed in this way, her days blending into one another. Christmas came and went. Rose turned six in February, and they celebrated in the park with her classmates, where Ichigo hid behind Eva and cried in jealousy. Eva made cupcakes for everyone and Rose received more toys than she'd ever had in her whole life. Sasha mustered up the energy to be there but not much else. She sat on the bench with Ichigo and held his hand, feeling sad for her son. She hoped starting school in September would help him to open up a little and not be so dependent on Rose.

It was April Fool's Day, when the doorbell rang just after Eva had left for work. Rose and Ichigo were sitting in the living room with their bowls of cereal, finishing cutting paper fish that Rose said everyone was supposed to bring to class. Both kids dashed to the door and Sasha put a hand out to block them.

"Get away from here! Go to the bedroom and don't come out until I call you, okay? Close the door and don't eavesdrop."

"What does Eaves-" Rose started to ask, a piece of tape on each of her fingers.

"How long mommy?" Ichigo asked.

"Until I call you."

The doorbell rang again, followed by a knock. Whoever it was, they'd gotten upstairs. She wished their building had security.

Ichigo took Rose's little hand and pulled her towards the bedroom. "Come on, let's go."

Rose began to protest.

"Rosalie! Right. Now." Sasha said, her words sounding scary even to her. Rose stuck her lip out defiantly but allowed Ichigo to pull her along.

Sasha went into the kitchen, looking for a weapon. Once again, she found herself with a mere butter knife. Another bashing on the door.

"Who's there?" She called out.

"It's me!" The voice was familiar and male, but that didn't put her any more at ease.

"Who's me?"

"Gabe."

"Gabe?" She unlocked each lock and wrenched the door open; swinging it towards her. The knife clanged to the floor. Gabe looked down at it. "We really need to teach you to shoot."

"What are you doing here? Is everything okay?"

He laughed. "How about a hug then, Alexandra?"

"Oh my god Gabe!" She hugged her friend's boyfriend, or whatever he was now.

"Daddy!" Rose cried from the hallway and came running towards them.

"Rose! I told you to stay in the bedroom!" Sasha snapped just as Gabe scooped her up into his arms.

"Okay, okay, I'm here, I'm here." Gabe laughed.

Balancing her on his hip, he closed the door behind him, confirming what she already knew: Hale wasn't with him. Gabe got down on one knee, Rose still in his arms, and beckoned down the hallway, "Come on, little man. Don't be afraid."

Ichigo looked up at her apprehensively, looking for permission.

"It's okay, Ichigo; go ahead." She sighed, still trying to gather her wits.

Ichigo came over reluctantly, and Gabe put his hand out to him as though he were approaching a frightened animal. Ichigo put his little hand in Gabe's, and Gabe pulled him in for a hug too, to which Ichigo let out a delighted little squeal.

"Okay then." Gabe picked up one kid per arm, dropping his backpack and shoes by the door and marched them all into the living room, where he flopped down on the couch with both.

"Where's Eva?" he asked.

"She went to work at Benny's today." Rose said before Sasha could say anything.

"What's Benny's?"

"A bar," Rose answered.

"Okay, Rosie, time to gather up your school things or we'll be late," Sasha cut in.

She rolled her eyes like a teenager and hopped down from the couch, gathering all of her paper fish and stuffing them into a plastic baggy. Sasha rubbed her eyes, pleading with whatever deity might listen that Rose was not going to say anything more about Eva's job.

"Did you want to stay here while I drop her off? It won't be long." she asked Gabe.

"Nah, I want to see where my little girl goes to school."

Sasha tried not to roll her eyes. She got the kids ready, tying shoelaces, zipping jackets and adjusting backpacks while Gabe watched her. She put her own jacket on, and the four headed downstairs. The old woman she met on the day she'd moved into the apartment cracked her door open and called the kids over to fill their pockets with hard candy. Gabe gave her a funny look but seemed to accept that Sasha was the authority and didn't intervene.

"That's my daddy!" Rose told the cranky neighbor, who gave Gabe a weary look and said, "Another one, huh?" Sasha bit her lip and hoped that had gone over the children's heads.

"Thank you very much." Ichigo said, and both kids headed down the stairs, now with lollipops, ruining all the work she'd done brushing their teeth. On the bright side, it made it harder for Rose to bombard Gabe with questions.

"Where were you before now, daddy?" She seemed to love saying daddy over and over again.

"I was on a secret mission to end the war," He said mysteriously.

"And you did, didn't you?"

"Of course,"

"So, will you take me to school every day now?"

"Sure,"

"Can I introduce you to my friends?"

"Sure, I'd love that,"

"Maybe not today, Rose. Your dad is probably really tired after saving the world and everything."

Sasha chimed in. She wasn't prepared to explain Rose's long-lost father to anyone at this stage.

"I don't mind."

Sasha rolled her eyes. "Fine, do whatever you want, Gabriel, like always." They arrived at the school gates, and Rose led Gabe into the schoolyard without so much as a "Bye Auntie Sasha" or a "Bye Ichigo." Sasha stood at the gates with her little shadow and waited for Gabe to come back out. To her surprise, Rose's little group of girls genuinely seemed excited to meet him for a moment before running off to play four-square. Rose hugged him and ran off with them, her hair bouncing as she skipped.

Ichigo pressed his face to the gate, watching.

"You okay?" She asked, putting her hand on his little shoulder.

"I'm okay." he said, giving her the tiniest smiles.

"It's weird, isn't it?"

He nodded.

"Don't worry. It's just new. Rose is just excited."

"I'm excited too."

"You don't look excited, sweetie."

"I'm okay." He repeated stubbornly.

"Well, it's okay if you're not. You can tell me."

"I know, mummy."

When Gabe returned, they stopped off for groceries, and she made sure to buy enough heavy food to make Gabe's presence worthwhile. Gabe also convinced her to buy a bunch of sugary and overpriced cereals, but didn't offer to pay for any of it. Ichigo was tasked with carrying a container of paper towels, which was huge for him. They'd almost reached home when Ichigo piped up.

"Where's Mr. Hale?"

Sasha stopped in her tracks.

"You don't have to call him that. Just Hale is fine, but you remember that he's your dad, right?"

Ichigo looked up at Gabe. "I wish you were my dad."

"It's okay; I can be your dad for now if you want." Gabe stuttered, glancing at Sasha uneasily.

Sasha was ready to stab Gabe. What the hell was he saying?

She took a deep breath to try and stabilize herself.

"Let's head on inside. Ichigo's favourite show is on."

"Will you watch with me, Uncle Gabe?"

"Sure thing, little man."

They hauled up the groceries, and she turned on the TV. "You start, Ichigo; I need to speak to Gabe for a minute."

Ichigo didn't argue, already pulled into the bright colours and happy songs on the screen.

She marched into the hallway leading to the bedroom and dropped her voice, turning to Gabe.

"What the hell are you thinking? You can't tell him you're his father. You're going to screw him up!" She hissed.

"Why? Hale's not here. It doesn't do any harm. He just wants to know he's not being left out."

"Just like you always do, you make all sorts of promises, then you suddenly have a mission, and then poof - you're gone, and we're here left picking up the pieces!"

"It's not like that this time."

"Listen to me, okay? I don't have a say in how you are with Rose, and Eva can decide how that will evolve, but there are rules when it comes to my son. I don't need you to have him love you more than he already does and then vanishes. He needs stability. You can hang out with him; you can be Mr.-Charmer-Rose's-Dad, okay? But you're not his father. Don't act like you are, don't give him life advice, or make him promises. No promises, none. I don't care if it's awkward for you. That's what it is to protect him."

Gabe raised both hands as though she were pointing a gun at him.

"Okay, okay, whatever. I didn't mean to throw you over the edge already."

"I'm not trying to ruin your grandiose return, okay? When it comes to Ichigo, I'm his mom, and I have to do what I think is right for him."

"And Rose?"

She took a deep breath. "I've been taking care of her for years. I love her like she's my own daughter, but I know she isn't. She's been through a lot, okay? She's yours, and needs her dad, but you can't be all 'Gabriel Wells' about this. Rose puts up a tough girl front, but she's just a little girl. She's super sensitive; she listens to everything you're saying, and interprets it in her own way. You have to think before you speak. You have to be, well, you have to be more."

"I've heard that a lot." He said bitterly.

She sighed. "I'm glad you're back, Gabe, even though I'm doing a terrible job showing it."

"You and Hale are the perfect match that way."

Her heart jumped into her throat.

"Do you know where he is? Is he...?"

He nodded. "Yeah, he's alive, as far as I know. He said he had some things to figure out."

"Do you have contact with him?"

"Not unless he wants me to. You know how he is."

She sighed. Unfortunately, she did.

"Is he coming here?"

"I don't know..."

"What did he say, word for word?"

She wished he would explain it in detail, that he'd describe the expression on his face so she could try and decipher the puzzle behind whatever he said.

"He said he'll see me later and had things to figure out, so I didn't ask more. That's never really worked out for me with him."

She wished the floor would open up and pull her in.

"So you have no idea where he is."

"I have some ideas, but that's all they are."

This conversation was making her feel murderous. "Okay, I'm going to go do laundry. You go ahead and watch that show. You did make a promise."

"Alright then."

He returned to the living room, where she could hear the TV set. Sasha walked into the bedroom, strewn with the laundry to be folded and buried her face in a pillow. She cried until she fell asleep.

Eva

She'd picked up groceries, assuming that Sasha would be too tired after working last night and a full day on parenting duty. Her legs felt like jello from the hour-long dance today, but what choice did she have? The street lights were just starting to turn on, which meant that Sasha would be heading home from the park with Ichigo and Rose. She was rushing to cross the street, the plastic bags twisting between her fingers, when the bag split open, and its contents spilled everywhere on the sidewalk, eggs smashed, milk dented, apples and clementines rolling in all directions.

"Of course," she muttered, getting on her knees and gathering up the mess.

From the corner of her eye, she saw a garage door open, spilling light onto the street and her groceries. Great, now her stuff would get run over too. She got up and stepped aside. Now her groceries would be run over too.

"Angel! Is that you?" An older man with salt and pepper hair and a scruffy beard greeted her. He wore overalls and was holding a dirty cloth on which he was wiping his hands, covered in oil.

She cringed. Was this a client? That was the last thing she needed. He walked closer to her, and she debated she should sprint towards. Back to the bar? Towards the bus stop? To a store?

"Rough day?" He asked. His voice sounded familiar, but she still couldn't place it.

"Just fine, thanks," she said, standing there like a deer in headlights.

"It's me, Charlie. Did you find your family?"

It hit her: This was the man who'd helped her when everything had blown up before she'd found Gabe.

"Oh, it's you! Sorry, I'm just tired."

"That's okay. Can I help you pick up your stuff?" He motioned at the groceries on the ground.

"Oh, no, it's okay."

He went back inside while she continued picking up clementines and returned with a more or less clean plastic bag. "Here."

He got down on his knees, which looked rather difficult for him, and together they picked up what they could as the sunset. A shadow appeared over them both from the open garage door.

"Charlie? Dinner's on!" A woman stood in the doorway, another familiar face. "Oh, it's Angel. I was hoping we'd see you again." The crow's feet around her eyes didn't make her look older but sweeter.

"I'm sorry. I forgot your name." Eva admitted.

"Emma. Don't worry about it. You look like you've got your hands full, again. Did you give her that bag? Oh, Charlie."

"What?"

She shook her head. "Come on, sweetie. Let's get you a clean one."

Eva laughed. "It's fine, really."

"Come on dear; I've just made supper too. You can bring Tupperware."

"You don't need to."

"You can't say no to Emma. She'll find you and make you take it." Charlie mocked.

The woman smiled. "He's not wrong."

Eva followed Charlie through the garage door, Charlie carrying her groceries behind her. She walked through a large warehouse, a few guys working on cars and motorcycles. One whistled at her as she went by, and Charlie barked, "Shut up, Bruce or Leanna will hear about it!" at him.

Eva looked up, inhaling gasoline and oil. It wasn't a bad smell overall. Emma led the way through a back door where the smell of cooking overtook the smell of the garage. The kitchen was tiny and painted bright blue. There were multiple pans on the stove, and before she knew it, Emma was spooning various foods into tupperware and stacking it in a large reusable plastic bag.

"I hope no one in your family has allergies, but here's a stew, some rice and my famous lemon meringue pie. I always make too much anyway. You're welcome to eat with us before you get on the road and tell us about your family."

"Oh, I really couldn't." Eva said, trying to find the words to express how overwhelming this level of kindness was to her.

"Then Charlie will drive you home, if that's okay. You shouldn't be walking alone after dark anyway. This neighborhood's full of hooligans. You do have to come by sometime, though; no need to be a stranger. Charles, you remember where Angel lived, don't you?"

Eva detected a very slight accent, but she couldn't place where it was from, so she didn't ask.

"Sure do."

Emma repacked her groceries into a separate bag as well. Eva looked around the small space. Just beyond the kitchen, she could see a bedroom with a double bed. She supposed this was where they lived. There were pictures on the kitchen walls, one was a photo of them in front of the garage, looking much younger, with Emma clearly pregnant. Another was a photo of a young man in a military uniform, in an almost identical pose to one she had of her dad at her parent's house. A pang of longing for a life she'd left behind hit her as she peered closer at the photograph.

"Is that your son?" She asked. He was handsome and looked close to her age, somewhere between 20 and 25.

There was silence in the chatter. She turned to look at their stricken faces.

"Oh, yes, that's our Andreas." Emma said, wrinkles appearing around her lips and eyes.

Charlie rubbed Emma's back.

"My dad's a soldier too, and my boyfriend, actually..." Eva said.

"Andy didn't know what he wanted to be. I guess he chose what he thought would get him out of here. He wanted to do something important with his life. I don't know if he did but I do miss 'em." Emma turned back to Eva. "That's how it goes sometimes."

"I'm sorry."

"Oh, it's alright. We wouldn't have his picture up if we didn't want to discuss him." Emma said, gently gazing at the photograph, her eyes shining.

"Maybe you can tell me more when I come back."

"Excellent idea. Okay then, hurry back before all this gets cold." She pecked her partner on the lips and walked them both back outside, through the warehouse and to the car, which Eva also hardly recognized now that it wasn't covered in dust.

"Okay, dear, we'll see you soon. You still have our phone number?"

"Yes, I think so...just one thing." They both looked at her.

"It's Eva. Sorry, I lied about my name before."

Emma laughed. "Oh, that's fine. People change names like socks around here. Whatever you're comfortable using is fine."

"Evangeline, Eva," she confirmed.

"That's beautiful, isn't it, Charlie?"

"It sure is."

Eva climbed into the car and watched as Emma waved them goodbye.

"So where you from?"

"Atlanta, well, sort of; I was an army brat, so we've lived all over."

"And you live with your folks?"

"No, with my friend, and our kids, and my boyfriend."

"Sounds hard at your age."

"We're getting the hang of it." She said.

They drove in companionable silence, listening to the radio. Charlie dropped her off in front of the house, and she thanked him profusely.

"I'd better hurry; my friend'll be worried."

"You come back soon, you hear?"

"I will."

She walked up the stairs, her heart feeling full for the first time in a long time.

It was too bad that she'd drop the groceries again when she reached her apartment, as Gabriel Wells was the one who opened the door.

Sasha

Eva's excitement filled the whole apartment as though they'd opened a bag of glitter, and it coated every surface. Gabe and Eva could sleep in the one bedroom, while the kids could sleep in the tiny second bedroom with Sasha on the couch. Eva argued with Sasha, but it was the most rational way to distribute everyone to get the maximum amount of sleep. Gabe could theoretically sleep on the couch, but Sasha didn't feel like standing in the way of their happiness, as miserable as it made her. She didn't want to be jealous, but the love glitter was a lot to handle.

Rose was over the moon and didn't seem to mind sharing her mom with Gabe. She treated Gabe like a superhero who'd fallen from the sky just for her. Gabe never seemed to get tired of her either, happy to listen to detailed, winding, nonsensical kid's stories for hours on end. She would play with his hair, paint his nails, they'd color on the floor for hours. He was prepared to say yes to just about anything she asked. He was a terrible cook but willing to try if Rose asked. Ichigo's reaction was more complex. He was happy to play along with Gabe and Rose every chance he had, but she'd often catch him frowning, looking up at her or Eva.

On one of the rare occasions when she got to be alone with her son - walking to the park alone while Gabe, Eva and Rose went to parent-teacher meetings - she asked him about it.

"Ichigo? I wanted to ask you something."

He'd been skipping ahead, trying not to touch the cracks in the sidewalk.

"Hm?"

"How are you feeling about Gabe being with us?"

"I like Gabe!" he said, "You don't like him, mommy."

"Why would you say that?" She did like Gabe; what made her five-year-old think otherwise?

Ichigo shrugged. "I don't know. So, you do?"

"Yes, I do like Gabe."

"Not as much as Auntie Eva."

"No, Auntie Eva and Gabe are in love. I'm not in love with Gabe; we're just friends."

Ichigo considered this.

"So you don't love Gabe?"

"I care about Gabe a lot."

"Do you love Auntie Eva?"

"Yes, very much."

"More than Gabe?"

She laughed. It wasn't often that Ichigo would get philosophical about emotions, which delighted her. It meant she was doing something right!

"Differently than Gabe, yes."

"Do you love Rose and me?"

"Yes, very much."

"I love everybody the same."

"Great."

"But Gabe is really cool."

"Yes, he is."

"Is he our family now?"

"Sort of; he's Auntie Eva's boyfriend and Rose's dad, so...yes, I guess so. You and I are biological family, though."

"So, real family?"

"No, just...biologically related."

He still looked confused.

"And Gabe isn't my dad?"

"No, Hale is your dad, and Gabe is Rose's dad."

"But he's not here."

"No, he's not."

"I guess he doesn't love us."

"He does Ichigo, he does. He's just had a hard life. He has a lot of things to figure out. Even if we never see him again, please know he loves us."

"How do you know?"

"Trust me."

"Okay, mommy. I'm gonna go play now."

She wondered if she was telling the truth. Did he love them? He didn't even know Ichigo. He'd only met him once, Ichigo, meanwhile, had run to the swings and pushed himself up with his little legs, lost to the world. She stood back and watched him. Did Hale love her? He'd never quite said as much. He'd said he cared about her. That was something, but it was so long ago. What was she going to do if he didn't come back? Would she keep living with Eva and her family? The endless third and fifth wheels? Gabe would need to get a job if she moved out. There were too many questions and worries for a park afternoon. She sat on the bench and took deep breaths, watching her son reach for the sky, closing his eyes until he felt the swing at the top of its axis and then opening them with a look of complete wonder.

Chapter 8
A New World

Eva

She was back to hiding big secrets. She'd sworn she'd never be in this situation again, and yet, how was she supposed to tell Gabe that she danced in a bar and took her clothes off? She couldn't even wrap her mind around how he might react. Of course, as per usual, Sasha was ready to throw in her take on the situation. They were walking to the bar across town, where she now had a half shift on Saturday afternoons. Having Gabe around to watch the kids was nice in some ways, but how long could she keep dodging his questions?

"You have to tell him before he finds out in some other way."

"He's going to freak out. Maybe I can change jobs and have him never find out?"

Sasha shrugged. "Well, if you find something, let me know. I'm getting pretty tired of paying half my salary to D. Also, I'm sorry, but Gabe has no leg to stand on. Remember what he was like in high school?"

"Yeah, but he likes this idea of me as this sheltered princess."

"And you want him to keep thinking that?"

"I don't know. I don't want him to think less of me."

"If he does, then he's a total ass. You have to give him a chance to prove himself, right?"

"Hasn't he already? He's here."

"He needs a job. Otherwise, he has to accept where we get our money. It wasn't our first choice either."

Eva knew Sasha was right, but it didn't lessen the uneasy feeling in her stomach. She wished she could talk about this with someone who wasn't knee-deep in it with her. Maybe someone with more life experience...that's when she thought of Emma and Charlie again. Would they judge her too? Would they react the way she knew her parents would have? She supposed it was worth trying. It would be practice.

That same week, she took Emma and Charlie up on their offer for lunch. She would never have been able to do it when it was just her and Sasha, but Gabe was happy to spend the day with the kids when Sasha was out with a client. Emma had pulled out all the stops, just like her own mother would have - there was so much to choose from, and everything looked and smelled absolutely delicious: cheese blintzes with sour cream, roast chicken, boiled potatoes with chives, sauteed vegetables. She'd even made homemade compote.

305

"This looks incredible!" Eva said.

"Have you had Eastern European food before?"

"My best friend is Russian, so yes."

"Ah, we're Polish, but the food's similar. So you live with your friend?"

"Sasha, yes - and my daughter and her son."

Emma smiled. "You're just so young."

"I know."

It wasn't judgemental, just a statement of fact.

"You should bring them with you next time. I can't cook for less than an army, apparently." Emma laughed.

"Actually, my boyfriend recently came to stay with us too."

"The one you said was a soldier? You mentioned that last time."

"Sort of, yeah."

"And how's that going?"

"It's been great in so many ways...but it's been a long time since Sasha and I were just the kids and us." Emma had filled her plate, and Eva told the story between bites. "We've basically been raising the kids together this whole time, and suddenly having another person in the mix is making it so complicated."

"How is he taking peacetime?" Charlie asked.

She hadn't really thought about it that way. "He seems happy. He loves the kids, and they adore him. It's just that, I've changed a lot, and I'm unsure whether to say anything. My job is sort of controversial,and I don't want him to think differently of me."

"Controversial?" Emma repeated.

"I dance at Benny's bar– the sixty-nine."

There was a pause during which Charlie took a long drink of the deep dark beverage in front of him.

"And you think he'll want you to stop?"

"I want to stop too, but we have to be able to pay for everything and Sasha, she does something even more dangerous." She was getting choked up just talking about it; she didn't realize how much this weighed on her.

"Eat, sweetie; it's the best thing for a heavy heart." Emma said. She patted her on the hand.

Eva laughed. "That's not what my mom would've said." As she mentioned her mom, she wondered if Gabe had kept his promise of finding her family. She would have to ask. Emma wasn't wrong, a few more spoonfuls of food stopped her from crying.

"And where is she?"

"I don't know. I left for California with Gabe when I was pregnant, and I haven't seen them since...I hope they're okay."

"They must be worried sick." Emma said, shaking her head.

"I just didn't know how to tell them, and now it's been so long."

"I'm sure they'd love to hear from you, no matter what. Any parent would, and any parent who had a lovely daughter like you sure would. I know I would."

"What does your guy know how to do?" Charlie asked.

"What do you mean?"

"Can he fix a car?"

"He can hotwire one, so probably." She remembered the red Mustang.

"Then why don't you bring 'em here? I'll give him a shot."

"Really?" She couldn't believe she hadn't thought of it! Gabe would do great as a mechanic!

"Sure, send 'em over tomorrow, round 9, and I'll see what he can do."

"Really? That's amazing! Thank you so much!" She wanted to cry again, but it was easier just to eat. She was so full by the time she left she thought she'd never eat again, but she still walked away with Tupperware full of food for the rest of the family. Charlie insisted on driving her home again too. Their city was so different from inside a car; grimy still but less intimidating, like it was coming out on the other side of the war too and figuring itself out alongside her.

Sasha

They were playing cards in the living room, which was fun with three adults and two kids. Rose and Gabe matched one another with drama, making it the world's most intense game of Go Fish.

"But you said you didn't haaaave kings!"

"I didn't theeeen."

"He did have kings. He was hiding them."

"Ichigo, don't look at people's cards; Gabe quit cheating!"

"So I have some good news." Eva said, "Do you have any sevens?"

"Nope!"

"You say, "Go Fish" Rose."

"Go get your fish!"

"Do you have 4s, Ichigo?"

"I found a job for you, Gabe."

"You peeked."

"Did not! Your 4s are mine!"

"Yeah?" Gabe looked surprised but not unhappy. When did Eva have time to look for a job for him anyway?

"My friends Charlie and Emma own a garage near here. They said they're looking for someone who can fix a car."

"That sounds alright! I'm down."

"Do you have any Jacks, daddy?"

"Go Fish, kiddo."

"Hiding aces, little man?"

"No, I mean, go Fish."

"Do you have any Queens, mommy?"

"Sure do." She handed Ichigo her Queens.

"Do you have any 4s, Rose?"

"Noooooooooo....I do, but I don't wanna give them!"

"So, how do you know Emma and Charlie?"

"I met them when everything...happened."

"I see." She thought they'd discussed everything that happened, and now there were surprise players in the game. She was getting tired of curveballs. Gabe having a job should make her happy...shouldn't it? It made perfect sense; they needed the money, so why did she feel so sour about it?

The doorbell rang.

"Who's that?" Sasha said, alarmed.

"Relax Sash- I ordered pizza."

"Good thing you're getting that job, Gabe." Sasha sighed as the kids gathered up the cards and took turns shuffling them.

Gabe shrugged. "Did you want my cooking instead?"

"No, guess not." She agreed. She was no great cook, but Gabe was the first person she'd ever met who had managed to burn pasta.

Eva had brought the pizza into the kitchen.

"Hands-washed kids!" She called.

"So, can I visit you at the garage, uncle Gabe?" Ichigo asked.

"Sure you can, little man."

"I like cars. Can I work at the garage too?"

"How about school?"

"I can't start until September, and if I work at the garage, maybe I don't need to go."

"You have to go to school, Ichigo." Sasha cut in.

"Did you go to school, uncle, Gabe?"

"Not much."

Ichigo grinned. He'd been telling her how nervous he was about spending the whole day away from home with so many kids he didn't know.

"School's not optional." Sasha said, "Now hop along and wash your hands if you want pizza."

Ichigo did as he was told, but she could see the little gears in his mind turning, considering his options, wondering if he'd found a way around his anxiety.

Sasha sighed and fetched the drinks from the fridge. She then had to go and bring an extra chair from the bedroom since they were still trying to fit five people around their tiny kitchen table. There was relative silence as they had their pizza, Rose picking off all the vegetables and leaving them on her plate, Ichigo starting from the crust as he always did, Eva and Gabe sitting with their chairs close enough so they could reach one another with their knees. It struck Sasha that her feelings were unrelated to Gabe getting a job. She wanted him and Eva to be happy. The problem was she didn't fit this picture anymore. It was always like this - Eva and Gabe circling one another and her on the sidelines trying to be the supportive friend. She loved Eva and Rose immensely, but being the third wheel again was just another reminder that her own life was still on hold. Her job was disgusting at best and outright dangerous at worst. She had to make a change, and the first step would be to find somewhere to live that wasn't face-to-face with what she would never have.

Eva

Charlie and Gabe got on like a house on fire. Eva wasn't sure why she was surprised, Gabe always did have a knack for fitting in. She'd walked him to Charlie as requested, and Gabe took it from there. Sasha had the kids for the day, and Eva had her dancing clothes in her backpack. Gabe acted as though they were just walking to the park, chatting the whole way about this and that while she mentally paced through all the things that could go wrong. What if Gabe was rude to Charlie? He wasn't great with authority figures, but she had to trust that he'd be okay, didn't she? And what about payment? What was a reasonable amount to ask for an unskilled mechanic? It turned out that she had nothing to worry about. Charlie put an arm around Gabe as though he'd known him his whole life and walked him into the shop, waving goodbye to her.

"He'll be home for dinner!" He called.

Eva stood in the doorway like a parent dropping off a kid at school on the first day until Emma came out of the backroom and turned her around.

"Come on, Angel, Evangeline, sorry, don't worry about it." She put a clementine in her hand and walked her out to the sidewalk.

"Charlie's so excited to have another set of hands in here. We're just swamped."

"Thank you, really." She said, "If he's rude or something, you can tell me or you can tell him off. He's not the best with people telling him what to do."

Emma laughed. "Sweetie, this is a garage. Do you think we attract the good-listeners types here? Charlie'll sort him out."

"You off to work now, sweetie?"

"Yeah..."

"I'm going to give you some advice. Now that you've got Gabe working, find something safer. You're too young for that world."

"I don't think that's how my clients see it." She bristled.

"Eva, I'm too young for that world, and I'm old. Get out of there before your daughter is old enough to understand what her mother's had to do to keep food on the table."

"Um, thanks." She wasn't sure what to say. Emma pulled her into a hug and sent her on her way. The truth was that she wasn't ready to give up the job, not yet. It had given her independence and a community when she'd had none. Some of the girls were awful, but others were sweet and asked her all about Rose and Ichigo, and brought her clothes they thought she'd look good in on stage. It wasn't what she wanted, but what she knew now.

Sasha met her outside the building with the kids. She was letting them ride their new bikes around. Gabe had splurged, as per usual, and brought them home. Watching them zooming around as fast as bicycles with training wheels would allow was great, and the rowdy teens who usually stood smoking in the alleyway by their building would hoot and holler when one of them zoomed past them. It made Eva a bit uncomfortable, but none of them had engaged further so she figured they'd keep to themselves too.

"How was Gabe's first day?" Sasha asked as Eva sat down and lit up a cigarette.

"Good! I think...Charlie said he'd be home by supper."

"I'm really glad."

"Are you? You seem upset."

Sasha took a deep breath. "I have some big news too."

"What is it?"

"I'm just nervous to tell you."

"Whatever it is, hon, we'll figure it out like always."

"Okay, I'm moving out."

"What?" Eva inhaled sharply, and the smoke went up her nose. She started coughing. Sasha patted her on the back.

"You okay?"

"Yeah, I'm fine, but what do you mean you're moving out? You don't have to do that. I know you're annoyed with Gabe, but we can make it work. I can talk to him about whatever's bothering you."

"No, it's okay. I just think I need some space, but I'm not going too far. Mirna from down the hall is moving in with her son now that the war is over, and she said I could take over her lease. It's much smaller than our place so that I can afford it."

"What about Ichigo?"

Sasha looked hurt. "I thought we could tell both kids together, sort of tag team it."

"Oh, are you sure?"

"Yeah, I won't be far, and I'll still take Rose whenever you want me to, and they can have sleepovers whenever they want. I just think I need to be able to stand on my own two feet here."

"You can change your mind at any time, okay?"

"Thanks."

There was silence. Eva put her arm around her friend as the sky faded from the pale blue of the evening to creamy pinks and oranges and, finally, to a cloudy dark Spring sky.

"Okay, kids, time to come in!" She called. Rose huffed but ran over.

"Did you see me on my bike?"

"I did! You're so good!"

"Daddy said I could have the training wheels off super soon!"

"That's great. You were great too, Ichigo."

Ichigo was looking at his mom. He always knew when something was the matter. Sasha picked up his bike, and Eva took Rose's. Gabe arrived home just in time for supper, covered in oil and wearing overalls she'd never seen on him before. She commanded that he shower before dinner, and he was happy to oblige. It had been a big day, and for once, the kids were just tired enough to be quiet through dinner. Then, it was bath time and bedtime for them.

As she lay beside Gabe in the dark that night, she tried to imagine living in a different apartment from Sasha and Ichigo - it seemed surreal. She was so tired of change that she couldn't sleep.

Sasha

Ichigo did not take the news well. She'd never seen him cry so hard. Rose patted him on the hand.

"Don't worry! We can hang out all the time! And soon you'll be at school with me, and I'll introduce you to everybody!"

Ichigo just cried harder; his little face squished up like when he was a baby, which he tried to cover with his hands.

"Oh, sweetie. Come on now." Sasha soothed. She untangled his little arms from his face and pulled him into her lap.

"We're going to be right down the hall Ichigo, don't worry. This is going to be good. You'll have your own room and your own toys." Eva tried to comfort him.

The front door opened, and Gabe walked inside, looking confused.

"Everything okay?"

Eva got up and went over to whisper to him.

311

"Where?" He said.

Eva whispered again.

Gabe's face reflected so many different emotions in seconds that she wasn't sure what he'd do now. He settled on a goofy grin.

"Hey there, lil' man? I hear you guys are movin' on up in the world!"

Ichigo stopped and peered at Gabe, bewildered.

"You're moving down the hall, right?"

Ichigo nodded, still choked up.

"That's great! You guys need more space now that you and Rose are getting so big, right?"

Sasha scowled. There was no way Ichigo was falling for this.

"What about you?" He sniffled.

"I'll be right here whenever you need me, kiddo."

Ichigo got up from her lap and stood before Gabe, who continued.

"You'll be the man of the house there, and I'll take care of your aunt and Rose here. We can tag team."

Ichigo turned to look at Sasha as though seeking affirmation with this stance. She wasn't sure she loved the message, but he'd stopped crying, so she wasn't about to look a gift horse in the mouth.

"And we'll even give you guys the TV. Now that I'm working," Gabe added.

Rose crossed her arms. "That's not fair."

"Rosie!" Eva reprimanded.

Sasha leaned back on the couch.

"Oh, one more thing." Gabe said. "I brought a little something..."

"What?" Both kids scrambled up to Gabe, who took two ice creams in their wrappers from his backpack. The kids quickly forgot unhappiness, and each grabbed one, heading to the kitchen, where they knew they were allowed to eat.

"What do we say?" Eva called.

"Thank you!" they chorused.

Sasha sighed. It was only an hour before dinner.

"Everyone okay now?" Gabe asked. She nodded. "Yeah, thanks."

"Great, I'm gonna go shower."

"I'll start on supper." Eva said, "okay, hon?"

Sasha nodded, hoping she wasn't being selfish.

Eva

The day Sasha and Ichigo moved out was a Sunday. It didn't take long - they didn't have much. After it was done, they all walked to the corner store for ice cream.

"How do you have so many books?" Gabe asked Sasha, stretching out his arms after hauling most of the boxes.

Sasha shrugged. "They're cheaper than cigarettes."

"Can you get some more friends to come and help us next time?"

"I don't have any friends."

"Don't say that mommy. What about all the people who pick you up for work?"

"Those are just coworkers, Ichigo. Not friends. We don't talk to those people when it's not for work."

"Lifts, huh?"

Eva elbowed her boyfriend in the stomach. "Stop, Gabe."

"Oh no!" Rose cried. The top part of her ice cream was on the sidewalk. Before she could start crying, Ichigo stuck his cone on top of hers.

"Don't cry, Rosie!"

"That's very sweet of you Ichigo. Come on, let's go back and get you a new one. We'll meet you guys back at, I mean, let's have dinner tonight. You guys come over and help us to break in my new kitchen table."

Eva nodded, realizing that "home" no longer meant the same apartment for them both. Sasha locked eyes with her, clearly thinking the same thing, then turned away and took Ichigo's hand.

"So, what does she do, exactly? Who are these friends?" Gabe asked once Rose was skipping up ahead, dangerously close to losing her ice cream cone again.

Eva sighed. "She's a sex worker, Gabe."

The silence wasn't very long.

"And we're all just...?"

"No..." The words were right on the edge of her tongue. She could tell him about her job now; maybe the contrast would make hers seem less bad somehow. She instantly felt guilty thinking it, but what if he said something and Rose heard him? What if it made him disappear again?

"So you're letting her do that?"

"Letting her? Gabe, I "let her" do that as much as I "let" you take experimental "serum" to fight a war I never agreed to and then raised our daughter with Sasha until you got back. What do you want me to say? Do you want her to stop? She needs another job."

He stopped and grabbed her hand, spinning her around to face him.

"Are you doing the same?"

She shook her head. "No, I'm not."

He looked relieved. "Okay, so you just work at the bar, right?"

"I work at the bar."

He didn't let go of her hand as they walked back home.

The apartment felt empty without Sasha and Ichigo in it. Rose, pumped with sugar, ran off to play "floor is lava," pretending Ichigo was with her.

"Um, babe?"

"Yeah?"

"What do you do at the bar?"

She sighed. "I can't right now, Gabe."

He brought her out to the balcony where they could keep watching Rose, but she couldn't hear them.

"Come on; we said no more secrets."

"You have a million secrets!"

"Ask me anything. I'll answer."

"Did you find out about my parents as I asked you?"

"I did."

"Where are they?"

"On a military base in Washington, DC. They're fine. Your dad got a promotion.They live in a pretty tightly secure place."

"Did you tell them where I am? Did you reach out to them?"

"No."

"Why not?"

"You didn't say you wanted me to do that! You just said to make sure they're okay."

"So the same way you've been checking on me then?" She knew she was picking a fight, but it also distracted him from his initial question.

"Babe, I'm here now, okay? I'm here now."

"Okay, but you weren't before, and that meant we had to make hard decisions without you."

"So? Are you going to answer me or what?"

"About what?"

"The bar!"

"Get off my back, Gabe." She said, feeling the burn on her cheeks. She sidestepped him and went back inside. If he wanted to bolt, he was more than welcome. She'd had a long enough day with her best friend and pseudo-son moving out. Why did she owe him an explanation anyway? He was lucky she'd found that job; they all were. It was what allowed her to raise Rose by herself. And how dare he judge Sasha? It wasn't her choice either. She'd been her only support system for all this time, and now Gabe appeared out of the blue expecting her to drop everything....

The sound of Rose crying coming from the living room interrupted her train of thought. She dashed out of the bedroom, but Gabe was already there, sitting next to Rose on the floor.

"Are you hurt, baby?" Eva asked.

Rose shook her head. "No!"

Gabe pulled his daughter up onto his lap, and she melted into his arms.

"I miss Ichigo." She said.

"Yeah, I get that. I miss lots of people too."

"Who?"

"Lots of friends - but you know what? Missin' 'em means you care about them, which is important. Do you know what we could do? We could repaint your room now. Get some posters up there, whatever you want, and you don't have to ask anybody."

She cried for a minute longer, then seemed to process his suggestion. "Can I get fairy lights?"

"Yeah, why not? Why don't we get on that now."

"Gabe, it's 7 PM." Eva said, depleted.

"Store's still open for another hour. You comin' babe?"

She looked at Rose to see if there was any apprehension about going alone with Gabe, but her mood had already shifted, quick as clouds parting, just like her father.

"You two go ahead. I think I'll just stay here and tidy up now that there's so much extra space." Moving all the furniture had created enough dust for it to be a good idea.

"All right, we'll see you in a bit." He got up and pecked her on the lips as though their argument on the balcony hadn't happened. Rose was already pulling her jacket back on. They really were two peas in a pod.

Sasha

She'd never lived alone. She supposed she wasn't alone, but five-year-olds weren't exactly a partner in crime. She imagined that many people in their mid-20s moved out on their own for the first time after finishing university and leaving campus, but this wasn't like that. Without Rose and Eva, the apartment felt empty. They were just down the hall; she saw them daily, but they felt a million miles away. Every time she came over, there was some warm family activity going on: Rose and Gabe making slime with shaving cream and food colouring on the living room floor, Eva and Gabe cuddled up on the couch with Rose wedged between them, a Christmas tree being hauled in through the front door. They celebrated Christmas at the old apartment, and she spent the night on the couch. She still needed to leave Ichigo with Eva whenever she had a client, but it wasn't the same as living under the same roof.

She felt herself having to reach further and further to muster up the energy to get up in the morning, to make meals,play with Ichigo , or even talk to him. She knew it was wrong; she knew it wasn't the sort of mother she'd wanted to be. She knew he needed her - but she needed someone too. Ichigo was endlessly patient and unbelievably sweet. He'd bring her lukewarm tea or snacks and leave them on her nightstand. He didn't cry when she forgot to pick up something he wanted from the grocery store. He would peer up at her with his deep, thoughtful eyes when they sat at the kitchen table doodling, expecting her to say something, but she couldn't think of what to say, so she just gave him an apologetic smile.

The more he tried to cheer her up, the sadder she felt. Here she was, waiting on a miracle that would never come and for herself to be strong enough to cope with a life that promised nothing but scraping by. Every time she saw a client could be her last. She knew it was dangerous and felt it every time she slid into a stranger's car or walked up a flight of stairs to an unknown apartment or hotel room. She'd gotten used to being afraid - afraid or unconsciousness, her two states of being.

Realizing how bad things had gotten came months after she'd moved out when she awoke to a knock on her door. She looked over at the alarm clock - it was 3 PM. She peeled herself off the bed.
"Ichigo?" She called. He wasn't in his room, nor the living room. She called again. Someone knocked harder.
"Sasha!" It was Eva's voice on the other side.
She ran to the door and swung it open, not caring that she was still in her pyjamas.
"Eva! I can't find -"
She found Eva carrying her purse on her doorstep with Gabe, Rose and her son.
"Ichigo! Where did you go?!" She fell to her knees and pulled him to her.
"Are you okay, mummy?"
"I am now! Where did you go?"
"The store." He said. "I got hungry, and you were soooo tired."
Tears burned her eyes almost instantly. Ichigo looked frightened. "What's the matter?"
"You can't just go out by yourself!" She cried.
"He wasn't by he-self, Auntie Sasha; we found 'em." Rose said, sporting two long braids like Anne of Green Gables.
Sasha finally looked up at Eva and Gabe, pulling herself up using the doorframe.
"Um, thanks." She muttered. Her heart was still pounding out of her chest.
"Kids, why don't you go with Gabe and see if you can figure out that gingerbread house we bought."
Both kids cheered and started pulling Gabe along to Eva and Gabe's door.
"You comin' babe?"
"Give me a minute." Eva said firmly, and Gabe nodded. Sasha wished the floor could open up and swallow her, but she allowed Eva into her

apartment and shut the door. She walked to the couch and pushed a pile of laundry she'd been meaning to fold onto the floor, sitting down and making room for her friend.

"Go ahead." She said, unable to keep the disdain out of her voice.

"Hon," Eva started.

"I know, I know. Things have been, not great lately."

"Do you want to talk about it?"

"What can I say? I'm just sitting around waiting for something, I don't even know what, for things to improve."

"Why don't you guys just move back in with us?"

"I can't, Eva. You and Gabe, I can't."

"I'm sorry about Gabe. I know he can be a lot. Did something happen between you guys?"

"No, it's just that...this is going to sound so dumb, but I just don't want to be the third wheel in your couple anymore. I want to move forward somehow."

She nodded. "I know, but you're not doing okay and ..."

"And I'm failing as a mom. I know." She looked down at the floor, digging her fingernails into the palms of her hands.

"I didn't say that."

"You didn't have to."

"I can help more. You know Ichigo's more than welcome if you just need some time."

Sasha pulled her knees up to her face and put her head down on her arms. It all felt so heavy. "I'm his mom."

"Yes, and you always will be."

She didn't know what else to say. It was as though all the colors had seeped out of the world..

"What do you want me to say?" She finally uttered.

"I want to help."

"How?" Sasha cried, "How do you want to help? I followed you into the dark, and now I'm in it alone!"

"You're not by yourself! Don't yell at me!"

"Then don't push!"

"Pot, meet kettle." Eva said.

"I didn't ask you to come over, okay? You can send Ichigo back home when you're ready. You can go back over there and play happy families now."

"That's not fair, Sasha!"

"Life's not fair."

It sounded stupid even to her own ears, but she wanted this conversation to end. She didn't want to talk to Eva about her bitter heart. She didn't want to discuss her failings as a parent, friend, or adult. Being with herself was bad enough, but being with someone else was worse.

"Fine." Eva got up. "I'll see you later."

She turned on her heel and left her apartment. Sasha cried harder until she was too tired to keep crying and went to sleep.

Ichigo came home after supper, already showered and smelling of Rose's pink bubble bath. She let him in when Gabe rang the doorbell and then closed the door again with a nod. Gabe looked like he'd had something to say, he always had something to say, but she didn't want to hear it.

"Thanks." She said,

Ichigo skipped inside until he saw her face.

"Mommy? I'm sorry I left by myself. Please, don't cry."

His hair was getting long, pushing into his eyes the way Hale always did. She pushed it back from his forehead and bent over to peck him on the top of his head. "It's okay; I'm sorry I wasn't doing what I was supposed to do."

"So you're sorry, and I'm sorry." He smiled. She got down to his level and gave him a big hug. He was getting so big so quickly all of a sudden. Where had the tiny squishy toddler gone? She wondered if he'd keep his rounded cheeks like hers, or if he'd thin out and stretch upwards like his goddamn father.

Eva

The phone was ringing non-stop. It was 4 am. Gabe reached for it before she could, his training making him much better at being alert in an instant than her.

"Unknown caller." His voice was rough from sleep.

"Don't pick up then." She muttered, eyes still closed.

He picked up. She could hear someone sounding hysterical on the other end of the line.

"You got the wrong number, lady." He said, then heard someone shouting on the other line. "Alexandra?" He finally whispered.

Eva's eyes opened as Gabe held out the phone to her.

"Sash?"

Her friend's voice kept breaking between sobs.

"Hon, what happened? Where are you?"

She could hear car horns and sirens in the background.

"I need you to come get me." Sasha sobbed.

Eva sat up, rubbing her tired eyes, "where are you?"

She hiccuped directions that hardly made sense.

"Sash, that's like 50 miles from here."

"I know, I'm sorry, he took my bag. I'd have to walk otherwise."

"Okay, I'm coming. Hang in there."

"Don't send Gabe!" She hung up.

"I have to go." She pulled herself out of bed, grabbing a pair of pants from a chair where she'd thrown them earlier.

"Where?"

"I have to go get Sasha."

"What?"

"She's stranded, and I have to go get her."

"From where?"

"Near the big supermarket on the North side."

"You're not going there right now." Gabe was braiding his hair quickly.

"Yes, I am, and you have to stay here with the kids."

"It's the middle of the night."

"Which is why I'm taking a cab."

"The hell you are. You stay here. I'll go get Sasha."

She pulled a big sweater over her head and put her hair in a bun.

"You have to stay here with the kids." She repeated.

"Do you know what kinds of people are out there right now?"

She turned to him in the darkness, unable to keep the anger out of her voice. "I know exactly what kinds of people, which is why I have to get my best friend."

"Let me go with you at least; we'll lock the apartment."

"And the kids'll just stay here by themselves?" They were screaming in a whisper.

"I'll go. You stay with the kids." He said, pulling on his pants too.

"Gabe, no. Listen to me, okay? This is what we've had to do all this time. While you were off fighting your war, this is what we've had to do, and now, I'm going to go and keep my side of the deal. You can sit here and worry for a change. I'm going to take Sasha back home, and you're going to stay here, and if the kids wake up, you'll take care of them until I come back."

With that, she was out in the hallway, grabbing her purse and pulling on her shoes. Gabe followed but was uncharacteristically speechless.

"Babe?"

"What?"

"Be careful."

She kissed him quickly and then ran down the stairs. There was a taxi station only a block away. She popped in headphones when she gave the driver the address and watched the city lights flash past her. She didn't want to talk. Her mind was entirely on the task at hand: Find Sasha. She was still groggy but had plenty of time to wake up as the car rushed past familiar streets and eventually changed to less familiar ones. As they made their way into the industrial sector, where tents of homeless people bloomed like flowers in every colour of the rainbow, a light rain began to patter against the glass. She asked the driver to wait and stepped out. He locked the doors behind her and tapped on the meter. She wished she'd brought an umbrella.

Industrial buildings were all around her, with all the lights off. She walked up and yanked on some of the doors, to no avail.

"Sasha?" She called into the rain and dark. Her heart was beating at a breakneck pace. Maybe she should've let Gabe come with her after all.

That was when she spotted a phone booth on the other side of the street. She walked straight to it, rain hitting her square in the face and soaking through her hair and clothes. Sasha curled up in the booth, her head in her arms, her knees up to her chest. As Eva pulled the door open, she startled, peering up.

"Oh my god, hon, what happened?"

Sasha pulled herself up from the floor. "I got robbed." She said, her voice sounding broken like it did on the phone.

"Are you okay?"

"I think so. I got into the car, drove for a long time, and parked here. I didn't see the driver. The guy in the back was, well, you know and then instead of paying, he told me to get out of the car, and threw my purse to the front."

"Oh, my god..."

"I told him I wasn't getting out until I got my purse back, so he shoved me out and drove off."

"Are you hurt?"

She shrugged. "I don't know."

"Do you want to go to the hospital?"

Sasha shook her head. "No, I don't have any ID, and that cab probably cost a fortune already."

"Oh, Sash...tomorrow? We can go tomorrow. I'll take you to the clinic."

The tall girl nodded, her jaw tight and her clothing torn and rumpled.

"Come on, hon." Holding hands, she led Sasha back to the cab and told the man to return them to where he'd picked her up. The meter kept going higher and higher, but all she could see was the darkness under her friend's eyes, the way she wore her pain like a blanket as she wrapped her arms around herself and stared up at the ceiling. She didn't say thank you. She didn't look happy to see her. She just looked so miserable that it broke Eva's heart.

"Sasha..."

"What?"

"You need a new job."

"I know."

When they went to the clinic the next morning (after she'd gone home to help Gabe get Rose off to school and given him the task of watching

Ichigo again), Sasha allowed herself to be poked and prodded quietly. She was given a clean health bill - a few cuts and bruises from the fall, nothing to worry about. Her pain wasn't physical, and they both knew it.

Chapter 9
Reunited

Sasha

After being mugged; it became harder to work, and scarier. She took on fewer clients, which left her with less money but more time - and somehow, time helped. She could wander to the sad little library around thirty minutes away while Ichigo was at school. She was able to scribble down her thoughts on paper. Her thoughts kept coming back to Hale, but less frequently than before. She'd lost hope in his return by the time it happened.

She had accepted that Hale wasn't coming back, so she'd decided that this was her life and she would have to make the most of it. She was going to find it in herself to be the mother she wanted to be, so when Ichigo started school in September, she stood proudly with him outside of the gates, both of them in brand new outfits, Ichigo squeezing the straps on his dinosaur backpack with his little fists. She could see how nervous he was.

"You're going to do great. You're so smart and so cool and so kind and fun. You'll make lots of friends."

He nodded, his chin wobbling. "Come on." She led him into the classroom, following the flow of other parents. Rose had already gone off to class. The Kindergarteners started later on the first day. This was it; this was the threshold. Parents weren't allowed beyond this point. She got down on her knees to be face-to-face with her son.

"Ichigo?"

"Mm?"

"I'll be right here as soon as it's over, and you'll tell me all about your day - good or bad and everything in between. If anyone gives you trouble, tell me immediately, and I will never let them hurt you, okay?" He nodded, a small smile appearing just at the corner of his cheek.

"You going to beat them up, mommy?"

"Yes, yes, I will."

He wrapped his arms around her neck, and she gave him a quick hug too, then turned him around and sent him off, walking back outside feeling like she couldn't breathe. She missed him so much already. She hadn't scheduled any clients today because she knew she'd be an emotional wreck.

She walked home and inhaled the Fall air; her birthday was just around the corner. She would be twenty-four years old. She felt so much older

322

than that and yet no wiser. All she'd learned was to keep putting one foot in front of the other forever, rinse and repeat.

She spent the day outside alone, popping into shops and browsing things she couldn't afford. She had lunch in the park. When she came to pick up Ichigo, he was quiet and clung to her knee as though he'd thought she was never coming back. They walked home together, and he held her hand all the way back. She made his favourite butter noodles, and allowed him to watch the same movie back to back on repeat. She let him have an extra long bath before bed, and only after she'd read him a story did he admit, "It wasn't so bad today."
"I'm glad. Are you ready for tomorrow?"
He nodded.
"And no one bugged you?"
"No, but Rose has a different recess."
"I'm sorry about that."
She kissed him goodnight and went to crash on the couch.

A solid knock on the door startled Sasha awake. It wasn't Eva's knock, nor Gabe's. She waited in silence; maybe the person would leave. There was another knock. She fetched the crowbar she kept in the kitchen and approached the door.
"Who is it?" She said quietly.
"It's me."
That voice...
"Me who?"
"Hale."
She unlocked the door carefully, the crowbar still in her hand.
There he stood, like an apparition on her doorstep. He wore a pair of dusty black jeans, a tight fitting long-sleeved sweater with a dark green jacket over it and carried a black duffel bag. His hair was shorter than when she'd last seen him. His face looked thin and dirty, like the rest of him.
She set the crowbar by the door.
"Hi." She said quietly. "Ichigo's asleep."
He nodded. "Gabe said he would be."
"You went to Eva's first?"
"I didn't know you'd moved."
"You're lucky it wasn't very far."
"Can I...come in?"
She hesitated. She wasn't sure why, but she stepped aside nonetheless, allowing him to step into the square-shaped hallway. He came inside and

pulled off his military-grade boots and lined them up by the door before closing it.. He set his bag down on the ground and pulled off his jacket.

"There's a hook there." She said, hovering by the door.

He did as he was told, his coat dusting hers a little.

They kept standing in the hallway awkwardly, staring at one another.

"You don't seem happy to see me." He said, his voice soft.

"I'm just surprised."

"I'm sorry."

"Just come in. Did you want something? Juice? Water? Food?"

"Water, please."

"Great, just go sit on the couch."

She walked into the kitchen, just off the hallway and took a moment to collect herself with her head in the fridge, the cold feeling good against her cheeks. This felt like a dream. She'd imagined it so many times, and now it was happening and it was overwhelming. Her mind was abuzz. How could he just appear at her door like that? What did that mean now? She had clients tomorrow. What was she going to do? She filled two glasses of water, spilling some on the counter as her hands shook, but didn't bother to clean up.

Deep breaths, Sasha. It's Hale. It's just Hale. Calm down.

She returned from the kitchen and held out the glass to him, which he took, his fingers brushing against hers in the process. She sat on the floor, cross-legged, not wanting to sit side by side. "Plus," she thought, "if I'm already on the floor, there's less distance to fall if I faint", given her head was already spinning.

"Are you okay?" He asks.

"Yeah, why?"

He shakes his head. "I don't know. You're acting...different."

"Well, it's been a long time Hale." His name feels like bitter chocolate on her tongue. She'd missed saying it. She'd thought about him so often since Gabe had gotten back, yet all she wanted was to snap at him. Why was this so difficult?

"That sounds more like you." He sips at his water and leaves a dusty mark on the glass.

"You need a shower." She says. "I'll get you a towel."

"Okay." He agrees and downs the rest of the water.

She closes Ichigo's bedroom door quietly and fetches a fresh towel from the closet in the hall. She brings it back to Hale, still sitting in the living room, looking out the window surrounded by all the things she hadn't bothered to clean up during the day: Ichigo's train set on the floor, clothes on the couch, candy rappers on the little coffee table she'd found on the street and dragged home, all of the debris of her life out for him to see.

She hands him the towel as he gets up, and he goes over to rummage through his bag for clean clothes. All the clothing in his bag is folded. Some things never change. She exhales once he's closed the door to the washroom, sitting back on the floor with her back against the couch.

She listens to the water in the other room and to the shuffling of little feet. Ichigo had been a good sleeper until the events of the last time Hale was here - but he'd been a very light sleeper since then. She suspected he was up and eavesdropping as best he could, but he hadn't come out of his bedroom and she didn't want him to see Hale, not just yet.

When Hale comes back, he's wearing a tank top and black sweatpants that she's certain he's had since the base. His hair is still dripping wet. He never dries it properly. He sits down on the couch, and droplets land on his shoulders. She turns to be seated in front of him again.

"Feel better?" she asks.

He leans forward, looking tired. "Yes, thank you."

"Are you spending the night?"

"Sasha." The sound of her name in his voice sends her heart racing. She wipes her sweaty palms on her leggings.

"What?"

"You told me to come back."

"I know."

"I'm here."

"I know that too." She can't help keeping some of the sarcasm out of her voice.

"I'm making you uncomfortable."

"A little." She admits.

"I'm sorry."

It pulls at her heartstrings like it always had, the way he tries to be a non-entity in the world, the way he doesn't believe he's allowed to take up any sort of space unless he's given permission or an order to do so. She had an inkling now of what brought him here, what environment made a man like Hale. The part she was missing was the aftermath. What kind of life could a man like Hale live now? Was it a life she could be part of?

"It's okay. I just thought you had moved on or decided to do something else." she admitted.

"I stayed with someone at the end of the war for a short time."

"A female someone?"

He nodded, which shocked her, but she still wanted to know more.

"And then she dumped you?"

"No, I left. What you said about Pythagorus...I found something, and I wanted to show it to you."

"So you came to show me."

"If you want to see."

"Yeah, I do. Enough with the suspense."

He reached into his big duffel bag and pulled out a small leather-bound notebook, tattered and tied down with a shoelace. He held it out to her, and she brought it to her lap, the leather pleasantly rough on her fingertips.

"What is this?"

"My father's journal."

"What? Your father? Like, your real father?"

He nodded. "You were right about Pythagorus."

They locked eyes. Her heart was pounding.

"Just open it." He encouraged her.

She nodded, her whole body feeling shaky. She carefully undid the knots on the shoelace and set the small notebook on the ground, flipping the pages. The handwriting was like chicken scratches, and the pages were stained. Whiffs of nicotine clung to the pages. There were capitals in the middle of words, no punctuation, and words scratched out and written over. Sometimes, the pen died, and another colour would appear.

"Where did you find this?"

"I'd rather not say."

She wanted to pour over the little book for hours, but it was only half filled. She flipped to the final page with words on it.

[crossed out] we shouldn't have called you that. should have named you after Aiko's father like she wanted, but we didn't want you to stand out when we went where everybody spoke English. I don't know why we ever thought we'd make it that far. I was young, stupid, in love, thought nothing could hurt me. wish i learned japanese to teach you. there i go, about me again. always been a bit of a selfish asshole, sorry. I did my best. It wasn't much. Damnit, back to me.[Stops being crossed out].

Hale - I am sorry. I wanted to tell you, didn't know how. I thought it was better if you didn't know. wanted you to have a normal life if you thought we were strangers. didn't want you to turn out like me. Truth is, you're my kid. Aiko's more than mine. Ours. you didn't seem ours without her, you just seemed hers.[Crossed out] it was my fault...she didn't deserve any of this, neither did you.[Stops being crossed out] Aiko was your mom. she was amazing. you have her smile and her skin and her patience. She loved you. i made a lot of mistakes, not you, you were a good thing i did.

She covered her mouth with her hands. "Oh my god."

He nodded. "Pythagorus was his employer after he left the military. He promised him protection."

"This is everything, Hale. This is your story."

He shook his head. "It's his story."

"You know who your parents are now."

"They're dead."

"I know, but this is the key to your past, and now you really don't owe anyone anything. You can move on. You can go back to whoever it is you lived with, or you can go and figure out who you want to be. This means you were loved. Do you get that?" She looked into his eyes, but if he felt a modicum of what she felt, he wasn't showing it. She supposed he'd had more time to process all of this. Tears had sprung to her eyes.

He looked caught aback, "You're crying. I'm sorry. Do you want me to leave?"

"No!" She jumped in, angrily trying to wipe the tears off her face.

"Why are you crying?"

"I'm just really glad you found this. It means so much to me to know."

"Why?"

"Because I care about you, dummy."

"But you don't want me here?"

"Why are you saying that?"

"Do you?"

"Do I what?"

"Do you want me here?"

She opened her mouth to retort but stopped. Her gaze fell back to the notebook, its old pages soft.

What did she want? At first, she thought she didn't know what she wanted, but she did. She knew exactly what she wanted, and she was done beating around the bush about it.

"I want you to either be all in or all out, Hale. I want you here with Ichigo and me, as a father and a partner, if you're ready. I want you to make a choice."

He was quiet. She realized he still wasn't making any promises, so she swallowed back her tears and ran her forearm over her eyes. If he just wanted to share, then he'd done it.

"I'm glad you showed me this. I hope it helps you to heal." She carefully placed the shoelace back over the notebook and returned it to him. He looked confused and a little hurt. His mouth was thin, his eyes steady on her.

"I don't know if I can give you all that, what you're asking for."

She shrugged. "If you're going to disappear again, it's a no. When I made that promise, I meant it; my door is always open, but Ichigo needs to feel that you're going to stick around if he's going to get attached to you. I can't let him experience...that." She pointed at the little notebook. "I want him to know you and to feel safe. Do you understand?"

He nodded.

"No, I need more than a nod." She got up and sat beside him, taking his hand in hers. It was cold as usual; Hale had a terrible circulation in his fingers and toes. "Are you going to stay? Because I need to speak to Ichigo and explain everything. It's been hard for him with Gabe back."

"What does Gabe have to do with it?"

"Rose got her dad. He only got me."

Hale's fingers ran over the side of the notebook. She could practically see the gears in his mind turning. "That's more than I had." He said.

"That's not what I'm asking."

"If you want me to stay, I will."

"Do you want to stay?"

He looked to be struggling.

"Hale, I need this to be your choice. Do you want to stay?"

"Yes."

She wrapped her arms around his neck and felt his arms go around her waist. He was different, but it was still him - and he'd come back. He deserved a chance, didn't he? Maybe she did too.

They scooted down to fit onto the couch, which was a challenge. The only way they fit was his arm holding her to his chest. She sighed. "This is never going to work. Come on."

She led him to the bed, and they each took a side, the way they had once upon a time when they'd had to share a slightly smaller bed. She didn't initiate anything, and when he did, she pushed him away gently.

"Not tonight."

It had been a long time since she could turn someone down, and it felt more intimate than everything she'd had to do with any man in recent years. It took her a long time to fall asleep while he closed his eyes and adjusted his breathing, like he was powering down rather than going to sleep. The difference between sleeping with and sleeping next to someone was strange. She watched his face. She definitely still felt pulled to him, but she'd seen the dark side of men now, and the last time they'd been close, really close, he'd still been so guarded, but it had also resulted in Ichigo, so half a decade ago.

How would they find one another again after so long? Had it just been proximity then? Was it just the natural consequence of being part of a group of four people in which the other two were so madly in love that they could barely keep their arms off each other? No, it had to be more than that and she had to believe that or this was never going to work. Did she want it to? She supposed it depended on who this new person was: Who was Hale now? The notebook was an incredible find, and she wondered again how he'd gotten ahold of it. She wanted to look over every page, but what she really wanted was to flip through the recesses of his brain. How did he feel about the notebook? What did he think of Pythagorus now? Did he still consider himself a soldier? Had he changed? Was he prepared to let her in further than he had when they had to hide all the time? So many questions, so few answers.

Her mind went back to her son: tomorrow, she'd have to reintroduce him to his father. Tomorrow would be a big day. Every tomorrow had been big for so many years now that her nervous system had learned to anticipate it. She was jumpy, on edge and anxious when she wasn't despondent and depressed. Perhaps he wasn't the only one with a lot to unpack. She thought about Eva's worries about how Gabe might react to the woman she'd grown up to be rather than the sweet girl he'd met at school. She'd always accepted Hale for who he was, or tried to, would he do the same for her?

Eva

She and Gabe had stayed up late talking. Neither of them could believe Hale had returned. Gabe was, of course, his usual level of "that's fate" about it all, but even he had to admit that he'd given up on seeing his friend again. He said he was used to losing friends in worse ways. They theorized about how Sasha would greet him and how Ichigo might react. At about 6, Rose climbed in between them and they all slept in until Eva got a foot to the face from Rose, which was enough to wake her up. She pulled herself out of bed, Gabe opening his eyes to give her a questioning thumbs up, which she returned.

"You guys sleep." she whispered. She gathered up her clothes and got herself ready for the day in the washroom. She peered into the mirror, trying to imagine herself through Gabe's eyes for a moment. The woman looking back at her was definitely not the high school girl he'd met all those years ago. Her hair had changed texture somewhat from being dyed - a go for her when she was upset about something. Her eyes looked tired, but she was still young, even though she didn't feel that way. Had she taken the path her parents would've wanted, the path she'd wanted too, she'd be finishing college by now and starting to work. She had no wrinkles yet and, miraculously, no gray hair. Maybe she wasn't so physically different than she was as a teen, at least not her face. It was inside that she felt like a different person, a stronger one, not someone who might've followed her boyfriend across the country. She would've told Gabe about the pregnancy before they'd gotten on the road, she might even have told her parents, though she supposed she could do that now. She washed her face, changed, brushed her teeth, and put on some makeup. It made her feel more awake.

She made breakfast and coffee, and even had time to smoke a cigarette on the balcony before Gabe and Rose came barreling into the kitchen, Rose wide-eyed and bushy-tailed, Gabe jovial and affectionate. Rose acted as though she'd known Gabe her whole life, giggling at everything he said and did, and Gabe was feeding into it entirely, making faces, laughing along with her, doling out compliments like they were confetti. They were both basking in one another's attention, which was beautiful to watch. She wondered how Sasha and Ichigo were doing. Hale had spent the night there so she supposed it was okay. When everyone had eaten, and the dishes were cleared, Rose began to ask to go to the park, and she saw her opportunity to find out.

"I think the park's a great idea. How about I get Ichigo and Auntie Sasha to join us?"

"Okay! Tell Ichigo to bring his shovel. Mine broke."

"I didn't hear a please in there, Rose."

"Pleaaase."

"Alright, I'll be back then."

She pulled on her shoes and headed down the hall to Sasha's apartment, knocking in their usual code. Sasha opened the door, already dressed.

"Good morning!" Eva said.

Sasha looked like she hadn't slept much, but she smiled anyway and opened the door to let her inside.

"Auntie Eva!" Ichigo ran up to hug her thigh. "Hi!"

"Good morning, kiddo. How are you?"

"The man is back."

"The Man" was sitting on the couch, holding a cup of coffee.

"Hi, Hale!" She said. He nodded at her.

She looked into Sasha's face, trying to read her mind, but all she could read was fatigue.

"Gabe and I were going to take Rose to the park, and we figured you guys would want to join."

"Um, yeah, that sounds okay. Are you still okay with babysitting tonight? I have work," Sasha said.

"Yeah, of course." Clearly, leaving Ichigo with Hale wasn't on the table yet.

"We'll meet you downstairs in about 20 minutes?"

"Great. Ichigo, don't forget your shovel, okay?"

Ichigo made his determined little face and nodded, running off to gather his things.

Rose and Gabe were ready to go by the time she returned, so they sat outside on the steps to wait. Gabe drew a hopscotch board for Rose using a stone and showed her what to do on it, making the group of teens that often sat up front smoking roar in laughter.

"Watcha laughin' at? Think you can do better?" Gabe goaded them. Two boys, and a girl were tattooed and pierced, heads shaved and hair dyed. She'd seen them many times before but never spoken to them. One of the boys got up from the floor and did a surprisingly good job getting across the hopscotch board in his giant Doc martens.

"Good job! You guys live here?" Gabe asked.

The kid shrugged. "We live wherever."

"How come your hair's that colour?" Rose asked, unabashed. It was pink and green, which stood out to her. Eva wasn't sure how she felt about Rose speaking to many homeless teens but felt fairly safe with Gabe present.

"Because I'm an alien." The boy grinned at her, squatting down to her level and revealing a smile with a missing tooth in the front.

"I'm missing a tooth too!" Rose declared, delighted, showing off where she'd lost a baby tooth last week.

"I'm Gabe, that's Eva, and this is Rose."

"I'm Avi."

Hale, Sasha and Ichigo appeared in the doorway, all three looking uneasy about one another. Ichigo ran to Rose, giving Avi a sideways glance. She and Sasha spent a lot of time telling the kids not to talk to strangers.

"What's that?" He said, pointing to the hopscotch board.

"My dad made it - and Avi's good at it. You throw a rock and then do this." Rose demonstrated cheating a little to accommodate her jumping abilities. Ichigo held his plastic shovel and bucket, looking worriedly up at Avi. "Okay, are we going to the park?"

"Yeah, for sure." Gabe answered. "Good meetin' you, Avi - and your friends."

"Do you have any cigarettes?" Avi asked, seemingly figuring out there wasn't much to lose. Gabe pulled a full pack out of his pocket and handed it over, making the two still sitting down stop their chatter and stare. Avi held the pack dubiously.

"Uh, I don't have any money..." He mumbled.

"That's cool. Enjoy 'em. Come on, Rose, say bye."

"Bye!" She waved, shoving the hopscotch rock in her pocket and taking Ichigo's hand so they could get ahead of the adults.

"Slow down, guys!" Sasha called after them before falling in step with Gabe and Eva. They split off to make room on the sidewalk, Gabe falling behind to speak to Hale.

"Sooo...?" Eva said, eager to hear how things had gone for her friend.

"I don't know yet." Sasha said, yawning. "It's just so weird having him here."

"Yeah, I felt the same way for a while."

"I guess it depends on how things go from here."

"You don't seem excited."

Sasha sighed. "He doesn't seem excited."

"He's Hale."

"I know, but Ichigo's all weird about him being here too. You should've seen him at breakfast. It was so awkward that I let him watch TV so we didn't have to sit there in dead silence."

"That bad, huh?"

"Just awkward."

"Give him some time."

"What was with the punk kids?"

"Oh, Gabe being Gabe. At first, I wanted to stop him, but then I saw that guy's face when he gave him his cigarettes, it's what I love about him. I didn't get it in high school, but he doesn't split the world up like we did back then. He knows everyone's out here just trying to get by. It's actually amazing."

Sasha smiled at her. "You're so in love."

Eva shook her head. "Hush you. Stop changing the subject. Did you um..."

"No."

"Why not?"

"I dunno. I guess I want to wait and see if he sticks around."

"I get that."

When they got to the park, Gabe followed the kids to the swings and pushed them so hard that Sasha ran over to get him to "take it down a notch" to Rose's loud complaining.

Eva hung back on the bench. Watching Sasha and Gabe squabble over parenting was annoying, but it was beginning to feel normal to her, and it was nice to stop and let that sink in. Hale sat beside her, watching too.

"Gabriel said you helped him to find work." He said.

"Was that a question?" She laughed. He was such an awkward turtle!

"He said to ask you first."

"You mean to get you a job at Charlie's garage? I don't see why not, if they're willing. Just go with Gabe tomorrow, and they'll let you know."

"He said they were your friends."

"They are. Charlie and Emma are amazing. They're the nicest people you'll ever meet, and you're going to be super polite to them, right?"

Hale nodded.

"How's it going with Sasha?" She asked.

He looked like he wanted to say something snarky but held back, "Fine."

"Not great then?"

He shook his head.

"Want some advice?"

"I suppose."

"Ask more questions. She wants to make it work, but she's been through a lot. We all have, we're just not the kids we used to be."

"Okay." He seemed to be genuinely thinking about her words, which was new.

"And spend one on one time with Ichigo when she lets you. You're a lot alike."

"Why did she give him a Japanese name?"

Eva smiled. "That's exactly the sort of question you should ask her, but maybe don't sound like you hate it when you ask."

"I don't hate it."

"Mommy, look!" Rose was calling her from the top of the play structure.

"Gotta go."

Hale stayed on the bench, but he hung back with Sasha on their walk home and looked to be trying to make conversation. It was a start.

Chapter 10
Connections

Sasha

Pro: the apartment had never been cleaner.

Con: She now had to hide her job from Ichigo and Hale, too, and he was a lot smarter than a five-year-old.

Pro: Hale was surprisingly good at cooking.

Con: Ichigo refused to make conversation at the table.

Pro: Sharing a bed was comforting.

Con: They still hadn't hooked up, and the longer they stayed on opposite sides of the bed, the more she worried about what it would be like when they finally did.

Pro: More money was coming in.

Con: They never discussed money, so he would bring back the cash that Charlie paid him weekly and hand it to her as though it were rent.

There was too much unsaid between them, and it all felt so precariously balanced that she was reluctant to get into it. She worked most nights, and while Ichigo was accepting of Hale watching him, she worried that one day he wouldn't be, and she would come home to him crying and Hale not knowing what to do about it. Hale worked during the day at the mechanic's shop, returning tired but content, seemingly pleased not to be idle. On weekends, they'd spend time with Gabe and Eva, playing board games or watching TV. In some ways, it felt like they were roommates again, like they had been at the base.

It had been a few weeks before either of them tried anything. They were sitting on the couch, Ichigo asleep in the bedroom, and discussing the day's events.

She'd had a client earlier, a regular, and had been happy to drag herself back home and shower. Her hair was still wet, so she'd pulled it up into a towel at the top of her head. She was also cradling a cup of tea. Hale had taken Ichigo over to Eva's for supper and put him to bed before she got home. It was sad to miss those moments, but it was comforting to know there was an extra adult to help, even if he wasn't Ichigo's favourite person so far. She knew she had to fix that somehow, but she didn't want him to feel like she was forcing their relationship. She wanted Ichigo to come to it on his own, which was probably naive of her. No one had ever accused her of being too cynical, unfortunately.

"So, what's it like working at Charlie's?" She asked, yawning.

"It's fine." He looked like he was done speaking, then changed his mind and continued, "Emma is a lot like you."

"How so?"

"She asks a lot of questions."

She chuckled. "Do you answer her better than me?"

"I'm...trying to do better at answering you." He admitted, looking serious. She hadn't meant to be hurtful.

"I know. I noticed." She put her hand on his and squeezed it.

"What about your job?"

"My job?"

"You never talk about it."

"Not much to say. It's not a great job, but it makes good money." He paused, something she'd done to him so many times she'd lost count; he was waiting for her to elaborate.

"We can all have our secrets." She said. She didn't want his judgment or his advice. She wasn't sure what he'd say, but it made her feel dirty to even think about it. Who knew what someone like Hale would think?

"Is it dangerous?"

She sighed. "Do you already know what it is?"

"No."

"Then let it go."

It was as though they'd switched roles. She had always been the one harping on him for answers. She knew secrets had a way of coming out, but maybe she could keep hiding them from him.

"Enough about that." She said and scooted over to him on the couch. If she'd learned one thing, it was that men were easily distracted. She knew what to do. It was a sort of choreography, especially with someone who was shy or reserved. However, this wasn't a client - and he made that clear quickly. The towel on her head and her shirt were on the floor. She'd climbed onto his lap and kissed him. So far, so good, but as soon as she began tracing his neck with her lips, he froze. He put both hands out in front of him, holding her back by her shoulders and looking down.

"What?" She asked, putting her fingers on his chin to make him look up at her.

"You never did that before."

"You don't like it?" It came out business-like, which she instantly felt embarrassed about.

"It feels different."

"What does it feel like?" She smiled, hoping they could both shake off the awkwardness.

"Like you're going through the motions."

At the moment, she felt as if she had been shot - an experience which she could now say wasn't uniquely metaphorical. Instantly dropping her gaze, she wrapped her arms around herself, got to her feet, and pulled her shirt back on.

"Sasha." His voice was soft, so different from what she was used to.

"Goodnight." She said, tears spilling onto her cheeks.

She locked herself in the bathroom and turned on the shower again, despite having just showered. In the warm water, she let herself cry, sitting down at the bottom of the tub where a rubber ducky had been left behind from Ichigo's bath. When the water ran cold, she dried herself off again and shivered and pulled her clothes back on. She wished there was somewhere else to go in the tiny apartment.

Hale was sitting on the bed when she entered the room, and all she wanted to do was flee. She grabbed a pillow and turned to go back out.

"Where are you going?" He said quietly.

"I'm not sharing a bed with you." She hissed.

"I won't do anything."

"Then what's the point?" She whispered. "You want to be my roommate? My friend? Which is it? I thought you wanted to be together, but I guess I'm not good enough for you anymore." She wanted to shout, but didn't want to wake up Ichigo, who was sleeping just down the hall.

"Alexandra..."

"What? Spit it out already."

"I'm sorry. I didn't expect you to wait for me. I understand."

"I did wait for you. I've only ever...I do it for money, okay? I do things for money. I know it's super gross, and you're right. We shouldn't sleep together."

The silence that followed was deafening. He seemed to be wrapping his mind around the concept. He had the face he'd had on when she told him Eva was pregnant. It was Hale's version of scared.

"Aren't you afraid?" He asked.

She nodded. "I'm always afraid."

She sat down on the side of the bed next to him, staring down at her bare feet, still feeling flushed with humiliation.

"You can stop."

She shook her head. "I owe that guy a lot of money, and it's not something you can just stop. There's a system. They know where I live, they know where Ichigo goes to school, they'd find me."

He seemed to be mulling over the information. There was another overly long pause in which they both just breathed.

"You're not the only one who had to follow orders to survive."

"We can leave."

"And go where?"

"Wherever you want."

She scoffed. He'd never struck her as optimistic. "You just got work. The kids are in school. Now that I'm not the only parent, I'm a little less afraid of what would happen if I don't come back." She could feel his stare, but she refused to meet it.

"I'm sorry," he said again, "I don't want that. I wouldn't know how to be a parent by myself."

"Then you shouldn't have had a kid."

"I didn't know...I'm just saying that I don't want history to repeat itself. He needs you, and I don't want you to get hurt."

"Let's just go to sleep." She said, lying down and adjusting the pillows. He put an arm around her and pressed her to his chest. It felt protective. She wished he had the words she needed, but if this was all he could offer, at least he was trying.

Eva

She was walking the kids to school and listening to them talk. Rose was recounting a make-believe game she had going with Gabe about spies and ninjas, while Ichigo kept exclaiming, "so, cool!" with diminishing enthusiasm. When they got to the school gates, Ichigo hung back.

"Auntie Eva, I have a question."

"Sure lil man, but we don't have much time. You don't want to be late for class." She was already going through her list of to-do's for the day in her mind.

"When is Hale leaving?"

The list paused.

"Why do you think he's leaving?"

The little boy rubbed his nose and tugged at the bottom of his sweater. "I know mommy likes him."

"What about you though?"

"I don't want to hurt your feelings."

"You won't. It's okay." She got down to his level.

"I liked living together, and I know mommy doesn't like Gabe so much."

"Did she say that?"

"No, but they argue."

"It's okay that they argue. They're still really good friends."

"Do you like Hale?"

"Ichigo, he's your dad. I know it's hard, but he really does love you."

"But he doesn't play with me or give hugs like Gabe."

"He shows how much he cares in other ways."

The little boy looked like he had a million things to say, but he glanced at the school gates.

"You should talk to your mom about this."

"I don't want her to get upset."

"She won't."

"Okay, bye, auntie Eva." He gave her a big hug and walked off to school. She waved, her chest tight for the kids. There was so much for them to process, and none of them had the skill or the time to dedicate to figuring it out. Frankly, she wasn't sure she had figured anything out either. Things were going well with Gabe, so much so that she felt guilty about leaving Sasha and Ichigo out. In times of concern, there was always a place to go now.

It was a warm and windy day, so she wore a skirt, one of the few she owned. Something about dancing for leering men had made her want to stay far away from showing off her curves. However, she had to walk through the garage to get to the back room to see Emma, which meant catcalls and whistles from the guys. She kept walking, rolling her eyes, until Gabe pushed and rolled himself up from beneath a car.

"Princess!" He greeted her, his hair covered in motor oil, wiping his hands on his shirt.

"That your girl, Gabe?" someone shouted.

"Yeah, so you'd all better shut your mouths when you see 'er." Gabe corrected, but the smirk on his face showed that he appreciated the compliment of having them looking at her. She wondered why it was so different when they did it here versus at the bar.

Eva put her hands in front of her.

"Hey, babe. Believe it or not, I'm not here to see you."

"Aw babe, you hurt me."

She chuckled. "Get used to it."

There was plenty of hooting and hollering at that. Charlie stepped out from the back room. "Alright! Alright! Back to work, guys! Eva! Come on in!" He was covered in a white powder which turned out to be flour. "You got here just in time. Emma was just sayin' I'm useless in the kitchen."

"You and Gabe have that in common." She laughed.

"She was gettin' Hale to help her, but then we got a couple of old bikes in, so he's back there working on those."

"Thanks, Charlie." She said with a smile. It felt as though everyone in the garage was his family.

She entered the little kitchen where Emma made dumplings, and the older woman cheered as though she were a miracle.

"Perfect! Charlie, you're off the hook. Now get out of here!" She practically shoved her husband out of the door and shut it behind him. They could hear the guys mocking him good-naturedly. She set Eva up, wetting the edges and folding the dough into little purses around her homemade fillings. She had three bowls: spinach, feta, ground beef, potatoes, and cheddar. She poured them both a cup of tea, and they sat down to work.

"So, how have things been?" Emma asked.

"Good!"

"Not great then?"

"Well, sort of great. It's great with Gabe."

"And your friend? Is she feeling better now that her soldier's home from the war too?" Emma's eyes were soft.

"She's glad he's here but..."

"That boy's scared to death." Emma said, shaking her head as she measured out a ball of dumpling filling in the palm of her hand.

"Of what?" Eva outlined a pre-cut piece of dough with water and began trying to close it with her fingertips.

"They're all like overstuffed pierogies, these boys, they have too much inside them, and I wouldn't even know where to start in knowing what got them to where they are today."

"But what's he afraid of?"

"Charlie asked him to fix an engine the other day. He changed the part, but then he fixed the broken part, too and put that back into the car. Then, he washed the car inside and out and reorganized the stuff in the trunk. Then, he polished the car. When Charlie said the client would probably ask if he owed more, he said the kid just stood there and stared at the floor like Charlie was going to throw him out or hit him."

"He thought Charlie would be mad that he did a good job?"

"No, he hadn't followed exact directions, so to him, it wasn't a good job."

"So what happened?"

Emma laughed. "Charlie gave him a pat on the back and he looked green."

Eva shook her head. "I'm not sure I'll ever understand him. At least I can talk to Gabe about things."

"Here's another example," Emma continued, committed to her cause, "if he were in here making dumplings with me, he'd still be on the first one, while you've got a dozen."

She held up a pierogi and closed a tiny unpinched part of the dough where Eva hadn't put enough water, "seeing this makes a kid like that want to cry, except he doesn't think he's allowed to cry, so he just stands there hoping someone will make him feel like trash."

Eva was amazed. In just a few short weeks, Emma had jumped past all of Hale's walls and understood him in a way that even she and Sasha had never managed. She wondered if Gabe saw it too.

"Wow..." she mumbled. "What's your read on Gabe?"

"I'm not a tarot card reader." Emma laughed.

"But you see things I don't."

Emma thought about it. "Hmm, different side of the same coin. Gabriel covers his fear by being charming and funny."

They made dumplings in silence for a minute while Eva took all this in. "How do I help?" She asked.

"Same as you, they need to feel safe, day in and day out, and eventually, that becomes normal. It seems to me that they're both adjusting."

"Gabe seems pretty settled."

"People who are settled don't need everybody to like them." Emma kept pinching pierogies, as though all this was nothing. Was this what it was to be a mature adult? She wished she could skip all this confusion and go straight to a time in her life where she could understand people the way Emma did. She wondered if it came from loss. She hoped not.

When she walked home with Gabe that day (Hale had insisted on staying and finishing up a car he'd been working on), Emma's words weighed on her mind. It wasn't that she hadn't known that there was something she could do; it was that it bothered her that she hadn't pieced it all together earlier. She'd now known Gabe for a big part of her life - and had spent full days together, yet it hadn't occurred to her that he and Hale were alike. The idea of being his safe space, he'd expressed it to her, those not in those words. She wondered how she'd know that they'd arrived; what would Gabe even be like if he brought his guard down?

Chapter 11
Decisions

Eva

Their little town was blossoming around them, or "gentrifying," as Sasha called it. The new government had a lot of ideas for making changes, starting with things she took for granted when she lived at home: investment in schools, medical facilities, and social housing. It felt like it happened overnight, but it was more like opening your eyes when familiar places turned into unfamiliar ones. It felt like every week, something closed, and something new popped up in its place. First, the 69 shut down. It would've been a disaster before the guys showed up. Still, with two salaries, Eva was fine working exclusively for Benny, who had significantly changed his tune towards her after saving her from the alleyway. He was almost protective of her - offering her day shifts behind the bar and fewer dancing shifts. Fewer people were coming into the bar for dances, which helped the other girls not to be too annoyed at this sudden favoritism.

Old, empty and industrial lots that had been there since she arrived were suddenly under construction, with posters of apartment buildings promising a future she couldn't imagine here. A high school opened up a few blocks from them, too, giving her hope that there might be somewhere for Rose to go when it came to that. She hadn't allowed herself to think that far before. It was always about today and the next day, but maybe she wouldn't have to move somewhere else or go looking for her parents for Rose to have a chance to be the best kid that she could be. Maybe right here could work. With all these new things, she finally gathered the courage to speak to Gabe about her work.

It had been a rough night. They'd had both kids, and, uncharacteristically, they squabbled. Rose was feeling territorial and kept trying to get Gabe to play with them, but also didn't want him to pay Ichigo any attention. When Hale had come from the garage to pick Ichigo up, Gabe had invited him in, hoping that might balance out the dynamics, but it had resulted in Rose climbing up on Hale's lap to try and win him over, which backfired spectacularly. Hale froze up, removed her, none too gently, from him, plopped her onto the couch, and then went to stand by the door. Rose wailed about the rejection and said she hated him, which made Ichigo cry too. It was up to Eva to comfort him because he wanted nothing to do with either Hale or Gabe at that point, and she was more than happy to pass the sad little boy on to Sasha, who finally came home from dealing with a client. Ichigo ran to his mom and wordlessly melted into her arms. Sasha looked apologetic, kissing the top of his little head. Once the little family of three was out the door and Rose was secure in knowing that her daddy was her own and finally put to bed, Eva made hot chocolate and sat at the kitchen table.

It took mere minutes for Gabe to appear in the kitchen doorway. She went into the fridge and added a bit of rum to her drink. Gabe laughed.

"It wasn't that bad tonight." He poured some into his as well. The perks of being adults.

"It's fine. They're still getting used to being two separate families. They were brother and sister for most of their lives."

"Yeah, but I was pretty pissed off there. Hale could've just let her sit. She wasn't doing anything."

"He's not comfortable with physical contact - you know that!" Eva shrugged. She wasn't sure why she was jumping to Hale's defense, maybe because of Emma. She agreed that Hale should've been better with Rose, but Emma's take of him being afraid of everything made her feel for him. Rose was a lot, as precious as she was to her.

"I wanted to talk to you about something." Her heart was beating hard.

"Yeah?" he sipped his drink, sitting on his foot as he often did, his version of comfortable.

"So, you know how I work at Benny's?"

He kept sipping. "Uh-huh."

"I think you should knowI didn't always work at the bar. I used to dance there and at the other bar too, I still do sometimes." She covered her face with her mug. The creamy sweetness and the burn of alcohol traveled down her esophagus, too hot. She slowly tore her eyes away from her cup and looked at him.

"But now you work at the bar?"

"Mostly."

"Alright. Hey, it's okay, babe." He hurried over and put an arm around her.

"I just thought you might overreact like you did about Sasha."

"I'm not reactin' that way because I've got some crazy moral thing goin' on. I've lived on the streets; it's not about that. I also don't have a problem with sex, obviously. It's that I know how messed up people are, especially with girls."

"Women." She corrected him.

"Babe, it's okay. You had to do what you had to do, but you don't have to do any of that anymore unless you like it."

"Of course, I don't!"

"Some do. Don't do nothin' you don't want to do. Not anymore. I want you to have it all, everythin' you would've had before you met me."

She exhaled. "If I hadn't met you, I'd be living a totally different life, that's true, but I'm glad I met you. It hasn't all been pretty, but we're here now, okay?"

He nodded and grinned. "I've actually got somethin' for ya."

"Oh God, Gabe, what now?"

He disappeared into another room and returned with an envelope.

"Gabe, what is this?"

"Open it!"

Her hands shook, so she took another sip of her drink and exhaled slowly. She pulled out three tickets - tickets to San Francisco, round trip.

"What is this?"

"Khal helped me pay for 'em."

"What is it?"

"Your family's heading there on vacation next week - and so are we."

She couldn't seem to form a word. Her tongue was doing something, but no sounds came out.

"How did you-"

"It wasn't that hard."

"Do they know?"

"Nope. Total surprise."

She laughed incredulously. "My dad...is going to shoot you."

Gabe laughed. "I'd probably deserve it."

"Gabe, this is amazing." Her heart swelled.

"And when we get back, if you wanna come back, your call what we do next."

She nodded. "I do...want to come back. I want us to help make this town better..."

She looked up at him, the familiar face she'd loved for so long. She leaned over the table, eyes closed, and kissed him like it was the first time.

Sasha

She stood outside of the medical clinic picking at her nails. Who was she to apply here? She had no training; she wasn't sure she was good with blood. Weren't they going to see right through her? A mom with just a high school degree? No, she was going in there. She closed her eyes and breathed. She counted down her senses from five: I see sliding doors, white walls, a blue sky, people walking in, and clouds; I hear cars driving past, someone coughing, ringing in my left ear, and a plane going by. I feel how cold my fingertips are, how quick my heartbeat is, my feet in my too-tight shoes, I smell the dust in the air, the restaurant down the street, I taste how dry my mouth is. She exhaled. It was time to go in there.

She walked quickly through the sliding doors and into the busy waiting room so as not to change her mind.

"Take a number." The woman behind the plexiglass said, motioning towards the dispenser for tiny papers.

"Number 42!"

A pregnant woman headed through the white doors, leaving them swinging behind her.

"No, actually, I want to apply for a job." She slid her CV underneath the glass, which she'd typed up at the local library, while Ichigo and Rose ran circles around her. Thank god for the librarian leaning over her shoulder and correcting the terrible formatting. The woman barely glanced up. She had no idea how important this was to her. She picked up the paper and added it to a stack of other papers.

"It's a CV." Sasha insisted.

"I got it."

"So, can you give it to someone who does hiring?"

"Yeah, have a nice day."

Sasha shook her head. "Thank you."

When she reemerged on the street, the wind blowing her hair into her face, she wasn't feeling hopeful. It was something, though, wasn't it?

She walked back home. She hadn't said anything to Hale or Eva. She didn't want the congratulations if nothing would come of it. It was time to move on, and she could finally afford to do so. She had enough money to pay D and was more than ready to turn the page.

She had a few hours to herself for a change, so she walked home, planning on washing the bathtub and then submerging herself in warm water and not thinking about getting called.

She unlocked her front door to the sounds of voices, which instantly made her heart jump into her throat. She paused, listened, and exhaled, hearing Gabe's voice as the loudest in the room. Who was the other male voice, though? Not Hale...

She let out a long breath and walked in.

Her living room was full of men. Hale was sitting on the couch next to Remi, who she recognized immediately. Both were silent. Gabe and Khalil were debating animatedly, standing in the center of the room. They froze as she walked in.

"Uh, hi." She said.

"Hey." Gabe said, looking sheepish.

"Remi, Khal, it's nice to see you guys...I think."

"Welcome home, Sasha." Khalil smiled at her, though it didn't quite reach his eyes.

"What's going on?" She said, setting her bag down but keeping her jacket on. Unfortunately for her, Khal and Remi, as gorgeous and kind as they'd always been to them, had always been harbingers of some disaster about to hit her like a bullet - sometimes literally.

"I'm sorry, Alexandra, we need Gabe and Hale to come with us. There's something we need to do."

"Something, huh?" Sasha said, "How specific and surprising."

She wanted to go right back out the door immediately. She didn't want to hear it. She didn't want another excuse for the goodbye she'd have to listen to and the cause she'd have to accept for some vague war-related speech. However, this was her apartment. She glanced at Hale, who didn't look up from the spot he was staring at on the floor. His face was frozen, that familiar dissociation she'd seen after the fight with Jason, when she woke him up from a nightmare, when she'd told him her plan to escape the base, when he'd realized what she did for work. It was the way he looked when he was overwhelmed. She wanted to sit beside him and tell him everything would be okay, but he wasn't even acknowledging her, which could only mean one thing.

"So, how many years will you need them for this time? Is my kid going to be done with elementary school?" she thought. Instead, she walked past them and entered the kitchen, where she found Eva stress-baking. Her friend looked up at her with bloodshot eyes. She was wearing a loose-fitting black sweater dress and leggings, both covered in flour, and it suddenly struck her how much she looked like her mom. She hadn't thought of Mrs. Whalen in a long time, nor her own parents, it made her too sad.

She walked into the kitchen and plopped herself down at the table.

"Drink?" Eva asked.

Sasha sighed. "Like it'll change anything."

"So, what's the verdict so far?"

"Apparently, there's still a pocket of their organization that doesn't agree with where things landed after the revolution, more anarchist...types."

"Are they still talking about the philosophers?"

Eva made a face. "No, I think Remi and Khalil are trying to tie up loose ends, making sure things stay stable."

Eva poured her a drink, and Sasha sipped the cheap wine. It tasted the way she felt, so she set it back down.

"That's enough, Khal." Remi said, his voice deep and firm. Gabe and Khal stopped speaking.

"We'll let you think about it. We'll be at the airport at 5 o'clock."

Sasha got up to say goodbye. "Come on; it might be the last time we see them."

Eva followed her out into the hallway.

Khalil gave Eva a big hug, not caring about the flour. "Goodbye. I'm sorry again." Khal said to them both, Remi handing him his jacket.

"Guess I'll send pastries." Eva said, unable to keep the sadness out of her voice. Sasha knew exactly how she felt. Her mind was already reeling with plans: Should they move back here, or should Eva and Rose move downstairs? This apartment was larger, but hers was less expensive. They'd probably need to call Emma and Charlie and let them know it was the right thing to do. She wondered if it was better for the kids to say goodbye or just to let the guys vanish the way they'd appeared. What was more traumatic? Should she ask them to write goodbye letters? Thinking of Hale's father's journal, she thought that might help. It would be something to hold on to, to reread in dark moments.

"I'm not going." Hale rose from the couch. He looked from Remi to Khal, to Gabe and finally, to her.

"You're not?" Gabe exclaimed though everyone's faces reflected the same shock.

"No, I'm finished."

Khalil nodded at him. "We understand. We'll be there at 5 if you change your mind. Gabe?"

Gabe looked to Eva, who said nothing.

"I need to think about it." He said, running his hand through his long hair.

Sasha's brain hadn't caught up to what was happening. Wasn't Hale going?

Remi and Khal left, the guys patting each other's backs, except for Hale, who stood by the wall and looked at the ground. She thought she'd finally figured him out, and now he threw this at her?

When the four of them were left alone, the falling silence was incredibly loud.

"I have the dough to finish." Eva said, walking past them and into the kitchen, the tension in her voice so thick it could be sliced with a knife.

"Come on, Hale." Sasha said. She looked at Gabe, whose expression was identical to the look he'd given her once upon a time in a dingy motel on the road, back when she thought they were just four kids heading to California for the summer, the night she'd learned who they were, the night everything had changed. She patted Gabe's shoulder, not having anything to say to him. It was a bit funny leaving her own apartment, but Eva had always had keys, and both couples needed to talk.

She took Hale's hand and led him out, down the stairs and across the street to the park until she found a bench. He didn't pull his hand away and kept apace. From the outside, they must have looked like a couple out on a date.

Despite the cold, she sat on the bench and turned to him, letting go of his hand to hold onto the edge of the bench.

"You're not going?"

He did not know what to do with his hands, so he crossed his arms.

"As I said."

"Even if Gabe does?"

"It's not about Gabe."

"You're not worried about what'll happen to him if he goes alone?"

She expected him to make a snide remark, but he paused instead. She waited.

"I am."

"Then are you staying for me? Listen, I know I made you feel terrible about being so late to come back. I know you're worried about...my job...but you don't need to worry about me. I actually applied for work at that new clinic today, and if that doesn't work out, I'll find something else. I don't want to be another person who manipulates you into something. You can go; we'll be okay until you come back."

He shook his head.

"I'm not going because I don't want to anymore." He looked out at the buildings across from the park. "I'm tired of there always being something more important to do...important to somebody else anyway."

"I thought this was your cause, the thing you said you'd die for."

"I'd rather live for something..."

Her vision blurred as her eyes filled. He shook his head.

"You're always crying."

"You should try it; it's great." She sniffed.

"I thought you'd be happy."

"I am!"

She took his arm and put it around her, leaning on his shoulder and wiping her eyes until she could get herself to stop.

"Is this what I should've done when you cried next to me in school?"

She laughed. "No, you should've done this." She leaned up and kissed him.

Eva

The door shut behind Sasha and Hale. She went back into the kitchen, Gabe hot on her heels.

"Babe..."

"It's fine, Gabe."

"Princess."

"Don't."

He reached for her, and she held both hands in front of her. She lifted her gaze to him.

"I'm done."

She'd forgiven him every step of the way: lying to her about who he was, leaving her alone to rebuild her life with a baby in tow, never checking in on her in all that time, making promise after promise to her and now to Rose - and she just couldn't take it anymore. She loved him, and she would always love him, but this was the final straw. He couldn't charm her into saying it was okay anymore. He couldn't reach her for warmth when he would tear it away again in an instant. She was tired of being his anchor.

"I didn't ask for this."

"What do you want from me, Gabe?" She finally shouted. "I have nothing left to give you! You want my permission, my forgiveness, what?"

"I want you to say you understand."

"No. I've always understood, and given you a pass because I know what you've been through, and what you think you're fighting for, but I am done. You want to leave? There's the door. I will take those tickets and disappear, just like you did."

"I'll find you, wherever you go."

"No, you can't have it both ways." She broke eye contact and went back to rolling out the last of the dough, which she stabbed with a fork a few times for good measure. She put the top on her pie and popped it into the waiting oven.

"Eva..." His voice broke as though he knew his words had finally run dry.

"What?" she huffed, piling dishes into the sink and using a cloth to dust flour off her. She imagined what he must see: a small woman with her hair in a tangle at the top of her head, covered in white powder.

"I don't want to lose you." He reached for her hand, and she stepped back.

"Then figure yourself out."

"I have!"

"Have you? You're making the same decisions over and over again."

"It's what I have to do."

"Great, then do it."

"Eva..."

"We're going in circles. Do you need me to find your suitcase?"

He sighed and took his phone out of his pocket. He went to the balcony, and the door shut loudly behind him. She washed the dishes, letting the warm soapy water soothe her nerves and finally sat down with a cup of coffee, moving her feet back and forth against the floor. She'd surprised herself. Even a few years ago, she never would've spoken to Gabe like that. She wanted him to be hers. It had been so important, but now she wanted something else. She wanted him to choose her, to choose this and to choose it over his trauma and this battle he was fighting inside of himself every day. She knew it to be true now. She really was done.

When she'd finished her cup, she washed it and went to the bedroom. The curtains were being pulled in all directions, swirling and rising like a wave. She could smell Gabe smoking outside. She shut the window and pulled out her old suitcase. It could be her parting gift to him. There wasn't time to go down to the laundromat, so she folded up what was clean of Gabe's and added a pair of extra shoes on top. She added some bar soap and shampoo. She paused, holding up a cross necklace he'd left on the floor beside the bed. They never did bother to buy a nightstand. It was strange for him to wear a cross. He didn't believe in God but loved people who believed. The smell of pie filled the hallway and reached her. Now wasn't the time to keep dwelling on the combination of idiosyncrasies that made up Gabriel Wells. She'd have plenty of time to unpack all that later, probably with a licensed therapist. She put the cross into the suitcase pocket and zipped it up, then made her way back to the kitchen.

Gabe was still outside, but she could see the first droplets of rain pattering the glass of the kitchen window. It made her think of his old apartment near her school, and the number of times they'd sat on his balcony. It always seemed to rain when they fought. Maybe this would be the last fight and the last rainy day they shared. She pulled the pie out of the oven, inhaling its warmth, sweetness and tartness. She wondered how Emma and Charlie would react when she told her that Gabe was gone again. She swept a towel over the dessert to keep it warm longer.

Was he planning to come inside? She turned off the oven, returned to the bedroom, and rolled the suitcase into the hallway. It was nearly four o'clock. He was running out of time. They'd gone through a number of goodbyes now, but this felt different. There was no pining, no holding onto one another. It was as though her heart had scarred over where it had been cut in the same place over and over again. The humidity made her arm sore, so she rubbed at her elbow as she sat on the couch. The rain was coming down hard now, and she could see Gabe's outline still on the balcony. She sighed and went to the only closet in the apartment to grab a towel.

She went to the balcony door and tapped on its window. She saw him jump as though he'd forgotten she was there. He turned to look back at her, rivulets of rain coming down his face, his eyes red. He opened the door and came inside, dripping onto the linoleum. He accepted the towel and wrapped it around his head; his hair was soaked through.

"I packed your bag." She said, pointing to the suitcase.

"Babe, I'm not going anywhere."

"You're not?"

"No, I can't do that to you again and to Rose."

"What about the cause?"

"I've done enough."

"Will we be enough though? Will I be enough this time?"

His hand was cold against her cheek. She leaned into it anyway.

"You've always been enough."

She nodded, her throat tight.

"I told Khalil I couldn't. He agreed."

"What did he say?"

"That he'd see us at our wedding." he laughed.

"Khal's a hopeless romantic."

"Is he?" Gabe said. He smiled, searching her eyes. She smiled back.

"Is that a proposal?"

"No, I'd do a better job of that."

"You're shaking."

He shrugged. "I'll probably be shaking when I propose too."

"Guess you should unpack." She smiled.

"Nah, we'll leave it for when we go to California."

"You'd better come and warm up then, you're dripping all over my floor."

"Guess so." His eyebrows rose.

"Shower?" She offered.

He laughed. "Pie in bed?"

She grinned, shaking her head. "Still incorrigible."

She felt the weight of the world lifting off her shoulders. It could have its battles, its causes, its excuses for turmoil, but she had her own two feet to stand on, and Gabe beside her and they would defend their little patch of happiness.

Epilogue

Ichigo could never sleep on planes, something he'd surely inherited from his mother. She was always pulling at her fingers, biting her lip and going through packs of chewing gum, every part of her uncomfortable with being so high up. It didn't make him anxious, though. It felt soothing somehow, like whatever was going on down below didn't matter, as there had never been a war or poverty or hunger, as if all that there was beyond the pod of the plane was sky and sunlight. Still, he could never get to sleep.

When they touched down, the other passengers clapped, which he didn't think was necessary. He wondered if he inherited his father's reluctance to participate in group activities. He sat quietly in his seat with his headphones in until the row in front of him rose before he fetched his carry-on backpack from the overhead bin and secured it safely on his back. He always traveled light. Anything he might need could be purchased, and if it couldn't be, he could live without it. A few people pushed forward or huffed their disapproval, but he kept his headset in and waited for his turn, eyes fixed on the young girl before him with a neck tattoo.

He hadn't seen them in 8 months, his parents, Auntie Eva, Gabe - and Rose. He'd video-chatted with his mother, and she wrote him long letters that covered just about everything from the weather to what every person he'd ever known was up to. Auntie Eva sometimes texted, just to check how he was doing, and he did his best to answer. He missed her way of making him feel at ease and, of course, her cooking.

He took his phone off airplane mode and found 5 text messages from his ex, which he skimmed. Isabelle was not a woman used to being told no. She was beautiful, ambitious, talented, clever and wealthy. He didn't want to answer. Any answer he gave her would just lead to the cyclical argument of her telling him what he was supposed to feel, him agreeing, but still not feeling it.

As he stepped off the plane, he took his headphones off and was met with the surge of human traffic: Children screaming, metal trolleys stacked with luggage clanging, and the swoosh of rotating doors. He followed the arrivals gate at a quick pace, knowing that everyone was waiting, that his mom would be worried sick, and that auntie Eva and Gabe would be telling her to calm down, which always just made her more nervous. He knew his father would stand beside him, assessing exit

351

strategies. He wondered if Rose would be there, but probably not. She hadn't so much as wished him a happy birthday while he was gone. She probably forgot he'd ever existed.

As he walked through the automatic double doors through the arrivals gate, he spotted them right away: His mother, hair up in a ponytail, wearing cut-off jeans and a tight-fitting t-shirt, Hale standing beside her, leaning forward to hear what she was saying but scanning the crowd nonetheless, Auntie Eva elbowing Gabe as he tried to pull her to him and beside him...Rose. Rosalie Erin Wells, with her hair in thick curls framing her face, the tips of it dyed pink, her eyes dark with makeup and her posture - arms crossed, eyes cast down - clearly stating a bad mood, was meeting HIM at the airport. His dad spotted him first and pointed toward him with his chin, his mom looking for him in the crowd right away. He smiled and waved, moving towards them behind the rest of the passengers. Once his mom had seen him, there was no more leisure strolling.

"Ichigo!" She cried and ran to him, winding between people, not caring if she knocked anyone over. He braced for impact and caught her, nearly toppling backwards on his willowy frame. She pressed him to her so hard that he could hear her heart beating through her shirt and his jacket.

"Hi, mom."

"Ichigo! Look at you!" She was glowing, craning her neck to see his face fully. Was she always so small compared to him? She wasn't so short really.

Leaning on him, she led him to the rest of the group. Auntie Eva ran up for a hug too. "Stop growing!" She mocked, even tinier than his mother, with the brightest darkest eyes he'd ever seen. She looked a bit tired. They all looked a bit older than he remembered. Gabe gave him a hug and a pat on the back too. "Welcome home, kid. It looks like England did you good. Not much of a tan, though." He laughed. Ichigo laughed too. He always loved spending time with Gabe. He turned to his father.

"Welcome back," Hale said, looking unsure. Ichigo held out his hand, which Hale shook with a nod. He turned to look for the last hug, but Rose was gone.

He looked around, turning on himself. "Oh, she uh, went out for a smoke," Gabe explained, nervously running his hand over the back of his now-short hair. It was still strange on Gabe, the mane of dark hair gone. Ichigo had never thought he'd cut it, but it seemed okay when he began going gray and finally did cut it. He'd always thought Gabe was like the story of Samson, but it turned out his hair had nothing to do with his strength.

"Where?"

"Probably not too far. She does need us for the lift home."

"Do you mind if I...?"

He turned to his mom, knowing she'd be the one to say no, leave her be, don't do this, but she just nodded, making the familiar face she always had when she felt conflicted.

It didn't take long to find Rose. She was the only one with tousled pink hair. She was standing right outside the doors to the outside, where taxis and limo services pulled up, a cigarette lit in her hand, inhaling deeply.
"Uh, hey." He said, standing beside her.
"Hi, did my mom send you?"
"No, I wanted to see you. I missed you." He felt bashful around her; he could feel the blush on his cheeks. She looked tired, with dark circles under her eyes and layers of makeup that she never needed. She wore a pair of denim shorts and a gray band t-shirt for a band he'd never heard of.
"What'd you miss?" She smirked, goading.
"Everything! Even the way you make fun of me." He didn't remember her being so much smaller than him, either in height or build. He wasn't exactly a big guy.
"Course I have to. You look like someone who sells Bibles."
"Well, I do go to an Ivy League school, Rose."
"I know. I just didn't think you'd wear corduroy." Her voice had a slight lisp that he didn't remember her having before.

"It's cold on the plane." He shrugged. "You should come visit me sometimes; you'll learn all about it."
"I don't think I'd fit in. You wouldn't want me cramping your style Ivy League Boy." On the last word, he caught a glimpse of the metal piece in her tongue, a stud.
"I don't have a style, and everyone at school is pretty dull compared to you."

She looked up at him sulkily, perfect lips in a pout, perfect eyebrows narrowed, those huge blue eyes demanding an explanation, a late slip for the past eight months.

"Did you get any of my letters?"

"Yeah."

"Why didn't you write back?"

"Not much goes on here. You know how I am about keeping in touch."

She finished her cigarette and crushed it with the bottom of her Converse. Ichigo sighed. "So you didn't miss me? Honest?"

"Of course, I did, you moron."

"Then, what's up? What did I do? What do I have to do?"

They were face to face, her looking up, him looking down, studying one another's familiar faces. He noticed a fresh batch of freckles on her nose, visible underneath the makeup.

He felt older.

She looked frail. She looked beautiful.

"Nothin'. Just stick around," she said.

"Stop being stupid." He pulled her into a hug

ACKNOWLEDGEMENTS

With thanks to the following people: A. Whalen, for always listening and being the one who told me to be courageous, to K. Chow, for humouring my special interests, E. Tremblay, for telling me to "do the thing", E. Zrajevski for daydreaming with me since childhood and to T. Pardo, for being the first person to whom I entrusted the manuscript early on. Special thanks to my husband, who patiently put up with living with an aspiring writer.

Milton Keynes UK
Ingram Content Group UK Ltd.
UKHW040217160324
439374UK00004B/304